GENELL DELLIN . . .

"HAS STYLE and she writes in such a way that the wild horses are beautiful and full of life."
—*The Romance Reader*

"Definitely WRITES PAGE-TURNERS that can't be put down."
—*The Romance Readers Connection*

"DELIVERS a powerful family drama with true in-your-face bluntness. Moving and riveting."
—*Romantic Times*

HONEY GROVE

Genell Dellin

BERKLEY SENSATION, NEW YORK

THE BERKLEY PUBLISHING GROUP
Published by the Penguin Group
Penguin Group (USA) Inc.
375 Hudson Street, New York, New York 10014, USA

Penguin Group (Canada), 90 Eglinton Avenue East, Suite 700, Toronto, Ontario M4P 2Y3, Canada
(a division of Pearson Penguin Canada Inc.)
Penguin Books Ltd., 80 Strand, London WC2R 0RL, England
Penguin Group Ireland, 25 St. Stephen's Green, Dublin 2, Ireland (a division of Penguin Books Ltd.)
Penguin Group (Australia), 250 Camberwell Road, Camberwell, Victoria 3124, Australia
(a division of Pearson Australia Group Pty. Ltd.)
Penguin Books India Pvt. Ltd., 11 Community Centre, Panchsheel Park, New Delhi—110 017, India
Penguin Group (NZ), 67 Apollo Drive, Rosedale, Auckland 0632, New Zealand
(a division of Pearson New Zealand Ltd.)
Penguin Books (South Africa) (Pty.) Ltd., 24 Sturdee Avenue, Rosebank, Johannesburg 2196,
South Africa

Penguin Books Ltd., Registered Offices: 80 Strand, London WC2R 0RL, England

This is a work of fiction. Names, characters, places, and incidents either are the product of the author's
imagination or are used fictitiously, and any resemblance to actual persons, living or dead, business
establishments, events, or locales is entirely coincidental. The publisher does not have any control
over and does not assume any responsibility for author or third-party websites or their content.

PUBLISHER'S NOTE: The recipes contained in this book are to be followed exactly as written. The
publisher is not responsible for your specific health or allergy needs that may require medical supervision. The publisher is not responsible for any adverse reactions to the recipes contained in this book.

HONEY GROVE

A Berkley Sensation Book / published by arrangement with the author

PRINTING HISTORY
Berkley Sensation mass-market paperback edition / May 2011

Copyright © 2011 by Genell Dellin.
Cover design by Diana Kolsky.
Cover illustration by Trish Cramblett; image of blue gingham © MedusArt / Shutterstock.
Interior text design by Laura K. Corless.

ISBN: 978-0-425-24153-0

BERKLEY® SENSATION
Berkley Sensation Books are published by The Berkley Publishing Group,
a division of Penguin Group (USA) Inc.,
375 Hudson Street, New York, New York 10014.
BERKLEY® SENSATION and the "B" design are trademarks of Penguin Group (USA) Inc.

PRINTED IN THE UNITED STATES OF AMERICA

10 9 8 7 6 5 4 3 2 1

In loving memory of Arthur David Dellin

Acknowledgments

I thank God for giving me my family, my friends and my agent, all of whom lovingly held me up so I could write through the hardest time in my life.

One

Sometimes a person just *will* break down at a funeral, no matter how hard they try not to. Like the time Claude Jenkins cried so hard at his wife's funeral he had to take off his glasses. He kept walking while he wiped them and stumbled into her open grave. They had to call the volunteer firemen to get him out.

Lilah Briscoe reached under her cuff and pulled out a handkerchief, just in case her granddaughter was going to pieces. She didn't know her well enough to predict, of course, because she hadn't seen her since she was six years old. But from the minute Meredith arrived at this graveside service, anybody with any vision at all could see that she was wound way too tight. If she took after her mother the least bit in the drama department, Lilah had her work cut out for her.

The pastor asked them all to stand for the closing prayer. As they got to their feet, Meredith leaned toward Lilah, who grabbed her by the elbow and held on tight, hoping to steady her.

Meredith whispered in Lilah's ear, "I'm amazed they'd use such a big coffin for a cremation."

Well. If *that* wasn't the last thing Lilah expected.

She tucked the hanky back in her sleeve to save for somebody who might actually need it. Then she hissed, "No daughter of *mine's* going to be cremated."

"*Not* your decision. In Mom's will, she specifically stated . . ." Meri's response held a sharp edge, even though it was no more than a whisper.

That just flew all over Lilah. Never mind the drama department, *here* was how this girl was her mother's daughter—ready to argue and criticize every time Lilah opened her mouth.

Lilah hissed, "No piece of paper's gonna tell *me* what to do with my own daughter's body."

The preacher glanced at them. Everybody was waiting, so they had to hush and bow their heads. While Pastor Gray prayed out loud, using that worn-out old verse about "dust to dust," Lilah prayed silently for the right words to set Meredith straight in her thinking.

Honestly. The child had been raised up north and in a city, no less. What could you expect?

But why bother? No matter that she *was* the only blood kin Lilah had in this world, she'd be gone by sundown. And Lilah would be alone again.

A breeze sprang up from the southwest, enough to flap the edges of the canvas tent shading the rows of folding chairs. With it, from the back of the tent Shorty's fiddle started to play softly. "Amazing Grace." That Shorty, you could always count on him. He surely did know what song to play when.

"Amen."

At last. And the preacher had done as well as possible, considering he was new here—he'd only been in Rock Springs ten or fifteen years—so he didn't know how to personalize his remarks about Edie Jo.

Which was just as well, considering.

Lilah couldn't even *count* the times Edie Jo's behavior had embarrassed her in this community of good people, so it was nothing but right that at least her funeral would be free of humiliation for her mother. Born beautiful—and

wild—her daughter—her only child—had gone wrong as
soon as she was big enough to step foot off the farm without Lilah.

But all that was in the past and none of Pastor Gray's
concern. She had to admit, though, that it might be the
main reason he'd had so little to work with for the eulogy,
despite his many earnest questions.

Meredith walked out into the sunlight and straight to
the casket. She touched it once, then stood still, looking
down at the bouquet of red roses she'd had Estelle make for
the family arrangement. Lilah didn't ask, but those flowers
had to have cost a pretty penny.

However. It was Meredith's money and she looked like
she could afford it, and if she wanted to throw good dollars
away to honor a mother who didn't deserve to be called
one, then it was nobody's business but hers. Tears stung
Lilah's eyes.

She blinked them back as friends and neighbors gathered
around, offering hugs, handshakes, sad smiles and sincere
words. Barbara Jane Carter, one of Lilah's oldest friends,
squeezed her hand. "It was a nice service, Lilah, don't you
think?"

Lilah nodded. She was watching Meredith, who must be
about to melt in that perfectly fitted black suit. She hadn't
known that anything black—unless it was faded black—
was not a good choice for an outdoor occasion in Texas in
the summer.

Comfort aside, the young woman cut a striking figure.
High heels with the bright red soles like in the movies, and
a scarf with a touch of color in it that exactly matched her
violet eyes—inherited from Lilah herself—made her look
like a movie star. Which Edie Jo had always wanted to be.

When Meredith came back, Barbara Jane hugged Lilah,
murmuring about how this step, the hardest, was over now.
Meri let herself be hugged, too, but she didn't seem real
comfortable with it. Same as with Lilah's hug when she
first got there. Not the touchy-feely kind, this girl. Self-
contained and tense as a fiddle-string.

Lilah wondered whether she was that way all the time or just because of the funeral. One thing she did know: A girl who grows up without a mother never gets over it.

Barbara Jane was all brisk again. "Okay. I'll get on over to the house and get the dinner whipped into shape. Meredith, will you bring your grandma? I need to take her car."

Meredith, clearly startled, nodded her agreement.

Great big sunglasses hid her eyes, but a sudden tear shone on one high cheekbone. She brushed at it and missed.

Lilah's heart cracked open. Bless goodness, she could kill Edie Jo if she wasn't already dead.

Doreen Semples came between them, then, trying to be her usual superior self, but Lilah had known her since the first grade. She knew that look. Doreen was feeling more than a little sheepish. As well she should.

All she said was, "Lilah, I'm so sorry."

"I know you are, Doreen."

Lilah let the words hang there for a moment so Doreen could take them whichever way she chose: as acceptance of her sympathy or as an evaluation of her character. Lilah meant them as the latter.

Then she smiled sweetly and said, "This is my granddaughter, Meredith, from Brooklyn, New York. I'm so proud of her. She tells me she's an attorney."

There. That'd give the haughty heifer something to think about next time she decided to file a lawsuit against Lilah over a perfectly healthy horse.

It was Lilah who should've filed a suit against Doreen, many years ago, over Edie Jo. What was it they called that? Alienation of affections?

Wrong as it was, Lilah could not forgive and forget. People were right to talk about her tendency to hold a grudge. She was ashamed of that.

Meredith's quick look jerked her out of her thoughts. It held both surprise and . . . resentment, maybe? As if Lilah had no right to be proud of her.

Well, she was. With Edie Jo such a mess and a high-school dropout on top of all her bad behavior, it was a miracle the child had made something of herself. Law school wasn't easy, according to those who'd been there.

And, to be downright honest, it gave Lilah a little thrill to have some family to brag on. Even if only for one afternoon.

Lord knew, she needed something to brag about right now.

She sighed. Then she stood straighter and squared her shoulders.

A young man in starched jeans and white shirt loomed over them, hat in hand. It was one of Jasper and Dulcie Burkett's four tall sons. One of the twins. But at this instant she was in such a fog, she wasn't sure which. Then she noticed the limp and those blazing blue eyes

Mercy, goodness! How could she not know that rascal, Caleb! She was more upset about this funeral than she'd thought.

Lilah hugged his neck. "Thank you for coming, Caleb. I got the azalea and it's gorgeous. Tell your mother I love her."

"Yes, ma'am. She's sad that this funeral caught her so far away she couldn't get home in time for it."

"Dulcie's here in spirit. She called me this morning. Now, Caleb, I want you to meet my granddaughter." As soon as the words left her mouth, she realized what a fine idea that might be.

Or not. Lilah was not one to matchmake or meddle.

Except, of course, when absolutely necessary.

"Meredith, this is Caleb Burkett. His mother and I have been bosom friends all our lives. Caleb, Meredith Briscoe, my beautiful granddaughter from New York City."

She was beginning to like this showing off her granddaughter.

It was like new breath in her lungs.

Don't get attached to this girl. She'll only go off and leave you like Edie Jo did. You don't have time for a granddaughter, anyhow. You've got a farm to run.

Of the four Burkett boys, this one had Jasper's smile. It could light up the dark.

"New York," he said, shaking hands with Meredith. "Let's see, now, that's a whole lot like our Rock Springs, right?"

Meredith stared at him. At first, Lilah thought she was going to be sharp with him, too. But after a second, she said dryly, "My thought exactly, when I saw your policeman watching the four-way stop."

Well, praise be. She had a sense of humor. And she was pretty quick on her feet. Of course, to argue cases in court, she'd have to be that.

Caleb gave her that grin of his but she didn't smile back.

"If y'all need anything, Miss Lilah, you know all you have to do is call."

Shorty appeared, bow in hand, fiddle tucked up under his arm. He gave them each a brief, formal handshake before he sent Lilah all the sympathy—and strength—in the world. In one hard, direct look.

"Well, our girl's come home at last, ain't she, Lilah? I'm just sorry it had to be in a pine box."

Meredith gasped a little at his bluntness.

It comforted Lilah, though. The truth, plainspoken. That was a trait she liked in all her friends. "Me, too, Shorty. Thanks for everything."

As he turned away, she saw the gleam of wetness in his eyes.

The mothers of two of her students were there. That surprised her. These were new people in the area, McMansion people whose only connection to her was that she gave their girls horseback riding lessons.

She was touched, too, that there was such a crowd of other farm and ranch people from all over the county and beyond. They'd left their never-ending work and taken the time to clean up and dress up and drive all the way into town out of respect for her.

To comfort her over this old, old grief.

It was like a recurring boil she'd thought was lanced and gone a long time ago, now come back in flames.

She closed her eyes and opened her heart. Gratitude for what she *did* have in life slowly filled her. *Thank You, God.*

The breeze freshened again and she caught the smell of rain.

* * *

A blast of hot air hit Meri in the face when she opened the car door. Squirming on the baking leather, she slipped into the driver's seat and turned on the motor and the air-conditioning. Lilah and the young man who'd insisted on walking them to the car didn't even notice. They stood beside the open passenger door, talking earnestly. Something about a loan and sources of credit.

Meri glanced at her watch. Eleven fifteen. The service had lasted half an hour and the rest of the time had been eaten up by condolences—which was all right, because she'd allotted an hour for the cemetery. But now it was time to move to the next item on her agenda, the reception or luncheon or whatever.

That would finish everything concerning Edie Jo and she, Meri, could get on with her life. She glanced at her watch. This time tomorrow, she'd be back in her office with the motions all done and the depositions analyzed.

If she could stick to her schedule and have the rest of the day alone in her motel room to work.

You should've planned to return to New York tonight.

She tapped her fingers on the wheel and willed Lilah to stop talking and get into the car.

You shouldn't've worried about driving the round-trip from the airport in one day. You aren't too shaken by the funeral. And you may not even be able to use the Internet from that motel.

Her nerves were rattling over her skin, though, under the thin layer of sweat that glued her clothes to her.

Edie Jo's gone. This time you know she won't be back. Put your mind on something else, Meri.

She took a deep breath and stared at her grandmother's tanned, knotted hand holding on to the door. When Meri had arrived ten minutes before the service, she and Lilah had exchanged the barest facts of their lives. *I'm still farming,* Lilah had said. *Mostly organic now.*

A grandmother/farmer. What a weird concept.

But, in actuality, it was more like stranger/farmer. Now they didn't even have the tenuous connection that had been Edie Jo.

You never had it anyway, Meri. Maybe Edie Jo kept her away while she was still with you, but after that, there was no barrier. Lilah was the adult. She could've found you if she'd tried.

Lilah certainly was connected to her friends, however. Meri had never known anyone who was so close to so many people. How did that happen?

Was it only a small-town thing? A live-in-one-place-all-your-life thing?

In New York, Meri had a few friends she considered close, along with her college roommate who lived in Seattle. And Tim, of course.

But nothing in her experience was anything like this. Lilah was pouring out her problems to this guy and he was truly trying to help her know what to do. These people were entwined in each other's lives like the branches of the enormous old trees overhanging the road.

Did roots like that make them feel secure? Loved?

Tim. He loved her, didn't he?

She really wished she hadn't thought of him right then. The replay of their disappointing date to the Yankees game started looping in her mind again. The perfect opportunity and he'd screwed it up. When would the next right moment ever come along?

He had damn well better hurry, after two years of talking about marriage and making plans and wearing her down to the point she agreed they wouldn't have children. What had he been thinking? Too much attention to the game?

Tim was a very private kind of guy who rarely talked about his deepest feelings. Had he lost his nerve?

It was the first long-term relationship for her; maybe she needed to encourage him more. She and Tim were so much alike that they were perfect for each other.

Meri gripped the steering wheel to take the light trem-

ble out of her hands. This funeral must be affecting her
more than she'd realized.

Or maybe it was this *heat*. She wanted to wipe her
sweating palms on her skirt, but this suit was silk and one
of her favorites. She made a big deal of reaching over the
seat for her bag and digging in it for the little package of
tissues. Good God! Couldn't Lilah take a *hint*?

Impatience clutched her stomach. She had to get this
done and get out of here. But in this wide, hot, different
world everything moved at the pace of a snail.

She took out her cell phone to check for messages.
Nothing from Tim. Nothing from work.

Meri dropped her bag into the backseat again.

She'd hardly slept since Tim hadn't proposed. Her hands
were shaky from exhaustion, that was all. And desperation.
Too many feelings here.

Finally, Lilah made a move. The man helped her into
her seat and left them with a good-bye that included Meri,
too. It surprised her that he bothered to bend over, stick his
head into the car and meet her eyes to offer his condolences
once more. And to welcome her to Texas.

She smiled at him. She had to admit that the hospitality
here was as warm as the weather.

Meri shifted into drive and steered the car up from the
side of the ditch, carefully, and into the narrow road. It
wound in an endless maze through the tall grave markers. Some, tilting with age, angled away from their marble
bases. Some had vases that held flowers.

"It's cool in here," Lilah said. "This AC works fast. I
love these SUVs."

"I tried to rent a smaller car but this was all they had left
at that time of night."

"Be glad. Around here, any kind of a wreck in a small
car is liable to kill you. Odds are, the other vehicle would
be one of these or a truck."

"So I noticed. Is it all right if I call you Lilah?"

After a beat, Lilah said, "When you were little, you

called me Gran. But Lilah's fine, if that's what you want to do. I want to call you Meri."

"All right. Lilah, could we talk about Mom's will?"

"Stop."

Meri gasped and hit the brake. She looked around but there was no danger. Sudden anger shook her. She hated being scared.

She turned to Lilah. "I don't mean to be disrespectful, Lilah, but why did you say that?"

Lilah pointed to the wrought-iron arch over the gate.

1846. OAK HILL CEMETERY. TEXAS.

"Our people were some of the first families to be buried here. Briscoes and Robinsons and Gills and Smiths and St. Clairs—some were heroes in the War for Texas Independence. Two of them died at the Alamo."

Meri looked at the arch, then at her grandmother with the silent question, *So?*

Lilah reproached that attitude with her tone. Tart, to say the least.

"Every time I give one of my talks about Texas history, I'm inspired all over again to live up to such loyalty and courage. Did you know they had to sign an oath of loyalty that said, Texas Forever? That wasn't so they could *enjoy* independence. They had to swear allegiance before they were even allowed to *fight* for Texas."

"No," Meri said, carefully keeping her voice polite. "I didn't know that."

"Well, now you do." Lilah looked her in the eye as if she were appraising Meri. "It's hard to believe, but on my side of the family, you're the last of the line."

Then she sat, waiting.

Meri wouldn't let herself break the look but more sweat popped out on her skin. She didn't need this now. "What do you mean?"

"You're a native-born Texan. Do you realize that?"

Meri resisted mimicking Lilah's tart tone. "Are you telling me that, as the last of the line, I should have children?"

A quick look passed through Lilah's eyes—violet colored, like Meri's own, so she must've inherited it from her—that Meri couldn't interpret. Surely not pity. Surely not regret. But yet . . . What was going on in Lilah's head when she looked at her granddaughter? Did Meri satisfy her expectations?

Meri hated not knowing, not being in control of the situation.

Lilah's look was all surprise and hurt innocence. "Why, Meredith! I would *never* tell you to do *anything*."

Meri rolled her eyes behind the protection of her sunglasses. *Why don't I believe that?*

"That's good," she said, and had to fight a sudden lump in her throat. "Because I . . . probably won't."

"You mean, have children?"

God! Was there any way to communicate with this woman? "Yes."

"Why not?"

Meri stepped on the accelerator and drove under the arch to leave the cemetery with a lump in her throat and a tsunami of mixed feelings washing over her. She jerked her mind away from it. How long was this drive supposed to take? Twelve minutes, according to the GPS. Could she survive that long in the same car with this nosy, bossy grandmother?

Lilah still had her interrogating gaze fixed on Meri's face. "Do you ever think about who you are, Meri? What people you come from?"

Meri's jaw clamped so fast she almost bit her tongue. "I can't even dignify that question with an answer."

Lilah waved that away. "No, no. I'm talking about the people who came *before* your mother and father. Those two are not the only ancestors you have, you know. Think about that."

Meri wanted to scream, but she retreated into her habitual control. "My *father*? How could I ever think about him, since I don't even know who he was. Is. Whatever."

"Turn right," the GPS announced. "One point five miles

ahead on Farm-to-Market Road 2317. Twelve point three miles to Old Briscoe Road."

Lilah jumped and glared at the instrument. "Good heavenly days, that *voice*! It's as bad as fingernails scraping on a blackboard."

"It's a great tool," Meri said. "And they don't all have the same voice. You might find one that you like."

Lilah sighed and got right back on the subject of family. "I just thought you might value knowing something about your heritage. You're named for my mother, you know."

Meri gasped. That tidbit nearly did her in. She didn't *care*, she really *didn't* want to hear about family, but somehow her heart was knocking in her throat. She wasn't *up* for this. How pathetic could she be to let it get to her this way?

She shook her head and forced herself to focus on her driving. But something in her was rocketing around.

No, I don't know that. She had hardly driven any car since college, much less a behemoth like this one. She must concentrate on safety. Think of nothing but the other cars and that slow-moving piece of farm equipment ahead on the highway.

Why have I never known this all my life? She didn't even bother to tell me that. Why didn't she tell me?

"Naming you after your great-grandmother is the only thing Edie Jo ever did for me. She wasn't much of a daughter."

Too much. This is all too much and I can't bear to think about it.

"Honestly, Lilah, I don't want to hear about her."

"I don't blame you one bit. The Good Lord knows that's perfectly normal, since she wasn't much of a mother, either. But, Meri, most everybody sooner or later comes to a place in life where they want to know the truth of their childhood. I might not be around when you get there."

"I *won't* get there. I never want to think about my childhood again."

The GPS said, "Left turn, eleven point five miles ahead."

"If this was your own car, I'd say take that bossy machine out. It's downright dangerous. That awful thing's enough to make a person run off the road and straight into a tree."

Edie Jo never bothered to tell me. It meant nothing to her.

Trying to keep her tone light, Meri said, "No bossy piece of technology's going to tell *you* where to go or what to do, right? Like no piece of paper's going to tell you how to bury your daughter."

Lilah looked at her.

"I'm sorry, Lilah, but I keep thinking about the illegalities here."

And I can't stop thinking about the fact that at the age of twenty-seven, I've just buried my forty-four-year-old mother and I didn't know until this minute that my name had any significance. I really am connected to a family. I am.

"That's because your mind runs in that direction. You're a lawyer."

"I'm not trying to *stop* thinking about it. I'm trying to say that the provisions of a will must be followed. It's the law."

Lilah sniffed. "Sometimes the law doesn't have a blessed thing to do with what's right."

Meri turned, studying this woman in pale blue linen who looked more like a Texas history professor with a good haircut than a woman farmer.

Lilah was waiting for her with those wise, violet eyes.

"Tell me," she said. "Why do you keep bringing this up about the burial, Meri, if you don't want to talk about your mother?"

"I'm not talking about *her*. I'm talking about the law. Since cremation was what she wanted and the directive for it is in a legally filed will . . ."

"What Edie Jo wanted, most all of her life, *also* had nothing to do with what's right."

Meri managed to keep her tone respectful instead of irritated. "But, Lilah, that's not the point . . ."

"Now, you just listen here to me, Meredith Kathleen. You're just gonna have to let that go."

Lilah's vehemence shocked Meri into silence. That was

true. There was nothing she could do now short of disinterment and she couldn't even contemplate that, so why talk about it? Why think about it?

Habit. Hardwired into the law, into work. Default into lawyer mode.

Pathetic attempt to prove that in spite of all these churning feelings you still have a brain, Meredith Kathleen.

Meri drove on, staring straight ahead, gradually lifting her foot off the accelerator as they came closer to the farm equipment creeping along the highway with two cars behind it already. As Meri slowed the SUV to a creep, Lilah spoke.

"It's done," she said. "And no harm done with it."

The flat authority in her tone and the simple truth of the words hit Meri hard. This time, she could name the feeling: unfamiliar comfort.

Like a moment of rest.

Two

But turning off the highway and driving beneath the arching sign for Honey Grove Farm made Meri's nerves come back to life. She wanted to throw the SUV into reverse and back right out again when she saw how many cars and trucks were there, parked on each side of the driveway. Dozens of them.

She'd already been pummeled with hugs and handshakes. *And* battered into insensiblilty by the words *your mother* and *Edie Jo*. They still hurt. She should've left for the airport directly from the cemetery.

"What is this? Were there this many people at the funeral?"

Lilah's sharp glance pricked the side of Meri's face; she knew she'd sounded ungracious and angry. Lilah possessed a tart look to go with her tart tone.

"Friends. These are friends, some as close to me as butter on a hot biscuit. Friends come to keep us company on a sad day. They know hardship is best met together."

With just the slightest emphasis on *they*.

Meri's face went from warm to hot. If a grandmother

was someone who shamed grown women into feeling like
a naughty child, she'd do without.

But it was true sympathy these people had offered her—
she didn't know them, but she did know that—and she'd
always hated feeling guilty or embarrassed or wrong.

Which was good because it motivated her to be the stu-
dent with the best preparation in any class, the girl with the
neatest room in any house where she lived and the attorney
with the most billable hours at Savage, Mitchell, Tung and
Fenton for the last three consecutive years.

And it led her to never be naughty. She'd learned that
early. Her mother was nothing *but* naughty, which brought
nothing but tears and trouble.

"They only want to tell you they're sorry for the loss of
your mother."

Bitter words popped out of Meri. "Too late. I lost her the
moment I was born."

Lilah sat silent while Meri shoved her feelings about
Edie Jo back into the vault where she kept them, slammed
its door and turned the wheel on the lock. She had enough
rage locked up in there to wreck the world.

Lilah sounded calm and soothing. "Just drive on down
to the garage and park behind my pickup." She gestured to
the truck sitting in a small, open building, really a farm shed,
not too far from the house. Behind it, perhaps the length of
a football field, stood a row of white boxes set up on legs,
another row stacked on top.

*You have to be sociable, Mer. You might as well start
now. You'll hate yourself if you don't live up to your own
standards.*

So she said, "That *can't* be a bank of mailboxes. What
is it?"

"Beehives. See that grove of trees back there? They're
sourwood trees, and sourwood honey is some of the best
there is. Ed's granddaddy named the farm Honey Grove
after those trees."

"Isn't it scary to take the honey from the bees? Don't
they sting?"

Lilah smiled. "I think not, but I'm no beekeeper. They're Audie Blaylock's. He's got bees all over this county."

There were lots more outbuildings besides the "garage," some wooden and some metal, scattered around the old house and out in the pastures, most painted dark red with white trim. The house and two small structures behind it were built of white limestone. It was a classic farmhouse with porches on three sides.

A faint sense of déjà vu tickled the back of Meredith's mind. A dim barn with good smells. A cow with huge brown eyes. Her six-year-old body sitting in a saddle, trying to keep her balance without clutching the horn, Lilah leading the horse. A dozen or so men were standing around in small groups in the front yard, talking and smoking. Keeping an eye on them, three fat horses stood with their heads hanging over the pasture fence, switching their tails. A smaller animal, sheep or goat, grazed near them.

"I still look for Ed when I see the men gathered like that," Lilah said, "and he's been dead twenty-eight years next Thursday."

As Meri parked the SUV, she felt Lilah turn to look at her. "Do you know what I'm talking about? That kind of heart-and-soul dangerous love that goes to the bone and never leaves you?"

If a grandmother was someone who gets to ask any personal question she wants, Meri could do without that, too. Did the woman really know what she was talking about? Wasn't that kind of love a fantasy?

"Your farm could be in a children's book," she said.

Lilah waited a beat. "It takes a lot of hard work to keep it going and a magician to make the profits come out bigger than the expenses. Even harder than that is finding good help—or any help at all, sometimes. I'm moving heaven and earth right now trying to find pickers for my tomatoes."

"Is that a goat over there by the horses?"

"It is. I'm boarding that bay horse and it's his goat."

"*What?*"

"Lots of people have goats for 'only' horses," Lilah

said. "Horses are like people, they need companionship."
She smiled as she opened the passenger door. "Oh, and *you*
can answer *my* question whenever you want."

Assuming that I ever will! This woman is incorrigible.

They got out of the SUV. At the back bumper, Lilah
stood still for a moment, looking at the house, waiting
for Meri, then surprised her by taking her arm. Meri sup-
pressed her instinct to pull away.

Sociable, be sociable.

"You might need a little support in those good-looking
heels. I've ruined many a pair out here on this driveway.
Let's go slow in this gravel or it'll chew them right up."

But it was Lilah who leaned slightly on Meri as they
moved toward the worn brick walk lined with flowers. Was
she, too, feeling a little shaky, thinking of Edie Jo and the
fact that once she'd walked this same path?

*Damn it, why? Why had she never bothered to tell her
daughter that she was named for her great-grandmother?
Why couldn't she have given Meri even that one tendril of
roots? When she was little, she'd wanted so much to be in
a real family.*

Lilah held herself straight again. "See that tree by the
corner of the back porch? It's a native persimmon. Almost
as old as I am, which is why it's over forty feet tall. Do you
like persimmons?"

Meri forced her mind onto that question instead of the
other. "I've never eaten one."

"The frost in the fall of the year is what sweetens them
enough to eat," Lilah said. "But I'll pick you some to take
home with you. There's a way to do it in the freezer."

Someone—Barbara Jane—opened the screened door
and held it with her shoulder, a stack of small plates in one
hand, forks in the other. "Come on in here, girls. Everything's just about ready."

Lilah insisted that Meri go ahead. Two steps into the
large, square kitchen and she was enveloped by the min-
gled smells of fried chicken and hot bread, the chiming of
women's voices rising above the clattering of dishes and

utensils, the onslaught of colorful food covering every surface. Hunger stabbed her.

She hadn't been hungry for weeks. Months. Half the time she didn't have time to eat. It'd become her habit to eat only one real meal a day.

The woman, Doreen, in her stylish floral silk dress that Meri had noticed at the funeral, was pulling trays of dinner rolls from an oven in the brick wall and sliding them into cloth-lined baskets. She looked up and beamed at Meri.

"There's our pretty girl," she said.

Lilah snapped, "What do you mean, *our*?"

There was a vibration in the look the two women exchanged. They had a past and they weren't exactly friends.

Why do you care? An hour from now, you'll never see any of these people again.

Another oven, this one in the stove, was giving up a large glass dish of cheese-topped casserole to a woman about Lilah's age with a dramatic white streak in her dyed black hair. Whatever it was, the food looked delicious.

Lilah was hanging her purse on a coatrack in the corner. She gestured for Meri to hand hers over, too, waiting while Meri dropped her sunglasses into their case, surveying the room in one long glance.

"Toncy, would you go call the men in so we can serve this King Ranch Chicken while it's hot?" she called. She looked at the drinks table. "Jessie Kate, my rose-glass tea pitcher's in that cupboard over there if y'all need another one."

"I already told her that," B. J. said. "I know your kitchen as well as I know my own, you know."

A woman with faded red curls looked up from cutting pies at a long table covered with desserts. "Why didn't you say so, Barbara? I can't find the pie server for the silver."

"Second drawer down in the pie safe," Lilah said. "I use it all the time, so I never do put it in the silverware box."

The dessert table made Meri's mouth water. She couldn't stop looking at the tall white cake and the long, flat chocolate one, a lemon-trimmed pound cake, a bowl of something that looked like fluffy clouds plus fruit pies and cookies and brownies and fruit with dip. It went on and on.

Meri tried to see everything at once. The countertop along one wall had dishes filled with all kinds of brightly colored salads and vegetables next to a beautifully crusted ham, a sliced brisket, a roast, chopped meat with barbeque sauce, the cheesy casserole—what had Lilah called it, King Ranch Chicken? On a round table nearby were platters of sliced tomatoes and onions, crystal dishes of pickles and relishes and two baskets of fried chicken.

Her stomach growled. "This is a feast," she said. "Does this happen with every funeral?"

Lilah said, "Out here, yes, but not so much in town anymore. The last funeral dinner at our church was nothing short of pathetic."

Barbara Jane agreed as she stepped around them to take the plates and forks to the dessert table. "Oh, my goodness gracious, *yes*. That was so pitiful. They only had *one* small ham and a store-bought lasagna for the main dishes. I was *mortified*."

Lilah said quickly, "Just so you know, Meredith, it wasn't our committee in charge." She flashed a teasing grin. "Doreen, was it yours?"

B. J. chuckled.

Doreen bristled. "No. You know perfectly well it was *not* my committee."

A hair-raising yowl erupted from the floor and interrupted all the conversations. Meri jumped and cried out before she could stop herself.

A cat. A tawny, imperious one, sitting tall with its large blue eyes fixed on her face. It cocked its head farther back and screamed again.

"Oh, Henry, get a grip, we're getting around to you!" Lilah bent over to pick him up. "You haven't met him yet," she said to Meri. "No one can come into this house without saying something to him."

"Paying homage to him, you mean," Barbara Jane called.

"He thinks he's the king of Siam instead of just a cat of Siam." She chuckled at her own joke.

Henry flattened himself against the floor, head tilted to keep his eyes on Meri. Lilah tugged but the cat held fast.

"He can just plaster himself down until there's no way to move him," Lilah said, huffing for breath from her upside-down position. "I don't know . . . how . . . he does it."

"Never mind. It's all right," Meri said. She could not *believe* this. "Leave him there, Lilah. I'm not an animal person. Really. Not at all. Please."

Henry meowed as if he'd understood her words. He had really long fangs.

"If I *were* an animal person," Meri said, "I really think I'd be a dog person."

"Can't ignore him," Lilah gasped. "He'll carry on . . . 'til we can't even eat in peace."

Barbara Jane said, "Meredith, forget him. If you give in to that cat once, he'll rule you from now on. Look how he's got your grandma on a leash. Think about that."

"Meredith," Doreen called from the drinks table where she was pouring tea, "don't pay any attention to Lilah. Next thing you know, she'll try to make you hold him. That wonderful suit you're wearing does *not* call for cat hair."

Lilah straightened up fast with Henry in her arms. She shot a killer look at Doreen. "Meri can make her own decisions, thank you very much. Now, Meri, here's Henry. Just stroke him under his chin."

Lilah smiled fondly at the cat.

Barbara Jane, who'd begun cutting the thickly frosted, flat chocolate cake, said, "Lilah, I hate to tell you this, but some people—mostly people with good sense—don't like that screamin' cat and they don't care *what* makes a difference to him. Let the girl alone."

Lilah—and everybody else in the room—looked at Meri. From the corner of her eye she glimpsed a couple of the men in the doorway to the dining room and others streaming in behind them.

This was insane, totally ridiculous. A standoff with a cat.

She didn't want to touch him but she wanted this over with, so she made herself reach out to stroke Henry. He had surprisingly warm, soft fur.

And the fastest paw in the West. He reached out, snagged her scarf with his claw, leapt to the floor and ran.

She plunged after him. The men at the dining room door tried to block the cat but he was too fast for them. It couldn't possibly be the real Meredith Briscoe screaming, yet the voice sounded like hers. "No! That's my new Hermès. Stop him. Catch him, *please*."

The men jumped apart to let Meri through, yelling to the others coming in from outside through the front door.

"Head 'im off, Clem, catch that cat!"

"J. T., you're a cat man. Git him!"

"Herd 'im into the corner."

"Shut the door. Don't let 'im out of the house!"

Everybody was laughing and scrambling either to stop Henry or get out of his path. Men were waving their cowboy hats, trying to turn the cat back while he ran past them, scarf flying like a flag.

Meri was through the dining room and halfway across the living room when the cat vanished beneath a crocheted afghan that floated out of the air and fell, reducing him to a startled lump beneath it. A tall, very thin white-haired man stood over the culprit, smiling at her.

"Come on, missy," he said. "Let's see naow if Ah can hold this thief heah while you recovah youah propahty."

His low voice and his Southern drawl were surprisingly calming. Or maybe it was the fact he'd rescued her scarf. Or the kindness in his eyes.

Despite that, she was embarrassed. Furious with Lilah. And herself. Why had she just stood there and petted the obnoxious creature as if she were an obedient child?

She thanked the man as they knelt on the floor to peel back the covering. The old gentleman held Henry by the nape while Meri freed her scarf, fighting the cat for it.

She finally won and stood up to examine it, blurting, "I bought this the day I got the news that they'd found her . . ."

To comfort herself? In memory of her mother, who also had violet eyes? Or as a token of how well she'd succeeded in making a success of her life in contrast to Edie Jo's?

No matter why she'd bought it, it was ruined now. A long rip. Two of them. And another, shorter one.

She realized her lips were trembling. This whole episode was *such* a metaphor of her life with Edie Jo.

Lilah and Barb appeared on either side of her. "I'll pay for it, Meredith," Lilah said. "Don't fret. This mess is entirely my fault."

"Yes, it is, and it serves you right that it'll cost you several hundred dollars," Barbara Jean said. "Maybe even a thousand."

Lilah gaped. "*What?* Barb!" She clapped her hands to her face. "Oh no! Surely not *that* much!"

The whole crowd laughed at Lilah's shocked dismay.

"You'd be a lot better off if you'd quit pushing your cat onto people," Barb said, raising a censorious eyebrow as she showed her the label. "I'll bet you'll think twice next time."

Meri, too, stared at the label numbly. How stupid. No way she'd needed that scarf. And she could in no way afford it. But when she'd heard the news that Edie Jo's bones had been found, her whole being had gone into turmoil. She'd just *had* to do *something*.

Like eating too much chocolate. Or drinking too much alcohol.

As usual, she'd spent too much money instead.

"I heard that scream in the kitchen and I thought somebody was cut or burned," the man named Clem said. "I sure am thankful there was nothing but money at stake in this deal."

Meri's face flamed. She looked up. Again, everybody was watching her.

"I'm sorry I made such a scene," she said, suddenly aware of her fast-beating heart.

"Hey, now," Clem said. "This here's a small town. We *live* for somebody to make a scene."

Everybody laughed and Barbara Jane put her arm around Meri's shoulders. Some other women comforted her, too, murmuring about someone who could repair silk and how it would never show and how sweet Meri had been to please her grandmother by petting Henry when she wasn't really an animal person at all.

Somehow, they made her feel . . . well, she didn't know exactly how to describe it. "Better" was the best she could do.

Clem was right. How important could a scarf be in the larger scheme of things? She agreed, she supposed, even though she couldn't recall when she'd ever heard the phrase *nothing but money at stake* or imagine when she might ever hear it again.

Barb announced it was time to eat, and Meri and Lilah went off to wash up. Then they led the way through the buffet line.

"Meredith, you look like you didn't have the first bite to eat this morning, so take a slice or two of roast and some of this barbeque buffalo brisket," Lilah said. "They'll be strengthening for you. Sample some of everything. Here, let me help you to this fried okra."

This was the woman who said she'd never tell Meri what to do.

But she meant well. Meri took a couple of deep breaths. Really, Lilah had more concern in her eyes than anyone else had shown her in a long time.

"I don't eat fried foods," Meri said.

Lilah served her some okra anyway. "Which is one reason why you're way too thin."

Meri scrambled to save herself. "Really, Lilah, sweets are my weakness. I'm trying to save space for dessert."

"Don't worry, you'll eat with a coming appetite. Now, Nettie and Wanda Sue and Lorine will all be hurt if you don't at least sample all three kinds of the potato salad. What you need to know is that this one—mustard and mashed potatoes—is the kind *our* family always makes."

There it was again, that voice of authority. *Our* family. Meri couldn't help but be drawn in by it, like stepping into a deep bath of warm water.

"Edie Jo loved my potato salad," Lilah said.

The water turned icy. There *was* no family.

"She hated potato salad," Meri said. "She wouldn't touch it."

Lilah turned and raised an eyebrow. "Your memory's faulty on that."

Meri opened her mouth to argue, then closed it again. It made no difference whose was the faulty memory. *Just get through this.* An hour from now it would over.

Edie Jo was mentioned again in the blessing of the food but, to Meri's surprise, no one spoke of her around the round oak table, where she and Lilah sat with Clem and his wife, Shorty, Barbara and some others.

"Can y'all believe the difference two weeks and three inches of rain can make?" Clem said, lavishing butter on a hot roll from the basket. "Meredith, I'm glad the country's all nice and green for you to see."

"We're comin' off a two-year drought," a man named Bobby said. "When the water started runnin' in the rivers, we couldn't remember what to call it."

"Yes, and now we've got bumper crops," Lilah said. "If we can find the pickers, we might accidentally stumble onto a little profit this year." She looked down at her plate. "I just hope it's not my last."

"It won't be," Shorty said. "Don't even think it."

They talked on about farming and the weather and the food.

Which was delicious. Every dish. Meri understood what Lilah had meant by the expression *eat with a coming appetite.*

"Have some more of these tomatoes," Barbara Jane said, coming from the kitchen with a replenished platter of thick-sliced tomatoes and a dozen varieties of peppers around the edges. "They're from your grandma's truck patch, Meri."

"Cherokee Purple," said a man called Tol sitting across

the table. "The best of the heirlooms, in my considered opinion."

That started a long discussion of tomato varieties and organic techniques and farmers markets. Meri relaxed and let it all wash over her.

Until she heard the tension come back into Lilah's voice. "Listen, y'all, somebody's got to help me find pickers for my Cherokees. Hector was supposed to call me but I haven't heard a word from him."

Clem and Tol said they'd ask around, and Lilah thanked them. Shorty said he might know somebody.

"I've got a big order from that fancy new restaurant in Brenham," Lilah said. "That guy named it the Local Table for a reason. He's determined everything'll come from within a hundred-mile radius of his place. He'll spread the word for me if I can keep him supplied."

"Yep," Tol said, "them organic folks keeps up with the news, all right."

After dessert—at which time Meri was able to eat only the smallest piece of the fantastic chocolate cake with layers of marshmallow called Texas Mud Pie and a bite or two of buttermilk chess pie—she tried to help with the kitchen cleanup but no one would let her. She absently straightened up the unused silver and stacked the clean cloth napkins, then sorted them by color as she accepted friendly good-byes and invitations to come back to Texas when she had the time and best wishes for her busy life all the way off up there in New York City.

A couple of people told her she was bound to come back soon, seeing as how she was Texas-born and -bred. The words, the warm smiles, yes, even the hugs and the pats wove a web of warmth around her despite her efforts to keep it all at a distance. She felt like Henry with the afghan tossed over him.

She didn't quite know how to process that. She needed something to *do*.

Finally, when only the closest friends were left, Lilah and Barbara let her work separating the silverplate from the

old real silver and put it back into the velvet-lined wooden
box, worn so smooth it felt like satin beneath her fingers.
Then she took it and the unused napkins to their drawers in
the sideboard Lilah pointed out and rearranged them while
the easy bits of talk—community gossip, family news, recipes, gardening—continued to swirl in her ears.

All of this took her back to that favorite memory of when
she was in second grade, visiting at Jennifer Kirkpatrick's
house. That house had been filled with this same kind of
chatter and smells of good food and sounds of laughter.

Meri had always loved to relive that time. She'd felt safe
at Jennifer's house, like when she was there things were
right in her world.

She'd never known until then what a real family was like.

Sooner than seemed possible, everything was cleaned
up, leftovers wrapped in the refrigerator or freezer or on
the counter and the last guests were leaving. She shook her
head. To her own shock, she didn't particularly want to go.

She'd better not let herself be drawn into this place for
even another second. It felt too safe.

She looked at her watch. Stared at it. Could it possibly
be nearly four o'clock? It was. So much for staying no more
than an hour. So much for her schedule. She must go. The
work waiting in her room had to be done by the time she
landed in New York.

Barb was last to leave, after hugging Meri first, then
Lilah.

"It's over now," she said, looking from one of them to
another in a way that said she meant more than just the dinner. "Y'all remember that Edie Jo did the best she could,
just like everybody else in this world. Then walk on."

Lilah took Meri's hand and started to squeeze it while
they stood at the screen door to watch Lilah's friend drive
away. Meri pulled back. She couldn't allow herself to make a
silent pact with this grandmother she'd just met, not even
an agreement to follow Barbara Jane's advice.

She couldn't let herself get too comfortable. She didn't
even know this woman.

Meri said, "I need to get going, too."

Lilah shook her head and untied her apron. "Kick those pretty shoes off and rest your feet. You want a ribbon to tie back your hair? Might even unbutton that little old skirt and let yourself breathe."

"Why?"

"We're gonna sit right here at this kitchen table under the best ceiling fan in the country and drink hot, fresh coffee 'til the sweat rolls in rivers down our spines."

Well. That was Lilah. With the authority in her voice, telling Meri what to do.

Lilah went to the counter, where Barb had put all the remnants of the desserts.

"*And* finish up what's left of Bobbie Sue Turner's hummingbird cake. I saw you didn't eat but one tee-ninetsy little scrap of a dessert. You have to do your part. You said you have a sweet tooth."

This woman's chatter was mesmerizing. Meri felt herself being sucked into its lilting, rocking rhythm when she should be on her way to her car.

She glanced at her bag, hanging on the coatrack. She felt naked without it. And she needed to check her phone for messages. Maybe there was one from Tim.

But, before she knew what she was doing, she obeyed Lilah and kicked off her shoes.

"I can't stay long," she said. "My room's in Rock Springs for tonight but I have to leave for San Antonio and the airport tomorrow fairly early."

Lilah smiled. "There's not *that* much cake left."

After a beat, she added, "Come by on your way out of town and I'll make sausage gravy and biscuits for breakfast. I . . ."

Lilah bit her lip. She held Meri's gaze.

"I'd really like it if you'd come for breakfast," she said. "But I don't want to push you into anything. I know your life is busy and far away from here. Just know that you're always welcome at Honey Grove."

She waited a beat and added, "Anytime. For as long as you like. You don't even have to call."

Meri tried not to acknowledge the new surge of warmth that ran through her.

"Thank you, Lilah."

What was the matter with her? Where was her defensive wall? Even to hang around for more dessert proved she was losing it.

Get a grip, Meri. Get going. You don't have time for this.

But something about padding around on the worn wooden floor in her bare feet made her think about that class on relaxation techniques. She'd paid good money for that.

She might as well enjoy the moment, something she was trying hard to learn to do. While she relaxed she would keep guarding herself. She didn't need a mother anymore *or* a grandmother. She didn't need anything she hadn't had before.

She had her life all carved out.

However, when her mouth opened it said, "Breakfast would be nice. Thank you."

Lilah smiled. "I'll show you how the other Meredith Kathleen made sausage gravy. Pass that recipe right on down to you. Be here at six thirty sharp—if that's early enough for you to make your flight."

"Yes, that's fine," Meri said as she went to the refrigerator. "May I have a diet Coke?"

"Help yourself to anything you want," Lilah said, lifting the glass dome off the tall white cake. "When you're here, you're home."

Meri wouldn't let that remark or the words *other Meredith Kathleen* sink in. She wouldn't think about anything at all for a little while. She'd just eat cake and drink diet Coke and feel the smooth, smooth floor with her feet. Then she'd go back to her room in Rock Springs and be alone so she could think.

She walked to the sink to open the soda can. As she pulled the tab, she saw a half-dozen ants scurrying over the faucets. She yelped and jumped back. First the cat and now these bugs.

"There're ants over here! Are they those fire ants that sting? Or bite or whatever?"

Lilah didn't even look up. She shook her head. "Those pesky things. I've been meaning to put a stop to that. I will. Later."

All right. It was Lilah's business. Meri wouldn't look at the ants anymore.

Lilah was cutting two thick slices of cake and putting them on transparent pink glass dessert plates. "I need to broaden my horizons," she said. "Tell me about life in the big city."

Meri didn't want to answer a series—or any—personal questions, like that one earlier about dangerous love.

She busied herself getting ice and a glass while Lilah carried their full plates to the table. Maybe she could start a different conversation.

But no. Not with Lilah Briscoe on the other end of it— Meri had learned something since she'd been here.

"Well?" her grandmother said, as they sat down at the cozy breakfast table guarded by a handsome ceramic rooster.

"Life in the big city," Meri said, as she took a bite of cake that melted her to her toes, "is the proverbial rat race, only everybody wears sneakers and black suits."

She tasted the cake again. "And it's completely lacking— at least my neighborhood is—in scarf-stealing cats and friends bringing cakes made in heaven."

"Ain't it so?" Lilah said. "I'm surprised there's a speck of it left. Bobbie Sue has given this recipe to half the county but nobody else can make it like she can."

"Secret ingredient?" Meri had another bite. Layers of the best white cake she'd ever eaten, then luscious creamy filling alternating with fresh strawberries, pineapple and bananas. And a jellied filling, too. With a thin layer of exquisite coconut icing on top.

"Has to be. But what?"

"We'll figure it out," Meri said, "if we have to eat every crumb."

Lilah, her mouth full, made noises of agreement.

Henry's loud snoring matched the rhythm of the fan's blades that were stirring Meri's hair. A small breeze coming in through the screen door brushed over her skin. Out in the pasture, one of the horses whinnied. Wasn't that the term? *Whinny*? Or was it *neigh*?

She sighed, twined her legs around the rungs of the chair, and ate another bite of cake. She had a third and savored it while she stared out the window over the sink. The sky was deep and blue today. She was a native-born Texan. That was a Texas sky. Maybe if she'd been here more often, she'd know whether or not it looked like this every day.

However, everything about this place and people was wrong for her.

I have to get going.

But her limbs felt too heavy to move. The silence stretched out until she realized this was the longest time ever without a word from Lilah.

She picked up her diet Coke. The older woman was staring off into space as if Meri had already left for the hotel.

"Are you all right?"

Lilah looked at her then, straight and hard. For a long moment.

Finally, she drawled, "I was just sittin' here thinkin' how exactly like Edie Jo it was for her to go off all the way down there to South America and get herself killed and then make us wait four years to find her body."

Meri, surprised and shocked by the frankness—it was like Shorty's pine-box remark at the funeral—snorted and spewed diet Coke out through her nose. Coughing, grabbing for napkins, she tried to talk but couldn't. Lilah jumped up and ran around the table to pat her on the back.

"I know you think I'm awful," she said, "but I've spent many a three o'clock hour in the night wondering why she couldn't just behave," Lilah said, her hand resting now on Meri's shoulder. "Why did she have to be always roaming around, always looking for something else, somebody else, someplace else?"

With a final pat, she went back to her chair. Meri's shoulder felt too cool without the warmth of her grandmother's hand.

When Meri got her dignity back, she said, "I know. I always wondered why she didn't . . ."

She clamped her lips together.

You've sworn never to talk about Edie Jo. Or think about her. You are completely out of control.

Don't come back for breakfast, Meri. Get on the road.

Three

All day, Meri had wished to be alone with her work but once she was back in her room at the Rock Springs Inn, changed into jeans and tee and ready to get something done, the faces and conversations that had filled her day came between her and the screen every time, no matter what folder she opened. Finally, she gave up and got out of there.

She drove into the heart of Rock Springs, an old town built around a square with an imposing county courthouse, and then out the highway to the east, a strange restlessness pulling at her. A winding gravel road caught her eye and she turned onto it. Tall trees met overhead and blue bluffs rose in the distance behind green pastures. Peaceful. Surely such scenery would calm her.

That hope shattered on the second curve. An animal—a deer—stood in the middle of the road. She was going faster than she thought. It jumped; she braked and swerved. One front wheel of the SUV dropped over the edge of a ditch and she came to a sudden stop that shook her to the bone.

At least the deer wasn't hurt. A brief comfort before the worries wiped it out. Rental car. Damaged? She put it in reverse and tried, several times, but no way was it going to do anything but spin the wheels. She'd have to call for help. But whom? She saw no houses on either side of the road.

But a truck pulling a trailer was coming down the road behind her. It began to slow. It pulled half off the road and stopped, hazard lights flashing. What to do? Could she trust just anyone who happened to come along?

She watched in the rearview window as a man in a cowboy hat got out of the truck and came toward her with his limping stride. Her ragged breathing caught. It was the guy she'd met at the funeral who'd joked about Rock Springs and New York City.

The guy with the blazing blue eyes and low voice. She admitted at that instant that she'd noticed his absence at the funeral dinner. She remembered his name, too. Caleb.

She opened her door only to discover the SUV was stuck at such a crazy angle she'd have to jump to the ground.

"Meredith," he called. "Don't even think about it. You break a leg now and we'll really have trouble."

We? His take-charge tone comforted her as much as it embarrassed her.

She jumped anyway, fighting to keep her balance with her sandals slipping on the grass. He reached her and held out a hand.

She shook her head. "I like to be independent," she said, and tried three times to climb out on her own, sliding back each time.

Finally, she put her hand in his large, callused one.

"That's right," he said, his voice so gentle it touched her. "It's a sign of strength to accept help when you need it. But then, you know that. You're a lawyer."

His hand was gentle, too. He let her go as soon as she stood in the road. He looked down at her feet.

"Why didn't you dig your heels in? Those look like mountain-climbing spikes to me."

"I didn't want to ruin them."

He shook his head sadly, then grinned. "Tell me. How did you independently end up in the ditch?"

Her breathing still hadn't calmed down since the accident. She tried for a deep breath.

"A . . . deer. It jumped the opposite way I thought it would."

"What're you doing all the way out here, anyhow? Where's Miss Lilah?"

He seemed genuinely surprised she was alone.

"At Honey Grove. I'm staying at the Rock Springs Inn."

His eyebrows went up, but he said only, "You're a ways from there, too."

She blurted the truth that she hadn't acknowledged until that moment. "I wanted to see the town where my . . . Edie Jo grew up. I just turned onto this road because it's pretty."

He nodded. "All right, then, let's get you back on the road. I can pull you out, but I'll have to unhook this trailer to do it."

"Oh no. Don't go to all that trouble. Just tell me who to call . . ."

"No way. I'd never live it down. Let me just get unhooked."

She noticed then that there was a horse in the trailer, looking out through its own little window. "Your horse looks friendly," Meri offered.

Caleb laughed as he took a block of wood out of the truck bed, set it on the ground and began cranking the hitching device. He stopped and looked at her.

"You know what? He'd be a lot happier if he could get out and move around a little. My brother Gideon has hauled him all the way from Whitesboro today. How about you walk him around a little while I get this done?"

Meri gasped. "Me? But I haven't been near a horse since I was six years old."

"No sweat. He's gentle as a lamb, just a great big pet. You don't have to *ride* him. Just hold on to a rope and walk him up and down. Any independent-minded person can do it."

She threw a sharp look at him. "That's hitting below the belt."

"Nope. Fair play. Come on, Miss New York City. If you can live there and make a career, you can surely walk up and down a country road exercising an old horse who's well known as just a sweetheart."

"I'd ruin my shoes on the gravel," she said. "And you know how I am about my shoes."

He stopped cranking and straightened up to look at her. "No danger to your shoes. Here you go."

He stepped to the front of the truck bed where—she saw for the first time—a pair of rubber boots hung by the soles upside down between the bed and the cab.

"These may be a *little* big." He looked thoughtfully, assessingly, from his feet to hers. "But I don't think you'll have any trouble wearing them."

"Well, thanks so much! Your feet are *lot* bigger than mine."

He brought the boots to her. "Just kick off those ridiculous things and slip into these. They'll be much more comfortable, and I don't care if you wear them in gravel."

He ignored all the protesting noises she could make, saying that walking his horse was the least she could do for him since he was doing such a big favor for her and laying on such guilt that the next thing she knew, she was standing in a pair of knee-high—huge—rubber boots holding a lead rope in her hand with an enormous brown horse on the other end of it.

"Just stay here, at his shoulder and walk slowly," he said. "Keep your rope just about this length. Like this."

She seemed to do fine, walking Old Bear up and down on the verge of the road. Really, it made her feel useful and competent somehow, wearing the clunky boots and doing something for the animal. As if she were a farmer, too. Or maybe as if she belonged here.

Caleb watched them closely from the corner of his eye as he worked on the hitch. Old Bear dropped his head and sneaked a bite of grass.

"Don't let him do that," he said. "It's a bad habit. When he's on the lead, he needs to concentrate on you."

"How do I keep him from it?"

"Pull his head up. Not too fast."

But Meredith jerked the rope faster than Caleb could talk and when Old Bear resisted, it slipped through her hands.

She screamed a little. "Oh no!"

Old Bear startled at that, jerked his head high and took all of the rope as he turned away. "Oh nooooo! No! Caleb, what should I do? Help me!"

End of fantasy. She was way out of her element here.

Caleb stood up straight to watch the show, and she could hear him fighting to keep the laughter out of his voice. "No, no. This is something you can do independently. You can catch him. *Go,* Meredith!"

Old Bear started moving faster but he never broke into a run. He looked back over his shoulder to gauge Meredith's speed and kept just ahead of her. Not even an arm's length ahead.

"Old Bear's the laziest horse I've ever known," Caleb called after her. "Speed up. You can catch him."

Meredith gritted her teeth. She wasn't about to give up. It was a matter of principle. She *could* catch this horse.

But Old Bear had other plans. She got close enough once to brush his tail with the tips of her fingers, but no closer. He avoided stepping on the rope, kept one eye out for her speed and did not move one bit faster than he had to in order to keep his freedom. It was almost as if he were taunting her.

To her own surprise, Meri felt laughter bubbling up. It did no good to rush at him because he still kept his position the same distance away. He was an old pro at this, that much was clear.

To her even greater consternation, she started *talking* to him.

"Hel-lo, horse!" she was calling. "Old Bear! Are you listening? Where are you going? Come back. I'll let you eat grass, no matter what Caleb says. Helloooo! Hey! Are you hearing me?"

She took little breaks to get enough breath to yell some more. Now it was a silly game.

Meredith Briscoe never played silly games. She did

whatever she set out to do. Caleb was watching her. She would prove that to him. "Grass! All the grass you want!"

Finally, though, she ran out of breath and had to gasp for it, but she made her legs keep moving. Insanely, she was bursting with repressed laughter just imagining how she looked flopping along in the boots.

That wasn't like her, either. She never, ever liked to look foolish or disheveled in any way.

But this was like being a kid again. She wasn't really worried because the horse clearly was not going to run away and get lost or anything. She stopped. So did Old Bear. Just out of reach. She ignored him. When he let down his guard, she would grab him.

She would catch him with no help from Caleb. She was *not* going to ask for help.

So, when she could breathe easily and Old Bear wasn't looking, she crept forward and made a grab for the rope. Before her fingers could close around it, he lifted his head and pulled it through them, taking one small step away from her. One small step that was just far enough.

Behind her, Caleb began laughing like a madman. "Hello, are you listening?" he called. "What did he say to that, Meredith? How about if you try 'Please give me the lead'?"

She turned and saw him wipe tears from his eyes before he started after them.

Oh, well, let him help. At least she hadn't asked for it.

Four

An early morning breeze began to rise out of the dark. Thank goodness for a little air stirring. Lilah lifted her face to it but, bad as she wanted to, she didn't let herself stand up and enjoy and take a bit of rest. Instead, she kept on picking tomatoes as fast as she could. She had to quit pretty soon and go cook breakfast for Meri.

She took a deep breath of the sweet scent of the fruit mixed with the bitter smell of the plants and moved on to the next one. The humid air was heavy to breathe and the temperature must not have dropped below the high eighties all night, so she was soaked. She'd feel a lot cooler if she didn't have to have the flashlight taped under one arm, but she'd still need the long-sleeved shirt to keep the leaves from irritating her skin. Even so, getting rid of the weight would help a little, but there wasn't so much as a glint of light in the east.

She took another breath and lingered on the fragrance of the rich black earth. There came a waft of the cedars up on the bluff, too. Early morning air always smelled new and fresh. And old and familiar.

Oh, Lord. How many more early mornings would she have at Honey Grove?

How could she *not* be here? She was Honey Grove and Honey Grove was her. They were one and the same.

This farm was Ed's inherited place and he'd loved it but he hadn't loved it like she did. He was always talking about buying an RV and traveling all the time when they retired. He'd loved every minute of the "practice runs" they'd made when they could get away from the farm work. Lilah, too, had enjoyed the Smokies and the Rockies and the mesmerizing Plains. But mostly she found that her heart had stayed at home.

She twisted sideways so the light would shine lower, and reached for a beautiful tomato hanging behind a leaf. Gentle as her touch was, when she pulled it, her fingertips pierced the skin. She straightened up, dropped it on the reject pile and wiped her fingers on her jeans. She had the overripes piled on the back end of the Red Flyer wagon that Ed had bought for Edie Jo so long ago, and the good ones in a plastic bucket on the front. They outnumbered the culls by probably double.

She let herself have a minute's break to feel the dark land stretching around her. Home.

But for how long?

Lilah used the back of her wrist to wipe off the sweat standing on her forehead between the rolled bandanna and her hairline and flung it away. She felt like she'd never gone to bed at all and she'd probably be better off if she hadn't. Sometimes four hours of sleep could make you feel worse than none at all.

She bent and started picking again, missing Shorty working down the other side of the row. Yesterday, after everybody went home from the funeral dinner, she'd roped him into helping her start on this patch and they'd worked until nearly midnight. But six acres was too much for two people.

Before he left, he'd lectured her. "Now don't you get up early in the morning and come back out here, Lilah. These tomatoes are right on the edge of being too ripe to haul."

He knew it wouldn't do any good to tell her that. They weren't *all* too ripe and she needed every single dime she could get her hands on, and she was going to gather the good ones until first light. That'd give her time to have breakfast on the table by six thirty.

Except for the gravy, of course. She'd wait to show Meri how to make it.

She smiled. That'd be a real grandmother/granddaughter thing to do.

By the time she'd finally quit picking and was back in the house, washed up and in clean clothes, Lilah could feel tension tightening every nerve in her body.

It was nothing short of pitiful how worked up she was over this breakfast. She didn't mean to be, she kept trying not to be, but somehow hope had slipped in under her skin. Right past her common sense and her learnings from hard experience.

She was old enough to know better. Did she expect to forge a bond with her granddaughter in the time it would take to eat one meal?

Ever since Meri had said she'd come to Rock Springs, Lilah had been having flashes of future phone calls from New York and a visit now and then. Images of a granddaughter who wanted all of the family recipes and maybe even this little glass pint jar Lilah held in her hand this minute as she measured out the dry ingredients for the biscuits.

She ran her thumb over the raised outline of Texas with the word *TEXAS* above and *MASON* below. No telling how old it was. All she knew was she was the third generation of women who'd kept their baking soda in it.

It'd be such a shame for it, not to mention all the old recipes (plus the ones Lilah had invented) and the photos and letters to go to somebody with no connection. Saddest thing she ever saw was family albums for sale at a flea market. She'd rather burn them first.

Her hand stilled, the pad of her thumb centered on the *X*. Was she about to become a needy old woman all alone in her house?

But she *did* need young life in it. She'd been cheated
out of that with Edie Jo. And with Meri, she'd cheated herself, hadn't she? Yes. Giving up like a sissy with no grit at
all when she should've been scouring the earth to find the
child, no matter what it cost.

She squinted at the clock across the kitchen, shadowy
because artificial light ruins early summer mornings. After
forty-six years, Lilah could cook breakfast blindfolded if
she had to.

Six o'clock. There was plenty of time and daylight now
to pick the persimmons. She'd had her shower and was all
crisp and clean. The sausage was fried and on the warmer,
drippings waiting in the iron skillet, biscuits mixed except
for the oil and buttermilk, coffee ready to set perking, table
set with the butter softening and the jams, jellies and honey
arranged around it.

Lilah smiled at her handiwork. At least Meri would get
one more good meal in her before she went back up north.
Bless her heart, she was skin and bones. Not to mention
pale as a ghost. She *needed* to learn to cook. Bad.

She exchanged her little apron for the fruit-gathering
one with the big pockets and stepped out onto the porch. A
big breath of sweet, grassy air caught in her chest and she
stood there for a moment, savoring it.

The rolling fields of her place were mostly green and
lush with all the rain they'd had. They bordered the hay
meadows. Curving around behind them like a protecting
arm were the high bluffs on the other side of the river,
rugged gray granite scattered with dark green splotches
of cedars and ever-changing movements of sunlight and
shadow. Every time her eyes came to rest on them, she had
trouble taking them away.

"I will lift up mine eyes unto the hills from whence
cometh my help."

*Thank You, Lord, for this place. And please, please
help me keep it.*

She stood for a moment longer, then moved across the
porch.

Pushing the constant money worries away, she headed down the steps. Another hour and it'd be too hot to enjoy being outside.

As she went, she tried to push away the other reality that kept nagging in the back of her mind. Yesterday, Meri had left in a hurry, acting a little bit strange. She might not show up for breakfast after all. She might call or she might not and she might be on the road to San Antonio this very minute.

Lilah grabbed the ladder from where she'd leaned it against the corner of the house and dragged it to the tree. All her life, she'd been an optimist.

Stop obsessing about the girl. You are old enough to know better, Lilah Briscoe, and you don't want to be pathetic. You don't have time for a granddaughter—you've got a farm to run.

A farm to save.

She breathed in deep. The cool early morning pulsed so sweet and fresh it went right through her. She savored it in her lungs, then breathed deeper.

No matter who came or went, this was a great day. Every day she woke up alive and still on the farm was a great day.

Sanders, her old rooster, crowed, agreeing with her. The sun was up and he thought he'd brought it.

She smiled as she stuck the ladder up into the thick branches and found a spot to prop it against the trunk. Yes, Sanders was a good old bird, but it'd taken years to break him of the habit of trying to drive his beak into her leg every time she went into the chicken pen. By rights, she should've wrung his neck long ago.

Maybe she didn't because, truth was, she kind of liked a good fight once in a while. It got the blood moving.

She balanced the ladder, then stepped on the bottom rung to set it in the ground, tied her apron strings tighter and started to climb.

The persimmons weren't thick on it, but that was all right—she didn't have enough trees for them to be a cash crop. Just this few would be a big plenty for her own uses, since she didn't have time or energy to do a lot of preserving while she tried to farm with the very fewest hired help possible.

True to life, the best persimmons were the hardest to reach. She climbed another rung and stepped one foot off into the fork of the tree, holding on to a branch with her left hand, reaching higher with her right.

Boy, she'd better never let Barbara Jane know about this. B. J. was such a worrywart and she'd warned Lilah more than once not to climb this tree. If she ever found out Lilah did it anyway, she'd pitch such a wall-eyed hissy fit Lilah would *never* hear the end of it.

She got the really nice, fat one that she was after, put it in her pocket and eased back down a rung for another one, nearly as big, that she'd just spotted.

Better not knock the ladder over. Gonna need it for the trip back down.

Something came at her, buzzing straight at her face, mad as a hornet. Which it was. Yellowjacket wasp. She jerked backward and took the ladder with her, falling faster than thought, clawing at the tree as she went, grabbing nothing but leaves and twigs and then empty air.

All she knew was that she needed to get away from the ladder before it landed on her.

She'd been wrong about the ladder. She *didn't* need it, after all, to get to the ground.

Five

Meri took a long step from the gravel of Lilah's driveway onto the brick walk to keep her nude Jimmy Choo sandals out of the damp grass, pressing the phone closer to her ear as if that could change what Tim was saying.

It didn't. The Century Rails Transportation team was meeting fifteen minutes from now.

"*Without me?* A strategy session? Give me a *break*, Tim. What's going on?"

Her voice shook a little, which told her she was right on the edge of losing control. Her shocked mind raced in all directions: Had she missed something in her research, pissed Alan off somehow? She could think of nothing, nothing at all.

He wasn't the partner who was lead attorney on this case, but he *was* the one with the power . . . and he was touchy and unpredictable.

She swallowed hard. "Look. My plane lands a little after noon. With any luck at all, I can be at the office by two at the latest. Why not *wait for me?*"

Now she was shouting because the horses in the barn

behind her were whinnying or neighing or whatever the hell you call it, at the top of their lungs. Who knew horses could make so much noise? For God's sake, why didn't Lilah shut their little windows at night?

And now somebody was yelling . . .

Her frantic brain finally took in the words.

"Help! Meri, is that you? Over here!"

Lilah? Then she saw her. Lying on the *ground*? With a *ladder* across her legs?

"Tim. I'll call you back."

She hit End Call and began to run. As fast as she could in a pencil skirt, her heavy bag clamped against her side.

Lilah lay in a heap, not moving.

Oh no! Don't let her be badly hurt.

That was Meri's first thought. Which made her feel a little less of a monster about the second one.

No! I do not have time for this. They're meeting without me . . .

"Help!"

"I'm here. I'm coming, Lilah."

Her grandmother just lay there, pale as paper. There was a sheen of sweat on her face.

Was she dying? A heart attack, maybe, had made her fall off the ladder?

What was first aid for a heart attack? Aspirin. Did she have any in her bag?

As soon as Meri came into her line of vision, Lilah gasped, "Move . . . ladder. I can't . . . my wrist's broke all to pieces."

Meri realized she still had the phone in her hand. "I'm dialing 911," she said, her thumb already in motion. "What *happened*, Lilah?"

"No," Lilah said, using a weak approximation of her vehement tone from yesterday. "Take me in the car."

"No," Meri snapped back at her. "I've had only basic first-aid training and all I know is you must *not* move at all."

She dropped her bag into the grass, tucked the phone into her shoulder and picked up one end of the ladder.

Tried to pick it up. "Oh my God, this thing is *heavy.*"

The phone was ringing at the emergency call center, wherever that might be.

"Don't take the Lord's name in vain," Lilah said.

The horses neighed again. And again. They should never be put in the barn. It was too close to the house.

A calm voice in Meri's ear said, "What is the location and nature of your emergency?"

The tone steadied her.

"Honey Grove Farm," she said, pulling up her skirt so she could squat and use her legs for more leverage. "A fall from a ladder. Yes, Lilah Briscoe. She thinks her arm is broken. Do you need directions?"

"No. Everybody knows Honey Grove. I'm sending help as we speak. Stay on the line and . . ."

But the phone slipped off her shoulder and fell into the grass when Meri put her weight into lifting the ladder.

"*Now* you've done it," Lilah said, "gone and alarmed . . . the whole county . . . and for no reason."

The horses sounded off again. Even more loudly.

"It's feeding time," Lilah said.

Meri didn't have the breath to answer. She managed to raise one end of the ladder enough to shift its weight—*some* of it—onto the other end and, grunting with the effort of holding it up, she began walking, swiveling it away from Lilah.

Her arms burned. She considered herself fairly fit, but . . . maybe not.

"You called Roy Jo and now everybody's gonna be calling and . . . coming by and taking up my time and asking me how this happened. You could take me straight to Doc's office . . . get a cast on this . . . and be back by nine o'clock."

Meri opened her mouth but she didn't have any more breath than Lilah did until the ladder cleared Lilah and Meri let it drop into the grass.

"Don't be silly," she snapped. Her arms were really shaking now. She *must* make time to go to the gym on a more regular basis.

"They'll take me . . . to the hospital and I can't stay there. I've got a farm to run."

"You are being completely unreasonable," Meri said, anger taking over from worry.

She retrieved her phone and dropped it into her bag. "Stop complaining. Your judgment's impaired. You may have internal injuries."

Lilah's face flushed with color at last. "I am *not* impaired! I don't have time for a big furor and the emergency room and all that."

Meri's temper flashed sarcasm. "What a coincidence. Neither do I."

How long would all this take? She looked at her watch, her fingers itching to call Tim but her mind warning that she'd better pay attention until the ambulance arrived. Like it or not, she was responsible for Lilah until then.

"Well, then, you just go right ahead on," Lilah said. "Help me sit up and then *go.*"

Lilah began trying to dig the heels of her flats into the ground for leverage, raising her shoulders a little, trying to do a sit-up without moving her arms.

"Give me a break. Will you be reasonable and lie still? It'll just be a few minutes until the ambulance arrives."

"Thanks to *you*. Right this minute, the news is already all over town."

"What is it with that? You're trying to keep a broken arm a secret? How're you planning to explain the fact you can't use it? That it's in a cast?"

"Don't stand over me with your hands on your hips. And don't take that tone with me. I'm your grandmother, missy, and I'll do what I think best."

Lilah was pale again, and gasping hard for breath between words. But she did stop struggling to sit up. Her eyes were sharp and bright on Meri's face, looking to see if she got the message.

"Is that how you fell? Doing what you think's best? Right now, *I* say what's best, and that's for you to lie still."

Lilah flushed even redder. "And don't give me orders, either," she said. "I'll get up if I want to."

"Not *even* if I have to sit on you," Meri said. "You think I *like* being responsible for you? I do not. I don't like being responsible for anyone but myself."

"Then you go on. *Right now.* Sissy and Buck will be here in a minute. You're the one started all this 911 business, so you might as well take advantage of it. Hit the road."

Meri was ashamed, but she *ached* to do just that.

"I finish what I start," Meri said.

"Maybe so," Lilah said. "After all, you did show up this morning."

That remark hit Meri like a slap. "Of course. Did you think I wouldn't? I accepted your invitation, didn't I?"

She would never admit that she *had* been tempted to cancel.

"Yes," Lilah said. "But as soon as you said you'd come, I had a feeling you wished you had refused."

"So on the basis of that feeling, you thought I would stand you up without so much as a call?"

"No. I thought you'd call. But you were raised by a mother who never did one thing unless she was in the mood for it that very minute, and I figured that today you'd wake up in the mood to get back to your work and your life."

The old pain surged and pushed the words out of Meri before she could hold them in. "My *mother* did not raise me. She left me with neighbors and sitters and acquaintances and strangers when I was little and then when I was fourteen, she left me at my best friend's house and never came back."

When would that ambulance arrive?

She threw up her head to listen. Had she really heard a siren in the distance?

She hoped to God it was true. And she was not taking His name in vain when she thought it.

Six

Meri finally made it to the hospital after following all of Lilah's directions: Bring her purse with the insurance cards in it, turn off the warming oven with the sausage in it, put the butter back into the refrigerator and throw some hay to the horses. She stopped just outside the half-open door to her grandmother's room to catch her breath and check her phone again for Tim's response to her text message.

Surely he'd texted since she last checked the phone when she left the car. Surely he could've found a second to reply, even if he couldn't take a call. Surely he had done that but the beep had been obscured by the elevator and other noises in the hospital.

Fumbling for the phone, juggling her bag, Lilah's bag and the loose mail that the rural carrier had thrust at her when they met at the end of the driveway (not only was the woman out working before seven A.M., but she'd already heard about Lilah's accident and suggested that Meri might want to wait a day or two before giving her grandmother the letter from the bank!), Meri dropped it all on the floor. She squatted to retrieve everything.

Inside the room, Lilah and Barbara Jane were talking. Meri heard her name.

"Meri should've cut me a switch from that persimmon tree," B. J. said. "You deserve a whippin', Lilah Briscoe, for not having better sense than to climb up in it. And at your age!"

"What I deserve the whippin' for is not moving heaven and earth to find that child when she was little and raise her myself."

Lilah's voice trembled. It held so much fresh pain that it froze Meri in place.

"B. J., listen to this. She told me this morning that Edie Jo completely deserted her when she was fourteen. *Exactly the age when a girl needs a mother most.* She just went off and left her with a friend's family when she was only *fourteen*! I tell you what, Barbara Jane, hearing that hurts me a million times worse than these broken bones are hurting right now."

Silence from B. J. Then a soothing tone. "But look at it this way, Lilah. She's turned out so well, it couldn't have been a bad home where she left her."

"It wasn't her *family*," Lilah growled. "I was her *grandma* and I was alive and healthy and I *failed* her. Even if the Good Lord forgives me, I can't ever forgive myself."

Meri's heart raced. She felt cold and then hot. Lilah had deep feelings about *her*? She would never have guessed. Lilah didn't even know her. But the pain and regret in her voice were almost palpable.

Meri's hands shook a little. It was so strange to think that someone besides Tim cared about her as a person, and not just for what she could do.

It was weirdly moving, like hearing she was named for Lilah's mother.

"You need some help?"

Startled, Meri tore her gaze from the envelope with the return address "Central Texas Bank of Rock Springs" that she was supposed to keep from Lilah, to look up at a pixie girl with short curly brown hair who looked to be about twelve years old. Well, maybe fourteen or fifteen.

The girl squatted down opposite her to help pick up the scattered mail. Her big brown eyes kept going back and forth from it to Meri's sandals.

"Are those Jimmy Choos? They are *awesome*. When I get my own business, I'm going to buy some gorgeous, famous-brand shoes."

Meri dragged her mind to the question. "Yes, they are."

"I'm definitely gonna make enough money to dress like you do," the pixie informed her in a tone that said she knew what she was doing. "I saw you at the funeral. You are so cool."

Meri blinked. She wasn't accustomed to being considered cool.

"Uh, and also, I'm sorry for your loss."

They stood up and the girl held out her hand. "I'm Dallas Fremont. I'm a volunteer here at the hospital for my FFA chapter. So is my brother, Denton. But if you meet him, I want you to know that we are *not* twins."

"Meredith Briscoe."

They shook hands and the girl handed over the magazine and grocery flyers she'd picked up. She glanced at Lilah's door. "Right now I have to go get a wheelchair because Banker Quisenberry's going home today, but tell Miss Lilah I'll be in to see her in a little while. She's my godmother, like in a book. I don't know if you know that."

Dallas disappeared as quickly as she'd materialized, and a nurse passed by Meri on her way down the hall. Meri glanced at her phone, which still had no messages, clutched all her burdens and went into Lilah's room.

She had to get through with all this and get on her way to the airport.

What was a decent length of time to stay? She *couldn't* miss her flight.

But she would like to hear a prognosis before she left. Lilah's face was pale again beneath her tan. What if she had internal injuries?

After all, she is your grandmother.

"Thank you, Meri," Lilah said, looking at her. "I know

you didn't really have time for all that but this hospital is on the San Antonio Highway, so it didn't take you out of your way any."

"I can still make my flight," Meri said. "Why don't you give me your cell phone number so I'll be able to check on your progress? Have you seen a doctor yet?"

She needed to get out of here. Not only to make the early flight but to think. It was unsettling to hear that Lilah had cared about her as a child. Meri had believed Edie Jo's story that Lilah didn't want either of them.

"No, but I've had enough broken bones in my life to know that my wrist is smashed. You go on now and don't miss your plane."

"Lilah's living in the Stone Age still," B. J. said. "I'll give you *my* cell phone number 'cause she doesn't have one."

Meri and B. J. exchanged numbers. "I'm glad to have a way to get in touch with you, Meri," Barbara said. "After all, you're Lilah's only blood kin except for her baby of a cat."

"I've got a farm to work," Lilah fretted. "I've got bills to pay. I can't be laid up for long."

Barbara said, "Well, who's fault is it you're hurt? Meri, did she admit to you that she'd fallen out of that tree? That she'd been climbing up in it like a crazy kid instead of a grown-up old enough to know better?"

Lilah scowled and clutched her upper arm. "Nobody's business but mine."

Barbara Jane snorted. "Not hardly. When Roy Jo called me to say you were on your way into town in the ambulance, I ran out of the Price Cutter like my hair was on fire and left a whole basketful of ice cream and fresh-cut meat and milk for poor little ol' Shuggie to have to put back on the shelves."

She smiled sweetly at Lilah. "Just so I could get over here in time to tell you good-bye."

"Don't be gettin' your hopes up, girl," Lilah said. "It'll be another thirty years, at least, before you inherit my claw-foot table. Remember, my grandma lived to be nearly a hundred and six."

Then she looked at Meri. "Where was Henry when you left, Meri?"

Meri, surprised, looked up from stacking the mail on the tray table. She had no choice but to leave the letter from the bank. What did the mailwoman think was in it? Anyway, Lilah seemed as strong as ever except she clearly was in pain.

"Henry? I don't know. I didn't notice him when I ran through the house to your bedroom. Why?"

"He's been declawed in his front paws, so he has to stay in the house, but he's always trying to get out."

Meri's eyes widened. "Oh no. I didn't look for him. I didn't realize I should. I have no idea where he was when I left."

"Personally, I don't believe in declawing a cat, but it'd already been done when I got him from the shelter. It leaves them too helpless if they come up against another animal, plus it affects their mind, is what I think."

"Oh, my God. I'm so sorry. I would've . . ."

"He's all right," B. J. said, "even if he did slip out the door. He's got his teeth, not to mention the heart of a snake. But you're right. *Something* affected his mind."

Meri looked at Lilah, who was frowning in worry.

"I don't know that I have time to go back," she said, glancing at her phone again. Still no message. "It's urgent that I catch the early flight."

"You catch it," Lilah said. "I'll send somebody else to Honey Grove. You might drive too fast and have a wreck with that hateful voice in a box telling you where to go and how to get there. It takes a bushel of concentration just to listen to that thing, much less to watch where you're going."

A nurse Lilah and Barbara greeted as Wanda Sue came in, fussing around with a blood pressure cuff. She said, "There's a bunch down there in the lobby wanting to see you, Miss Lilah. But I'm keeping them out because you sure don't need company before you can even see the doctor and get something for pain. Doreen's having them all sign a list she can give to you later so you'll know who came."

Lilah glanced at Wanda Sue and said, "Doreen likes to be helpful."

She rolled her eyes at B. J.

"Oh, and your pastor is here. He wanted me to tell you that he's praying for you."

Which made Lilah ashamed of herself for being catty about Doreen.

Wanda gently removed Lilah's good hand from clutching the hurt arm and slapped the blood pressure cuff on.

"Yeah, well, they're all just really worried about you. Betty Tolliver rushed in because she heard you broke both legs and dislocated your back trying to get Henry down off the roof."

"Heaven help us all!" Lilah said. "I hope the Limestone Fire Department boys don't hear that and rush out to Honey Grove to save him. I don't have the money to pay for that kind of foolishness."

B. J. said, "Don't worry, nobody but you would try to save that cat."

"You're just jealous, Barb. Admit it: Your dog has no personality at all."

"So *you* say."

Meri looked at them, completely unruffled by the insults to their pets. Was this how it was between old friends?

"We'd better be getting some help lined up for the chores," Lilah said. "We need to get ahold of Shorty. He was going to the river today."

"I've already sent Earl Thomas to go get him," Wanda said. "I thought about that first thing when I heard they were bringing you in."

"Thanks," Lilah said. "My horses have only had hay this morning. Shorty can feed the grain and turn them out." She looked at Meri. "I didn't want to put all that on you, Meri."

Meri couldn't tell if that was a hint to her or not. No matter. She had to get back to New York, and Henry and the horses could just wait for Shorty to take care of them.

But the question about Henry bothered her.

Lilah truly did love that cat like a baby. But really, he

hadn't been Meri's responsibility, had he? Not if she didn't know he should stay in the house.

She tried to wipe him off her list of worries.

"X-ray," somebody said, from behind Meri. "Excuse us, please. We have to take Miss Lilah to X-ray but we promise to bring her right back."

"Take your time," Barbara Jane said with a chuckle. "Give us a break."

Meri stepped up to the bed. "Lilah, I'll have to say good-bye now. I'll give B. J. my card and leave one for you. Keep me posted about your condition."

Lilah looked up at her earnestly as the techs started rolling her bed toward the door. Meri followed it, giving B. J. her card and a quick good-bye as she passed.

"Remember, you're welcome at Honey Grove anytime," Lilah called to her. "No need to phone first, Meri. If I'm gone to San Antonio for a movie or anything, I'll be back soon."

At the doorway. Lilah's gurney almost collided with a man in a wheelchair. Dallas was pushing it and she swerved just before they collided.

"Lilah," the portly man said, "you know you can't farm with only one arm. This may be a sign that it's time for you to give it up."

"I heard you got your bunions fixed, Buford. Congratulations."

And Dallas whisked Buford away so fast he didn't have a chance to reply.

Meri hurried out of the hospital before any of Lilah's friends in the lobby could stop her, ignoring the fact that Doreen was coming toward her. Without stopping, she got past them all by calling, "She's in X-ray right now. Yes, she's holding up well. Thanks for asking."

She felt as if she were barely escaping. Small-town life in Rock Springs was sending tentacles creeping and curling into her brain, tugging at her with a vague feeling that she was leaving unfinished tasks and unanswered questions here.

Why didn't cute, smart Dallas want to be mistaken for her brother's twin? What was going on with that letter from the bank? Was officious Buford the banker at Central Texas Bank of Rock Springs? What would be the X-ray results for Lilah? What was between Lilah and Doreen? What time would Shorty get back to feed the noisy horses?

Out of here. I've got to get out of here. I'm not responsible for any of that. None of it matters in my life.

But then there *was* the matter of the surly cat. Damned cat.

Not my problem. I cannot miss my flight, or I'm toast.

Cold fear for her job ran in her veins.

Maybe I already am toast, knowing how unpredictable Alan is. But what could he possibly have to use against me? Why take me off the most important case of my career? God! Why don't I hear from Tim?

She broke into an awkward run, fumbling in her bag for her phone. She pulled it out and stared at its face. No messages.

Her jaw locked as she got into the steaming car and ran the windows down while she turned the AC up to full blast. Tim, who was Savage, Mitchell's golden boy, *always* knew the latest gossip. And he wasn't telling her.

That chilled her faster than anything else could.

She wouldn't even think about what this meant to their quasi-engaged condition.

On the way through the parking lot to its highway entrance, she texted Tim one more time and nearly ran into an oncoming car doing it. That was all she needed right now—a fender bender in a rented car. She threw the phone into her bag and stared at the road ahead.

At the highway, she stopped and looked both ways. An eighteen-wheeler coming on the right. Which didn't matter since she would be turning right, into the empty lane.

But she waited, her foot hard on the brake. Right to San Antonio. Left back to Honey Grove and the cat. The scarf-destroying cat.

She didn't owe Lilah anything. And she wasn't falling for that guilt-and-regret performance about not finding

Meri when she was an abandoned child. People did what they wanted to do. Lilah had been the adult in the situation. Lilah didn't love her any more than Edie Jo ever did.

The truck passed with a huge swish of wind and noise. The highway was empty both ways.

Her heart pounding in her ears, Meri sat, squeezing the wheel with both hands.

Seven

What was she thinking?

If only she weren't so obsessive-compulsive. She was working on that but evidently she was making no progress. If she were, she would've asked one of Lilah's friends standing around in the hospital lobby to go to Honey Grove and check on Henry. They were there because they wanted to do something to help.

But she had to see with her own eyes that Henry was safe. Otherwise, she'd worry all the way to New York and she'd never be able to stop thinking about the cat. It was critical for her to arrive at the office with her mind sharp and focused.

She shifted her butt in the lush leather seat of the SUV and pressed down on the accelerator just a touch more. She *did* have enough time before her flight, yet not a lot to spare in searching for him, so she began planning ahead. Park at the end of the brick walk, that'd be a few steps closer, run in, and probably she'd find him in his little bed in the corner of the kitchen. If not, she'd check the windowsills.

Cats liked to sun themselves, right?

She added a little more speed, just one mile more on the speedometer, reached for her phone and hit redial. It was her strong opinion that no one should talk on the phone while driving, but this was an emergency.

Voice mail. Again. "Call me the *instant* you get out of the meeting. I have a right to know what this is all about." She paused, anger rising in her throat.

"Tim, what are you keeping from me?"

The words settled like cold pebbles into her deepest gut as soon as they left her mouth. Something was very, very wrong.

If not, Alan would've called beforehand to brief her, and it would've been an urgent, incredibly important reason that the CRT team was meeting without her.

Every cell in her body was leaning toward the airport, then New York, urging her to turn this car around. But, from the moment Lilah asked about that awful cat, Meri had fixated on him. She would get no peace until she saw with her own eyes that he was safe.

She had a flash of Doreen in the waiting room, asking how long Meri would be in Texas and the surprised ripple that ran across the room at the news she was on her way, leaving today. She'd caught the muttered words "grandma in the hospital."

All she could deduce was that local custom must be for a patient's family to stand vigil indefinitely. Well, she was *not* a local here.

You're her only blood kin. You and that baby of a cat.

She was not going to think about that or let any of this touch her emotions. Lilah didn't want her any more than Edie Jo had.

Meri was doing this for her own sake. She always fulfilled every responsibility as perfectly as humanly possible.

This was for her own peace of mind.

Lilah hadn't been shocked Meri was leaving, she'd told her to go.

Lilah was accustomed to taking care of herself.

She sat up straighter behind the wheel and started

slowing for the turn into Honey Grove. Lilah didn't care about her—why, she'd assumed Meri was as unreliable as Edie Jo and might not even show up for breakfast.

Well, right now she wished she hadn't.

She laid her phone down on the console with a feeling of cutting off her arm and tried to forget everything but finding the damned cat. The stress was tying her up in knots and she'd learned in relaxation class that worry was a waste of time and energy.

Her childhood, however, had taught her that many times worry was justified by reality.

She'd wait and call Tim again when she was boarding the plane. Maybe they'd go for a late dinner at that new Italian place and he'd tell her in person what was really going on.

He was banking on the CRT case as his ticket to an early partnership and once set on a goal, nobody could focus like Tim could. He was focused on work right now and not his . . . no, *their* . . . personal life.

She was halfway down the driveway toward the horses— still hanging their heads out of the barn with their big eyes looking for breakfast—when she caught a movement in the corner of her eye. She turned just in time to see a tawny streak flash into the driveway. Literally, she had no time at all to react. The bump came in the same millisecond she saw the movement and then she heard the terrible thud.

She jammed the brake and sat, clutching the wheel in both fists, her whole body trembling. What was it that she'd hit?

Meri tried to block it out, but the thought came clear: Whatever it was, it was the same color as Henry.

No. She would not *let* it be Henry.

Desperate hope flooded her as she forced herself to move, to turn off the motor, to get out.

Could it have been a . . . what? Rabbit? Were there tawny rabbits? What wild animals lived around here? A raccoon, maybe. They were black and white, though, weren't they? What was that one with the long, skinny tail?

She looked under the vehicle. Nothing. Hope rose with her as she stood up and tried to take in a deep breath.

Scanning the grass on both sides of the road, she willed her eyes to see some animal running away.

Stupid. That bump had sounded sickeningly final.

She walked down the driveway toward the barn, looking for a body thrown forward. Nothing.

But when she turned, she saw it. A tawny lump on the silver bumper, pale against the dark blue paint of the SUV. Yes, oh, God, it was the exact color of Henry.

Legs shaking, she started toward it even though her body begged to go backward and away. Her whole *being* ached to leap into the car and drive like a maniac straight to San Antonio, to the airport, to throw herself onto a plane.

If only she could get that lump off the bumper.

She started trying to run in that damn skirt. If only she'd known that she'd spend this day running.

Henry. For sure. If only there wasn't that long, skinny tail that grew darker and darker toward the tip.

Henry. Motionless. Miraculously silent. A trickle of blood coming out of him somewhere. She couldn't bring herself to look close for details.

Oh, God, she'd killed him!

You should've been paying attention to your driving, Meredith. You weren't even thinking about it. You could've prevented this.

No, no. How could she ever tell Lilah that her "only blood kin" had killed her "baby of a cat"?

He could *not* be dead. He was only stunned. She would not *let* him be dead even though yesterday she'd wanted to kill him herself.

You should've left town when you had the chance.

She ripped herself out of her jacket, threw it over him, and made herself pick him up. Ruining the jacket was what she deserved for being so stupid.

This is all your fault, Meredith. You should've checked on him before you left the house.

She shut out her critical inner voice and focused on

exactly where she'd seen that veterinary clinic a little outside
of downtown. She cradled the bundle in one arm, opened the
passenger door and laid him on the leather seat. She thought
he moved one paw but she couldn't be sure. She couldn't see
him breathing. She didn't have the guts to touch him.

Was it possible to give CPR to a cat? No. *No.*

She'd rather tell Lilah she'd killed her baby dead. It was
not possible.

She threw herself in behind the wheel, then slammed
the car into reverse, and backed it the length of the drive at
a dizzying pace. No traffic coming. She shot out into the
highway and headed toward Rock Springs.

There was a clinic with a gaggle of smiling animals
painted on its wooden sign at the edge of town . . . *yes*!
Next-door to the Dairy Queen.

She floored the accelerator and flew past Leroy's Store,
its BEER, BAIT AND AMMO sign nothing but a blur. Who *was*
this woman who'd taken over her body? The real Meredith
never drove recklessly and never took chances.

Well, except when it meant the difference between winning and losing. At work, in crucial situations, she'd taken
plenty of chances. She hated to lose and she would not
lose now.

If there was a breath left in this cat when she got him to
the hospital.

This might cost a small fortune. Selling the Hermès
scarf might've paid for it if the obnoxious creature hadn't
torn it to shreds. Were animal doctors as expensive as people doctors? What if he needed surgery?

She glanced at the static bundle on the other seat and
convinced herself that Henry really *did* move his paw
when she laid him down. She stared. The yellow silk jacket
was moving. Or was it? She reached to uncover his nose.

Then she slapped both hands around the wheel and just
drove.

The parking lot holding that silly sign was covered in
thick gravel and her tires threw it everywhere, including
all over the car, when she flew in, sliding on the back tires.

The paint job would be damaged, for sure. Good thing she always took out the insurance when she rented a car.

She braked right in front of the door, cut the motor and ran around the car to pick up the bundle in a gingerly way. Her heels clattered on the steps like warnings as she rushed him inside.

The girl behind the desk looked up. Too much—way too much—black eye makeup.

"A doctor," Meri yelled. "I need a doctor *now*. I hit him with the car and this cat may be dying . . ."

He probably *was* dead. He hadn't moved at all in her arms.

The girl jumped up, came to Meri, and lifted the jacket with an air of full medical authority.

"Henry?" She turned furious flashing eyes on Meri. "How come you don't learn to *drive*? *Give him here*."

She took him away from Meri and vanished through a swinging door, which she opened with her bottom so as not to hurt him further.

Meredith, breathing hard, stood staring after them.

This girl had *recognized* the cat?

Oh no! The Rock Springs grapevine moved information faster than instant messaging. It'd be terrible if Lilah heard this from someone else—that would make Meri feel completely dishonorable on top of all the guilt.

But she couldn't call her grandmother now. First, she had to have a prognosis to give Lilah some hope. If there wasn't one, then the bad news needed to be delivered in person.

Please, God. Let him be alive.

When the Goth girl, Zoe, according to the sign on the counter, came back, Meri would warn her to maintain the doctor-patient privilege. Surely veterinarians had one of those, too.

Especially if it turned out that the hateful cat *died*.

Breathing hard, perspiring profusely all over the sleeveless silk top that matched her butter-colored jacket, she brushed at the bloodstains on her skirt. Good luck with that. They were as permanent as the gravel scratches all over the toes of her new Jimmy Choos.

Amazingly, only some small part of her even cared about the damage.

She only wished she still had the money she'd paid for these clothes.

But if she had to, she'd borrow to the limit of her income to pay whatever it took to save Henry.

And she'd do it not only to assuage her guilt and protect Lilah from the sorrow of losing him. She would have to do it to save her own life. This girl would probably lead a town posse to hang Meri at sunrise if the obnoxious cat died.

Eight

Meri had paced the reception area from one end to the other, twice, when she glanced outside and saw the car still sitting in the parking lot with both doors hanging open. Her bag, her phone, her briefcase, her *life* clearly visible and unprotected!

My God, what is the matter with me? This is still not me. I never do anything like this.

"Incredible." She was so far gone she was muttering aloud to herself as she rushed out the door.

She made it a tenet of her life never to let her emotions get the best of her. Her rigid control was one of her biggest assets—in her career and in her personal life. Example: She'd never brought up the subject of her and Tim's life plans together since that night when he didn't propose—despite the fact that he'd passed up the perfect moment.

Therefore, she could handle this crisis and keep her dignity, too. No more talking to herself aloud.

Meri might've been in Texas only one day and she might've run down her grandmother's cat, but she wasn't completely stupid, so she did take time to drive across the wide parking lot and leave the SUV beneath a huge old tree. At the dinner yesterday, after the funeral, she'd heard laughter at the remark ". . . and I told him: In Texas, the most valuable parking place is *not* the one closest to the door. It's the one in the shade."

She left the windows down for whatever cooling the breeze could bring, dropped her phone into her bag and went back in. Goth Girl could come back any minute with news.

How did such a rude employee keep her job? Surely Meri wasn't the only victim of her wrath. No way could Henry be *that* special. Could he?

Meri resumed pacing so she wouldn't let herself call Tim again. He *had* to be deliberately avoiding her calls or else the entire firm had imploded.

Then the girl, Zoe, came back and sat at her desk. She began answering the phone, ignoring Meri thoroughly as she pushed the buttons and spoke to each caller. Finally she deigned to inform Meri that the doctor would be with her shortly.

So Meredith sat down on the windowseat bench, calculating what time she'd need to leave Rock Springs to make her flight. Finally, her margin dwindled down to five minutes, there was still no doctor and she decided it would never happen. She booked herself on the next one out, leaving San Antonio at four that afternoon and texted that arrival time to Tim.

Then she practiced deep breathing as she tried to read the dog magazines and the horse magazines and the ads for ointments for mange and worm medicines and creams and pastes and sprays to create stronger, harder, hooves. Longer, glossier manes and tails. Shinier hair coats.

And tried not to call Tim again.

She got up and resumed pacing.

You should've checked on Henry first thing when you went into the house.

This is all your fault that you're in this situation.

She stood at the windowseat again, agonizing over The

Meeting, aching to be on her way back to New York, wishing for enough time to get to the office before it was over. Her heart was pounding as if she'd been running. Maybe she should just *go*. Henry was with a doctor now. There was nothing more she could do.

She started searching through the names on her phone, looking for somebody else in the office who'd tell her *something*, either facts or gossip.

But whom could she trust? Everybody at the firm was highly ambitious and out for him/herself and if they felt the earth shifting beneath their feet, too, it might do more harm than good to talk to them.

It'd be embarrassing if the whole firm knew she'd been trolling for info from someone besides Tim. Humiliating. The secretary assigned to Meri was a notorious gossip. She scrolled through her contact list, passing over name after name. Her head felt about to explode.

Finally deciding to take a chance on Stephanie Schwabe, her best woman friend at the firm, she touched that name. The swinging door opened behind her. She hit End Call and whirled to face it.

Caleb came through it.

Meri did a double take.

"What are *you* doing here?"

"Saving lives. Looks like you're working against me, at least among the cat population."

Meri felt her face flame as she rushed across the room to meet him.

"What are you saying? *What?* Are you telling me Henry is . . . *dead?*"

"No! Oh, Meredith, I'm sorry. I didn't think about your taking it like that. He's alive. For now."

Her heart was racing. "Is he about to die?" Then she recovered half her brain. "Is the veterinarian working on him right now?"

"That would be me."

He looked and sounded perfectly serious. Taken aback,

she stared. "You're a veterinarian? Why didn't you say so before?"

"The subject didn't come up. You were too busy rounding up horses last night for the conversation to wander . . ."

"Don't even start with that again." Meredith tried to grin ruefully. She didn't want to recall her embarrassment now. Not when all her energy should be focused on Henry "How badly hurt is Henry?"

He took her by the arm and led her to the windowseat, where they both sat down. Worried as she was about the cat, she noticed that he wore battered boots instead of polished ones and well-used jeans below a scrubs shirt but still looked as handsome as ever.

"Zoe said you hit Henry with the car."

"Well, yes. He ran into my wheel and there was no time to stop."

She waited for a remark about her problems with animals, or a dig about her driving skills, but he was completely professional now.

"Henry's urinary bladder is crushed. Cats have stupendous powers of regeneration but those are very individual, so we can't make a firm prognosis for several days. Obviously, if his bladder doesn't heal . . . well, he can't live."

Tears sprang into her eyes. She tried to blink them away.

"Why am I shocked?" she said. "I thought he was dead when I saw him on the bumper."

She blinked back tears. "This makes no sense." She sniffed. "I don't know why I'm so upset, he's not even a pleasant cat. Most of the time we don't even like each other."

Now this agony over whether or not she'd killed Lilah's cat would go on and on. She'd been dreading to hear he'd died but at least that would've been final. But, oh, Lilah had enough suffering. She didn't need the loss of her "baby," as B. J. called him. That would be so sad. Meri would hate to do that to her.

"How long?" she said, her voice a bit shaky.

Meredith. Get control of your emotions.

She cleared her throat and started over. "How long until we know about his . . . regenerative powers?"

She *really* resented Caleb Burkett for seeing through her façade to her upset inside. He did. She could see it in his eyes. And hear it in his voice as he said, "Couple of weeks. Henry's going to need constant care until we see whether the bladder will function normally again."

Bladder crushed. Couple of weeks. Constant care.

She thought about what was going on in New York and felt like screaming hysterically. But instead, she tightened her jaw.

"Isn't there a surgery or anything else you can do?"

"No. You'll need to monitor his urinary output," Caleb said. "Change the litter every time he goes—I mean every time—and estimate the amount as accurately as possible. Keep a log. Call it in every day. In ten days or two weeks, we'll know."

Meri's pulse beat still faster as random words from the instructions filtered through the wild tangle of self-recriminations and possibilities in her head. Yes, she should've been more careful and this was all her fault, but no way could she deal with this, even if she *were* staying at Honey Grove.

"I can show you how to . . ."

All of it—the bad timing of Lilah's fall, the rotten bad luck of hitting the damned cat—all of it turned her need to get out of this town into a panic.

"Don't bother to train *me* as a nurse. I'm on my way back to New York as we speak. It's urgent that I land there in time to get to my office tonight. I'll have to leave Henry here with you. What is the per diem?"

Her tears wrapped themselves even tighter around her throat muscles as she turned away to get her bag. What was *wrong* with her?

"I'll let, um ,.. . Zoe . . . run my credit card. I'll be happy to pay for the very best care for Henry."

When Caleb didn't answer, she turned to look at him.

His gaze held an intensity as strong as his smile. But he wasn't smiling now.

"You're leaving *today*? With Miss Lilah having surgery tomorrow?"

"She *is*?"

"You didn't know?"

She raised her eyebrows. "Well, *no*," she said. "I've been a little busy since I, um, ran over her cat."

He looked at her thoughtfully, as if he'd misjudged her somehow, then shifted his gaze to the cell phone in her hand.

"Listen," she said, "I couldn't talk to Lilah until . . . uh . . . I heard his prognosis," she said, hating the way her words stumbled over each other while she looked him in the eye. "I'll stop by the hospital on my way out of town. I don't want to give her bad news over the phone."

He continued to study her. For God's sake! What *was* it with these people? They thought she should camp out at the hospital?

"I can't keep Henry," he said, and she thought she detected pleasure in his tone. "We don't have the staff for twenty-four-hour one-to-one care. Miss Lilah will need care, too, when she comes home. She won't be able to take care of Henry."

She blinked. She stared at him. Glared.

His look said she should be the one to take care of them both.

He wouldn't let her look away from his powerful blue eyes.

He was bringing out primal instincts in her, some that she'd never known were there. She did not believe in violence. Of any kind. But she wanted—very badly—to slap his handsome face for judging her when he knew next to nothing about her as a person.

Or . . . maybe she wanted to touch his mouth with her fingertip. His very nice mouth. •

Meri, you are going insane. Get out of here.

She stood up and so did he.

"The cat is the only part of my life that's any of your concern," she said, every word coming out cold and hard.

She had to put distance between them. "I'll let Zoe run my credit card right now and be on my way."

"Nice try," he said. "But we can *not* keep Henry here. You'll have to make other arrangements."

"That's vindictive," she said, "and judgmental. Just because I can't give up my entire career to stay here and play nursemaid to a . . ."

"You're right that the rest of your life is none of my business," he said stubbornly. "But this is about the cat. We can't keep him here."

"You didn't say that until you heard my plans for leaving town today." She glared even harder. "Plans of which you disapprove."

He returned her stare. Waiting. For her to capitulate.

Well. She'd been in negotiations before. With tougher opponents.

"*I* can *not* care for Henry." She tapped herself on the chest for emphasis. "*You* are running a business here, one that purports to offer medical care and compassion to animals. Hire some more *staff*."

"Not my decision, not my clinic. I'm just filling in for Doctor Vincent while he's on vacation."

They glared at each other. It had become a stand-off. She had no way of knowing whether or not he was telling the truth and no time to find out.

And no intention of taking care of Henry herself.

"Is there another veterinary clinic in Rock Springs?"

"No."

"All right, then. Keep him until I can make arrangements in San Antonio."

She looked at Zoe, then back at him.

"I'm asking you both not to mention this to anyone. I don't know the patient-doctor privilege code for veterinarians, but I'm sure there is one. I'm learning how fast news travels in Rock Springs, and I need to be the one to tell Lilah that I hurt her cat."

Caleb, she thought, looked at her with perhaps a modicum of approval. *Something* new glinted in his blue, blue gaze. For only a heartbeat.

Then again, she might've imagined it.

No matter. She couldn't care less about his opinion of her.

It was certainly no worse than her opinion of him.

He had had way too much fun when Old Bear got away from her last night. She couldn't even be sure that he hadn't taken the horse out of the trailer for that reason.

Meredith wasn't a trusting person by nature; Caleb Burkett had given her more than one reason to be wary of him.

Nine

Meri held Henry at arm's length, closed the passenger door with her foot and ran for Lilah's back door, a distance that looked twice as long as it had yesterday because, any second now, this cat might pee on her. It wasn't easy to do, and still keep her bag from sliding off her shoulder but she didn't dare leave it behind in case Tim finally did call.

If Henry *did* pee on her, she refused to be responsible for what happened to Caleb Burkett.

Determination to commit shocking malpractice was how he'd won the standoff. Meri was seething. What kind of a veterinary clinic didn't have staff to take care of an injured cat? And what kind of a veterinary clinic didn't even have an extra animal carrier lying around? A towel was *not* an adequate substitute.

"Better than your jacket, though," he'd said to her, with that maddening grin that he used like a weapon.

Really, just thinking about him during the endless, harrowing drive back to Honey Grove while worrying that Henry might leave the rental car permanently reeking of cat urine—insurance almost certainly would not cover *that*—had made her realize that, contrary to her usual view of herself, she *did* have a strong potential for aggressive behavior.

It would come unleashed. She'd have to drive back to town and wreak violence upon *Doctor* Burkett's handsome body. She tried to ignore the fact that he'd pushed her into this trap simply by having the stronger will. Meredith hated to think that any opponent could hold out longer than she could. Persistence was the key to success in everything, and she'd proved over and over, since she was a little girl, that she had it in spades.

No, he must've sensed the quivering button inside her marked "guilt" and pushed it. He certainly had seen how upset she was, even though she'd been perfectly—well, mostly—cool on the surface. That, too, made her furious.

She would've never expected that kind of sensitivity in a man. Who would? Tim never had a clue about her emotional state.

She reached the porch steps and ran up them, heedless of more damage to the toes of her Jimmy Choos, while watching Henry constantly for signs of returning consciousness. First on the agenda: get him in a basket, the litter box, *anywhere* but in her arms. She'd scream if she couldn't be *rid* of him.

One step onto the porch and the screen door to the kitchen flew open. Meri squealed and stopped so suddenly she rocked back on her heels, which made her squeeze Henry, probably too hard. An *intruder?*

Oh, God! In addition to forgetting about the cat, she'd been in such a hurry to get to the hospital and then the airport that she'd forgotten to lock the house.

It was yet another person she'd already met. Doreen, in a crisp, black-and-white pinstripe dress, straight, short, sleeveless and as stylish as the floral one, standing back to hold the screen door open for Meri and Henry.

"How's he doing?"

Meri's heart stopped. Word was out. Trust the Rock Springs grapevine.

Caleb was a liar. Or Zoe was. They'd both assured her they wouldn't tell anyone. For God's sake, whatever happened to fear of malpractice lawsuits?

The shock destroyed her capacity for diplomacy.

"How'd you even know he was hurt? What are you doing here, anyway, Doreen?"

"Oh, just gathering up some toiletries and your grandma's blood pressure medicine and a couple of her good nightgowns to surprise her with."

She followed Meri in, patting her shoulder, which Meri jerked away from. But the older woman's comforting tone did actually soothe Meri slightly. For a millisecond. This was pathetic. She had to get control of herself.

Doreen bustled around, trying to help as Meri laid Henry in his basket in the corner and tucked the towel around him, thankful that he was still out cold. If he woke and needed to go, surely he could get himself to the litter box.

"Who called you, Doreen? How'd you hear Henry was hurt?"

It's your own fault. You should've called Lilah yourself when you left the clinic.

"Calm down, Meri, honey. Don't worry so. He must not be dying or he'd still be at the clinic."

A sound almost like a growl came from Meri's throat. "That's where he *should* be."

"Doreen. Have you told Lilah that Henry is hurt?"

"*Lilah* told *me*."

Oh, damn. No.

"Now, Meredith, I don't want to upset you even more, darlin', but your grandma's just a teensy bit disappointed that you didn't call her as soon as it happened."

Meri felt that old clutch in her stomach like she used to get in first-year law school when the professor called on her.

"I took up for you. I told her you were busy trying to save her cat."

"Who called my grandmother?"

"She was talking to Caleb Burkett when I walked into her room."

Meri's whole brain went up in flames. Oh! She *could* understand the need to do physical damage to another's person.

I will make him pay.

Yes. She *owed* him, big-time. Not only for this, but also for the taunting grin when he said, "Change the litter every time he goes—I mean every time—and estimate the amount as accurately as possible. Keep a log."

She ought to sue his butt. For impersonating a veterinarian. For not having the best interests of the patient at heart when he pushed him into the arms of an incompetent caregiver.

Doreen was talking a mile a minute. "But don't worry, Meri, about your driving. I won't say a word to Lilah about that because she's already got enough to give you grief about."

Meri had to work at processing the words while she pulled herself back into the conversation. She was so far gone in her imagined threats to Caleb, it was as if Doreen were speaking in Mandarin.

"My *driving?* What are you *talking* about?"

"Well, when I left the hospital I stopped by the Grab It 'n' Go to get her a copy of the new *Western Horseman* and some Krispy Kremes . . . to try and sweeten her up, you know," Doreen said with a conspiratorial wink.

"And . . . ?"

"Tol Weddle and some of his Dairy Queen coffee buddies were in there. They said you peeled off the highway at the clinic throwing gravel like the Dukes of Hazzard, and when you left it running without even closing the door of your car, they knew it was bad and . . ."

I should be on a plane to New York this minute. I shouldn't even be here, in Nowhere, Texas, listening to this insanity.

Meri interrupted her. "Tell me, Doreen. Was Lilah terribly upset about Henry?"

"Well, yes, she was, but you know, it took her mind off her pain. And she was *deeply* relieved when Caleb assured her that you are going to be the one taking care of Henry."

"Oh no. I'm not. I have to get back to New York today. I'm looking for a qualified pet-sitter. If you know anybody . . ."

"Your grandma said that a person has to be the really picky, thorough kind that leaves no stone unturned to get to be a lawyer, so you'll be just the one to do it. She believes in you, honey, even if she is just the least bit disappointed, too. She says if anybody can save Henry now, you can."

Great. Now my entire relationship with my grandmother is riding on my keeping this *&%!$ cat alive.

"Knowing that you're his nurse is what's giving her the strength to get through that surgery tomorrow," Doreen said. "Now don't you worry, Meri, about not calling to tell her right away. I know from personal experience that Lilah can hold a grudge for thirty years. But she won't do that to you. I'm sure of it."

Meri's head was spinning. She absolutely could not deal with this another second. She no longer cared what the weird dynamic was between Lilah and Doreen.

Or what was going on between the Fremont twins . . . uh, siblings.

Or what the deal was about a loan, Lilah and Buford Quisenberry or whatever his name was.

The only relationship in Rock Springs that mattered to her at the moment was the one between her and Caleb Burkett, the pseudoveterinarian. He was not getting away with this.

Since she'd lost the argument and let him foist the cat on her, he must have no respect for her at all.

"Doreen, tell me about Caleb Burkett. Is he considered trustworthy?"

She went to the refrigerator for a diet Coke and glanced over her shoulder as she opened the door. Doreen was looking for something in Lilah's cabinets.

"Of *course* you want to know about Caleb! Every

woman who ever met him wants to know more about him. That smile of his melts them in their shoes."

"I'm *not* attracted to him. I'm asking if he's generally considered to be trustworthy. As in, if he makes a promise he holds to it."

"Oh, honey, don't bother to deny it," Doreen said. "You're only human. But to answer your question, yes, even the black sheep of the Burketts is an honorable man. Except in his romances."

Meri took out the cold can of soda and held it to her forehead. She was raging hot all over from the run and from her temper.

She didn't care about his romances.

"I don't see how someone can be partially honorable."

Doreen shrugged. "Well, most of his many conquests admit he never made them any promises but still . . ."

Meri pulled the tab on the can and drank.

Doreen took down a little tray from Lilah's cabinet, pocketed a prescription bottle from it then put the tray back. She opened another door, picked up a glass and went to the fridge to fill it with ice.

Meri took another drink.

Doreen lifted the can from her fingers and poured the diet Coke into the glass. "I know customs are probably different in New York, honey, but around here well-mannered ladies don't drink straight from the can. It's just not done. It's almost as bad as neglecting to send a thank-you note. And I don't mean e-mail."

Doreen leaned against the counter and smiled sweetly as if taking the sting out of correcting a child.

"I heard you," she said, "but Caleb Burkett has his ways of getting what he wants and there's no man on earth who wouldn't want you. Just be careful. He's liable to do anything."

Meri drank from the glass while Doreen gave her a straight look for emphasis.

"What? You're not saying he's dangerous?"

"Only to your heart. No, he just does crazy things like

get a veterinary degree and then spend ten years working every rough job in the West and Alaska, when he's got enough inherited money to never work another day at anything."

"So why is he back here now?"

Doreen shrugged. "Trying to settle down, I guess. He just bought the run-down old Connor Ranch out across the river. And that's another example. Instead of hiring someone to have the renovation done right, I hear he plans to do it himself."

Quickly, Meri said, "I'm just curious."

Do not ask another question, Mer. She'll think you're too interested.

Her phone rang. She set down her glass, ran to her bag she'd dumped on the kitchen chair and grabbed it.

Oh, God, it was Tim. At last.

"Excuse me, but I have to take this," she said, walked to the door and out onto the back porch.

She looked out across the green yard and fields, flowers and vegetable plants or whatever they were, and slid her finger across the phone. "Hi, Tim."

He went right to the point in a flat, tight voice. Later, she tried to replay the conversation in her head but she couldn't. All she could remember was standing there after the call ended, staring at the deep blue Texas sky, right where it met the curve of the earth.

Alan and the other partners had pulled her off the prestigious CRT case and reassigned her to second chair on some obscure tax dispute she'd never even heard mentioned. Alan would be calling her shortly to break the news, but he'd asked Tim to prepare her.

Tim's thought was that she might want to stay in Texas for a few days to get adjusted to the idea before she returned to New York. Alan had said that'd be fine.

Her thought was that this news certainly put all of today's other troubles into proper perspective. Her staying in Texas had been Alan's thought, not Tim's, and what

Alan was telling her was that she was no longer needed at Savage, Mitchell, etc.

Her life was spinning out of control. Her almost fiancé was helping Alan turn it.

Not urging her to come to him for comfort, not offering to help her fight for her rights. Not talking about their future.

Her temper roared to life. She'd gone way beyond the call of duty for that damned firm—and for Tim, too. She'd won awards and cases and accolades. Her work could not be faulted. In her free time, of which there was basically none, she'd done things Tim's way, tried to please Tim.

Why, she'd even gone so far as to give up her desire to have children because he didn't want them! Still, he'd hesitated to make the big commitment to her.

To hell with him and Alan both. She was not going to take this lying down.

When she could speak in a normal voice, she walked back into the kitchen and told Doreen that she'd been called back to New York on urgently critical business. Doreen heard that, took one good look at Meri and volunteered to take over Henry's care until she could hire someone.

Meri repeated Caleb's orders for Henry's care. Doreen wrote them down.

Then Meri ran to her car for her overnight bag. She got out of her blood-streaked suit, showered and dressed in the one pair of jeans she'd brought—designer, way too expensive but perfectly fitted—and a white tee. With the black Louboutin stilettos and the black silk jacket from the funeral suit, she'd still look in control and powerful for a meeting with Alan.

Ten

"This'll get your hackles up even more, but I have to say that Doreen was right," B. J. said, in her most maddening, righteous tone of voice. "Meri *will* call you. She just didn't have time when it happened, Lilah. Think, won't you? She was busy trying to save your furry dictator's life."

Lilah wanted to throw something at her. From the way she was situated in the bed she couldn't even see her friend, plus it hurt too much to move and she did *not* want to hear this. She rang the bell for Wanda Sue and said over the intercom, "I'll take that pain pill now, Wanda Sue, if you please. I've got to get easy so I can think."

Then, to Barbara Jane, "She had time to call me while she waited for Caleb to examine him."

"Naturally, she wanted to hear the verdict before she upset you. She's not been here long but she knows you're a plumb fool over that cat."

Lilah set her jaw against the tears that kept threatening. What was the matter with her? She was tougher than this. "No. What she's doing is trying not to own up to her mistakes, just like her mother. I tell you, Barb, I'll miss that onery cat so much if he . . ."

"He won't. Some cats, like some people, are too mean to die. He's one of 'em."

"Siamese cats were specially bred to guard the royal city walls in China. He thinks he's royalty. He's *not mean*."

"Only when he doesn't get his way. But back to Meri. This'd be an awful time to give her one of your famous tongue-lashings, Lilah. Think how bad she feels already and how scared she—your own, only human, *granddaughter*—has been about that *animal*."

"I am so mad right now I could turn her over my checkered apron and blister her bottom. How would you like to hear about a big event that happened in your family from an outsider?"

What if she's turned out just like Edie Jo, deep down where it counts?

And, oh, Lord, what if I could've prevented that if I'd kept on looking until I found her?

Wanda Sue came in with the pill and Lilah took it.

"Earl Thomas called," Wanda Sue said as she handed her the cup of water. "Shorty's on his way in."

Lilah heaved a sigh of relief. "Good. After he turns the horses out, I'll set him to organizing the work until I can get home. For starters, we need to call and cancel Taylor's and Madison's riding lessons for tomorrow. That's another fifty dollars I'll lose."

"Don't be worrying about all that," B. J. said. "You just concentrate on getting well."

"And we'll *have* to start hunting pickers for the Pink Beauties. They're nearly ready to come off. Looks like we're gonna lose the rest of the Purples."

Just saying those words hurt her heart. It was the worst kind of cold comfort to remember what Shorty had said while they were picking last night. 'Even if we saved every one of these tomatoes, Lilah, and sold 'em tonight, that money'd be nothing but a drop of water in the Gulf of Mexico. That note's for seventy-five thousand, ain't it?'

Wanda Sue popped the thermometer into Lilah's mouth.

Yes. It was. And trying to nickel-and-dime it was not going to work. Time would run out in just a few weeks. She didn't have time to save up for it, even if she could squeeze out more profits, so she was hoping against hope she could get it renewed for another year.

If she could talk Buford into giving her more time, maybe he could convince the board that ran the bank to approve it. Jasper Burkett sat on that board. He, for one, would do all he could for her cause.

Lilah wasn't used to debt because she and Ed had always lived within their means. But that long drought that finally broke last year killed so many crops and stunted so many others that she'd had no choice but to borrow money to keep going or quit farming right then.

Honestly, sometimes she thought the worry would do her in, never mind the hard work. Debt made her so vulnerable.

Shorty said it made her cranky, which was why he'd started bringing his fiddle over several evenings a week to play for her after supper. She told him he was coming over so often because he couldn't resist her cooking.

Both of them were right.

She smiled. She didn't know what she'd do without Shorty to keep her balanced. She wished he'd hurry up and get here, even though he'd tease her forever for falling out of a tree.

Her stomach clutched. Why had she taken that risk? She knew better.

But she'd done it to create one more thread of connection with Meri. To give them one more thing to talk about during the fantasy calls from New York that Lilah's desperate imagination conjured up.

To give the girl something from her rightful heritage to carry forward. An experience that would tie her to ancestors she'd never ever heard of, who'd eaten persimmons after the frost had sweetened them.

Instead, in real life, Meri hadn't even bothered to call

from here in Rock Springs, much less New York. And Lilah was broken up and laid up with big bills to pay.

Wanda Sue finished taking her blood pressure and the rest of her vitals.

"I'll pass the word that you're gonna need pickers," she said, stopping at the door, "but there's a lot of people with the same problem is all I can tell you."

Somebody was pushing that door open every minute, so Lilah lowered her voice when Wanda Sue went out. She had to make B. J. see the truth, but she didn't want to set the whole town to talking about Edie Jo again, now that the funeral was behind them.

"It reminds me of when Edie Jo wouldn't tell me she was pregnant and I had to hear it from Doreen."

"Oh, *honey*," Barbara said, "that was such a bad time. Dulcie and I barely pulled you through it in one piece. That was too long ago to even remember and you're just borrowing trouble, anyway. Meri is *not* Edie Jo."

The door flew open. "Miss Lilah, I've brought you some fresh water and more ice." It was Dallas Fremont, for the third time in thirty minutes, competing with her brother, as always.

"Sugar, thank you so much, but Denton just refilled all those pitchers about five minutes ago."

Dallas flashed a quick smile as she moved Denton's offerings from the bedside table to her work cart and replaced them with her own. "Yeah, but he didn't know you can have a Snickers. I asked Wanda Sue and she said you can eat until midnight tonight, so look what I got you out of the candy machine."

The last thing Lilah wanted was a candy bar, but she tried to look excited. Honestly, if she'd known this was community service week for the FFA, she would've waited until next week to fall out of the tree. These little Future Farmers of America were so good and helpful, they were about to kill her with kindness.

Especially Dallas and Denton, who'd been born thirteen months apart while their shiftless parents were parking their ramshackle trailer on Honey Grove land, supposedly working for Lilah. Happily, their children were proving to be great people, naturally ambitious and energetic. Several people in Rock Springs and around the county took an interest in them now, following the examples of Lilah and Dulcie Burkett, who'd done so from the beginning.

Lilah leaned back against the pillow and forced a smile. "You are the sweetest girl, Dallas," she said. "When I get well, I'll have y'all over for cowboy cookies and lemonade."

"We'd love that. Are you coming to see us team-rope for the championship? This is our last year in the eleven-to-fourteen age division and we might win a truck."

One of life's testaments to the old saying that blood is thicker than water was the amazing way these two little archrivals combined all that competitiveness when they wanted to. They were great team-ropers and they played music together, too. They had a chance of winning that truck, for sure.

Lilah narrowed her eyes and accepted the candy bar Dallas had torn open. It did smell good. "A *truck?* For eleven to fourteen? Do they expect y'all to drive illegally or what?"

"Or we could sell it and use the money for college," Dallas explained. "If we win, will you help us handle all that, Miss Lilah?"

"Yes, darlin'. Of course I will. Or maybe Miss Dulcie should, since they're her horses y'all are using."

They visited a minute more, then Dallas left to tell Denton she was one up on him. B. J. watched her out the door. "Those kids are amazing. You and Dulcie get a lot of the credit."

Lilah shook her head and bit into the Snickers. "No. The Good Lord gets the credit—it's nothing short of a miracle that those kids are not carbon copies of the parents."

"I thought you said you were sick to your stomach," B. J. said.

"I was, but the smell of chocolate's easing the nausea, somehow."

B. J.'s phone rang. She pulled it out of her pocket, looked at it and smiled as she answered.

"It's for you," she said, and held it against Lilah's ear.

"I'm not helpless," she said as she put down the candy and took the phone in her good hand, shifting her shoulder to try to ease the pain.

Meri's voice said, "Lilah? I'm *sorry*. I don't have words to say how sorry I am that I hurt Henry, but that was an accident. The fact I didn't call you immediately was a choice, the wrong one. Please forgive me."

Like a rehearsed speech. Delivered fast in an extrafirm, distant tone with a hard edge to it, as if this were business she had to take care of and nothing more.

That tone hit Lilah like the kick of a mule upside the head. Worse than hearing Henry was hurt.

Yes, and you remember that, Lilah Briscoe. You need not feel anything for her, either, not even guilt about her past. She's a grown woman now. It's way too late for wasting time and energy on those kinds of foolish hopes.

Anger flashed heat through her.

"Well," she said, "you took your time about calling. With me up here in the hospital getting terrible family news from people not even my blood kin."

"Of course. I understand completely. I tried to prevent that."

Did her voice tremble a little? It sounded a tad more sincere, at least. Lilah might as well take this as an opportunity to try to educate her granddaughter.

As long as you aren't trying to form any kind of attachment.

"It was a red-faced embarrassment to me, Meredith Kathleen. It makes it look like in our family we don't trust each other."

There was a long silence. Good. Maybe Meri was taking that to heart.

But no, she shot back, "How could we? We don't even know each other."

Lilah's anger erupted. "*Blood*. You trust your blood kin

until actions prove you can't. I had judged you as different from your mother but she never owned up to her own mistakes, either."

"My *mission in life* is to be different from my mother! I *am* trustworthy."

Meri had a temper like Lilah's. Hot words pouring out now with no cold edge to them.

"Lilah, I didn't even know whether or not Henry was dead when I picked him up and started racing to the clinic. I wanted to get a prognosis, then give you the news in person and break it gently. Today, especially, you didn't need another shock and more uncertainty. But if you are unable to appreciate that . . ."

Lilah interrupted. "I can. I do. I'm not that unreasonable . . ."

Meri talked over her. "I'm *sorry*. I apologize again, and you can forgive me or not. Now, I do need to mention that Doreen said you're expecting me, personally, to take care of Henry, but . . ."

Lilah's pulse jumped. "*Doreen?* What are you talking about?"

"Doreen is at your house getting your toiletries and lingerie and medicine to bring to the hospital. While I was talking to her, I got a call from Tim. I have to be in New York immediately. Doreen volunteered to watch Henry until she can find a full-time paid caregiver. I, of course, will take care of all expenses."

"*What? I'm* the one who decides who's in charge of Henry."

"Fine. Tell Doreen to get out of your house. Do whatever you want. But Doreen is happy to help and I'm on my way to the airport as we speak."

Lilah was so mad she really thought she might smother. Her heart was beating so fast she could barely breathe.

"You've put Doreen right in the middle of my business, where she loves to be, and she's pilfering through my closets and drawers and reading my mail and looking at my farm records right this minute to see if I can pay my note that's coming due or if she'll buy it at the foreclosure auction."

Lilah said all that so hard and fast that she ran the words together but Meri got it. That didn't make one whit of difference.

"Sorry. I couldn't leave Henry alone, but I couldn't stay with him. I had no choice. I changed my flight to a later one and I can't miss it."

A whirlwind of feelings blew through Lilah, all mixed up and strong enough to blot out the pain in every part of her body.

This was that same tone Meri had used when she was lecturing Lilah about the law and Edie Jo's will—flat, unbending and sure beyond any doubt that she was right. *Nobody* talked to Lilah that way. *Ever.*

"Don't tell me that. *You could've called me.* My cat, my house, my business. You had no right to take over my life and give it to her."

"*Take over your life?* How unreasonable can you be?"

Lilah bristled. Goose bumps of anger popped out on her skin and here she lay, helpless and trapped in a hospital bed.

Through stiff lips, she said, "Caleb assured me that you'd take care of Henry until I can get home. It's only a couple of days."

"Caleb had no right to speak for me."

"And Doreen, of all people for you to leave him with! *I* should be the one to decide who . . ."

"I've got to go. I'm sorry for hitting your cat, I'm sorry for taking responsibility for him and I'm sorry I didn't call you sooner. I hope your surgery goes smoothly and you recover quickly. Good-bye, Lilah."

Meri was gone.

Eleven

"She hung up on me."

"I wonder why."

B. J. sounded more sad than mad.

Lilah looked at her.

"I told you." She was shaking her head, looking into Lilah's eyes. "Lilah, I wouldn't blame her if she never spoke to you again."

"Well you didn't hear how . . . distant she sounded! How businesslike and rushed. B. J. . . ."

"What?"

Tears sneaked into Lilah's eyes. She looked at the ceiling instead of her friend's face. "Lately I'm sorta like I was right after Ed died. Remember I told you I couldn't regulate my emotional thermostat sometimes? I'm at one extreme or the other in a red-hot minute, my feelings are so fierce."

"Well, at least you're aware of it. And you've got enough on your plate to explain why. But don't take it out on that girl. She's doing the best she can."

Lilah let her battered bones sink into the bed, sucked down by the maelstrom inside her. Here she was. Her wrist was shattered, her whole body was bruised and wouldn't be at full strength for weeks and she had a farm to run. It was about to go under and she didn't know what to do next.

It'd been a long, long time since her spirit felt this low.

Dear God. She really *hadn't* been this vulnerable for twenty years.

But no matter how bad she felt, the only way out of this trouble was through it. She used her heels to push herself up and higher to sit against the pillows.

She looked at B. J. "Meri's gone and it's for the best," she said. "She *is* like Edie Jo. Undependable."

"Meri didn't get to where she is in life by being undependable."

"Well, too bad it doesn't carry over to her personal life."

Barbara Jane wasn't going to cut Lilah any slack. "You're not exactly perfect, either, and you know it." She came closer to the bed and stood staring down at Lilah. "Give her a chance, is all I'm saying. You know that's the right thing to do."

Lilah turned her face to the wall. When did they start painting hospitals mauve and that weird gray rose color and putting flowered borders around the walls? Institutional pale green was better. This was enough to make a person sicker.

"Lilah?"

"B. J., go away."

"No. You need to think about the way you treated your granddaughter. Truth?"

Lilah locked gazes with B. J. and used what felt like the last of her strength to make hers defiant.

"I don't have time for a granddaughter. I can't concentrate on trying to understand her and build some kind of a relationship with her that'll always be one-sided. *That's* the truth."

"I wouldn't blame her if she never spoke to you again, after the conversation y'all just had. You're the one who owes the apology."

Lilah managed to drag in enough breath for a sigh.

"This is all a monumental waste to even talk about it. I'll never see or hear from her again."

"You're just hurting right now, worried about yourself and Henry, so you let your temper get ahead of your good sense. You'll get your optimism back after the surgery's all over."

That was said in a tone so calm it was maddening.

"I can't control Meri or her feelings or anything about her and I have to look at what's real. I've got a big loan payment coming due, I have three new restaurants on my list that I have to impress, I've got to . . . "

B. J. interrupted, "All I'm saying is don't let fear get in the way of letting love into your life."

Lilah hooted. "She doesn't want to be in my life. And who knows if she'd ever love me? I don't have it in me right now to get attached to somebody I'd hardly ever see or hear from. I don't need that."

"But you don't know that it'd be like that. Where's your faith? Maybe God sent her here for a reason. After all, you didn't think she'd show up for the funeral and she surprised you then."

Lilah just looked at her.

"She might surprise you again."

Lilah rolled her eyes.

"And you can forget that nonsense that she's just like Edie. She isn't, and do *not* say that to her anymore. There was just something born in Edie Jo, that restlessness. A person could nearly hear the ticking clock inside of her and feel her waiting for it to tell her to move on. Meri's not like that."

"How do you know? Hush, B. J., and let me be."

She closed her eyes and tried to drift off on the pain medicine.

But B. J. was right. Lilah was a coward, so scared she wouldn't get the love she deep-down wanted from her granddaughter, she wouldn't even reach for it.

She should be ashamed. God and so many people loved her so much. She should pass it on with an open heart and never think for one second about whether it would be returned.

Here she was, sixty-eight years old and full of experiences, acting like life had never taught her one thing.

Most likely, though, she'd missed her chance with Meri.

The door opened and Wanda Sue came in pushing a cart that held three flower bouquets and a book with a blue-and-white-checkered cover and one of those plastic-ringed spines. She brought the book to Lilah.

Lilah forced her mind onto looking at it. Just as she'd thought, it was *Rock County Cooks*. The Women's Study Club—which mostly met to study the social life of Rock Springs instead of American literature as the founders intended—was selling these books for their yearly fund-raiser.

"Parmalee Parsons wanted so bad to bring this book up to you herself," Wanda Sue said, "but I've started telling everybody you're asleep, knocked out by the pain meds. They don't come any more stubborn than Parmalee. If she hadn't had to get home to give Verna Carl's granddaughter a piano lesson, we'd still be there arguing while you had plenty of time to wake up."

"It's her *great*-granddaughter," Lilah said. "What is that child's name? It's one of the presidents."

B. J. said, "Kennedy? There's lots of little girls nowadays with the most surprising names and they aren't family surnames, either. Is it Kennedy?"

"No," Lilah said, glad to have something else to occupy her mind. "What is it? Oh, yes. McKinley."

She started leafing through the cookbook while Wanda Sue and B. J. arranged the flowers in the room.

"Look at this," Lilah said. "It's a disgrace and I told them so, but here they are—casserole recipes with canned soup in them. And I just flipped past a cake recipe that starts with a mix. If you want to cook like that, well, all right, but don't tell the world by putting it in a book with your name on it. That's just not done."

"Oh, quick, Wanda Sue, change the subject or she'll go off on that old rant," B. J. said. "I've heard it a thousand times."

Lilah ignored her. "To tell you the truth, I'm downright embarrassed to have my recipes in the same book with them. I came within a hair-bit of not giving them any because of that very thing."

Wanda said, "What did you give them, Lilah? Any of your secrets?"

"Not her summer surprise peach pie, if that's what you're looking for," B. J. teased. "I haven't seen the book, but I can tell you *that* right now."

They all chuckled.

"I do like to think my recipes will live on after me, though," Lilah said. "I gave them my braided Christmas sweetbread and my cowboy cookies."

"'Cause nobody'll be able to make either one of them as good as you do, anyway," B. J. said. "You are so selfish, Lilah."

Lilah scowled at her. "But I am *not* vain about my cooking."

Both of the other women dissolved into laughter at that. Finally Lilah did, too.

"Well," she said, "maybe I am. Just a tiny little bit."

Then the laughter died and Wanda Sue left the room.

After a long silence, Lilah said, "B. J., you have got to pray for me every day."

"I always do."

"I know. But now I need so much wisdom. And strength. How am I going to meet the note coming due? Buford Quisenberry has put me off every time I asked for more time. I think it's because, just like Doreen, he covets my farm."

"I still say let Dulcie loan you the money like she wants to do."

"Absolutely not. I might never be able to repay her."

"In the world of the Burketts, seventy-five thousand dollars is pocket change. You know that. If they had to write it off it'd probably help on their tax bill."

"I will not take charity. That'd change the whole balance of our friendship."

"Lord help, what are you thinking? It's not charity. Dulcie is like me, she's your heart-sister and has been ever since we were all six years old. Nothin' in this world can ever change that. Think of all the ups and downs and fusses and fights and carryings-on we've all been through."

"It'd change *me*," Lilah said. "Nobody in my family has ever taken charity."

B. J. heaved her long sigh and said, "I give up. Lord knows, you just can't help some people."

A bad case of the blues was coming at Lilah from every direction.

"Oh, B. J., how am I going to take care of Henry and change his litterbox all the time? No telling who Doreen's already hired to do that job. And I'm not going to have just anybody in my house. He or she will have to sleep there, too."

B. J. nodded.

"And how can I farm all crippled up like this? One-handed, for goodness' sake. B. J., I can't even dress myself. I can't even fasten and unfasten my bra."

Barbara Jane came and sat on the side of her bed and bent over to look her in the eye.

"You are so pitiful, you're breaking my heart, Lilah Briscoe. And you're also making me mad enough to spit. You sound like you don't have a friend in the world, when Rock County is full of people who'd give you the shirt off their back."

B. J. shook her finger in Lilah's face. "What you need to do is put that pride of yours aside and accept help for once in your life. Think how much help you've given to so many other people during your long, *long* life."

Lilah grinned at the taunt in spite of herself.

"If only fallin' out of that tree could've knocked some sense into your head. *I'm* gonna sleep at your house and take care of that awful cat if I don't strangle him first and *I'm* gonna fasten your bra. Be careful not to cross me, or you'll have to go without one and that'll scandalize the help, not to mention your customers."

Twelve

"I broke open a new bale," Shorty said, "so you're in good shape for hay for a couple of days, but I still say I oughtta feed for you in the morning."

He stopped in the wide barn door on his way out and turned to give her the look he always did when he thought she was being unreasonable—disapproving, but not the least bit surprised.

Lilah dumped the scoop of sweet grain into Molly's feeder. "Feeding's one chore I *can* do."

"I'll go up to the house and change the litterbox . . ."

"I already did. It's possible with one hand if you don't put very much litter in to begin with. You've got your own chores still to do and it'll be dark in a few minutes. Go on."

But he just stood there, looking at her. "Don't worry yourself sick about them tomatoes. Every farmer loses a crop now and then."

"I'm not. I'm looking ahead now. I'm thinking of other ways to bring in money—maybe a part-time job in town. I could ask Doreen if I could help out at the dress shop. A broken wrist wouldn't hinder me in selling clothes."

"I've said it before," he drawled, shaking his head, "we're gonna have to think bigger than that. I doubt Doreen'd pay you more than ten dollars an hour at the very most. So what would you need? Seventy-five hundred hours? Buford gonna wait that long? You gonna *live* that long?"

She made a face at him. "I hate it that you always have to be so logical. But any amount would help and I have to do *something.*"

He looked into her eyes. "Lilah, I hate it that I couldn't find you some pickers in time to save 'em."

"Shorty, you did everything that could be done. Thanks for that and for the plowing today."

She hated this for him as much as for herself. It was hard on a man to feel he'd failed at anything.

"B. J. ain't stayin' tonight?"

"No. I sent her home. It's been nearly two weeks. She's coming by in the morning to help me . . . get dressed. Look, Shorty, I have got to have some time to myself. I need my freedom. B. J.'s always telling me what to do and not do."

"Well," he drawled, "I know somebody else who's kinda kicked by that same cow."

She walked to him, brandishing the plastic scoop. "You better not be talking about me. It's cruel to insult a sick person."

He raised an eyebrow. "I didn't mention a name, but if the shoe fits . . . And you keep tellin' me you're healing fast."

His sharp brown eyes searched hers to find the truth about how she was really feeling; the sweat-and-tobacco nearness of him comforted her. Her breath hitched and she drew it in deep, the hot and humid air of the old dog days of summer. If it hadn't been for the scoop in her only usable hand, she'd have reached out and patted his weathered, familiar face.

Even with B. J. there all week, she'd been feeling that core lump of loneliness that lives inside every human.

"Don't fret," she said. "I'm no weirder than normal."

"I dunno. Them pain pills they give you might've kicked it up a notch or two."

He gave her the full benefit of his slow grin. "But I have to say you're not real noticeable yet."

She laughed. "Get outta here. Save your skin while you can."

He said the same thing he always said when they parted. "You need me, you call me. Hear?"

After Shorty was gone, she straightened up the tack room and moved down the aisle again, puttering, willing her mind to drift away from the worries of the past and future both while the horses finished eating. Muttering pleasure, big teeth crunching, rough tongues licking the sweet grains from the sides of the feeders, they enjoyed every bite.

They were good company, always. Partly because they didn't use words to talk.

Lilah took long, slow breaths of the old barn's smells, the eternal pungent mix of horse, leather, manure, hay, sweet feed and shavings.

Flashes of memories came. Taking turns with Ed to keep foal watches long before there were baby monitors and TV screens so you could stay in bed until a mare's time came. Edie Jo, letting herself get trapped in that corner over there by a new horse who tended to kick . . .

Meri as a little girl, riding with a beatific smile on her face while Lilah led the horse around the yard.

That little girl loved Lilah.

The grown-up Meri didn't even call—after all that fuss about getting B. J.'s phone number—to see if Lilah had lived through her surgery.

Lilah sighed, grabbed the broom standing against the wall and made awkward, one-handed stabs at sweeping the aisle. It was just as well Meri was gone for good. Even if they kept in touch, they'd never have a real relationship. Meri was all ambition, which was borne out by her attitude during the phone call she finally did make on her way out of town. What comfort would she be to Lilah?

*   *   *

Lilah put the broom away. These feelings weren't really about Meri. This was the loneliness rearing its head again and she wouldn't allow that. Give it an inch and it would take a mile, especially for a widow wanting more life in her house.

She grinned to herself. When she'd said that to B. J., she'd replied that Henry was life enough for anybody.

And, on the other hand, Lilah truly was wanting some time to herself, like she'd told Shorty.

Lilah turned on her heel and started for the house and air-conditioning. She'd meant to stay and turn the horses out for the night but she could come back in half an hour. The barn stood with every window open, but out in the pasture they might catch a better breeze or two, especially early in the morning.

Lord have mercy, but it was *hot*! Sweat was running down her arm inside her cast. Talk about itching now. She'd have to fight her mind not to think about it or she'd be trying to scratch it with a coat hanger again.

She rubbed her arm above the cast, hoping to fool herself into thinking that'd do some good. Doc had warned against the coat hanger remedy, but she'd done it anyway, and found out he was right. She'd scratched through the skin and the sweat *really* stung after that. Those first few seconds were bliss, though.

A few feet from the open door she stopped. Dusk was fading fast into dark but she could see enough to know somebody was standing in the doorway.

"Shorty?"

She knew it wasn't. He would've come on in. He'd have said something.

Anybody friendly would've said something.

Thoughts of escaped prisoners and foot travelers and wishes she had a manure fork in her hand or kept a gun in the barn pelted her racing brain. She willed her tone to come out fierce and rough.

"Who is it? What do you want?"

"Lilah. It's Meri."

Hot as it was, the breath froze in Lilah's chest. Was she imagining this? Hallucinating?

She reached for the wall and flipped the light switch.

It *was* Meri but she looked like hell. That was the only way to put it. Her hair all messy in a lopsided ponytail that was fast coming down. No makeup. Jeans, a thin jacket, and under it, a tee shirt so wrinkled she must've slept in it. A pair of those ballet slippers that were so flat they must be like nothing between your foot and the ground.

"Well. Knock me over with a feather."

Same expensive black bag on her shoulder. Same great big sunglasses pushed up on her head.

Meri took a step farther into the barn's light. Dear God in heaven. Her eyes were like burnt holes in a blanket.

"Did you drive in here?"

"Yes."

"Lord! I didn't even hear you."

That was worrisome. She'd been too far gone in those memories to hear a car drive up, like she was a hundred years old instead of sixty-eight. She'd better get a grip.

But the look in Meri's eyes sucked Lilah's selfishness right out of her head. A couple of weeks ago, the confidence in those violet eyes never wavered. Now they were pools of pain.

Sweat was running down one side of Meri's face where a wet strand of hair was hanging. She tucked it behind her ear with a hand that shook.

"You said I could come anytime." She swallowed hard. "Without calling."

Meri was tied in knots and loose-jointed as a rag doll at the same time because she was desperate to collapse. She was in a worse state—much worse than the tension she'd carried before.

The child would explode if she wasn't too weak to.

Lilah believed older people ought to stay calm in the face of trouble as a help to the younger ones.

That they should show by example that panicking always did more harm than good.

That they should behave as if they'd all get through it just fine, whatever it was.

So she had to act that way and be convincing about it, even now when she was close to being a basket case herself.

"Come on," she said. "I was just headed to the house. Let's go get in where it's cool."

She flipped the lights out so the bugs wouldn't gather so thick in the barn, and they walked up the slope to the yard through the growing dark.

Meri shifted her bag on her shoulder and cleared her throat. "Uh, did Henry survive?"

"He did. Caleb thinks he's on the mend."

Meri let out a sigh of relief. Well, that was one small burden lifted off her skinny shoulders, but it was plain to see that she had plenty more. Big ones.

Lilah was dying to ask what was wrong but Meri seemed so nervous she knew she had to let her settle down first. Something really bad had happened to her. And she'd come running to Honey Grove.

To Lilah.

An arrow of warmth shot through her heart.

"Did you hit the rush-hour traffic?"

"Yes. It shook me up. But it helped that my driving skills aren't quite so rusty now." She managed a sickly grin. "At least I didn't hit any animals."

She looked at Lilah's wrist in the cast to the elbow. "How are you feeling?"

"Now you ask."

"I did call, Lilah. The nurses' desk. Twice. After your surgery and then again after you'd gone home."

Lilah stopped. "Why not call B. J.? You've got her number."

Meri kept walking, slowly. Lilah caught up.

"I didn't have the emotional bandwidth."

Whatever that was.

Lilah followed her up the brick walk. "Something going on at your work?"

"Yes."

She waited but Meri didn't say another word. Miraculously, Lilah restrained herself from pushing it.

Once inside the cool kitchen, Meredith went straight to the coatrack and hung up her bag. "Take off that jacket, too," Lilah said. "How can you stand it in this heat?"

Meri didn't answer but she took the jacket off and hung it with the bag while Lilah went to the refrigerator to check on its contents.

Henry came climbing out of his basket in the corner, mewling a little bit, heading straight for Meri.

"There's fresh sweet tea and Coke and diet Coke. Cream soda, RC Cola—I have some moon pies, too—and orange or cranberry juice."

Meri squatted down to greet the cat. "So, Henry, you forgive me?" she asked him. "I didn't mean to hurt you."

She stood up and looked at Lilah. "Diet Coke," she said. "But I'll get it, Lilah, as soon as I wash up. You only have the one hand. Sit down."

They crossed paths as Lilah headed for the sink in the mudroom and Meri for the bathroom.

"I thought you might need some help," Meri said low and quick as she passed.

Was that all the excuse she was planning to give for coming here?

By the time they met in the kitchen again, Lilah had the drinks on the table. Meri sat. But she didn't relax and she didn't talk. She drank half the Coke in her glass, then started straightening everything she could get her hands on—the napkins in their holder, the stack of mail Lilah had thrown there, the magazine Lilah had looked at while she ate her lunch.

Lilah wanted to grab her hands and hold them still.

Instead, she tried to soothe her with calm conversation. "To answer your question, I still have some pain, but I'm all right. Doc's thinking about taking the cast off tomorrow, if the bones are healed enough. Then I'll have it in a sling for another eight weeks."

Meri nodded. "Good." Then she drank the other half of her diet Coke and poured more over the ice in her glass.

"You need some food in your stomach with all that caffeine," Lilah said. "Or you'll never sleep tonight. We don't have Bobbie Sue's cake, but people are still taking turns bringing me dinner. We have ham and potato salad and meat loaf and pinto beans and chicken salad and B. J. cooked a roast when she was here. I'll make you a sandwich."

Meri shook her head. "I can't eat. But thanks. I should make you a sandwich. Do you want one?"

Lilah shook her head. "I had supper with Shorty. He was here all afternoon plowing the Cherokee Purples under."

"Did you ever find any pickers for them?"

"No. I put out the word and let people have as many as they wanted to pick for free, but only a few showed up. They took maybe twenty bushels or so and Shuggie Landry picked another two bushels to make chow-chow with and the rest rotted on the vine. It nearly killed me to see those beautiful tomatoes go to waste."

"And you lost the money you would've had from selling them?"

"Yes. And a couple of new customers because I couldn't fill their orders."

Then she shut her mouth and waited.

Finally, Meri got up from circling her glass around on the place mat, walked to the sink and ran some water into it, then turned and locked eyes with her grandmother.

"I'm sorry to just appear like this, Lilah. But I had no place else to go. I mean, that's not right—I could've gone anywhere in the world that I could scrape up the fare, but . . ."

Lilah spoke in her calmest tone. "I told you you could come here and stay as long as you like."

"Thank you."

That was all she said.

"For whatever reason," Lilah said.

Meri leaned back against the kitchen counter. From across the room, Lilah could see her tear up. "I . . . I don't exactly know why, but I couldn't think of going anywhere but here, even though I know you're angry with me. I'm sorry I upset you."

It was costing her a lot, but she was holding herself together, holding back the tears, holding back the words, thinking about them before she spoke. Lilah had to admire that kind of control. But it was killing Meredith.

"Look," Lilah said. "I'm sorry, too. I overreacted. It's true you should've called me before I heard about Henry from somebody else, but you were trying to do the honorable thing and tell me in person. Let's forgive and forget."

Meri nodded and said, "Done."

She came back to the table, sat down and started in on the napkins again. This time she took them completely out of the holder and squared the stack meticulously, over and over again, her motions brittle as peanut candy.

It was a true wonder that she'd been able to drive.

"I'm glad you got here safely."

Meri nodded, her eyes meeting Lilah's for a second, then shifting to the mail again.

The girl was in a terrible shape. She could not go on like this.

Lilah made sure she spoke softly, no pressure, as she said, "Do you have something you want to talk about, Meri?"

Meri looked up, her eyes dull. "My life's over. That's all I can say."

Lilah's heart stopped. "Are you sick? Do you have cancer?"

That would explain the lack of flesh on her bones. Her tension, her worrying . . .

"No, no. I don't mean my health. Although I probably developed an ulcer during all this hell I've gone through."

"You said it was about your job."

Meri nodded, then looked down and picked at the table-cloth.

"I'm sorry, Lilah, but I can't talk about it."

"And that's all right." Lilah couldn't resist adding, "Don't worry. You can tell me in your own good time."

Meri looked up at her, startled. But she didn't say she'd never tell.

"Whatever's wrong at your job, it doesn't mean your life is over. Didn't you mention you were dating someone when B. J. asked you at the funeral dinner?"

Meri's eyes flashed hurt. But she didn't answer. Didn't even nod her head.

Her lips started trembling. Lilah didn't let her break the look between them.

"Dear girl. You don't know nothin' yet about life. You'll feel better after a good night's sleep."

She pushed back from the table with her good hand and stood up.

"Listen to your old grandma, now. You are a successful, smart, downright *wonderful* young woman and a self-made one, at that. You'll be just fine."

Meri shook her head. The band around that poor little ponytail was just about to fall completely out of her hair. She didn't even try to talk; Lilah knew she couldn't.

"Hey. Don't let the bastards bring you down."

That brought a startled look and a trace of a smile to Meri's lips. And maybe a flash of gratitude in her eyes.

Poor child. Most likely, she'd never had anybody in her life to take her side and stand up for her.

"We can talk more in the morning," Lilah said, trying to be brisk and get Meri moving. "Let's bring in your bags, then I'll go let the horses out while you get into a good cool shower. And then go to bed. It's only nine o'clock, but you need sleep."

Meri looked up. Her eyes were full of hurt and confusion. And pain so fierce it flamed.

"I *can't* sleep. I've hardly slept since I left here."

Lilah could believe that. She looked it.

"We all go through periods in our lives when we can't sleep and then we start worrying about that and the more you think about it, the harder it is. But don't even *think* you have to sleep. If you'll lay it down, your body will rest. You're worn smooth out, Meredith Kathleen."

Meri didn't say one thing.

"I have comfort tea or milk we can warm. Either one, with some of that good sourwood honey I told you about stirred in will help you unwind."

Meri shook her head and got up from the table fast, as if she were scared Lilah was going to try to hold her nose and pour one or the other down her throat.

"I'll get my things," she said. "If you don't need me to help you with the horses tonight. If you do, I will. I can learn how to do all the chores around here."

"You won't have a choice. Honey Grove's like the first colony of the Pilgrims. No work, no eat. As soon as you get to feeling a little better, you'll have to hit it."

"I will."

Lilah turned and started for the door. She didn't look back but she could sense Meri following.

"You know that old saw, 'Time is the great healer'?"

Meri came up beside her. She nodded.

"Time helps, yes. But it's *work* that's the great healer. We should be thankful every day that the Lord told Adam and Eve we'd all have to work to survive."

"My work's gone."

"Don't you worry, honey. There's plenty more work everywhere, all different kinds of work. I'll give you some of mine."

Lilah came to her senses on the way to the barn. After she left Meri at her car, it was the first time she had a minute to herself to think.

But, oh, Lord, what was she doing? She'd better be thinking.

Deep down, she didn't know this girl from Adam's off-ox. She didn't know the first thing about her life or what she should do next to try to help her.

And what was she doing to herself? Yes, she'd like more life in her house. But she'd just had two weeks of Barbara

Jane and she was really craving her early mornings all to herself.

Besides, she and Meri probably would get along like cats and dogs. Good Lord, they *both* thought they were right all the time!

They were kin, all right. Whether or not they could ever be family was another question altogether.

Lilah Briscoe, you're old enough to know better. Good gravy, if sixty-eight years haven't taught you not to jump in a swimming hole blind, then there's no sense in you trying to live 'til you're 106.

Thirteen

When Lilah woke up the next morning, Henry was sitting on her cast, staring down at her like a sphinx and—no surprise—that entire side of her body was hurting six ways to Sunday. She pushed him off onto the bed, then rubbed her arm above the cast and wiggled her fingers the little bit she could to try and relieve the pain.

Then she threw the sheet off herself and over Henry. Sometimes he would burrow up and sleep for hours.

"Rest and heal," she told him, "even if you won't let me do the same."

The house smelled like bacon and coffee and, for a second, she thought it was B. J. in the kitchen. Then she remembered Meri and Lilah's call last night to tell B. J. she didn't need to come help her this morning.

But, goodness gracious, there was something wrong with this picture. Would Meri really take it upon herself to cook breakfast? She *must've* slept, because in the shape she was in last night, she couldn't have held the percolator under the water faucet.

Lilah pushed herself up one-handed and sat on the side

of the bed for a minute. She still wasn't completely adjusted to getting her balance, cast and all, so she stood up slowly.

At the funeral dinner, hadn't Meri said she couldn't cook?

Lilah's heart lifted. Well, now, maybe . . . just *maybe* . . . Meri would get interested in good food and accept—or even *ask* for—cooking lessons from Lilah. Once the child got some confidence and learned what good food was, she would value the scrapbook of old recipes and quotes and poems Lilah's mother had lived by.

Then the scrapbook and the soda jar could be passed down to their rightful owner—the next generation—and someone who treasured them.

With that happy hope, Lilah got up and headed to the bathroom. Henry, wide-awake, came out of the covers and off the bed to go with her as soon as she got to the door. She was surprised that Meri was taking hold like this. Maybe she *did* know how to cook a few things, after all. Maybe what she'd said at the dinner was that she didn't know how to make gravy.

When you got right down to the cold hard truth, there were lots of people who were halfway decent cooks but they couldn't make gravy fit to eat. Take Bobbie Sue Turner as a case in point. She could make that wonderful, delicious, *heavenly* cake like nobody else in the county could do, but her gravy was so bad it'd make a pig gag.

Biscuits were another delicate proposition; Bobbie didn't have the touch for them, either. Hers were little rocks. At last year's 4-H Horse Club fund-raising breakfast, Shorty had whispered to Lilah that he could throw one far enough to hit a snake in the eye. Lilah had started planning right then to put Bobbie to serving instead of cooking this year, so they wouldn't have people by the dozens wasting enough food to feed an army.

Lilah used the bathroom and washed up awkwardly. It was amazing how much a person missed having two hands. After that, she headed straight for the coffee, sniffing the air the same way Henry was doing as he led the way down the hall. Was it just her or was the good smell of bacon starting to give way to a *burnt*-bacon odor in the air?

The next second, Lilah totally forgot about bacon. The sight of her own kitchen just about floored her. She had to grab on to the doorjamb with her one good hand, it was such a shock.

For one thing, the table and chairs had vanished in the night. No, there they were looking strange on the opposite side of the room, under the south windows with the sunlight falling across two place settings on . . . were her eyes deceiving her or was that . . .? Yes. It *was* her grandmother's embroidered tablecloth.

Her mind boggled. Merciful heavens! That hadn't been out of the drawer since she'd hand-washed and ironed it a year ago Christmas when she'd used it for her ladies' Christmas luncheon and Johnnie Kay Loudermilk dripped cranberry punch on it. It'd taken three tries, but Lilah got the stains out.

Her pulse jumped. On the table, there was not one sign of her invoices or receipt book or the orders for produce. *Or* the mail. None of that was anywhere to be seen.

Oh, Lord. There were already more jobs on the list for today than could get done in two. She couldn't bear to think about taking time to redo what she'd organized yesterday.

"What've you done?" she wailed. "I don't have time to sort all those invoices again."

Meri jumped about a foot and whirled to face her.

"I knew where everything was in all those stacks. Now you've got everything all mixed up. Where is it?"

"Oh! Hi, Lilah. Uh, in there." She gestured toward the mudroom. She looked like she was about to cry. "I put them in there on the desk. I'm going to help you with them today."

"I don't need any help. I had them in order."

Meri went back to peeling the paper towels loose from the cooking rack where she'd cooked the bacon to a fare-thee-well.

"Really, we should put them all into your computer, Lilah," Meri said. "I'll start on that this afternoon."

"Lord, have mercy, that's worse than moving my furniture and using my grandmother's tablecloth—can't you see that's an antique?—and now you want to put my business on a *computer*? No. I can't deal with that."

Meri shook the rattling, ruined bacon slices off onto the little earthen platter Lilah always used for bacon and sausage. How'd she know to use it?

"It's the only way for a business to survive now. It's a computerized world, Lilah. I was surprised to see you're still doing all that on paper."

"Why'd you move the table?"

"It'll be easier there for you to manage your chair with only one arm."

Lilah threw up her hands. As best she could. "When I said you could stay, I had no idea you'd take over the furniture arrangement."

As Meri carried the awful bacon to the table, in a light tone she said, "You said I have to work. I'm working."

It was then that Lilah saw her mother's scrapbook open on the apron of the Conestoga cupboard.

"That's a keepsake from my mother."

"Are you afraid I'm going to harm your book?"

She wanted to just fly in and put everything back to rights but here she was, her broken arm trapped in the sling. Her whole self suddenly felt trapped in this new situation. Meri was a strong-headed girl.

Which, overall, was good. It meant she'd recover faster from the loss of her old life. But it might not be so easy to live with.

"I wouldn't do that," Meri said. "Give me a little credit for good sense."

The whole thing made Lilah want to go lie down with a cold rag on her head. Or grab this girl up and throw her out of this kitchen.

You're the older woman here. This girl is a wreck of her

*former self and she's trying to do something nice for you.
She's the nervous kind that has to be moving all the time.
Nothing's done here that can't be undone. You are so set in
your ways it is pathetic.*

But still, Meri was overstepping her bounds.

*Ten minutes ago, you were hoping she'd fall in love with
that scrapbook. Make up your mind. Get your priorities
straight, Lilah.*

"I'd planned to show you the scrapbook myself," she
said, "and see you discover it."

Lilah walked over to the cupboard and closed the scrapbook.

"Was I not going to be touching it?"

Lilah grinned. She turned to the stove, picked up the
bowl of scrambled eggs and took it to the table. The toast
popped up, so she went back for that.

Meri went to the refrigerator with two little glasses.

"Let's both have orange juice," Lilah said, then added
in a significant tone, "cranberry's harder to get out of that
tablecloth."

You are so beyond tacky, Lilah. Petty's *a better word.*

"I was just trying to make you a nice breakfast," Meri
said, her voice fragile. "A thank-you for taking me in.
Please tell me what I can do and cannot do in your kitchen."

Lilah's anger softened. "I'm sorry if I made you feel
bad, honey. I appreciate this, I really do. Did you sleep?"

"A couple of hours." Meri poured the juice. Her hand
wasn't quite steady.

They sat down at the table.

"Let's have the blessing," Lilah said, and they did.

Meri passed the bacon. It wasn't fit to eat, but Lilah took
a piece.

"I'll show you how to fry this in an iron skillet," Lilah
said. "It's hand-cut, applewood-smoked, homemade bacon
from Randy Lee Turnipseed's butcher shop. The micro-
wave's no way to cook decent, thick-cut bacon."

Meri didn't jump at the chance for a cooking lesson. She
just smiled to herself.

"You were cooking a special breakfast for me before you fell out of the tree, remember? Now we have a second chance."

She said every word of that in a patient, slow tone as if Lilah had dementia or Old-Timer's or something.

But. *Second chance.*

That took quite a bit of the wind out of Lilah's sails. Sometimes, last night, as she fell asleep thinking about Meri, the guilt had nearly overcome her. If she'd raised the girl, maybe she'd have been stronger to face this upheaval in her life.

And maybe she wouldn't have been quite so rudely pushy. But it was her way of pitching in to help. She didn't know how to do that because she had no yardstick to go by in any kind of family experience.

"Thank you," she said quietly. "It was just a shock to me to see the furniture moved. This breakfast table has stood over there in that corner since I came here as a bride."

Meredith ate one tiny bite of toast, then said, "So maybe it's time it was moved. Right?"

Lilah's eyes flew open wide. "Oh no! Are you saying I didn't clean under it?"

The horror in her voice tickled Meri. She actually grinned.

Then she shrugged. "I'm sorry. But I *did* find a dust bunny or two in the corner."

Lilah smiled, too. It was a good sign that Meri could tease.

"I've got a broken wrist. Not an excuse, but you should take it under consideration."

"I'm kidding. No dust bunnies."

They laughed. If they could hold on to their senses of humor, they'd do all right. It was nice to have companionship at breakfast.

"No, really," Meri said, "how many years has that been since you moved here as a bride? Forty? It might do you good to change all your furniture around."

"Are you saying I'm stuck in a rut?" Lilah shook her head. "I just don't feel the need."

Meri's reply was a raised eyebrow and a twinkle.

They smiled at each other and Meri nibbled at a stick of bacon.

"You'd better eat," Lilah said. "Even if you have to force yourself a little."

"I don't eat breakfast."

"Well, there's your trouble."

"Meaning . . . ?"

"Meaning your body needs the food so you can work. My grandpa used to say, 'Always eat your breakfast, 'cause you never know where you'll be by dinnertime.' Now we call it lunch. On a farm, you can get into a situation where you're too far from the house or into too urgent a job to get to eat at noon."

Meri nodded at that. She took another bite. "I love bacon, but I never let myself have it. This is a treat."

"*If* it's cooked right. Leave it to me tomorrow morning; you can do the eggs. These are scrambled just the way I like them. Bacon's a great appetizer, and you need to eat hearty to get to feeling better."

"I used to cook eggs for Mom and me but now I can't even do it as well as when I was ten years old."

A sudden image of the skinny little girl standing at the stove while Edie Jo slept off a hard night's work of show-girl parading and dancing tore Lilah's heart out.

Meri went on, "Bacon appeals to lots of people. Did you know it has its own Facebook page?"

Lilah took another bite of the eggs—they weren't as bad as the bacon—and stared at her granddaughter.

"I didn't understand a word you just said. A *Facebook* page? What's that?"

Meri's eyes widened. "You've never heard of Facebook?"

"No. Does it have something to do with computers?"

"Yes. It's a social networking site. You can meet people there and talk about bacon, if you want."

"Save us all! Why would I want to do that? Strangers? What do they say about it?"

"Oh, how much they love it, ideas for using it in recipes . . ."

"I wonder if they know there's a concession stand that sells chocolate-covered bacon at the fair."

Meri was getting all excited. "See? You'll have to get on there and tell that to the bacon fans. And then you could mention they should also come to the Honey Grove booth at the fair. If you've never been on the site, I'll show you how to join. Right after breakfast."

"I don't have a computer."

Meri's eyes flew open right in the middle of another bite. "*What?* Lilah! You *must* buy a computer. You have a business to run."

"Nope. I don't have the money for foolishness that I don't need."

"But you *do* need it. You could keep all your records on it, the orders for produce, the invoices, the receipts. It'd all be so much faster and neater than all those papers you had scattered around on your table."

"No. I can't afford it. And I know what I'm doing without it. Besides, my operation is small."

"But I can put up a good website to bring in new customers . . ."

"Whatever that is, I don't need it. I've gotten three new restaurants for customers just this year."

"What it *is* is a way to get three *hundred* new customers. Maybe in a month."

She took another bite of her eggs. "Lilah, I can put up some gorgeous pictures and great text and make Honey Grove Farm known all over the *world*. The organic food movement is worldwide."

"No. Hush. Let's finish our breakfast. Every time I think about learning to use a computer or one of those fancy phones or a gadget like you have in that car telling you where to go, my head starts to hurt and my skin crawls."

Meri stared at her in disbelief.

"No, really, it's true. If somebody tries to show me how

to do one thing on one of those electronic gadgets, my mind starts screaming, 'I don't want to hear this. I don't want to do this.' "

But Meri truly was her granddaughter. She wouldn't give up.

"I can coach you. You need to do this, Lilah. It'd be a great way I can help you before I leave. I'll get it all set up and teach you how to use it."

"No," Lilah said. "And that's final. No telling who might come out of the worldwide woodwork that we wouldn't *want* to know."

"But it'd be the most valuable, lasting help I could give you. I feel so bad about Henry and causing all that emotional pain on top of your physical suffering. I want to try and make it up to you. Getting a website for Honey Grove could make all the difference. Wouldn't you like hundreds of new customers?"

"I couldn't *handle* hundreds of new customers. What we need to do after breakfast is pick green tomatoes for one of the new customers we already have."

She took a deep breath to settle her breathing after the computer scare.

Meri looked crestfallen.

"I don't want to hurt your feelings, honey, I really wouldn't do that for the world. But I can run my business a lot faster and better the old-fashioned way."

She grinned at Meri.

"*If* you'll quit hiding all my papers from me."

Meri's smile trembled. "I'm sorry. But you can still show me the scrapbook, Lilah. I just flipped the pages looking for the biscuit recipe. I didn't read it at all."

Lilah heard the tremble in her granddaughter's voice, too. She reached across the table and touched the top of Meri's hand.

Fourteen

Having Meri as Lilah's cooperative little shadow during morning chores turned out to be pleasant. Like at breakfast, it was nice to have company.

Lilah was certainly used to doing things alone but she decided she was going to enjoy this for the weeks or however long Meri might be at Honey Grove. She seemed eager to learn the chores and this was a good way to put her desperate need to *do something* to good use.

Better use than moving the kitchen furniture, that was for sure. And she followed Lilah's directions very well.

They got the horses in and fed them, gathered the eggs and picked some fresh cilantro to add to the delivery for the Local Table restaurant. Meri took the brunt of the work and Lilah did what she could with her one useful arm and hand.

"Ever since I broke my wrist, I've been paying Jimmy Ransford to work more than usual," she said, "and too much of what he's done has been just these basic chores. For the time you're here, we can hire him mostly for picking. Today I'll start him on the Pink Beauties."

Meri said, "Sounds like a plan. I can do the computer work in the evenings."

Lilah stiffened. So the computer scare wasn't over, after all.

"I thought I made myself clear about that," she said, separating the cilantro into bunches and handing them to Meri to wrap in wet paper towels. "I can't afford to buy something I'll never use after you're gone."

She used her firm voice but it didn't faze Meri.

"Some of them aren't expensive at all, especially the used ones. I'll buy it with part of my severance package. My old one isn't working right and I'll have to have a dependable one for my new job search, anyway."

"Buy whatever you want, but don't expect me to use it."

Meri looked up from the wooden crate where she was stacking the fragrant, spicy bundles.

"Fair enough."

But then she added a smile that said she wouldn't stop trying to change Lilah's mind.

Oh, well. Let her try.

The day passed even faster than usual. The two of them worked together with a little bit of getting-acquainted talk along with all the work-talk, but not much. Lilah hoped Meri would tell her all about all the trouble in New York, and hinted around the subject but when Meri didn't respond, she didn't push.

The child is a bundle of raw nerves. Let her be.

After the deliveries were done and they ate a late lunch, Lilah insisted that Meri lie down since she was trying to keep going on so little sleep. Lilah found her business papers and got on the phone to take tomorrow's restaurant orders and schedule one of her Texas history talks with a young middle school teacher.

Meri popped up like a jack-in-the-box, so they talked about the farm some and Lilah showed her how the order and invoice system worked.

She almost told her the worst—all about the looming

debt—but she held back. If she started talking about it now, she wouldn't sleep a wink tonight.

And Meri did not need more worries right now. Not even as a distraction from her own troubles. She needed to get through some of them first.

She hated to tell her, too, because it'd make her think her grandmother didn't have good business sense. She'd been so stupid to wait so long to figure this out, but she still could hardly believe that Buford wouldn't think it over and, for old time's sake, persuade the bank board to approve an extension on the loan.

But even if she'd known all along that he was an ungrateful wretch, what could she have done to get the money? She had put every cent she could back into the farm because it took all of them just to stay in business.

But she didn't get into all that right then.

She pushed back her chair and said, "Let's go pick some of the Pink Beauties. Jimmy's quit for the day but we can get a few more before suppertime."

Meri was still skimming through the stacks of papers. "I'm no accountant," she said, "but I'll study all this and at least I can give you a second take on things."

"Let's not get all wrapped up in worry about it now, though," Lilah said. "If we do, neither one of us will sleep a wink tonight. Come on. I'll show you how to pick tomatoes."

Shorty thought he had found some reliable pickers for the next day, but Lilah knew how fast that kind of plan could evaporate.

Once they were into their routine picking Pink Beauties and laying them carefully into the plastic buckets, Lilah began telling Meri the harrowing story of the Cherokee Purples that had mostly rotted on the vines while she was back in New York. Possibly, Meri would reciprocate with her own story of the same time period.

Not that she needed to think about *that*, either, and then try to sleep tonight.

Lilah was so selfish. She had to fight her curiosity all the time to try to keep out of other people's affairs.

But how was Lilah ever going to help Meri come out of this nervous state she was in when her mind was a thousand miles away? Meri was obviously thinking about her troubles anyway, so she might as well talk about them.

In fact, it'd be much better for her if she would.

She had to get it out. The girl had just lost her job—evidently, if she was going to get a severance package—and maybe her boyfriend, too. Bless her heart, she needed to talk.

Trying to take the subtle, roundabout way rather than the straight, blunt approach that usually popped to the tip of her tongue, Lilah began.

"You know, Meri, all my life I've been a worry magnet."

Surprised, Meri looked at her as if she'd lost her mind.

"Even when I was just a girl going back and forth to college, I could get on a bus and sit down by a perfect stranger and, before the driver even pulled away from Pauline's Diner, which was also the bus station then and still is now, my seatmate would be telling me all his or her troubles. Before we ever got halfway to Brenham, I'd know that person's deepest secret or worst worry or both."

Meri gave her the look that said, "Why are you telling me this?"

"I'm a good listener," Lilah said, "even though I've talked so much today—I guess I must have lonely-person syndrome—you probably can't believe that I *can* listen. I just want you to know that you can talk to me anytime about your troubles up there in New York if you'd like a second take on things."

Meri gave her head a quick little shake and went back to work.

"I know, I know," Lilah said. "It's probably way too soon."

Meri kept picking, arranging each tomato gently on top of the ones in the bucket. Then she quit with one in her hand and stared at Lilah.

"You know . . . New York life is a little like farm

life—faster, because of all the people and the noise—but we work morning, noon and night just like you do. Tim and I didn't have much time for a love life. For these past six months we lived together but it didn't bring us any closer, except that our home desks faced each other.

"On Saturday nights we'd go out for dinner with friends from the office and we were all so exhausted we always made it an early night. The rest of the week we'd grab a pizza or pick up Chinese takeout . . ."

Her voice trailed away into her thoughts.

Were they still together or not? Lilah kept quiet but she didn't turn away to start picking again.

Finally Meri said, with her pretty eyes full of puzzlement and pain, "I don't want to think about it."

Her voice broke. Tears swam in her eyes but she blinked them back.

She cradled a green tomato in the flowered cotton gloves Lilah had loaned her. With them on, plus the big chambray work shirt shrouding her skinny body from the sun and the straw cowboy hat, she looked like a kid in a farmer costume.

Lilah saw the little girl who should've grown up at Honey Grove knowing that her grandmother loved her.

That would have made all the difference.

Lilah's heart left her body.

Meri turned away fast, as if she couldn't bear to hear any response. She was so tense she was shaking a little as she bent over to lay the tomato carefully into the bucket.

She popped back up and threw it instead, screaming, "Snake! Snake!"

Lilah got a glimpse of the long green garden snake wiggling away, but before she could get the word *harmless* out of her mouth, Meri had already knocked over the bucket and was running down the row, yelling back over her shoulder.

"Lilah, get out of there! There's a snake! Run! Run!"

Lilah finally caught her breath to holler after her. "It's a garden snake, Meri. It won't hurt you."

She saw Shorty and Caleb appear at the end of the row but Meri was not only running deaf but blind, too, and she ran right into Caleb's broad chest. She threw her arms around his neck, knocking her hat completely off and his loose. He grabbed for it with one hand while he tried to manage Meri with the other because she was climbing all over him, trying to get both feet off the ground, looking back over her shoulder for the snake.

Caleb was staggering under Meri's assault while he and Shorty were hooting and laughing loud enough to be heard on the square in Rock Springs. Lilah was trying not to laugh, with the girl so scared and all, but she couldn't help it. The whole thing was like a silly scene from that old TV show *Green Acres*.

Shorty yelled at Lilah over Meri's noise, "You know that for sure? It was no copperhead?"

"Yes! No! It was that old garden snake that hangs around the backyard. Tell her it's gone. I saw it go."

Meri hushed, like somebody'd turned off a radio. But not because she'd heard what Lilah said. She froze in mid-air with her long legs bent at the knees and pulled back to look into Caleb's face.

"You!" she cried. "What're *you* doing here? Take your hands off me. Let me go."

He opened his arms and she dropped, landing on her feet, staggering a little in the soft dirt.

"*I* should be the one complaining," he said, still chuckling. "*You* grabbed *me* and clamped on like a dog on a bone!"

Even from where Lilah was, she could see the color flood into Meri's pale face. Her mouth worked but nothing came out, so she whirled around and rushed, albeit a little shakily, back toward Lilah and the overturned bucket, her face flaming redder by the minute. Bless the girl's heart, she was embarrassed half to death.

And still looking for snakes on both sides of the row. She'd lost her ponytail holder along with her hat. She used her hair to half-hide her burning face.

"I'm s-sorry," she said, when she got to Lilah. "But I'm so scared of snakes . . ." She shuddered.

Lilah reached to rub her granddaughter's upper arms and Meri let her do it.

"Bless your heart, honey. Don't be so hard on yourself. Everybody's scared of something."

Before she could try to hug her, Meri squatted down to set the bucket upright, muttering, "I'll pick these up. I hope I didn't ruin any of them."

The men were right behind her. She refused to look up.

"Oh, Meri, don't be embarrassed," Caleb said. "You can run into my arms anytime you want."

That got her head up. "In your dreams," she said, eyes blazing.

She captured the last spilled tomato and stood to face him. "I'm glad you're here," she said, "because I intended to talk to you, you liar."

That set him back a step. "What?"

"You broke your word. You called Lilah with the news about Henry before I could even get back to Honey Grove. Whatever happened to confidentiality? I should file a suit. What a shock for a severely injured elderly person lying in the emergency room suffering from a hard fall and twelve broken bones!"

Lilah blurted, "*Elderly?* Hmph!" at the same time Caleb recovered enough to talk.

"Around here, *liar*'s a fightin' word," he said, nailing Meri with a killer look. "You're in Texas now. You better watch what you say."

She didn't waver one bit under his glare. No doubt she was excellent in court, just as Lilah had suspected all along.

Well, when you thought about it, she'd needed to say "elderly" in order to make her case stronger. Fast thinking.

Now she'd moved on to challenging her opponent. "*Fighting* word? Are you the kind of man who'd hit a woman?"

Oh, Lord! That was an even *worse* insult. Now Caleb was going white under his tan.

Lilah's hopes for a friendship—or maybe even more—between the two of them went rushing past her mind's eye in a series of romantic images going down the drain. Only then did her mind click into gear on what the heart of the trouble was.

She threw up her hands. "No, no, now y'all listen here to me. I called Caleb that day, not the other way around."

Meri turned her lawyer glare on Lilah. "Nice try," she said. "But I don't believe you. Not to call you a liar, though, since we *are* in Texas."

"Listen to me. I'm your grandma and I wouldn't tell you a lie. Somebody has told you wrong about that call."

It came to her then. She slapped her forehead.. "Doreen. Oh, dear heavens, I should've known all along. You said she was at my house. You left Henry with her. She'd been at the hospital when I was talking to Caleb. *She's* the liar, and always has been!"

Meri blinked. She thought about that. "Doreen," she said, recalling the day.

"I asked her how you already knew about Henry," she said slowly, remembering as she went, "and Doreen said . . . oh no!"

Meri sort of wilted. "If my memory's right, what she said exactly was that you were talking to Caleb on the phone when she walked into your room."

"You're sure? Nothing about who called who? Whom?"

"No. She probably didn't know. You were already talking when she came in."

"Then I have to take back calling her a liar."

Lilah was disappointed. She'd like to have something fresh on Doreen. They hadn't had a good old, clear-the-air, knock-'em-down, drag-'em-out fight in a long time.

"So you were lying there in the emergency room and you just picked up the phone and called Caleb? To chat?"

Lilah looked at her straight. "No. Tol called me from the Dairy Queen, sittin' there looking at your car with the doors still hanging open."

Meri's eyes widened. "What?"

Lilah nodded. "Yep. Ever since Tol got that mobile phone, he's an even bigger menace to society than he used to be."

"But *you* don't have one. How'd he know to call the hospital?"

Lilah wagged her head. "Oh, honey. Don't ever do anything around here that you don't want the whole world to know about, because *somebody* will see you and tell. Guaranteed.

"Shuggie at the grocery store called her cousin Darla while she was putting B. J.'s groceries back on the shelf and Darla called her brother to say I *fell out of a tree*, no doubt, was the way she put it, and *his* wife called *her* cousin's husband, Junior Thompson, who knew he'd best report the news to Tol or Tol would never forgive him. He and Tol are fishing buddies whenever Tol can tear himself away from gathering gossip long enough to *go* fishing."

Meri blinked and tried to figure out what she'd just heard.

Then she sighed. "I . . . I admit I may have jumped to conclusions," she said meekly. She didn't even sound like herself and she looked miserable. "I'm sorry I doubted you, Lilah."

She looked at Caleb. Lilah and Shorty did, too. He was still a little bit ticked off but his twinkle was coming back. He was holding the look between him and Meri, not letting her break it.

"I . . . I was mistaken," she said.

He waited, not moving a muscle.

"I . . . I misjudged you, Caleb."

Caleb wouldn't let her escape. "And . . . ?"

"I apologize," Meri told him. Anyone could see the words were hard for her to say. He was getting a little grin at the corner of his mouth and a righteous look with a cocked eyebrow.

Lilah smiled to herself. Caleb was never going to let Meri live this one down. Well, it'd be good for Meri to have to take a little teasing once in a while. She was way too serious.

Neither of them said anything.

Cale hooked his thumbs in his belt and stood there.

After a beat or two, Meri swallowed hard. "I'm *sorry*," she burst out.

He nodded. He waited some more.

"All *right*. I apologize for calling you a liar. Will you forgive me?"

She didn't sound very gracious but her tone was sincere. Lilah had already learned that Meri hated to be wrong about anything.

Cale gave her the full benefit of his megawatt grin. "I forgive you. If you'll let me teach you how to talk Texan. You could get in some serious trouble around here and if you did, me and Shorty'd be the ones to have to get you out of it."

"Yeah," Shorty said. "And we ain't got time for foolishness such as that."

Lilah was watching Meri close. It was the strangest thing. She smiled, and Lilah would've sworn that the girl let go—just for a sliver of a second—and actually relaxed for the first time since she'd known her.

Meri blinked. She couldn't believe that she'd let herself be drawn in. For a moment, back there in the Pink Beauties, she'd felt . . . delusional, or something like it. As if that silly chatter were real and she had people to . . . watch her back or whatever.

Whatever Tim was supposed to be doing for her but didn't.

That little wisp of emotion, fantasy that it was—how did Caleb Burkett unfailingly jerk her deep feelings to the top?—had put her here, in the backseat of Shorty's truck with Caleb in the backseat, too, on the way to some restaurant several miles on the opposite side of Rock Springs from Honey Grove.

"You'll love the atmosphere at Taylor's Inn, Meri," Lilah said from the front seat. "It's been a dance hall and steak house since the thirties and the Prohibition days, and it's still the original building, big screened porch and all."

Shorty said, "Back then, people came in cars and on horseback from miles around to the Friday- and Saturday-night dances. Me and a lot of other kids were raised around there playing hide-and-seek in the fields and woods next to the parking lot and sleepin' in our folks' old cars while they danced all night."

He shook his head and smiled at the memories. "Hard times, tough lives and anybody would drive across Texas for some fun."

"By the time we were great big kids, it was pretty seedy and wild out there. Always was, really. My folks forbade me to go anywhere near the place," Lilah said. "I'm still glad we sneaked off that time to see Bob Wills, aren't you, Shorty?"

They exchanged sideways glances and Meri had a flash of them as teenagers. She surprised herself by blurting, "Were you dating?"

Shorty said, "Buddies, mostly, I guess you'd say. That night she's talkin' about? It was me and her and Ed Briscoe."

"I seem to recall a brown-eyed girl named Nina Whitlock in there somewhere," Lilah teased.

"So you both grew up in Rock Springs?"

Shorty nodded. "Known each other all our lives. Ed Briscoe just barely beat me out by a hair when it came to capturing her heart. Ain't that right, Lilah?"

"Shorty," she said, "you always did have a mighty high opinion of yourself."

Shorty winced, pretending hurt feelings, then turned and winked at Meri over his shoulder. "She'll tell you how the cow ate the cabbage, your grandma will. Are you the same way, Meri?"

"I don't know anything about cows *or* cabbage."

The others laughed.

"See?" Caleb said, "You need a lesson in Texan right now."

"That means she's not one to mince words," Shorty said. "She'll tell you the truth straight out."

Meri thought about it. "I usually say how I think things should be done."

Caleb laughed. "That's the understatement of the year."

She turned to look at him. "But some people refuse to hear straight talk," she said. "They don't understand words like, 'I can't stay here and take care of this cat,' or 'I don't know how to hold a horse.' "

But rushing back to New York hadn't saved her career. Her stomach clutched, as usual when she thought about her losses. She didn't want to even try to eat. She couldn't, with her stomach knotted like this.

The guilty stammer in Tim's voice and the look on his face when she first realized he hadn't tried at all to persuade Alan to keep her on the team were burned onto her brain. Alone in Tim's office after leaving Alan's, she'd been quizzing him, trying to put together the time line of events and the process of how she'd been pushed off the team.

She hadn't even heard his words. Her gut was screaming that it was a lie.

Too bad they weren't in Texas at the time. Maybe she could've turned him over to Caleb to mete out whatever dire fate awaited a liar. A duel at sunrise, maybe?

Nothing was too silly to think about if it kept her from remembering that moment when she realized that all of her world was crumbling beneath her.

They drove into a gravel parking lot in front of a low, rambling frame structure with porches everywhere. Clearly, it had had a lot of use but, ramshackle or not, it was freshly painted white and it gleamed in the falling dusk.

"Back in the doo-dah days," Lilah said, "people flew in from all over Texas just for lunch or dinner here. They landed their planes in that pasture over there across the road."

When they crossed the porch and went in, they threaded through the tables slowly, speaking and being spoken to, stopping to visit here and there and introducing Meri to people she hadn't yet met. Even they seemed to know already that she was here to stay awhile and welcomed her warmly. The county sheriff and the Methodist minister both tried to charm her.

The tables filled one half of the huge open room; the

other half was the dance floor. A Western-dressed band was setting up in front of the wide windows. The crescent-shaped bar, with most of its stools occupied, curved along the back wall of the whole room, the bottles and glasses catching the last rays of sunlight.

Caleb took them to a round table in the corner. The whole place smelled delicious, like smoked meat. Onions and peppers, too. And sweet barbeque sauce. Fried chicken.

Surprisingly, she did feel a touch of hunger. Like when she'd walked into Lilah's kitchen after the funeral. Usually, she ate only to survive and hardly ever felt hungry, probably because nerves tied her stomach into knots.

But, somehow, that feeling had lessened on the drive out here.

Meri tried to push all thoughts of New York, Tim and Alan out of her mind. She'd had a long day today and a terrible fright. She deserved some free time. This was another perfect occasion to practice her live-in-the-moment skills.

Caleb gave Meri a flash of his grin as he pulled out her chair. When he sat beside her, she turned to look at him— oh, honestly, his eyes were as blue as Paul Newman's—and she looked across the room instead while she took deep breaths to try to clear her mind.

The band struck up a fast opening number, the lead singer stepped up to the microphone and several couples got up to dance.

Meri opened the napkin and spread it in her lap for something to do. A waitress came with menus and personal recommendations. Since yes, Lester was the cook tonight, the best dishes were the T-bone, the pulled pork barbeque, the beef enchiladas and the chicken-fried steak.

As soon as the ordering was done and the sweet tea was flowing, Caleb turned to Meri.

"Do you know how to two-step?"

"I don't dance."

"Why not?"

Annoyed by his persistence, she glared at him. "I'm a terrible dancer."

He gestured at his leg. "As a limping gimp, I'm not too graceful myself. Who cares? I can still teach you."

How embarrassing would that be? Public dance lessons?

From across the table, Shorty said, "What's the matter, Cale? Won't she dance with you?"

Caleb glanced at him. "No, and I don't know why," he drawled. "I put on my good-smellin' stuff and my new pearl-snap shirt, too."

"Maybe you oughtta sweet-talk her a little."

Caleb leaned toward Meri—indeed, his cologne *was* heavenly, but she'd never tell *him* that—and his cheek brushed her hair. His breath tickled her ear as he whispered, "I need to talk to you. About Lilah."

Meri pulled back, startled. His eyes weren't teasing anymore. He was deadly serious. Worried.

She nodded. They got up and he took her hand, heading for the dance floor, passing a couple Caleb greeted as Clem and Flora—Meri remembered their faces but not their names from the funeral dinner at Lilah's house. They were coming to the table to speak to Shorty and Lilah, who got up to hug them.

But that didn't necessarily mean they hadn't seen each other in a long time. Meri had already learned that much about this strange, new world.

The fast song ended. A waltz began. The West Texas Waltz, according to the singer, who did have a pleasant speaking voice, too, but not as appealing as Caleb's.

Once on the dance floor, Caleb stopped and took her in his arms. Her ear was just level with his lips. He murmured into it, "I'm thinking you probably *do* know how to waltz."

His warm breath tickled. His low voice sent a frisson of a thrill down her spine where his hand rested warm and sure in the small of her back.

She was wearing the spaghetti-strapped sundress she'd bought on sale in New York when she'd gone shopping to try and comfort herself. Being jobless had ruled, though, and she'd been glad when she threw the dress into her bag that it was the only thing she'd bought that day.

In spite of the terrible state she'd been in when she was shopping *and* packing, she'd remembered it was hot in Texas. But not *how* hot.

"What *about* Lilah?" she said.

"She's headed for ruin," he said. "She'll lose Honey Grove if she can't pay the note that's coming due in about thirty days. I'm trying to loan her the money and she won't take it."

Meri pulled back and stared up at him while they moved awkwardly across the floor.

He glared at her but it wasn't personal; it was frustration with the situation.

"I care about her, damn it. Maybe you can talk her into letting me help."

Meri heard him but she couldn't think and keep her feet moving at the same time while a scared shock was creating a dozen questions scrambled together in her head. Lose Honey Grove? What would happen to Lilah? And then where would Meri find refuge? Thirty days wasn't much time to find a job. How long would an eviction take?

She blurted, "I couldn't bear to go back to New York so soon."

Caleb's blue eyes showed surprise, then steel.

She felt heat pour into her face. At least, unlike after Lilah's fall, her first thought hadn't been for herself. What would be an inconvenience for her would be a tragedy for Lilah.

"Oh, God," she said. "Honey Grove and Lilah are one and the same. Where could she go?"

"Good of you to think of her, as well as yourself," he said. Some insane corner of her brain noted that was the first sarcasm she'd ever heard from him. It was cutting.

It hurt.

"I'm sorry I didn't mention Lilah first," she said, not letting herself look away from the disgust in his eyes. "I did think of her first, however."

The confession helped soften Caleb's look a little.

"But I don't see how I can influence her. Every time I

offer an idea or a suggestion, Lilah accuses me of trying to take over her life."

He nodded and negotiated a turn around a couple who had stopped dancing to gaze into each other's eyes.

"You'll have to get her past that. She admires you, she thinks you're smart."

"You're out of your mind. I have no influence over her."

"Look—you're a lawyer and your job is to persuade people to agree with you. Right?"

"Well, yes, but with the law as a basis for argument. There's no code saying she has to accept help if she doesn't want it."

His hand tightened on her back. "I'm at the end of my rope. Help me out here. She says it'd be charity. She says it could ruin our friendship. Ridiculous."

Meri forgot she was trying to dance while she tried to sort that out.

"Imagine it," he said, his hand pressing harder against her back. "Lilah in a rented house in town. In one of those new apartments on the west side. Lilah in some other town. Can't you see how miserable she'd be?"

"Why are you interfering in her affairs?" Meri cried, letting him whirl her around without even thinking about it. "What's it to you what she does or, come to think of it, what *I* do?"

He stopped still, glaring down at her. Another couple bumped into them, and he started dancing again, fire in his eyes.

"It's the cold, hard truth," he said tightly, "because Miss Lilah's like family. You get in trouble, I'm there. My dad and brothers, too."

"Because?"

"I told you. Miss Lilah's like family. You're her grand-daughter."

He looked her over, his beautiful eyes cold as glaciers.

"You'd have to go some length to break that connection, but now that I see how distant you are about her, I believe you might accomplish that in record time."

He looked away, then back at her again.

She said quietly, holding his gaze, "The real question here is why do you care so much? Maybe you have designs on Honey Grove for yourself."

It took him a second. Shock showed in his eyes, then pure anger.

Then, pity. That surprised Meri so much she stopped dancing.

"That is so pathetic," he said. "Such a sick life. It may be big-city, but it's not real."

A couple danced past them. Caleb held her gaze with his determined one. He took her upper arms—so gently it almost felt like a threat—into his large, callused hands as if to make sure she stayed where she was and heard what he said.

"I care about Miss Lilah because she cares about me. She always has taken up for me. In Texas, we call that a *friend*."

Meri blinked. " 'Taken up for you'? What does that mean?"

"Anybody'll tell you I'm the black sheep. Miss Lilah's given me hugs and tongue-lashings and cookies when I needed them and, when I was a crazy kid, a place to stay when my daddy wouldn't let me onto the ranch."

He studied her. "We're wasting our time."

He let her go and put his hand on her back again to escort her back to the table before the song was over.

Fifteen

Meri took her coffee out onto the back porch and settled into the cushions of the swing. She'd never consider herself an outdoor person, but here she was, for the third day in a row, outside to watch the sunrise. She liked the shapes of the trees against the sky and the smells of sweet, fresh-cut grass and the soft feeling in the almost-cool air that came with this time of day that Lilah called first light.

She liked the way that first light didn't creep over the landscape or arrive gradually with the rising of the sun. It just was. One moment it was night and the next was first light.

She even liked—sort of—Henry's lounging in the windowsill behind the swing, muttering royal catly comments at her from time to time. He was peaceful, too, this time of day.

But the rest of it would be busy, sometimes hectic, and she had a decision to make. Meri wrapped both hands around the mug and sipped coffee. Should she mention Caleb's request to Lilah?

She wished she'd asked him the amount of the loan. Showing that much concern might've raised his opinion of her a little, but more to the point, she might be able to withdraw enough from her 401(k) to save Honey Grove.

Probably not, though. It must be a substantial amount if the whole farm hung in the balance.

And she didn't care what Caleb thought of her. She cared whether or not Lilah could keep Honey Grove, and she was going to concentrate on that.

She'd been trying to talk Lilah into getting into the business records with her, hoping that would cause her to confide the bad news, but they'd been too busy trying to can and preserve everything they didn't sell. In addition, because of Lilah's arm in a sling, both of them had to give the riding lessons to the teenagers. Meri did all the driving and deliveries and hadn't even had time to look for a reliable computer.

Still, Meri had tried other ways of getting into the subject and Lilah hadn't responded. Either she was in denial or Caleb had exaggerated the urgency of the loan payment.

Or Lilah simply didn't want Meri to know, for some reason.

Suddenly, Meri knew how Lilah had felt when she hadn't called to tell her about running over Henry.

The screen door creaked. Meri jumped up to help Lilah, but she held the door with her foot and managed her cup with one hand.

"I still can't get used to that table being where it is," she said. "Every time I walk through the kitchen—my very own kitchen I've had for forty-five years—and see that, it rankles something fierce."

"Because it was my idea."

Meri dashed past her grandmother to hold the swing still for her to sit down.

Lilah said, "I don't need any help," at the very moment she sat and splashed a little coffee onto the porch floor.

Meri took her place again, rubbing a sudden ache in the

middle of her forehead. "I'm thinking *that* is the most rankle-causing angle of the unexpected tragic rearrangement of the kitchen at Honey Grove."

"What is?"

Meri looked at her, teasing her with a grin. "The fact it was my idea. But with the table where it is now, you're not in danger of hitting your broken arm on the wall. Just turn your chair a little bit and you're in. Only eight weeks and then I'll put it back where it was."

Lilah suddenly smiled. A thin, sickly smile, but she was trying.

Meri touched the floor with the toe of her flip-flop and tried to take comfort from the movement of the swing. She hated when Lilah was grouchy. It reminded her of Edie Jo.

"I'm sorry," Lilah said. "Worries troubling my sleep gave me bad dreams."

Meri smiled back. "Worries about the farm finances? You've mentioned that a time or two."

Lilah narrowed her gaze. "Yes. But you can tell Caleb that I'm still not accepting charity."

She pushed the swing harder and, startled, Meri splashed out a little coffee of her own while she stared at Lilah.

"Keep this up and we'll have to mop the floor," Lilah muttered.

"How'd you know?"

Lilah waved that away. "I knew what he was after before y'all even got up to dance. He's a typical man—hardheaded as Shorty's old blue mule."

"Not completely typical," Meri said. "He can make me angrier faster than most."

Lilah laughed. "You're not the only one. Just try not to shoot him in the other leg when you lose your cool."

Startled, Meri stopped the swing. "Is that why he limps?"

Lilah nodded. "Ronnie Rae Hardesty. She always was a hot-tempered little thing. But he swears he never once promised her she was the one and only so, truth is, she crippled him without justification."

She looked Meri in the eye. Meri had learned that was a sign she should pay careful attention.

"Cale doesn't blame Ronnie Rae, though," Lilah said, "and he won't listen to a bad word about her. Says it was all his fault because he knew her temper—*and* her marksmanship—when he got tangled up with her in the first place."

Meri tried to sort that out. "That's . . . unusual, but it seems admirable . . ."

"You might as well get that doubt out of your voice. Caleb Burkett is fair and he takes responsibility for his own decisions and he will not lie to you."

"He won't even be *talking* to me. He doesn't like me."

"He doesn't even know you yet."

"There *is* no 'yet.' He doesn't like me. Not one little bit. I don't like him either, and that's the way it is."

Lilah raised one eyebrow and stared out across the pasture. "Hmm."

The grass smelled like the watermelon Lilah had cut for dessert when they got home from Taylor's Inn. The scent floated full on the breeze. Then it grew weaker. The air was getting heavier. And hotter.

"That's the way it is, huh?" she drawled. "Well, yes and no. It's a funny thing about life, Meri. It's short but it's broad. You never can tell what's around the next bend."

Meri could still feel the warm strength of Caleb's hand on her back from when they danced. And she could see the steely judgment in his eyes when he looked at her.

Her lips parted and her mouth said, "He told me he's a black sheep. I didn't know anybody our age even used that term anymore."

"Well, he's heard it from his daddy all his life. You know, some men are jealous of their sons and of the four fine boys he has, Jasper picked Caleb, his spitting image, to be the goat." Lilah shook her head. "I always thought it was because Jake considers himself so special that he thinks he's one of a kind."

No, I don't know. I don't know anything about men and their families.

The sound of a motor and wheels on the gravel driveway made them both turn to look.

"Donovan's Delivery," Meri read, from the side of the panel van that drove up to the end of the brick walk and parked.

"Jerry's on the job early," Lilah said. "Oh, Lord, and here I am in my nightgown and no bra."

"You're fine," Meri said. "Just stay right there and I'll take care of it."

She got up and walked over to the steps.

A moment later, the driver started up the walk with four battered-looking boxes stacked in his arms.

"Not the feed supplements," Lilah said. "And I haven't ordered anything else."

Jerry called, "Where do you want me to put these for you, Miss Lilah?"

"Right there beside Meri will be fine, thank you, Jerry," she said, "if you're sure they're mine. Where are they from?"

For some reason, the minute those words floated on the air, something inside Meri contracted.

"Looks like South America," Jerry said, curiosity in his voice.

That something inside her exploded. No! Just when she'd thought she was through with Edie Jo forever. This had to be her things, right? The remnants of her pathetic life.

The boxes were battered, haphazardly tied with red string, the brown paper wrappers covered with inked postmark circles and colorful paper stamps.

Meri gripped the porch post.

Too much. I can't take this now. I refuse to look at this.

Jerry was a chatty guy and Meri wanted to turn and walk away, but she responded as best she could. Lilah introduced Meri, and then, finally, he went back to his truck.

Lilah and Meri looked at each other, then at the hellish boxes.

As the truck backed up the driveway, Lilah got up and came to stand beside Meri. She bent to peer at the postmarks. "Does that say 'São Paulo'?"

Reluctantly, Meri bent close enough to see. "Yes. Makes sense, since they found her bones in Brazil."

"There's absolutely no telling what's in them."

"Why would anyone go to this much trouble and expense?" Meri said. "How could she have this many possessions that somebody wouldn't steal instead?"

"I'm dying to know." Lilah picked up the top one by the string. "Not very heavy. I wish we had time to open them but Raul's got to have his peppers and tomatoes by eight."

"And who would send them? Lilah, she'd been missing *four* years before her bones were found. After all this time . . ."

"Let's just open this one right quick and . . ."

Meri turned away. "No. I don't want to see or know anything right now. But I'll have to look at them sometime. Let's do it together. Promise me."

Lilah, maddeningly, pretended to be deaf. "It has to be stuff she collected down there. Edie Jo was always one to travel light."

Meri snapped at her. "Yes. Whenever we moved, she abandoned furniture and cookware and toiletries and clothes . . ."

And a child.

But neither of them said it. They looked at each other.

Lilah's face softened and the look in her eyes made Meri want to cry, so she turned and walked away.

She opened the screen, then stopped with its handle in her hand. "You know?" Meri said. "I have to have your promise. I don't want to see what's in there alone. Will you wait until I'm ready?"

"Well," Lilah said to her back, "yes. It goes against my nature, but I will wait until you're ready. We'll look at them together."

It pleased her that Meri needed her. She'd think about that when she was tempted to peek.

"Come on, and let me help you get dressed," Meri said. "I'll carry them someplace else for us to open when we get back. I'll fasten your bra and then I'll load these orders and move the boxes."

She turned around to see if Lilah was listening.

Lilah said, "Back the truck up to the steps for the produce. Don't try to carry them any farther than that. Even if you are talking about fitness all the time, that'd be too much too soon.""

But then they both just stood there.

Meri did not, did *not* want to touch the South American parcels, but it seemed odd to just walk away and leave them.

"Don't you want me to carry these boxes into the house?"

"Not until I know what's in them," Lilah said, moving to follow Meri in through the door. "There could be South American jumping spiders or fruitflies or God knows what coming into this country that might spread all over Texas. And beyond. I'll have to take 'em to the old springhouse to open, just in case. For now, leave 'em where they are."

"If you're sure."

"I am. On second thought, I'll holler at Jimmy to come here instead of to the barn. He can load the deliveries for us. You look a little shaky, sugar."

Meri wanted to argue with her, but she couldn't get the words out as she went into the kitchen and headed for her room. She hated to admit it, but she felt a little shaky, too.

Well. Here she was, down to one arm and watching the young ones do the work. Old and in the way, that was just all there was to it.

With the remnants of her wayward child's wild life for her to sort out. And now that she'd promised, she had to wait for that, too.

Lord, what possible good can it do for those pieces of a misspent life to end up here? Curious and nosy as I am, there may be things in those boxes that'll hurt me and Meri in the heart. I'm sure there's more than one secret of Edie Jo's that we'd both be better off not knowing.

Lilah sat like a big, helpless sissy in her air-conditioned truck in the parking lot behind Raul's, staring at the brick wall and the open door Meri had gone through with the deliveries. They were right on time with the tomatoes and peppers this morning, so he could make his famous salsa in time for the flavors to "mature," as he put it, before the lunch crowd came in to eat gallons of it.

When you got right down to it, Raul's salsa came within just a hair bit being as good as Lilah's own. Almost. But not quite.

The culls from this batch of tomatoes and peppers would have to be used somehow. She'd ask Meri to chop for her and they'd make a batch of Lilah's salsa later in the afternoon. After she'd looked at Edie Jo's things and got that over with.

After *that*, she would double down on the loan business. She could not lose Honey Grove. She would not, as long as there was breath in her body.

In her dreams, she woke up with tears in her eyes if she'd dreamed she lost it. She and Honey Grove were one.

Surely she could work it out with Buford, somehow, to get some more time.

She wiggled in the seat and readjusted the sling on her arm. Maybe next week, her bones would be healing better and she'd get the cast off. That thing was a misery.

But she had to think of the good things in her life right this minute.

At least she had Meri here to drive for the deliveries. And Jimmy was working part-time again. Plus she had bumper crops of nearly all varieties of tomatoes, and the peaches were going to be plentiful, too. All she had to do was get them picked and sold.

And figure out how to save the land that gave them to her.

She shivered. *Lord, I just couldn't stand it if I have to live someplace else.*

But she could, of course. Her mother always told her she could stand anything she had to, and Lilah had proved that statement true more than once.

Poor little Meri, she hadn't lived long enough yet to

know that she could, too. The fact she'd raised herself so
well proved that.

*If I lose Honey Grove, though, I don't know if I'm tough
enough for that. Lord, if that's going to happen, please
prepare me.*

Meri came out the back door of the restaurant and ran
toward the truck, the invoice still in her hand. Lilah sighed.
That's what she got for being lazy. She should've gone in
with her.

When Meri opened the door, Lilah said, "If you couldn't
find Gail Bee, you should've left that invoice on her desk.
Anybody in the kitchen could've showed you where the
office is."

"I found it," Meri said, handing the paper to Lilah as
she climbed in behind the wheel. "She wants us to send it
online."

"On what line?"

"By e-mail. Lilah, you have no choice. You *must* get a
computer and learn how to use it."

Carefully, Meri backed the truck around, drove out into
the alley and turned down it toward the square.

Lilah stared at her. "This is insane. Raul wants my
tomatoes but to sell them to him I have to send the bill on
a *computer*?"

"Basically, yes. They're going to do all their business
online. Orders, invoices, receipts, payments. They'll pay
for your tomatoes by sending the money straight into your
bank account."

Lilah was never so flabbergasted in her life. "Meri. I
can't do this. I don't have money to buy a computer and I
don't have time to try to learn how to use the darn thing.
I'll just have to find some other customers."

Meri stopped at the end of the alley to look for traffic.

"Okay, which way is our next stop? It's Suzy's Cafe."

Lilah pointed. "Go left. It's just around the corner there."

"You can't *find* any other customers who'll want to con-
duct business on paper. The whole world is already online,
Lilah. You have to get with the program."

Lilah leaned her head against the window, then she rolled it down and let the breeze—hot, now—wash across her air-conditioned face. That was hard to believe, but she didn't say so because this minute she didn't have the strength to butt heads with Meri.

She tried to take comfort from looking at her own hometown. Its majestic courthouse ruled in the middle of the square with the familiar huge, old trees scattered across its grounds and along the streets around it. The shops and stores did business in buildings that were much older than she was.

It was all familiar and real. And yet, another whole world existed somewhere in space and it wasn't real—online, wherever that was—and somehow it was changing everything in this real one. It was craziness.

Meri said, "You'll have to go digital if you're going to stay in business. But don't worry. I'll do it. I'll get it all set up and show you everything you need to know before I leave. You'll be surprised how easy it is."

For once, to her credit, she wasn't being bossy or pushy or a know-it-all. She actually seemed to sense Lilah's despair and this was an offer of help.

"But if you do it on your computer, then when you're gone . . ."

"The hard drive went out on my personal computer. I need a new one. The good laptop belonged to the firm."

The stilted tone in her voice hit Lilah harder than if it had been one of open pain. Poor girl. Her job *was* gone.

And it'd been her life. Lilah'd known that first thing. And she'd said she lost her fiancé, too.

Bless her heart. Someday, she'd have to talk more about all that pain and pour it out or it'd always be a rock in her gut. Lilah could tell her all about that.

Meri spotted the sign for Suzy's, parked in one of the slanted spaces in front of it, carefully making sure she was within the lines on both sides, which, Lilah was learning, was typical of her granddaughter. She took the last box of tomatoes inside for Suzy to put on sandwiches and hamburgers and in salads.

It tickled Lilah to think about all the people her crops were feeding every day. All she needed was some pickers and more mouths to feed and she could change the world.

She looked around the square. It was fairly busy. They were fortunate. Rock Springs was on hard times because of the national economy but it definitely wasn't dying like so many small towns.

One example was Doreen's Dress Shop, one door down from Suzy's, and, despite the fact that some women hardly ever wore dresses anymore, still in business for what . . . forty years? Thirty? Meri was twenty-seven now. Doreen's shop had been just three or four years old when Edie Jo had her out-of-wedlock baby and scandalized the town.

Back then, in the same flowing, fancy script, the sign had read the same as it did today. Doreen said that store name fit her "brand"—as if she burned it into the clothes she sold—and she wasn't about to change it. She even had special labels made for the most expensive suits and dresses. And always for the wedding dresses.

Doreen always was one to keep up with the times. Not to mention other people's affairs.

But she was also one to keep up with business. It wasn't her wealthy husband's money that had kept the store open all these years. Lilah couldn't help but admire her for that. Somehow, by sheer determination, Doreen had made her business succeed.

Probably her secret was making herself such a pest and a flatterer at the same time. Customers gave in and bought everything she pushed at them just to get free of her and out of the store.

She was to be pitied, too, though. Sheer determination hadn't helped a bit during all those years she tried to get pregnant. And the deepest regret of her life, right now— since everything was always about Doreen—was that she had no grandchildren.

When it should be that she had aided and abetted Edie Jo in all her foolish mistakes.

Which brought a person to the real truth of "Be careful

what you wish for." Lilah, too, had badly wanted children, and look at the grief the one she had had brought her.

Although, there *had* been wonderful times when Edie Jo was very small—feelings then and memories now—that Lilah wouldn't trade for anything.

The door of Suzy's opened, and Doreen appeared as if Lilah's thoughts had called her out onto the sidewalk. She was carrying one of those paper drink trays with three tall, lidded cups in its pockets and she headed straight for Lilah.

"Come on, Lilah, get out and come in. I just talked to Meri. We're all three gonna have coffee at the shop and get caught up before opening time. We haven't even seen each other since she came back to Honey Grove!"

Damnation. The woman really was determined to court Meri just as she had Edie Jo.

"I don't have time, Doreen. I've got a farm to run."

Doreen laughed her little tinkling giggle. "That's exactly what Meri said you'd say. But I won't take *no* for an answer. Y'all got your deliveries done, so give the girl a little break. We agreed. Thirty minutes. That's all."

Doreen balanced the tray in one hand and used the other to open Lilah's door. "Let me help you down, now. Step on the running board and I'll steady you."

"It's my wrist that's broken, not my leg," Lilah said. "Don't ever believe I'm helpless, Doreen."

"That sounds like a threat," Doreen said merrily. "I want to show y'all some tops and capris that just came in. There's some gorgeous tunics in that collection that you could wear, Lilah."

Lilah got out, unassisted but with Doreen hovering.

"Well, at least you didn't say muumuus. You think my figure's so far gone I have to wear something loose?"

Doreen chuckled. "You said it, I didn't. But no, Lilah, I think your farm work has kept you"—she threw Lilah a quick, sideways glance as they walked to her store—"surprisingly . . . in fairly nice shape."

That rare concession made Lilah laugh. "I'm honored," she said, "with that coming from you. But the great thing about getting older, Doreen, is that I don't really care how I look anymore."

Doreen hooted. "Don't try to tell me that. You do, too, or you never would've made yourself that gorgeous lace-trimmed top. It looks like a million dollars with your old concho belt."

Lilah rolled her eyes. Doreen must want something, for sure.

Meri appeared as they went into Doreen's and they all sat down around the little wrought-iron table Doreen decorated every day with fresh flowers.

Lilah looked over today's selection, which was expensive and tropical. "I tell you, Doreen, Estelle would kill me for saying this, but you're wasting your money on these foreign-looking flowers."

"I think they're pretty," Doreen said, clearly miffed.

"I've told you and told you. Why don't you just plant a few tiger lilies in that bed by your garage? And maybe a camellia bush and some of those knockout roses everybody's so crazy about? Good heavens, woman. Pick some every morning and be done with it!"

Doreen rolled her eyes. "But I don't have a green thumb like *some people* who tell other people what to do."

"Pot callin' the kettle black, I'd say."

Doreen confided to Meri, "We've had this conversation a hundred times. Your grandma doesn't know how to mind her own business."

Lilah snorted so fast she nearly spit coffee on the table.

"Look who's talking," she sputtered. "Queen of Minding Other People's Business, that's who."

"Well, I heard y'all went to Taylor's Inn for dinner, so you've seen a little bit of Old Texas, Meri," Doreen said. She sighed. "And, of course, Caleb Burkett, who acts like he *lives* in Old Texas, fistfighting in bars and hunting wild hogs with his bare hands and all that nonsense. Honey, you be careful with him."

Lilah's temper flared like a flame in a high wind.

"No. We're not going to go there. You don't want to start

a fistfight in your own store. Hush your mouth about Caleb, Doreen."

Doreen shrugged daintily. "Then I'll just say this, Meri: Your grandma has been overly partial to Caleb all his life. Remember, her view of him is warped."

"You're the only woman on the face of the earth who doesn't like Caleb and you won't cut him any slack because he ignores your flirty ways, Doreen Semples. He may be a little rough around the edges but he knows appropriate behavior for an old woman and he don't see it when he looks at you."

That got her. At last. Doreen snapped, "I should've strangled that horrible cat of yours when I had the chance instead of staying with him and finding a caretaker and trying to save his snarly little life."

Lilah was ashamed of herself for flying off the handle like that. It wasn't a becoming example to set for Meri at all. So she took another sip of her store-bought coffee and smiled.

"I thought you said you have a new shipment in," she said in her sweetest voice. "Is that pansy-print dimity dress something that was in it?"

The only thing Doreen liked more than fuss-fighting and gossiping was making a sale. She set her cup down and got up.

"Well, yes. In fact, the minute I saw it, I thought of you, Meri. It's *you*."

Lilah really hated to agree with Doreen on anything, but this time she'd nailed it.

The flowers in it had shades of violet to match Meri's eyes and bits of black like her hair. It was a delightfully old-fashioned style with a full skirt, sweetheart neckline, and wide, gathered straps over the shoulders, which formed little cap sleeves. Lace trim. Oh, it would be so sweet on Meri for a date with Caleb.

If that should ever happen, of course.

Doreen pulled it off the rack and swirled it in front of her.

"Come on, Meri. Would you please let us see it on you?"

Lilah could tell Meri liked it, too.

She looked like a different girl when she came out of the dressing room: relaxed and smiling like a woman who knows she looks good. Not too dressy, not too plain. Not too young for her but still, it made her look about sixteen.

Meri tried to resist temptation but not for long. As soon as Doreen finished the credit card transaction, Lilah got up and got them out of there.

On the way back to the truck, Meri said, "I shouldn't have done this. With no job, I can't afford it, but buying something new and gorgeous really lifts my spirits sometimes."

"Once in a while, once in a *great* while, mind you, that's all right. When it's something that is so perfectly made for you that it lights you right up. This is one of those times. Regrets would spoil it."

Meri gave her a surprised look, which Lilah pretended not to see.

"Doreen does bear watching, though. I'm not talking about this dress when I say that. It's just that she can push anybody into anything before they know what hit them."

They climbed into the truck and Meri turned to put the fancy Doreen's bag on the backseat of the crew cab. She left it with a little pat that made Lilah smile.

"Take me, for example," Lilah said. "She's pushed me into a lot of situations I would've liked to miss."

Meri met her eyes as she started the truck and turned to look behind for traffic.

"I'm sorry, Lilah. I knew you wanted to get back to the farm but she was insistent, and a lot of people were listening in, and I didn't want to refuse her coffee invitation in public. I owe her because she agreed right away to take care of Henry that day when I had to rush back to New York."

Lilah held back the long, loud sigh that was pushing at her lips.

Here we go again.

Trust Doreen never to miss a chance to dig in her hooks.

Sixteen

Meri drove around the square at a snail's pace.

"You've been driving this truck long enough now that you know you can do it, so relax and kick it up a little," Lilah said, glancing at her watch. "Hector and his crew are supposed to be at Honey Grove around ten."

"Don't worry, I'll bet they know what to do until we get there."

Meri turned and smiled at Lilah as sweetly as if she knew what she was talking about.

"Or does Hector carry a cell phone? You can use mine to call him if you want. I just have one quick errand."

She started easing into a parking place. Lilah looked at the store in front of it: LONE STAR COMPUTERS, SALES AND SERVICE and threw up her hand in a totally useless attempt to signal Stop.

"Now, listen here, do not go in there and buy me a computer. I can't afford that, and besides, I'd be like a hog with a hat. I'd ruin it first crack out of the box."

That didn't faze Meri. "I'll teach you."

"You're every bit as stubborn as your grandpa Ed. I think you got that from him."

Meri glanced at her. "Really?" She looked surprised. And pleased.

Bless her heart. What would it be like to grow up in limbo without anybody telling you how you fit into your family tree and where you got your temper and who passed down those big, violet-colored eyes and whose nose you'd inherited?

It must be sort of like floating in space, untethered.

Oh, Lord. What all had this child been through in her short lifetime?

She reached over and put her hand on Meri's wrist as the girl turned off the motor. "I haven't been just whinin'," she said. "I am short, very short, on money. Even without considering the note Caleb was telling you about."

"I'll be getting the severance package soon. For now, I have a credit card. And, even though I just bought this dress, I can afford a used laptop and still pay the bill at the end of this month."

Lilah's grip tightened. "No. When I said I won't take charity, I wasn't just whistling Dixie. I'm telling you just like I told Caleb, and I mean what I say."

Meri turned to fully face her and looked straight into her eyes.

"Do you want to save your farm? There'll be *no* chance of that if you lose your customers. Think. Any new ones are going to be online, too."

Instead of throwing Lilah's hand off her arm, she took it in both of her own to plead her case. That scared Lilah.

"Please, look at reality. Computers are like cars, Lilah, a monumental shift in the whole world. It's the same thing as if you still drove a horse-drawn wagon full of produce into town for farmers market."

She opened her door, then remembered to turn the motor on again for the air-conditioning. "I won't be long." She jumped out and ran like a deer.

Lilah's head was just whirling, full of worries about

paying that ungrateful Buford Quisenberry for the note he'd refused to extend, swirling thoughts of her grand-daughter and her farm and prayers that the two of them could save it—and that Meri would think it was worth sav-ing after Lilah was gone. What happened after she was dead and gone was none of her business, Dulcie always told her, and she was right.

Lilah sat and stared at the orange and yellow zinnias and blue salvia planted by the garden club in huge earthenware tubs placed at intervals all around the square. She and Dulcie had driven one of the Burkett Ranch trucks down to Mexico to get those tubs, and they'd had a tubful of fun doing it.

They still looked good.

Dulcie, too, had had a lot to deal with here in this world. Not financial troubles, but nearly every other kind. Of course. Being the mother of four boys and then four grown men, which she said was *so* much harder, was more than enough to turn her hair white early, not to mention having a difficult husband like Jasper.

Lilah heaved a big sigh. Dulcie was back from that cruise now. They'd talked on the phone but she needed a big hug and a good, long face-to-face visit with her.

She looked at the computer store again. There was no stopping Meri and this computer tear she was on. Well, she could get the Honey Grove business organized and *online*—wherever that was—all she wanted to, but teach-ing Lilah how to use the doggone thing would take nothing short of a miracle.

Fifteen minutes later, Lilah was watching the time—what did Meri know about whether Hector and crew could get started without her?—Meri came out of the store with a bag.

"They don't sell Apple, so it's a rental until I can order online. No problem. I'll just do a little research today and we'll go from there."

"*We* will?"

Dear goodness, this girl was one to step right up and take control, wasn't she?

Lilah couldn't let that happen. "Even if I had the money *and* the desire, I do not have the time or the energy or the mental space to learn to work a computer right now."

"Bandwidth," Meri said.

"What?"

"It's a computer term. Remember the other day you asked me what it means? It means exactly what you said, as in, 'You don't have the bandwidth for this right now.'"

Lilah shrugged. "Well, I guess I can learn the vocabulary, even if I can't learn to work the machine."

"You are going to be so surprised at how easy it is."

Meri was so excited she backed out into the street and drove away with none of that irritating creeping around.

"Really, Lilah. Not to worry. Even if I weren't concerned about Honey Grove, I *have* to have something to do. This is the first time I've been at loose ends since I realized Edie Jo wasn't coming back to get me."

Lilah's jaw dropped. "That didn't put you at loose ends?"

"No. Once I internalized that fact, I decided I would *not* grow up to be like her. I made a list of all the ways I'd be different, then a list of what I had to do in order to get into college, then a list of what I wanted to buy when I got my first job."

Every word socked Lilah right in the gut and drove everything else out of her mind.

She managed to sound fairly normal when she said, "That is admirable, Meri. Extremely. For a fourteen-year-old."

And especially one who hadn't had a drop of good raising. Which I could've supplied if I'd had the good sense to keep on searching for her.

All she could do was stare out at the green-and-brown fields flowing past on both sides of the truck and try to hold back the tears.

She thought about her Cherokee great-grandmother, who famously (within the family) started off her edicts with, "I am an old woman and I have lived many winters . . ."

Well, Lilah was getting there. *Her* many winters had

taught her the bitter truth that of all the demons that can torment the human heart, the cruelest is regret.

The least she could do was let Meri try to show her how to use that infernal computer. It would make her granddaughter feel good and like she was helping save the farm.

Standing on the ground, Lilah could wrestle the boxes of Edie Jo's things off the porch and onto the Gator with only minimum use of her casted arm. She'd been in the mood to get right to them and out of Meri's sight, but this was the first private moment she'd had. Once they got home with the blasted computer, first there'd been Hector and then turning the horses out and then gathering the eggs, on and on, all the chores with Meri right beside her, determined to figure out a way to pay that dratted note hanging over their heads.

Caleb should never have told Meri about that. Surely, surely, Lilah could bring enough pressure to bear on Buford and the bank board—public relations, the new bank coming to town, the fact Jasper was on *his* bank board, memories of Ed's help when Buford was starting out—all the workings of a small town that he'd renew the note for five more years.

On top of that, she would also give him a solid repayment plan, talking about good crops and a growing business.

She thought about what to say to him and how to say it while she struggled to put the boxes where she wanted them. It was better than speculating about what all was in them and what that would tell her about Edie Jo.

Meri was so skittish about even looking at the boxes that Lilah didn't want to ask her to move them to the springhouse. Finally, she tipped the last one off the porch and let it half-fall onto the passenger seat of the ATV. She got in, and awkwardly put it in gear with her good arm.

Meri'd had her head in that computer ever since they'd come to the house. When Lilah went through the kitchen,

the girl was at the desk in the mudroom starting in on
Lilah's business papers. It was just as well that she didn't
want to be in on this. That poor granddaughter of hers had
enough on her plate in the present without dragging the
past into her head right now.

The white limestone springhouse sat on the edge of the
yard where an underground spring ran aboveground for a
few short feet. In the past it had been the refrigerator for
the milk and butter. Now it was a cool, stone haven used
only as a storm cellar. It had been her refuge more than
once when she had to cry over Edie Jo and Ed didn't want
to hear it anymore.

One of the greatest blessings for both of them was
that he'd passed before Edie Jo got pregnant. If he hadn't
already been dead, that would've killed him. Right there
was one problem that went straight to the head, heart, gut,
pride and ego of the daddy of a girl.

It didn't take two hands to swing the door open, thank
goodness, and not too long to unload the stuff because,
luckily, none of it was very heavy. If it had been, whoever
sent it probably wouldn't have paid the postage.

She looked at the postmarks again. Some word that
looked like it might mean *police*. They'd kept all this on
file while they looked for her bones? Were they that efficient down there?

Well, who or how didn't matter now. Her daughter's last
possessions were here and had to be dealt with.

But not now. She had promised Meri, and she'd not
break her word. The girl had a hard enough time trusting
people to begin with, and all that mess back in New York,
whatever it was, hadn't helped one bit.

Even if she couldn't trust another person in the whole
world, she needed to be able to trust her grandmother.

Seventeen

The next day was Saturday, which meant farmers market and always hectic, but this one was a doozy from the get-go. The minute she opened her eyes, though, Lilah had no idea that *this* Saturday would take her from the minor irritation of Henry yowling her awake to near-panicked desperation *and* a washout by noon.

She sat up in bed and rubbed her shoulder. It had developed some shooting pains from carrying her arm in the sling and somehow, they were usually worse when she first woke up.

Edie Jo's boxes were the first thing she thought of. Could she talk Meri into opening them today? *No. Let the girl get used to the idea first.*

Meri helped her get dressed. They grabbed a quick breakfast of ham biscuits and fresh peaches. Lord knew, they'd *better* eat 'em because, this time around, it was a bumper crop of all three varieties that Lilah grew.

Once, last night before supper as Lilah showed Meri how to make corn bread—teaching her, of course, *never* to use one of those heretical, Philistine corn bread recipes that call for sugar—she'd mentioned, in passing, that she was dying to open Edie Jo's boxes. Meri froze with the cup of buttermilk raised, ready to pour, looked at her to make sure she got the message and said, "I. Can't."

The tone of her voice was cold enough to freeze Lilah's heart. Bless her. For once, Lilah would have to be patient.

Jimmy came over to help load. Lilah couldn't afford him much longer, even part-time like he was, but she couldn't do the lifting herself and wasn't about to let Meri ruin her insides tugging at bushels of peaches and plums, boxes of tomatoes, peppers and okra.

Mercy! They had a lot to sell today. If they could get hungry customers swarming into the square like they had last Saturday, the money would be great. Maybe they'd pick up a little word-of-mouth restaurant business, too, because this Honey Select yellow corn was really sweet. Meri had made a cute sign with colored markers and drawings of cornstalks advertising Honey Select from Honey Grove. She had a real talent for selling, Lilah thought.

On the way into town, while Jimmy drove and Meri listened to the music on her phone with its wires stuck in her ears, Lilah thought about how she wanted to arrange the fruits and vegetables in the booth. Then she considered what to say to Buford Quisenberry if he was there—as he usually was, working the crowd for new bank customers that he could give a toaster to and then fleece with a dozen fees every time they used their Rock Springs Bank account.

She'd decided to feel him out one more time about giving her more time to pay the note. They had always irritated each other to some extent, but this was a small town, after all, and morally, he owed her some extra time. Ed had gone out of his way to help Buford when he came to Rock County and started his bank and everybody knew that.

Jimmy helped them unload and set up in the square. He put up the open-sided tent with Meri's help and they off-loaded the produce, with Lilah telling them what went where until Meri got so irritated she installed Lilah and her cast behind the cash box.

Sad thing was, Lilah didn't fight it. Wagging a couple of pounds of cast around all the time wore her down, and it had been a hard week. Getting old was not for sissies. She was feeling it now, but she wouldn't let Buford see that.

The good breeze picked up, smelling like pines. And rain. If it would stay with them, the heat would be so much more bearable today. Trouble was, if it rained the customers wouldn't stay.

It seemed like heresy in Texas to wish it wouldn't rain, when the heat always sucked the moisture out of the ground so fast, but they'd had an unusual amount already. That was why the crops were so good. But, oh, Lord, she needed a dry day to sell this fruit. If it did come, maybe it wouldn't rain for long.

Get your priorities straight, Lilah. Figure out what to say to Buford and leave the weather to the Good Lord and Channel 6. It'll rain or it won't.

There were less than thirty days left now until the note came due but Lilah refused to look at exactly how many. Deep down, she'd been counting on Buford doing the right thing all along, and she was going to keep focusing on that.

But, just in case, she was also going to talk to Shorty about finding a buyer for her tractor. If she sold it and the haying equipment, she'd have a fairly good amount. Maybe half of what she needed. She could always hire out the haying.

No tractor, though, would be a problem. Maybe she could find an old relic that would still run.

But how *could* Buford refuse her and still hold up his head in this town? Everybody knew full well that Lilah was good for the money. Someday.

Jimmy left, heading for his buddies who hung around Harlan's Sale Barn Saturday auction, to see how the prices were, listening to the auctioneer and watching the cattle sell. He said he'd be back at three to break down the tent and load whatever was left but he might not show up. That would depend on whether he came back by the Cold Springs Bar and how many beers he had. He and Lilah both left that unsaid.

Meri began arranging everything to suit herself and she seemed to be enjoying the work, so Lilah kept her comments to herself. Well, except for showing her how to stack the corn. Meri was so precise and she did make it all look wonderful—the golds and oranges of the peaches and plums all in one sweep of color and then the red tomatoes and all colors of peppers in another corner. The white and gold and yellow corn fanned out across the end of the table.

Business picked up and was fairly brisk. In spurts. The same could be said of the wind. It smelled a little more heavily of rain.

In the slow periods, Meri went wandering around, talking to other vendors, trying to get a feel for the "whole organic farming scene," as she put it. Lilah watched her, gorgeous as a model in a magazine, introducing herself to that family of dairy farmers with their refrigerated trailer, then moving on to the guy from Chapel Hill who thought he was an onion expert.

No telling what kind of ideas she'd come back with. Probably enough fodder to preach Lilah several more sermons about the magic computers could do for Honey Grove.

Lilah sold two quarts of plums and some sweet red peppers to Sadie Morrell, who was going to try them instead of the green ones in her stuffed pepper recipe. Lilah shared hers, too, including the fact that she usually made a heavy, slightly sweet tomato sauce to spoon over them for the last five minutes in the oven.

As Sadie moved on, Lilah spotted Buford working his way toward her, glad-handing people. She decided right then that the gossips were right: He was gearing up to run for some office, whether it was in the legislature or not.

When he got to the Honey Grove booth, he touched the brim of his hat to her. He always wore boots and a Resistol with the cattleman's crease to make himself taller, even though he wouldn't get his hands dirty or his boots dusty if he could help it at all. For all she knew, he might not even be able to tell a cow from a horse.

She reached for her best, most confident smile. "Hey, Buford. Good to see you."

He used his deepest voice. "How's it going, Lilah? Reckon we're gonna get a drop or two?"

Rumor was, he was going to run against Cummins Matheny for the Texas House of Representatives. If he did, the voice would do him good, but poor Buford didn't have a good smile. Even when it was sincere, it made him look wolfish.

"I'm thinking the storm's about to go around us," she said. "For once in our lives, we aren't really craving rain and I don't want to haul all this good produce back home again."

Her stomach went tight. Now, how should she broach this?

He was looking over her wares. "Looks like a picture in a book."

She latched on to that positive sign, took a deep breath and hoped her vocal cords hadn't tightened up, too.

"Thanks, Buford. I'm blessed with big yields this year—even a third cutting on my hay. I've been meaning to drop by your office for an official visit to talk about maybe extending my note 'til everything's harvested and sold."

His thoughtful gaze flashed from the produce to her face and stayed there. The expression in his eyes was neutral, but nothing about the look made her feel any better.

"You know, Lilah, if it was only me, that'd be no problem whatsoever."

Her heart sank. There was a flat rock under that deep tone now.

He heaved a big sigh. "But you know what? Considering everything that's going on in the economy across the entire country, I'd have to take somethin' like that before the entire board. Most of them are of the considered opinion that mom-and-pop farms are a thing of the past."

Lilah's stomach went from tense to sick.

He lifted one arm and swept it over the market as if he were king.

"Selling cucumbers one at a time? Look around you, Lilah. Does this look like farming's still what it was?"

Those words had enough steel they rang against the rock in his voice.

It was hopeless. He wasn't about to give her more time. Or even consider it.

Lilah held herself together and stayed cool. Two minutes later, she couldn't imagine how she did it. Desperation, she guessed.

"Everything's changed," she said, nodding. "You're right about that, Buford. Remember back in the doo-dah days? When Ed introduced you to all those ranchers and farmers?"

She waited to make him acknowledge that. Finally, he nodded.

"Why, there must've been fifteen or twenty of them that opened accounts with you who were running *big* operations. Now, on the ranch side, the Burketts and the Daltons are the only ones left—I guess in the entire county. And I can't even name one on the farm side."

He frowned thoughtfully, nodding. "That's about right. Those days are long gone and they're not comin' back."

He adjusted his hat and finally looked her in the eye again.

"Well, Lilah, I'd better get going. But do drop by my office anytime you want, you hear? It's always great to see you."

Really, it was an insult to the wolf to compare its face to Buford's. That sickly parting grin of his looked more like an egg-sucking dog.

On the way home in the driving rain, Meri and Lilah rejoiced that people had helped them save most of their produce and tried to get their breath back. The whole cab reeked of wet corn husks, plums and peaches in the backseat and, in the front, of wet clothes, wet hair and a smashed tomato Lilah had smeared against her shirt trying to save it from the pavement. All of those odors mixed together made Lilah want to vomit.

She wished. But no, it wasn't the smell in here that was making her sick.

The due date for the note was coming, no matter how much she tried to ignore it. And, just like the days that were flying past her, any hope for help from Buford was gone.

Meri slowed abruptly when a sudden heavy gust slapped the windshield.

"You'll get us killed if you keep that up. Somebody'll run over us from behind. Jimmy might've done better even half-drunk."

"*I'm* driving."

Lilah was so lost in her thoughts that she heard that but it didn't register on her brain.

Denial. You've been in denial.

No, I've been foolish enough to expect that kindness and morally right behavior would mean something nowadays. I've been an ostrich with my head in the sand, not seeing that times have changed and the old ways of honor and obligation are gone.

Evidently they'd been banished from the culture along with any song that had a melody and all rules about dressing appropriately for business, church, school, reading the news on television and shopping. Why, she'd seen grown women in their pajama bottoms and house shoes at the Walmart more than once, and that wasn't the half of it when she remembered all the short-shorts at the high school band concert.

Meri did it again.

"If you're too scared to drive, pull off up here at Leroy's. This won't last long."

Where would she get the money? What else could she sell besides the tractor that would bring anything anywhere near what it was worth?

"I don't know how you can say that," Meri said, her lips as tight as her fingers around the wheel. "It's already lasted an hour, at least."

"So?" Lilah snapped. "It's bound to be over soon."

"You hope."

Lilah shut up. If they died, they died. What *she* had to worry about was if they lived.

No, she couldn't sell her tractor or the ATV. She'd been out of her mind to think of that. She'd get pennies on the dollar. And besides, she couldn't farm without her equipment. She could do without the haying machinery, maybe.

Her mind darted in circles. If only old Doff Fritzenburg hadn't died! That thrifty old farmer had made a practice of lending his private money to give other people a hand up. He'd saved many a farm from foreclosure. Early in their marriage, he'd been a lifeline for her and Ed.

She had no more lifelines now. She wasn't about to take money from that precious Caleb. Lordy! What a thought! She'd lose the farm before she'd hinder some young person just trying to get started, *especially* Caleb, no matter how much money he had. He was just now settling down to get serious and make his own mark on life. He needed to invest in some businesses that were new and modern and had a bright future.

Meri didn't move her lips or her head, as if any motion of hers would wreck the truck, but she muttered, "I think it's getting a little better."

And so it was. The rain and the wind were both letting up.

"Well, thank the Lord for that. I don't know what we would've done if Aud Blaylock and Doug Martin hadn't come by right when they did. If they hadn't stopped to help us, we'd still be trying to save our fruit and our tent would be in Oklahoma."

Meri said, "Which brings up the question of what are we going to do with our fruit now. Not to mention all the ripe tomatoes."

Lilah heard her as if from a distance.

Looking at the situation coldly, nothing she had to sell could bring enough to pay the note, unless it was land. She might have to let go of her pretty little meadow, but yet she needed the income from the hay.

She might have to do that but it wouldn't be easy to find a buyer that fast. Plus, when you started lopping off land to sell, it always signaled the beginning of the end.

Hello! Would you rather go straight to the end of the end?

Jasper and Dulcie would help her in a heartbeat and never miss the money, but no way was she going to impose on their priceless friendship.

She fled back into the moment. "The plums and peaches are the most critical. We'll make jam this afternoon."

Might be the last time in my kitchen.

She looked out across the sky she loved, the whole heavens filled with the Texas wind chasing the gray-blue clouds away from the sun.

They took the Dog Creek curve and she could see Honey Grove from here. Its hills and tree lines, striped by the sunlight and shadows, all green and lush with bounty—for this one season, at least—opened up to her loving eyes. The familiar sight reached out and pulled her, spirit and flesh, into the old, sweet rhythm of coming home.

Home.

Lord, I can't give this up without a fight. I'm asking for Your help. I can't save this place by myself.

By the time they reached the end of the driveway, she knew what else she had to do. She sucked in a hard breath and turned to her granddaughter.

"Meri," she said, "can you really find us a lot of customers with that computer?"

Eighteen

When Meri walked into the kitchen after she'd showered and changed into dry clothes, she couldn't believe her eyes. Lilah stood at the sink washing plums with her one free hand and putting them into a large pot.

"Meri, you'll have to carry this to the stove for me. And see that one over there with the jars on the rack inside it? Would you fill that with water high enough to cover them and put it on to boil?"

Meri stopped still on her aching legs. Holding on to a tent in the wind had been a challenge like no other.

"All this before we eat lunch? Give yourself a break, Lilah, please. You need food and at least a couple of hours rest. I'm *tired*; you must be wiped out."

"Because I'm so *old*?"

Meri mimicked her tone, lightheartedly. "Because you have *one arm in a cast*."

Meri went to carry the pot full of jars to the stove, watching Lilah's fast, jerky movements from the corner of her eye.

"What's wrong?"

Lilah flashed her an irritated look and kept working. "What d'you think? You were there when the farmers market blew away."

"Yes," Meri said, soothingly, "and I'm here to see to all the leftovers out there on the porch. Face facts, Lilah. If we have to boil the *jars*—I didn't even know about that—*and* cook the fruit, there's no way can we preserve it all before it spoils."

Lilah's face became even more grim. "Maybe not, but we'll go down trying."

Meri had not seen her grandmother this nervous the entire time she'd been at Honey Grove. She kept hitting her knuckles on the top of the tall pot when she threw in a handful of plums.

And Lilah's face was flushed. What if she had a heart attack over all this?

Meri took a deep breath. She had to try to take charge, but in a way that wouldn't bring out Lilah's contrariness any further.

"I don't care if there *is* a five-dollar fine for whining," she said, quoting a silly sign Lilah had hanging in the barn for her riding students. "I'll pay it because I'm exhausted. I need a couple of hours at least just to regroup, so why don't I make sandwiches?"

Lilah surprised her by agreeing. "Go ahead. I'll let you know when this pot's ready to go to the stove."

Meri headed for the refrigerator and the delicious roast beef Lilah had cooked the day before.

"We'll try to finish the plums today," Lilah said. "They're the ripest. Then we'll start on the peaches early in the morning. I hate to miss church tomorrow, but wasting good food is worse and the Good Lord knows our ox is in the ditch."

"What ox?"

"It's just an old expression, taken from a Bible story. It means we have an emergency situation."

"Well, then, we definitely qualify," Meri said, still using the light tone, watching Lilah as closely as she could without being obvious.

Maybe she could handle this as if she were trying to get Alan to name her the lead attorney on an important case.

Her heart constricted. She wished she hadn't thought of that particular analogy. Would she ever argue in court again?

She found the roast, placed it on a cutting board and reached for the meat knife.

"Lilah," she said, "on the way home, you asked about finding new customers on the computer. Before I begin, I need to know what particular crops . . ."

Lilah made a strange noise. Meri dropped the knife and ran to her.

Lilah was frozen in place with tears running down her face. Meri's stomach clutched. Even when she'd found Lilah on the ground with a broken arm, her grandmother hadn't shed a tear.

Oh! She cared about her.

"Are you in pain? Lilah! Do I need to call someone?"

Lilah shook her head no and dropped her face into her plum-stained hand.

Meri touched her arm. When had she tried to comfort another person? She didn't even know how. Aware of her awkwardness, she patted Lilah's shoulder. At first she thought her grandmother was going to shake her off but she didn't. Lilah turned to look at her instead. "You need to know," she said. "I'll have to tell you. Put these plums on to cook—medium—and let's sit down."

Meri took care of the plums and finished making the sandwiches while Lilah went into the mudroom to wash up and compose herself.

"I don't like to break down like that," she said as she returned, "but I've been living in such a dreamworld. Now I'm about to lose this place."

Meri felt a strange chill. Lilah had never behaved this way, never used this tone of voice. Lilah dropped into her chair without even looking.

This is partly your fault. You should've urged her to accept Caleb's offer or at least to consider it.

Lilah reached for a napkin from the holder and wiped her eyes.

"I thought all I had to do was ask for more time to pay my loan, but Buford Quisenberry has no sense of obligation. He would never have survived as a young businessman from outside Rock County if Ed hadn't taken a liking to him. What he saw in him, I'll never know."

Anger had made Lilah's voice stronger with every word but she looked extremely pale beneath her tan.

"When is it due? What's the deadline?"

"I counted it up when we got home. We have twenty-four days."

Meri amazed herself as Lilah recounted this morning's conversation with Buford and recited the hard facts of the case. Her legal brain noted every detail but a sweeping rush of emotions took over her heart.

True to her selfish roots, somewhere in there, she was upset for *herself*, but that was in the distance. Her heart ached for Lilah.

She would leave, go back to New York and find a new job and a new life. Lilah would be here but she would not be living at Honey Grove. That would be torture for her. Honey Grove *was* Lilah. This couldn't happen.

"But you haven't formally *asked* him for more time," the legal part of her said.

Lilah shook her head. "It'd only be an embarrassment for us both. We communicated. That's his final decision. I believe he's telling the truth about the attitude of the board toward small farms."

She dabbed at her eyes again. "I still think, though, that if *he* would get behind my request for an extension and take it to the board, Jasper Burkett would push for it, too, and the two of them could get it done. This is still a small town, after all, and Jasper's involved in a lot of its businesses."

"But if you're right that he isn't going to do that, we have to find the money elsewhere. And we don't have much time."

"Not Caleb," Lilah snapped. "That precious young man

is trying to get started on his own with no help from Jasper.
I won't do it."

Mentally, Meri rolled her eyes. *Precious young man!*

"Then, my severance package . . ."

"*No.* You're young and jobless. No."

"But if the bank forecloses, where will you go?"

Lilah sat up straight and visibly pulled herself together.
She took a long drink of sweet tea.

"A full stomach always makes the world look better.
Let's finish our lunch. There's two pieces of that lemon
chess pie leftover from yesterday, and we've got three
weeks to figure where to get the money. I won't give up yet.
I'll pray on it some more."

After lunch, Meri cleared the table and took the plums
off the burner when Lilah pronounced them done. Meri
obsessed on the problem silently.

"They need to cool before we put them through the colander," Lilah said. "I'll make some phone calls while I find
the wooden spoon I like to test the jell. Go on out and sit in
the swing and rest yourself a minute."

But Meri continued putting their dishes in the dish-
washer and then began to rearrange the canisters on the
counter above it.

"Sugar, you are so particular about little things that it
eats up a lot of your time. I need a little breathing space and
so do you. Get on out there now."

Evidently she was getting on Lilah's nerves, so Meri did
as she was told. She touched her toe to the porch floor and
started the swing moving as soon as she sat down.

Honey Grove looked green and peaceful. The storm-
cooled breeze moved across the tops of the tall grass in
the pasture and made the tops look golden. The storm
had washed the humidity out of the air, providing a great
respite from the heat.

When had she even started noticing things like that?
When, before today, had she ever really *seen* a thunder-
storm?

She'd loved that storm, even if it scared her, too. Coming

in, the menacing clouds and billowing winds full of ozone had been magnificent. The whole thing had felt like a big adventure, complete with knights Aud and Doug riding to the rescue before everything blew away or was ruined.

She'd hated this place a few minutes ago when she realized all the work involved in trying to save these vegetables and fruit jumbled all over the porch.

No matter. She could feel Honey Grove reaching around and settling its hold on her.

"Yowrrr?"

She turned to look at the open back door. Behind the screen, Henry sat looking at her. Pleading, actually. Wanting out.

He'd been much worse about that, according to Lilah, since he'd escaped on that fateful day of her fall from the persimmon tree.

"Think about the last time we were outside together and what a disaster that was," Meri said. "Go take a nap."

He refused, verbally and physically.

"Stop staring at me."

She was in big trouble. Now she was actually talking to animals. First to Caleb's horse and now to this awful cat who hated her.

Well, not so much anymore. Lately he'd been following her around and using a less antagonistic tone in his conversations.

She looked away, hoping he would hush if she ignored him. Her gaze fell on the little white rock building called the springhouse.

Inside it were those boxes from South America. From time to time, Lilah hinted that they should look at Edie Jo's things. Soon, Lilah would probably move on from hinting to telling her to do it. But that was an order Meri wouldn't obey.

Meri stared at the faded green door with its worn iron hinges and handle.

Was there anything, anything at all, of her in there?

Nineteen

The next morning, as Meri fastened Lilah's bra for her and helped her retrieve the hairbrush that had fallen behind the dresser, Lilah declared Meri experienced enough to make the restaurant deliveries on her own.

"You know where to go and what to do," she said. "There's no sense in both of us going when I could be here getting the barn chores done. Jimmy needs to be mowing, so I'm going to weed the flowerbeds, too. That always helps me think."

"Well, thanks," Meri said, laughing a little try to lighten Lilah's mood. It seemed almost somber. "I consider this a promotion."

Lilah chuckled, and Meri left for town. When she returned, around nine o'clock, Lilah was nowhere to be found.

Meri looked for her in the front flowerbed first, but she wasn't there, so she ran down to the barn. Nobody there or at the chicken coop. Then she realized she was hearing the noise of the mowing machine, although Jimmy's truck was nowhere to be seen.

She spotted it near the beehives and recognized Jimmy as the driver, so she opened the gate and ran down into the pasture. When he saw her coming, he turned off the machine.

Meri called to him, "Do you know where Lilah went?"

He shook his head and yelled back. "She just asked to borrow my truck. Didn't say why."

"She's *driving?*" That came out as a screech. "She's not supposed to drive yet."

Jimmy shrugged, lifted empty hands to show it was all a mystery to him and went back to work.

Meri retraced her steps. As she was closing the gate again, she heard a vehicle coming down the driveway and hurried to see if it might be Jimmy's truck. It wasn't faded red, so it wasn't Lilah coming home.

In the corner of her eye, she saw something move in the yard and turned to look. She stared. *Pigs?* No. One was huge, the other three large. Hogs.

They were definitely hogs, with their noses in the dirt, moving steadily while pawing and snuffling, seriously busy tearing up the ground as they went. When they reached the persimmon tree, they continued ripping up the grass as fast as their hooves could work, gobbling up the fallen fruit and digging in the ground for more. Lilah would be so upset when she saw her yard. Meri froze, watching them, wondering what to do.

The truck screeched to a stop behind her but she could hardly look away from the hogs to see who had arrived. *Hogs?* Lilah had none. They must've escaped from a neighbor's place. Would yelling drive them away?

"Meredith!"

Caleb's voice. What was he doing here?

She whirled away from the ugly scene. Yes, it was Caleb and he was already out of the truck, moving so fast he left the door open, rounding the front of the truck with a long gun in his hand.

"Stay right where you are," he yelled. "Don't move."

The urgency in his voice froze her. She remembered a gun like that hanging on a rack in his truck when he pulled her SUV out of the ditch.

He gave her an abrupt nod of approval when he saw she was going to obey his order, and walked up to her with barely a glance. His eyes were on the hogs.

"Whose are they?" she said. "Lilah doesn't have any hogs."

He lifted the gun to his shoulder and squinted down its barrel. "Cover your ears."

"What?"

The big hog lifted its head suddenly and stared at Caleb for a second before it charged, picking up speed as it ran toward them.

Caleb fired.

Meri covered her ears too late; the noise was deafening. The dead one fell in a horrible heap of bloody flesh and the others ran, fleeing across the yard and into the hay pasture like the wild things they were.

Meri realized she was pressing her ears against her head so hard they hurt. She was trembling all over.

"Caleb! Why would you kill somebody's hog like that?" Her voice shook, too. "That's terrible!"

He lowered the gun and reached to put an arm around her. He pulled her closer and she leaned on him for just one heartbeat, before she knew what she was doing.

It was like leaning on a rock. It was a far-too-seductive comfort.

She jerked her body away from his, forced her mind to try to work again. But all she could think or say was, "You killed it, Caleb."

"That sounds like an accusation," he said with a glint in his eyes. "I *aimed* for the kill. You'd be a lot more bothered if it had you down on the ground right now, stomping and chewing you into little bitty pieces."

"I didn't mean . . . I mean, I just never saw anything killed before. And now look at this mess in the yard."

He made a noise halfway between a snort and a laugh and teased, "No more sympathy for the hog?"

She had to sit down. Her legs had gone weak under her and she wasn't quite sure why or what to do next.

Meri forced her legs to carry her to the back steps and up them, then across the board floor to the swing. She dropped into it. Caleb took his gun back to the truck and hung it in the rack.

Good. Maybe he'd just go away. He always saw right through her and she needed to be alone.

But he closed the door of the truck and came up the brick walk to her with a purposeful stride. Without a word, and without asking, he walked to the swing and sat down beside her.

"They're feral hogs," he said, his voice as steady as his body had been when she leaned on him. "They're thick on the ground around here, trying to tear up this whole county. Don't waste any tears on him."

Meri sat up straighter. "I'm not. I am not crying for him. *I am not crying.* He was the meanest-looking creature I've ever seen when he started toward us. I know you had to do it."

"Just so we're clear, I'd have shot more of them if I hadn't had you to consider. They need to be thinned out." His voice gentled. "Real life's not always pretty, Meri."

She turned on him. "Believe me, I know *that*, Caleb. Just so we're clear."

Their eyes locked in a hard look.

He asked, "Why don't you just say it?"

"Say what?"

"That you're holding it against me that I laughed so hard at you and Old Bear ambling down the road in the twilight that night," he said, and that irresistible grin began at the corners of his luscious mouth, "but really, Meri, it was mostly at *him*."

He paused to gauge her reaction. She showed none.

His grin grew bigger. "He's the laziest equine on the face of the earth and he never broke a sweat or a trot—just stayed an inch beyond your reach. I would *never* laugh at *you*, flopping along behind him in your stylish rubber boots."

She tried to hold her face straight but failed. She felt such a mix of irritation and embarrassment she hardly knew what to do with it but she wanted to laugh, too, and his chuckle was contagious.

"I'm *not* holding a grudge . . ."

"Don't lie," he said. "I'd hate to have to call you out."

She fought back a smile, but he saw it.

"Then it's because I made you take care of Henry? Why hold that against me? You pawned him right off on Doreen."

Meri pulled herself together. "I don't know why you think you're so important," she said. "I'm upset about Lilah."

"I know. But she'll be all right. Miss Lilah can take care of herself—and the whole county, too. And the sight of a dead feral hog won't bother her a bit. Believe me."

Meri was horrified. "*What?* Are you leaving it as a yard ornament?"

He gave her a disgusted look. "I'll take care of it. First, I just wanted to make sure that we were all right."

She drew back, startled. "*We?* There is no 'we.' "

His raised one eyebrow. "We'll see," he said with a significant look.

Her heart jumped and she felt heat in her cheeks. She blurted, "I'm upset because Lilah doesn't trust me. Not enough to tell me where she was going."

"What's the story here? What'd she do?"

"She borrowed Jimmy's truck and left. Doc hasn't cleared her to drive yet, so she's illegal behind the wheel and I don't have a clue where she is."

"Maybe it was just a spur-of-the-moment thing."

"No. She sent me on deliveries alone for the first time. She was getting me out of the way."

Just saying those words made Meri want to cry. Caleb was watching her with sympathetic eyes. She couldn't stop the words crowding on her tongue. "It reminds me of my . . . Edie Jo. She never trusted me, either."

Meri clamped her lips together. Had she really said that? To anyone, much less to Caleb?

Yes, she had, and to her own consternartion she went even further while she looked into his blue eyes.

"Not for one minute or for one decision did she trust me, despite the fact that I was cooking her breakfast and cleaning the apartment from the time I was eight years old. And I made good decisions, too. I had to, in order to survive."

"I hear you," he said. "Jasper, my dad, never trusted me, either. Still doesn't. Miss Lilah thinks it's because he's jealous. Maybe your mom was jealous of you."

She stared at him. "Well . . . maybe . . . I know some mothers are jealous of their daughters."

"Like the old studs want to kill the young ones."

"They do?"

He nodded. "Natural instinct. Try to hold on to power as you age."

"I'm worried Lilah'll have a wreck trying to drive with one hand. She could hurt herself or someone else and end up with a lawsuit on her hands . . ."

"Or she could drive down the driveway right this minute," Caleb said, and Meri turned to see Jimmy's faded red rattletrap truck coming toward them.

Lilah parked it behind her own, got out and came around the truck. She came up the brick walk looking fabulous in black linen pants and a long tunic with a string of rough-cut turquoise stones.

Her face was grim and her mouth tight. She waved at them, then she saw the pig and stopped still to exclaim about it. Meri and Caleb walked out to join her and tell the whole story.

The whole time, though, Lilah wasn't herself. When they'd exhausted the feral hog story, she said, "Well, kids, I've been to San Antonio to try to get a loan. And failed."

Before either of them could take that in, she went on, "I'd love to help y'all butcher your hog, but I need a little time to myself right now. I'm going to call a special meeting of my prayer group. Don't worry, we'll think of something."

Caleb and Meri stared after her, then at each other.

"We've gotta get on this," he said.

It was the strangest thing. That "we" felt more good than strange or scary to her.

Twenty

Meri finished dumping ice over the big tub full of soda cans—around here they said *pop* or *soda pop* instead—stuffed the bags into the trash then drifted to the back corner and her laptop, hoping Lilah wouldn't notice. That idea lurking at the edges of her mind was pulling at her again. A little more time cruising the web and it might crystallize.

At the front of the rickety wooden concession stand, Lilah was talking to Shorty about trying to lease some of her land along the highway for commercial purposes, but he was saying that kind of deal would take way too long to do any good with this loan coming due. And word of it would only encourage encroachment on the cropland out this way.

Meri's heart ached for them both. Shorty wanted to help so much. And Lilah was so much more desperate since returning from her secret trip to San Antonio.

She got online and continued her surfing through organic-farm websites, looking for whatever had triggered her creative juices earlier in the day.

From behind the concession stand, mouthwatering aromas emanated from a huge smoker. Shorty had pulled the machine into the fairgrounds with his pickup truck earlier. A bunch of his buddies were sitting around it in folding lawn chairs, "shooting the breeze," as they put it, and spitting tobacco juice into the grass.

Who would've ever thought that she, Meredith Briscoe, would be in the middle of all this? It didn't even feel strange anymore—and that was scary.

She'd also been looking for jobs online and she needed to update her resume and start applying for the most promising ones. But how could she, when she wasn't sure when she could leave Honey Grove?

It couldn't be now, with the loan problem looming and Lilah in a state of continued panic.

Meri sat on the high stool at the fold-down counter and tried to concentrate on the screen of her laptop instead of worrying. Lilah and Shorty seemed to be giving up on that, too, for the moment.

"I've got to get to the arena and my girls," she was saying to him. "Look at them up there lollygagging around, with flag team practice in thirty minutes! They need to be warming up their horses instead of sitting there gossiping."

"Well, hurry back," Shorty said. "We're gonna have some hungry buzzards circlin' around here pretty soon and I've got to pay attention to those ribs *and* grill the hamburgers for y'all. I'll be too busy to help Meri if she needs it."

"Well, then, send one of your lazy cohorts over here if it gets too busy. I'll be back as soon as I can, but I don't know how long the practice'll take."

Meri clicked on the site she'd been exploring when Lilah asked her to take care of icing the drinks. It came up, the home page background a gorgeous shot of a lush cornfield. She liked it, yet for the Honey Grove site, she wanted a photo with more points of interest or some action, maybe.

"Meri! You know what I forgot? The onions! We'll need some for the devil's hot sauce if you have to make another batch, and also some for people who want onions but no sauce. When you get customers standing in line out here, there won't be time to chop them."

"In a minute," Meri said, scrolling down the side for the farm wife's blog she'd been reading earlier. "I'm looking for the Pioneer Woman."

"Oh, honey, don't get started on that now. From what you showed me of that one, it's too interesting. You'll be in there looking at all of it for an hour."

Meri sighed and closed the laptop. Lilah was right.

She concentrated instead on the instructions for running the concession stand: which containers Lilah always used for chopped onion, which knife was best for the job, which cutting board was for onions only. Meri mustn't chop too many at a time (if so, some might get too hot and spoil before being used) and she could follow the written recipe for devil's hot sauce to make another batch if this one should run out.

Meri hated to chop onions because they always made her cry, but she didn't mention that. If she got everything done and there were few customers, she could still work on clarifying her vague business plan.

"I've got it. I can do this," Meri said.

"Remember when the onions make you cry, hold your hands under cold running water."

Meri chuckled. "The key word being *running*, which we don't exactly have in this concession stand."

"Then just pour some out of the cooler and stick your hands in it."

"I will." Meri glanced toward the arena, across the little fairground road in front of the stand. "You'd better get over there. Those girls are doing nothing but talking."

She hated to rat them out, but fifteen more minutes online would be great and it'd be a while before the onion situation would be critical. Lilah was turning to leave when the bread truck arrived.

Lilah snorted. "Bobby Kyle Albritton. It's about time he got here."

The driver got out, his head down, texting on his phone. "Where do you want your order, Miss Lilah?"

"He shorted us six dozen hamburger buns last year,"

Lilah muttered to Meri. "Then had the nerve to argue with me about it. And all over him not paying attention to business because he was fingering that *phone*.

"And hello to you, too, Bobby Kyle," Lilah called to him. "Are you having a good afternoon?"

To Meri, she said, "I tried to teach him some manners when he was just big enough to work for Shorty. I cooked for them while they hayed my meadow twice that summer. Bless his heart, he's just had no raising."

The young man lifted his head and looked at them with a sheepish smile. "Yes, ma'am, thank you, I am. And how're you? How's your wrist?"

"It's much better," she said. "Thanks for asking."

He shoved the phone into his pocket and went to the back of the truck to take out some boxes.

"Right over here," Lilah said, going to the open side door. "Stack them separately, if you would, hot dog and hamburger buns, right here by the door."

Bobby Kyle glanced toward the arena. "I think Addison will win the trail, hands down," he said as he followed directions. "She looked good at practice last night."

Lilah's head jerked up and so did her eyebrows. Meri smiled to herself. It was rare to see Lilah surprised.

"Bobby Kyle! Do I have a bug on my grapevine?"

He shrugged. "It's no big deal."

He straightened up and added, with a grin, "Yet."

Lilah looked at him, eyebrows still lifted. "Isn't she way too young for you?"

He shrugged again as he held his clipboard for her to sign. "Addy's very mature for her age."

"Does her mother know about this?" Lilah said.

"About what? We're just friends."

"Let's see," Lilah said, "time goes by so fast. Was it three years ago or four that I was shopping for your graduation present?"

"Four," he said. "Next year'll be my five-year class reunion. Can't believe it. Seems like I oughtta still be playing football."

Lilah signed for the delivery and they said good-bye. He threw his clipboard into the truck and strode across the road to the arena. Addison, smiling, sitting her horse by the gate, talking to Chelsea, tried to appear completely unaware of him.

"Well, I'll be switched," Lilah said, looking to see if Meri was watching them, too. "Deep down, Bobby Kyle's got a heart as big as Dallas. And that Ryan Stamps who Addison's been dating is a purely arrogant ass. But, still, this will never do."

"Five years *is* a lot of difference at her age."

"Too much. Her mother will pitch a hissy fit."

"Lilah," Meri said, "I don't think you can say anything. You'll only make things worse and besides, it's none of your business."

She had to admit, though, that she, too, had a strange new urge to try and help Addison, whom she barely knew, manage her life.

"Tell me, now. When did *that* ever stop Lilah?"

They whirled around and saw Doreen standing in front of the fold-down front counter. "I'd like a hot dog with the famous devil's hot sauce, please," she said with an irritating grin, "and a large sweet tea with lots of ice."

Lilah looked her up and down. Meri noticed that Doreen's dress was as stylish as usual but just a bit too tight.

"I wouldn't, if I were you," Lilah said, "since that dress could split up the side seam the next time you take a deep breath."

Doreen's smile didn't change. "Really, Lilah, Meri's right, you know. You can't say anything to Addison or Bobby Kyle because words of advice from an adult only fuel teenage rebellion."

Lilah stiffened to her full height and enmity vibrated in the air between them so palpably that Meri could feel it.

"I know all about teenage rebellion." Lilah used a low, dangerous voice that was new to Meri. "And about how advice from an adult can inflame it. Get out of my sight, Doreen Semples, before I come around this counter and snatch you bald-headed right here in front of God and everybody."

"You sound like we're still six years old."

But instead of staying, Doreen spotted a woman walking past, and called, "Oh, Lottie, I need to talk to you. Wait just a minute, okay?"

She looked back over her shoulder at Meri. "Good luck with taking care of your grandma, honey. She can be *such* a pill when she gets overwrought like this."

For a long minute after she'd gone, Lilah just stood there staring into space. Her face was red and Meri noticed that her hands were shaking.

Impulsively, her arm went around her grandmother's waist. Lilah's rapid breathing pushed the edges of the conchos on her turquoise belt up and down against the skin of Meri's arm.

"That was about . . . my mother?"

The words, like the gesture, came from nowhere, as if Meri were having an out-of-body moment.

"Edie Jo never would have taken you to Vegas or Hollywood or *anywhere* else, at least not out of Texas, if it hadn't been for Doreen sticking her nose in where it didn't belong."

Lilah's voice went rough and hard. "Telling her she could be a *star*, for goodness' sake! Telling her to marry money, telling her she had so much talent she could shoot straight to the top in Hollywood, when everybody with ears and eyes knew she couldn't sing or dance *or* act her way out of a paper bag."

Lilah clamped her mouth closed, took a ragged breath and patted Meri's arm. "I've got to get over there to the arena. Just watch yourself with Doreen, Meri. If she tries to get close to you, I can't be responsible for what I might do."

She turned to go. "Now that'd be a real Rock County scandal! Me going to jail for attacking a member of my Sunday School class!"

"Definitely a bad way to get publicity for Honey Grove," Meri said dryly.

"Not to mention for the Sunday School class."

That made them laugh and Lilah gave her another pat—
on the shoulder, this time—before she walked away. Meri
stared after her. There'd been such regret and resentment in
Lilah's voice for all those terrible, long-ago decisions that
had torn up her life. And Meri's. Who would she be if she'd
grown up here?

Lilah had loved Edie Jo very much. That had been evi-
dent in her voice, too.

Love was such a treacherous thing. Tim had proved that
to her, just as Edie Jo had done all those years before.

But it was Lilah she needed to focus on. She'd already
had enough stress with the loan trouble and the work of
trying to save the leftovers from the farmers market and
everyday life on the farm. She needed to forget about the
past right now and so did Meri.

"Five Frito chili pies, please."

She turned to see a group of preteen kids in green and
white 4-H tee shirts proclaiming ROCK COUNTY LIVE-
STOCK JUDGING TEAM standing at the front of the booth,
money in hand. She hoped they didn't want onions.

But of course they did. Meri chopped a big purple one
while she tried to remember what Frito chili pie *was*. Even
with her working fast, her eyes were streaming tears before
she finished. She tried to decide whether or not to yell to
Shorty for help.

But as soon as she reached for corn chips instead of Fritos, the two girls at the front of the group, amazed by her
ignorance, started coaching her, alternating directions.

"It has to be *Fritos*."

"Tear the bag open on a paper plate . . ."

"Pour some chili on, then put onion and cheese on top . . ."

Soon she had five bags opened and was dipping chili
from Lilah's Crock-Pot, sniffing back the tears, trying not
to wipe her eyes on the shoulder of her pale pink shirt. Her
mascara would ruin it.

A man spoke, close behind her. "I'll take the drink
orders and the money."

Startled, Meri whirled around, ladle in hand, chili

flying off it onto the counter, then the floor and finally his shirt and hers when she stopped its trajectory.

"*Caleb?*"

Her pulse raced wildly. How ridiculous was that? She definitely was *not* the type to scare easily.

"Looked like you could use some help."

He glanced down at the red-brown spots staining his white shirt. It had pearl snaps and smile pockets. Very retro. Very good fit.

His cologne was the same. Irresistible.

No, that was a silly choice of words. She wasn't even attracted to him—much—and she could resist anyone and anything.

Tantalizing probably would be a better description, considering . . .

"You okay?"

She blinked and nodded. "Of course."

Heat crawled up her neck and into her face. The 4-Hers had gone quiet and were listening and watching intently.

"Didn't mean to sneak up on you. Sorry."

Starched jeans, big hat. Scrubbed, suntanned face. Eyes full of mischief.

He was *impossibly* irritating.

"Well, you did make it sound like a robbery!"

The kids laughed at that.

"How many robbers offer to pour the drinks?"

That was funny, too. Then their audience was waiting for the next line.

Meri felt heat bloom in her cheeks. "I can handle this," she said, meeting his twinkly look with a firm one of her own. "Thanks for stopping by."

No doubt, he was here to bug her some more about helping him with Lilah. Right now, she didn't want to talk about the foreclosure or even think about it with her conscious mind because of that niggling idea still lurking in her subconscious. It would come out if she left it alone.

Instead of leaving, Caleb went to the tub filled with ice and cans.

"You'll have a rush to deal with in a few minutes," he said. "The cutting contest is nearly over and the crowd'll be fogging up this way for Shorty's barbeque. Okay, kids, let's get y'all outta here. Who wants Dr Pepper? Cream soda? Coke . . ."

Meri turned back to her Frito chili pies and added a dollop of chili to each so they'd still be hot. *He* was the one who needed to be outta here.

While the kids paid Caleb and he made change, Meri cleaned up the spilled chili from the counter, then wet a paper towel and squatted to get it off the floor.

"Here," he said, squatting beside her, a little awkwardly because of his leg, reaching to take the towel from her, "let me do that."

"Stop it. Why are you trying to take over here?"

She vaguely acknowledged the words were an echo of Lilah's frequent, unreasonable complaint, but he was too much for her to deal with right now.

He caught the end of the towel. She jerked it back and it tore. She stood up, fast.

He used his half to wipe out the last spot and looked around for more. Only then did he unfold his long frame and stand up to face her with the most irritating nonchalance in the world.

"You go on ahead and get organized to sell a lot of drinks and chips," he said. "Shorty's got enough meat smoked out there to feed the whole county."

"*You* go on ahead," she said, "and get out of here. I can do this."

They glared at each other.

More accurately, she glared and he twinkled. He was, hands down, the most infuriating man she'd ever known.

His face was the strongest. Most handsome. His air the most confident.

No surprise that women were sometimes moved to shoot him.

The feel of dancing with him flashed through her memory. He'd held her so firmly, they could've danced off the edge of the world.

Get a grip, Mer. You're losing it.

"How do *you* know what we'll sell and how much?"

Her tone came out so belligerent she could hardly believe it was hers. But didn't he always push her to the edge?

"The cuttin' contest is down to the two final runs."

"And?"

She set her hands on her hips.

Now you're hopelessly bitchy.

She dropped them. She put them back again.

His eyes were laughing at her but she chose to ignore that.

"It's the most popular event of the whole fair."

"So?"

"Shorty wins trophies for his barbeque."

She squinted at him. "You're predicting that *all* the spectators of the 'cuttin'' contest, whatever that is, will eat barbeque for supper?"

He beamed like a caricature of a proud parent, which in itself made her want to slap him. "Good job, Meri! I don't know about all, but a large percentage of them will."

Meri shook her head in disgust. "Riddles are so juvenile. Do you think I'm stupid or what?" She went to put more sodas in the tub. "As if I care."

"I think you're smart as the proverbial whip," he said, throwing the paper towel into the trash box, "which is why I want you on my side when it comes to saving Miss Lilah's place for her. What'd she say when you talked to her about it?"

Meri whirled around with a bag of ice in her hands. "You're assuming I discussed it with her just because you asked me to?"

His eyes, boring into hers, smiled at the taunt. Briefly.

"What'd she say?"

The heavy patience in his voice set Meri's priorities straight. The trouble was real, it was coming fast and if they couldn't stop it, she and Lilah both were out on the street.

Where would they go? She could take care of herself, even if she had to wait tables, but what about Lilah? Would Meri be responsible for her? Morally, yes. They were connected now.

They could use help from any source they could get, no matter how Meri happened to feel about the giver.

Caleb must've read her feelings yet again because he came to her, took the bag, cut the top off with a knife he took from the front pocket of his jeans and poured the ice over the soda cans. Without saying a word.

"A little more over here on this side," she said.

He did it. She felt stupid because, after all, what difference did it make? But she had such a desperate need right then to control *something*. Done, he shook out the bag and took it to the tall plastic trash container.

Meri took a deep breath to try and drive the cold from her veins. "She said, and I'm paraphrasing, something to the effect that she would lose Honey Grove before she would ever take money from that precious young man or anybody else who's just trying to get started in life."

He turned, his thoughtful gaze going straight to hers. His eyes were a darker blue than she'd ever seen them.

"So. What can we do?"

She relaxed a little on the inside. He was staying in this, determined to help.

She panicked on the inside. Why was he staying in?

"What do you mean, 'we'? Look, Caleb, I'm not really comfortable sharing Lilah's financial details with you. I don't have her permission and I . . ."

He finished the sentence for her, ". . . don't trust you."

She held his gaze, trying to read him but also searching herself. It was true. Nobody ever did something like this unless something was in it for him.

"No problem," he said. "We need to come up with a possible idea. Today. If it's yours, you can have the copyright with no protest from me."

"I've got a ghost of one but it'd take four or five years, at least, to make enough profit to pay off this loan. We don't have that kind of time."

He nodded abrupt agreement and said, "I'm thinking maybe we could funnel my money through you and get this done. Miss Lilah's always swearing that she won't take charity but family help wouldn't be charity. It'd be survival."

"She won't take money from me, either."

He frowned. "All right, then. Trot out your ghost."

She had to reach for courage to say her idea out loud. She always hated so much to be wrong about anything. "I don't know anything about farming or business or anything else but . . ."

"Come on. The bare bones."

As if to say she was too wordy! She bristled.

"Unsold produce. There's a niche there, but I'm not sure what it is. Family farms can't sustain the losses. Demand for organic food. Prevent waste, salvage the damaged foods, turn them into commercial products, jams, jellies, other goods like that."

He blinked, nodded. Thought about it.

At least he wasn't laughing.

She shrugged. "But so what? It'd take too much money—a commercial kitchen, lots of equipment and time."

He cocked his head. "Yeah. But it's something to think about . . ."

From the corner of her eye, Meri glimpsed another customer walking across the grass.

"No copyright," she said, moving toward the service window. "I don't care about that. If Honey Grove goes down, I'll never be on another farm."

Caleb waved to the approaching man, who happened to be angling toward Shorty and his helpers instead of the concession stand.

When he turned to Meri again, he caught her gaze with that electric force of his that wouldn't let her look away.

"So," he said, with that devilish glint in his eyes, "let's think about this idea and then get together to see what we've got."

Meri stopped still.

*Careful. You're getting into something here. With Caleb
Burkett.*

*Impossible. You won't be here for four or five years,
so it's stupid to even start with this. Even if you weren't
insanely attracted to him.*

He gave her a smile and a nod. "Good," he said. "Then
it's a deal."

"No, I . . ."

The smile widened and became his lethal grin.

It worked. Or worry did. Whatever the reason, her
mouth opened and her voice said, "Deal."

Twenty-one

Meri stumbled into the kitchen in her pajamas, still half-asleep and with her computer under her arm, aiming for an hour alone with it accompanied by coffee. Lilah had let her sleep late, and the even larger miracle was that Meri had done so. She had even missed first light today.

A glance at the kitchen clock told her it was eight thirty, which was mid-morning on farm time. The horses weren't sounding off, so Lilah must've thrown them some grain and then let them out. If Jimmy was too busy, Meri'd clean the stalls later but first, she wanted to surf the organic-farming web.

She hadn't had any more chances to get online last night because Caleb had been right about the onslaught of customers for the concession stand after the cutting contest. Apparently, that activity involved cows and horses instead of knives. When it was over, the 4-H Club had a lot of money to count. Meri had been exhausted by the time they'd celebrated their success and cleaned everything up.

She took a mug from the cabinet. As she poured it full of fragrant black coffee, she became aware of a hum of voices floating in from the back porch. Lilah liked to open the kitchen windows whenever possible and this morning wasn't *too* hot. Yet.

Meri leaned on the edge of the counter in front of the sink and peered out. Oh, yes. This must be the special prayer-group meeting that Lilah had mentioned.

Apparently, the group consisted of two women in the swing and two in rocking chairs pulled up on either side. Meri felt like a Rock Springs native because she could name all four of them. Dulcie, Caleb's mother, and a sweet-faced woman named Parmalee were two of the new people Meri had met just last night at the fair. The third guest was Lilah's friend B. J.

All of them had coffee cups and paper plates with muffins. The paper plates sat on their laps, the coffee cups rested comfortably in their hands.

"Well, you might try praying for another perspective on it," Dulcie was saying in her husky voice, which held a note of humor, much like Caleb's did. However, he didn't look like his mother at all. Idly, Meri wondered if his twin brother had a different type of personality.

Dulcie surely couldn't have that lilt in her voice if she had *two* sons as irritating as Caleb.

Meri would have to see him again, and all because she'd told him her germ of an idea that might not be any good at all. He'd said he'd think about it, and he would. That was one thing about him she knew for sure—he would do whatever he promised.

How could he know so instinctively how to push her buttons? There was arrogance under all that teasing. He wanted to charm everyone, including her. *Especially* her, since she wasn't falling for it.

If he only knew, he might as well give that up. She wasn't going to succumb.

It was just her luck that he, of all the men she'd ever met, roused her senses as much as he did her temper. But she could resist.

"Lilah, maybe you should pray on this differently. Why

don't you pray to see Doreen and y'all's relationship from her point of view. Think what her life's been like."

What? Why weren't they working on saving the farm? Or maybe they'd done that first, while Meri slept.

Lilah made a sound something like a growl. "She's had a good husband who's lived as long as she has, and money and business success and . . ."

Dulcie held up her hand. "*Pray* to know how it feels to walk in her moccasins before you say another word. This month, why don't we all pray that way with you . . ."

She stopped and looked for B. J. and Parmalee's nods of agreement, then finished, ". . . before we really double down again on praying that you can forgive her and forget."

Lilah was sitting facing the window, so Meri could see a dozen different expressions flit across her face, ending on the stormy, stubborn one that Meri had come to know well.

Meri sipped at her coffee, which was still very hot, and waited. She might learn something from Dulcie about how to handle her grandmother.

Dulcie said, "Look at it this way, Lilah: We all know God has a sense of humor. You might end up actually sympathizing with her."

Everybody except Lilah broke into raucous laughter. She scowled at Dulcie.

"Being your *friend* is a challenge," Dulcie said in an earnest tone. "You're such a handful for us to try to keep in line—always bossing, always wanting your own way and poking into our business telling us what to do about everything. Honey, it's exhausting, let me tell you, so . . ."

Everybody was chuckling except Lilah. She was starting to smile, though, in spite of herself.

". . . just think how much more of a strain it must be on Doreen to be your enemy."

All four women shouted with laughter and the hilarity went on to the point that the dignified Parmalee bent over double and then had to grab the chain to keep from falling out of the swing. Some of her coffee splashed out of the cup.

When they finally settled down again, Lilah was still

smiling. Grudgingly, she said, "Well, all right. I guess it's worth a try."

Silence fell. Dulcie gave her a thoughtful look. Lilah returned it.

"I *will* try. I promise. Y'all please pray for me to be able to listen for guidance with an open heart."

She shook her head ruefully. "The Good Lord knows how stubborn I can be. But I will try my best to listen and look for His guidance about Doreen and also about what to do to save Honey Grove. All of y'all please keep praying about that. Every day. That's the biggest problem I've ever had."

"We will. We always do," the three friends said in chorus. They sipped coffee.

"Well," Parmalee said, "it's gettin' hot now and we all have things to do today. But let's talk about the pie contest just for a minute before we break."

Lilah said, "I hope, at my appointment this afternoon, Doc says my arm's healed enough to use. I haven't missed a contest since . . ."

"You can *not* enter this year, not with your arm in a sling," Parmalee said. She had a sweet voice to go with her sweet face. "How about if we all enter a different one of your pies, Lilah? In honor of all the years you've won first place?"

Lilah's eyebrows flew up, her eyes wide open in shock.

Parmalee threw up her hands and said quickly, "I know, I know. We couldn't make them come out as good as *you* make 'em. But your recipes are so good, at least one of them is bound to win the rooster."

Meri had a fleeting but forlorn hope that Parmalee was talking about Lilah's real-live, hateful rooster, Sanders—it'd be great if he went to live with someone else. But, probably not.

Dulcie smiled. "Great idea. But, Lilah, you'd have to give us the authentic recipes with all the secret tips and tricks and *definitely* all ingredients listed."

Lilah bristled. "I take offense. Exactly what are you

implying, Dulcie Burkett? I've never given out an altered recipe in my life!"

The laughter started again. It was infectious. Meri chuckled. The look on Lilah's face was priceless.

"I wouldn't touch that one with a ten-foot pole," B. J. said. "Lilah's lying at a prayer-group meeting, and I don't want to be the cause of her gettin' in any deeper headed in the wrong direction."

Lilah made a face at her. "I haven't said yet that I'm not plannin' to enter for my ownself."

That brought a chorus of protests as they all stood up at the same time, as if at an unseen signal that it was time to go.

"Don't you *dare*."

"You'll hurt your arm again. Even if Doc says it's healed, you shouldn't use a rolling pin yet."

"Be generous. You can stand to let somebody else win the rooster *for once*."

Lilah waved all that away and picked up the muffin basket while the others gathered cups and Bibles and started clearing the small table.

Meri stepped back from the window so she wouldn't be caught eavesdropping. Her gaze lengthened to sweep across the yard and came to rest on the small springhouse building.

She knew what it was like to be unable to forgive. She would *never* be able to forgive Edie Jo—and she wasn't going to try because she didn't like to think about her mother.

But the old, familiar question that had been with her since the day Edie Jo left pulled at her again.

In those battered boxes sitting behind that thick green door, was there *anything* to prove Edie Jo ever had *one* thought about her little girl?

Twenty-two

Meri parked in the shade of the old tree at the back of the garage/shed and rolled down the windows. She had the driver's door open and one foot out of the truck when her ringtone sounded.

"Hey, Mer. You called?"

Caleb's careless tone in her ear sent a sent a shock through her, even though she'd seen his name on the screen. Something about his low voice always rendered her unable to think for a second.

That, and the fact that no one had ever called her *Mer* except her own conscience.

"I'm just arriving home with groceries," she said. "Ice cream. Can I call you back?"

"Headin' into a no-service area here pretty quick," he said. "Gimme a hint."

As usual, he was a force like the wind now whipping through the truck.

"Lilah's trying to sell antiques that've been in the family for generations and she's pushing Shorty to find her a cheap used tractor so she can sell her good one. She'd only get pennies on the huge dollars that she paid for it. Have you had time to think about my idea?"

"Better," he said. "I'm all over it with a broom. Why don't I pick you up tonight around seven?"

She could feel the shape of his warm hand against her back, guiding her across the dance floor.

"I'll buy you dinner."

Dangerous.

"Why don't I meet you somewhere? What place would be good?"

He laughed. "What? You don't get into cars with men? You don't stay out after dark? You don't trust me?"

I don't trust me.

"Ask anybody," he said, still chuckling. "I've had good raisin' and I'm a perfect gentleman. We'll drop by the pie contest for dessert and the dance. See you at seven."

He was gone.

Good raisin'? Ha! Meri was sure Dulcie had tried, but this son of hers needed a refresher course. He didn't hesitate to be arrogant and controlling when it served his purposes.

Meri grabbed the big bag of groceries and ran up the walk toward the back porch. There had never been two men more different than Caleb was from Tim.

She'd thought Tim was trustworthy in his personal life. And she'd been wrong.

She thought Caleb was trustworthy in business. Why? Because so many people who knew him well had vouched for him.

Because she really believed he cared about Lilah.

She'd been hearing around town that Caleb had started a couple of small business ventures since returning to Rock Springs after several years away. He should be able to show her how her idea could become reality.

Meri ran up the back steps and across the porch, her stomach growling, mind racing, making a mental list for her afternoon. First, *lunch*, then enter into the computer all the produce deliveries she'd been making since dawn, and after that, organize her folder full of the info she'd found online and print it to show to Caleb tonight.

She balanced the bag of groceries in one arm, threw open the back door and dashed into the air-conditioned coolness of the house. But the kitchen was *not* cool. The oven was on, a pot of something mouthwatering that smelled like delicious sweet peaches was steaming on top of the stove and . . . the floor was a mess. *Lilah's* floor? In the *kitchen*?

Lilah herself sat on a tall stool grimly rolling out dough on the antique butcher block. She looked up. Her face was sweaty.

"It's about time. Where've you been?"

"What're you *doing*?" Meri wailed. "Oh, Lilah, Doc said your wrist isn't fully *healed*. No one's expecting you to enter that pie contest! You don't have to do this."

Lilah glanced down. "I'm wearing my sling."

"But you're using your hand to hold the dough. He said don't put any strain on it. I heard him say it. Lilah, please take care."

Lilah flashed her an angry look. "I'm not. I am."

"I beg to differ."

"I didn't promise Doc not to enter the pie contest. I promised to take care and not overdo."

Meri heaved a disgusted sigh and hurried toward the refrigerator to take care of the ice cream. Incredibly, the countertops, the sink, the stovetop and the kitchen table were all even worse than the floor. Overwhelming to neat-nik Meri.

"Lilah, this is nuts. Absolutely *nuts*. This kitchen's a wreck. I can't believe you're putting yourself—and me, since I'll have to clean up this mess—through all this just to enter that silly contest . . ."

Her heel hit something slick and she slipped, one arm pinwheeling, the other clutching the groceries to her chest, but only for a second. She did the splits and went down hard, groceries shooting out of the sack like missiles, cans banging into the cookstove, round Blue Bell ice cream boxes rolling like wheels into the cabinets.

Her bottom stung like fire. And her best chinos were sticking to the floor. The best, most expensive chinos like she'd never be able to afford again.

White stuff . . . flour? Sugar? Along with Henry's paw prints, pieces of dough and some dark, syrupy drips here and there near the stove made up the landscape down here on the kitchen's lowest level.

"I don't know whether to laugh or cry," she gasped. "But I know you can forget about your reputation of being so clean someone could eat off your floor." She laughed, then sighed. Poor Lilah. Of course she had to do this—she'd felt helpless for much too long.

"You hurt?"

Meri twisted around to look at her grandmother. "What I am is worried, Lilah. I wish you'd let it go. You know nobody can make a pie with one hand."

"*I* can."

Meri looked around dramatically. "This kitchen looks like the scene of a food fight. You're going to have to let me help you."

Lilah thumped the rolling pin on the hard wood. *"What?"*

Meri peeled herself free, got up and went to the sink to wash her hands. She tore off a paper towel and wet it, then picked up the empty grocery bag to serve as trash bag.

"I don't think we can make a pie in this wreckage and I want to make this fast. I have to do other work this afternoon—an idea to save the farm, for one."

"Hmph. You don't have to help me, missy. I'll clean up my own mess and make my own pie."

Meri ignored the bravado and started washing up sticky spots, picking up pieces of pastry and a stray peach pit, then a whole strawberry, working her way toward the broom closet in the mudroom, willing Lilah to listen and actually *hear* her.

"Try not to drop anything else on the floor and think what part I can play."

"What'd you hear in town about the contest?" Lilah used a conciliatory tone to try and change the subject.

"Everybody in town's talking about it and, to a man—or woman—they're assuming you're out of it. Most people are saying that this is Doreen's one chance to win."

Lilah glared at the piecrust, thumped her rolling pin, then rolled furiously.

Meri found her most persuasive tone of voice. "So that means Doreen can win, just this one time, and your reputation won't suffer," she said brightly. "In the future, if she brags about being champion, everyone in town—Suzy, Raul, *everybody*—will always say it was because *you* didn't enter."

"Hmph." Lilah tossed her head.

She was holding her one good hand flat on the middle of the rolling pin to push it over the flattened dough. How effective could that be? Surely she'd give it up soon. Or let Meri do it.

Meri worked all the way to the mudroom door.

"Careful when you open it," Lilah said. "I shut Henry in there because he kept trying to get up here and help me."

"So far, the most prevalent rumor Doreen's spreading— according to Shuggie at the grocery store—is that you always use canned filling when you make a fruit pie."

"She's slipping," Lilah said. "Nobody in their right mind would believe that. No, wait. She's desperate. She's trying to find out from Shuggie what groceries I've bought so she can figure out what kind of pie I'm making this year."

Meri opened the door, slowly, silently. It had barely moved two inches when Henry came shooting out as a tan blur, knocking the trash bag from her hand, spilling some of it, heading for Lilah, protesting his imprisonment as he went.

He jumped from the floor to the other kitchen stool and tried for the butcher block. Lilah, screaming, tried to fend him off with an awkward swipe of the rolling pin and missed.

Instead, she hit the steaming pot on the stove.

It tilted sideways, spilling a pinkish syrup onto the countertop to ooze toward the edge. Before Meri could get to it, the liquid was running down the front of the cabinet, dripping onto the floor. So was water and a couple of ice cubes from a glass that fell off the butcher block on Lilah's backward swing.

"Henry didn't do that, I did," Lilah said as she set the pot upright. She looked stricken. "I'm so glad I didn't hit him," she said. "Oh, Meri, I could've hurt him bad with this rolling pin."

"But you didn't. Don't worry. He's only used two of his nine lives."

Obnoxious cat! It was a good thing he'd already vanished down the hall.

"Thank the Lord, I didn't spill the peaches, too. I don't have any more of them peeled."

One glance at Lilah's stricken face made Meri feel more sorry for her, even if she *was* being unreasonable. Her grandmother could not do this by herself.

Lilah wadded up the dough she'd been rolling and threw it to one side.

"It's noon and this pie has to be at the VFW by five o'clock," she said, clearly desperate, "and I've yet to get a good do on this dough. This batch is too short, so it's coming all to pieces."

Disgusted, her face red from exertion, she swept the dough off the butcher block into the wastebasket, which sat half beneath one end of it instead of in its usual place under the sink.

Meri saw that it held more crusts than the ones Lilah had just thrown in. Lilah had to be exhausted. Why couldn't she admit that she had enough stress worrying about the crops and the loan without adding this stupid contest?

"Look," she said. "Sit there on your stool and tell me how to mix it up. Let me roll it out for you, too, Lilah. Nobody can do that with one hand."

"Against the rules," Lilah said, pursing her lips and shaking her head as she turned away to go for more shortening. "Now I've got to hurry and get a crust that won't tear, mix the berry/rhubarb syrup into the peaches and put a pretty lattice crust on top. It'll have to bake and then cool enough for us to carry."

Lilah stopped still. "But first—oh, Lord, we may not have enough of that syrup left. Here, let me see."

She turned quickly in mid-stride. "And listen. Do not ever, ever breathe the word *rhubarb*."

"That's your secret ingredient?"

"Yes. It's been years and no one has guessed."

Meri showed her how much was still in the pot and Lilah gave a short nod. "That'll do. You'll have to hold the peaches there in that Dutch oven and I'll stir the syrup in."

Then, "Where's that flour you brought? Let's get another batch of dough. It'll have to be right this time. When I roll it, Meri, you can hold the edge of the dough . . ."

Meri turned and looked into Lilah's eyes. "Let me do it, and you tell me how," she said. "*You* can hold the edge of the dough with your uninjured hand."

"Against the rules," Lilah said.

"Hold the dough, hold the bowl, what's the difference?" Meri said. She turned back to her cleanup work. "Oh, Lilah. *Please* give this up. Shorty'll take you to the dance, anyway, and . . ."

"I'm not going a step unless I take a pie, and that's that. I *always* win the pie contest."

Meri closed her eyes and resigned herself to leaving the deep cleaning for later. She sighed.

"Sigh away, missy. Sling on my arm, broken wrist or not, I'm not giving Doreen Semples an inch. Not a chance of bragging rights."

There was no reasoning with her grandmother. Meri wanted to scream.

What in the world would happen if Lilah didn't win? Meri couldn't even bear to think about it.

Lilah found the flour, picked it up and wrestled it to the butcher block, opened it then stopped short. "Mercy! I've got to have a clean bowl to mix this in. And more ice water to sprinkle on it. Wash and dry that bowl over there and then get me a glass of water in the freezer to cool right fast."

"What about the rules?"

"Helping in the kitchen is not the same as doing the baking, smartypants."

Meri went to find a clean bowl. Lilah sat slumped on the stool.

"B. J. and Shorty are right," she muttered. "I oughtta get a whuppin' for climbing up in that persimmon tree in the first place."

Meri turned to look at her. "Lilah? Are you all right? What's *wrong*?"

The sweat rolling down Lilah's face was really heavy and her cheeks were too bright.

Her voice was normal, though. Tart as sour apples, but normal.

"What's *wrong* is, I can't make a decent piecrust to save my *life*! It's *noon!*"

Maybe her voice *wasn't* normal. It was rising to a screech at the end of every sentence.

Henry answered each one with a yowl of his own from the bedroom or wherever he'd gone to hide.

"How long have you been at this, anyway?"

"Ever since right after morning chores. I've gone through five pounds of flour but I just can't seem to . . ."

"Lilah." Meri tried for a calm, soothing tone. "Think about it. Who *can* make a piecrust using only one arm?"

"*I* can, as God is my witness," Lilah said, through gritted teeth. "I just can't make one that'll hold together when I *pick it up* with one hand. And I'm not even *trying* to get it big enough for a cobbler. Just a deep-dish pie."

She gestured at a pot on the stove. "I may've spilled the sugar trying to measure it, but I still got the best syrup I've ever had and there's still enough of it to make the flavor just right. If I can make my usual crust and bake this pie the perfect length of time, Doreen Semples will find out, once again, that when it comes to a pie contest, she might just as well go to the house."

Meri tried to think before she spoke. Lilah's expression was fierce enough to scare even Shorty. *Or* Doreen herself.

Meri would keep the tone light. And maybe try to appeal to Lilah's sense of humor. Usually, it was there, even in the worst situations.

"It smells wonderful. What is it?"

"Texas summer peach pie. It's famous. Remember: Don't you *dare* ever breathe a word about the rhubarb."

"I won't. I promise. Don't worry about that."

Lilah gestured for Meri to help her measure the flour, added some salt and shortening, then drops of cold water and started mixing it with her hand, telling Meri how to do each step.

When it felt ready, she formed a ball on the butcher block, sprinkled a bit of flour on the rolling pin and flattened it to roll. Meri did hold the edge and Lilah rolled it out to fit the fluted pie plate with the picture of a peach in the middle.

But when Lilah picked up the crust, it split. She scooped it up and wadded it viciously in her hand, then dropped it to one side.

"Measure me some more flour."

"You're making more dough? But look, when you squeezed these pieces they stuck together. Could we just roll it out again and . . ."

"Absolutely *not*." Lilah turned around and wiped her face with her apron. "Rolling it twice makes it tough. You don't *ever* want to do that, but this is one time we *cannot*. I got this last batch too short to handle, *once again*."

"I'll measure it. But, Lilah, you need to let me roll it out *and* pick it up this time."

"Against the rules. I'm *not* gonna be DQ'd on a technicality."

Her voice shook a little bit, Meri was sure of it. Lilah took a deep breath and went to the bathroom to wash her face.

When she returned, Meri said, "Please don't take this so seriously. The rules *can't* be as important as your stress level and I'm going to make this piecrust. Sit right there and tell me every step to take and it'll truly *be* your piecrust . . ."

"Listen to you! And you're little miss letter-of-the-law! Always lecturing *me* about what's legal and what's not."

They looked at each other for a long beat, then burst into hysterical laughter.

Finally, Meri said, "Come on, Lilah. I hardly ever, almost *never*, had the chance to be a naughty little girl. I deserve to try to get away with something."

Lilah hesitated.

Meri looked around. "Nobody will know, except maybe Henry, and he won't tell. And I'd like the pleasure of helping you beat Doreen, since she's spreading such vicious rumors about what we're doing here in the kitchen at Honey Grove."

Lilah studied Meri's face.

"You know we have to uphold the farm's reputation," Meri said. "Honey Grove's future depends on it."

A flash of quick despair in Lilah's eyes made Meri fear she'd said the wrong thing.

But then Lilah's usual spark drove it away. She grinned at Meri, her eyes twinkling.

"Well, you know," she drawled, "there's lies and then there's damn lies. This'll be just a plain lie, and for a righteous cause. Are you good enough to pull off a denial if Doreen accuses you of helping me?"

Meri nodded.

"It's crucial. If I get DQ'd, I'm disgraced forever."

"Never fear. I'm your granddaughter the attorney, remember? If you have to go to jail, I'll get you out on bail."

Twenty-three

Even though God was on her side, human slipups could occur.

Lilah tried not to be a worrywart, but she was risking her reputation for honesty here and she was old enough to know that anything could happen.

For one thing, she could ruin her reputation for good manners and scream at poor Shorty, walking close on her heels across the VFW dance hall parking lot, driving her crazy as a Bessie bug.

Not to mention Caleb, who'd driven into the parking lot at the same time as she and Meri had arrived from the opposite direction. Now he and Meri were walking together, talking in low voices behind Lilah's back. She heard "dinner and dance" and "here for Lilah" but hard as she tried, nothing about any idea to save Honey Grove.

She'd remain firm on one thing: They'd not risk their financial futures for her sake. She wouldn't take their money, so if that was it, they might just as well save their breath.

Shorty nattered on, "You need to let me carry that pie,

Lilah. Or Meri or Caleb, if you don't trust me. You'll end up damagin' it yourself just tryin' to impress everybody with your one-handed trick."

Thank goodness they were nearly to the door or she might kill him, which would ruin her reputation for patience on top of everything else.

"Shorty, I have to carry this in. It's a psychological thing. It's *my* pie."

That flummoxed him. "What craziness are you talkin'? You don't know it's your pie unless you carry it? That don't make no sense at all."

"Not *me*," she hissed. "I want the judges and everybody else to know it."

He shook his head sadly as he opened the door for her and Meri.

"Sounds to me like you might be on the road to the Old-Timer's disease, Lilah, my girl. You know as well as I do that if I was carryin' that pie, there ain't a soul here who'd think *I* made it."

"Oh, Lord, give me strength," Lilah said, and she *meant* that, six ways to Sunday.

She walked into the big room with the pie tables set up down the middle and probably fifteen people already there, bustling around, laying out the smoked meat and potato salad, baked beans and all the trimmings along the bar on the wall. A few hungry early birds were hanging around, too, ready for supper. Lester Salzman's five-piece band was tuning up over in the corner.

And there must be two dozen other entrants waiting to be judged. Doreen wasn't there. Could it be she wasn't *entering*? No. It could not be. Not unless she'd had a wreck on the way here or tripped and dropped her pie.

Lilah paused for a moment, smiling and holding her head up high, hearing her father's voice in her mind.

When in doubt, walk fast and look important.

"Lilah, don't worry, you're going to win," Meri murmured at her shoulder. "I just know it."

The girl was sticking to her as close as Shorty was. Good Lord, they were about to smother her. She had to have some room to breathe.

"Y'all wait here," she said. "I'll be back in a minute."

Meri, bless her heart, was so young and inexperienced in navigating the tangled dealings of a small town. She could hesitate to answer a question or respond incorrectly to a remark about the making of Lilah's pie and bring the whole thing down on their heads. Lilah would need to stick as close to her as she could all evening.

Thank the Lord, they hadn't let Shorty in on their secret. If they had, he'd be winking and grinning to beat the band and everybody would get suspicious. He was a firm believer that Lilah could do anything, once she set her head to it, even roll piecrust one-handed. Well, she'd *almost* got it done.

Lilah took a deep breath, walked across the room to the check-in table and set her pie basket directly in front of Elbert Carson, an old county court judge who loved her Texas summer peach pie better than anything in this world except bourbon. This was a sign. She was meant to win the rooster tonight.

It came to her to ask Elbert to lift the pie out of the basket so he could really smell its aroma and she wouldn't look so awkward doing it, but she caught herself in time. Somebody might think she *couldn't* do it and ask, so how could she have made the pie?

"Elbert," she said, "you picked the right job for today. Sign me in."

He twinkled at her, but kept his judicial face on. "Lilah. You're just in time. We're about to start the tasting."

Judges' identities were always kept secret until the check-in so contestants wouldn't deliberately make one of their favorite pies. She'd done it by accident, but Doreen would never believe that, either.

The other judges, who were already walking around the tables marking their cards on "eye appeal," were Callie Turner, that young hairdresser at LaDonna's shop, and Pete Suggs, who owned the greasy-spoon diner out on the highway. That was ridiculous. Pete wouldn't know a good pie if it walked up and slapped him in the face.

Elbert took a deep breath of peach aroma—the Firegold variety always had such a delicious smell—and beamed at her as he took a card from the stack at his elbow and wrote her name on it in his fancy, flowing script. Then, thank goodness, he voluntarily pushed away the tea towels that cushioned it and picked up the pie.

"Lilah. Thank you. I'll just set this over there on the fruit pie table and we'll start slicing these beauties."

Quietly, Lilah took a long, deep sigh of relief and began a circuit of the tables to see who all she was up against. There were two tables, one of two-crust fruit pies and one of meringued cream pies, which also held the chess pies and the other miscellaneous ones without meringue. The pecan ones were on the fruit table, which was appropriate.

There was Mildred Radner's blackberry cobbler in the white ceramic pan, Aunt Bill's apple and walnut with the top crust made out of tiny pastry leaves, Truby's Dutch apple with the streusel top—when would people ever learn that basic, plain apple pie was the best?—and Josie's cherry with a raw cherry on a stem in the middle. Somehow that didn't look quite right.

The one to really worry about was Betty Ward's butterscotch silk. And it probably wasn't a problem tonight because Callie hated butterscotch. Lilah knew that for a fact because they'd talked about sweets one time while Callie was cutting Lilah's hair.

Not very many fruit pies, really, considering it was summer. So many of the women had made cream or silk pies and worried with the meringue that always tried to wilt on the way. Well, that was their lack of foresight.

Her own pie was gorgeous, if she did say so herself. The lattice top was perfectly browned and glistening from the sugar and milk she'd brushed on it. And, oh, nothing ever smelled so good as it did.

When Lilah finished her assessment and turned to look for Meri and Caleb and Shorty, Doreen's fake-cheerful trill rang out. She was hurrying in at the door with her own pie basket in hand.

"*Lilah?* Oh, Lilah, honey. How could you . . ."

She crossed the room fast as a freight train.

"Oh, *I* know," she called, loud enough for the whole town to hear. "You're here entering for *Meri*. What *fun*! We have to give these young girls their chance, don't we now?"

She arrived at the table at such a speed her pie slid against the side of her pie basket when she skidded to a stop.

"Careful there, Doreen," Lilah said dryly, "or you'll break your crust. And the check-in table's over there."

Instead of looking at her, Doreen looked at the pies and saw Lilah's card. Her eyes bugged out.

"Surely you can't be serious," she snapped. "You could not possibly . . ."

Dramatically, she leaned toward Lilah and lowered her voice to a stage whisper loud enough for the judges to hear as they walked around the table.

"With only one *hand*? Come on, Lilah, surely you're kidding!"

Lilah fixed her with her sharpest look. "Doreen, you're not even entered and it's straight up five o'clock right now. Your tendency to get into other people's business is about to lose this contest before your pie can do it for you."

"I'm going to beat you this year," Doreen said, with her insufferable Cheshire-cat grin. "This is a new recipe that you've never heard of and it tastes like you've died and gone to heaven."

"Well, you're gonna wish I had done exactly that before I made my pie, because mine will taste even better and you know it. I *always* win the pie contest."

Doreen's face went hard. She lifted one perfectly plucked eyebrow.

"Not this time, you won't. I'm going to break your winning streak, Lilah Briscoe."

Lilah wanted nothing more than to slap Doreen's self-satisfied face.

Instead, she snapped, "That mess you've got there looks

like something the dogs dragged in. And with a *graham cracker* crust! Help us all! If that isn't perfectly cowardly, I don't know what is! Afraid your pastry can't compete with mine, are you?"

Doreen, in a cocky mood, was more than a saint could stand.

"This pie is *delicious*, I'll have you know. It's my own original recipe."

Lilah snorted. "Your ass is grass, Doreen."

Doreen's mouth and eyes flew open in surprise. Lilah hardly ever cussed, and she shouldn't have given Doreen that advantage, but she hadn't even known she was going to say that until the words left her lips.

There went her reputation for propriety.

She could just hear her grandmother's voice: *He who angers you conquers you.*

Another reason she shouldn't have done it was that it'd make Doreen so mad she'd be even more likely to accuse her of cheating. *Damn!*

She clamped her mouth tight, turned on her heel and walked off. Nothing she could do now but keep her fingers crossed and pray like crazy.

Lilah! Listen to you!

Well, she wasn't exactly asking God's help with a *lie*, just with keeping Doreen in her place.

The Good Lord knew full well that *that* would be a service to all humanity.

On the way to the dance floor, Meri noticed Lilah wandering around looking lost. Before she could say anything to Caleb, Shorty found Lilah and took her over to join another couple who were just arriving;

Meri looked up at Caleb as they reached the line dance that was forming. The music was loud, so he bent down to hear her.

"Thanks for being so good about postponing our business date," she said, her breath catching a little at his sudden closeness. "I just felt I should be here because Lilah's so tired and tense, not to mention so into this contest."

"No problem," he said wryly. "I know Miss Lilah. She's a pistol, ain't she?"

"No question. With all she's got on her plate about the farm, she's still not giving an inch on the pie front. Her competitive spirit's inspiring."

He drawled, "Or flat-out intimidating."

"Let's hope that's how Doreen feels. For the good of the community at the end of this evening."

"Hey, and what d'you mean, 'business date'? "There's no such thing. What I asked you on is a date. Steaks, candlelight, slow dancin'. We'll talk about those ideas before we go."

Meri raised her eyebrows. "I thought we agreed . . ."

"Right now, we need to get serious about the important stuff," he said. "You can't live in Texas if you can't do the Cotton-Eyed Joe."

"She don't know how?" the guy in the couple next to them called. "Well, here, we can show her."

Meri nearly panicked. She hated to be embarrassed. To Caleb, she said, "A line dance? Caleb, I can't. I'll mess it up for everyone."

His teasing smile warmed her. He shook his head. "No worries."

From the instant he put his arm around her shoulders and they began to move with the music, others offered advice, hooted encouragement or smiled at her, and what seemed like a dozen people showed her moves in what seemed an endless swirl of words: "Stick your right leg out and tap your pretty high heel on the floor three times—where's your boots?—really, girl, you need a pair of boots." With a look at Caleb—"Man, why don't you buy her a pair of them full quills like you've got on?" Then, "Eight counts with your feet together," and "Bend your left knee and cross your foot over . . ."

Words mixed with the fast flow of Caleb's feet taking hers with them and his arms and upper body twined with hers, his big body wrapped around hers and his laughter in her ear. She was so into it—to her own consternation—and the man and the music were so compelling that she shocked herself by completely letting go and whirling into the unknown with him as her guide.

She had no clue what she was doing, but he seemed to be very good at it, as best she could judge, so she did what he said and let the worries go.

When the music stopped so the bandleader could announce that the serving line would form at the north end of the bar, Meri was out of breath, slightly sweaty and definitely sorry to come back to the real world.

"That was fun," she said.

Caleb's eyes were sparkling. "It was. But I can promise you this: I'm taking you to San Antonio for our first date. There's a limit to the benefits of small-town togetherness, is what I'm thinkin'."

First date. She wouldn't even think about the implications of that word, first. *Not now. She was loving having fun.*

Laughing, she and Caleb went to reserve the table Lilah had said she wanted so they'd be close to the podium for the presentation of the rooster trophy.

Caleb said, "You've got to hand it to the woman. She may not have money for her loan, but she does have the confidence when it comes to her cooking."

Lilah was feeling absolutely punchy by the time dinner was done. Merciful heavens, she didn't even know the world she was in.

Meri and Caleb were over there on the other side of the round table with their heads together and Meri was behaving, for once in her life, like she was glad to have his attention. As Lilah watched, his hand brushed hers as she was holding the napkin he was writing some numbers on and Meri didn't even jerk it away.

Numbers. He probably *was* talking about Lilah's loan

but at the moment she was too tired to care who got into her business.

Shorty was carrying on the conversation with Treva and Lester Sloane so she didn't have to, and she was free to just sit there, zoned out, without feeling like she had to get up and do some chore right now. She'd worn herself smooth out with that pie.

She needed to stir around, though. Relaxing was her body's—and mind's—way of letting her know how tired she was. She had to hold on to her nervous tension because the real battle with Doreen was still to come. Results would be announced right now, at dessert time, after everyone had chosen a slice of pie at random.

People who picked pieces of the winner won door prizes, awarded with great fanfare by dear old thing Gladys Thomas, the contest organizer who'd run it for at least thirty years. Clearly, Gladys didn't have enough excitement in her life, so she always made the contest last as long as possible.

What she needed was a few money worries like Lilah's and a full day of trying to make a pie with one hand. Then she'd be willing to move things along and get on home to bed.

Exhaustion pulled at Lilah underneath her jangling nerves, and her wrist ached to beat the band. She should never have used it as much as she'd done today.

Mercy! She must've made a dozen failing tries at that crust. Which made her think about her wreck of a kitchen. She closed her eyes against that image. No rush. That mess would still be there tomorrow.

"Miss Lilah, can I bring you a slice of pie? Any particular kind if I can get it?"

Caleb and Meri were standing up, taking orders from the others at the table (the old folks) and Lilah snapped to.

Wake up and get ready. No telling what Doreen will do or say.

"Oh, thank you, darlin'. Nothing with a graham cracker crust for me," she said. "Anything else is fine."

She was so sick of pie right that minute she never wanted

to see another one, no matter what kind. Didn't even want to hear the word *pie*.

But, of course, there was no hope for that because Gladys rang her little bell and started the ceremony, thanking the judges and everybody who'd done so much as fold a napkin or set up a chair for the Thirty-first Annual Rock County Pie Contest. At long last, the dear old thing had run through her whole stack of notecards, everybody had a slice of pie sitting in front of them and Gladys turned to Elbert for the official results.

This, too, could take a while, even though there were only three placings now instead of the original fifteen. A couple of years ago, the judges had insisted on that change so they would have fewer complaints from people who entered. Weird as it was, it worked. It seemed most women didn't expect to be in the top three but they were mad as hornets at not getting at *least* in the top ten.

Lilah, sick of pie or not, ate the dish of Mildred's blackberry cobbler Caleb brought her. It was surprisingly good. Millie was a moody cook who scorned recipes, so her desserts tended to swing between the extremes of either very good—probably none had ever rated as high as "delicious"—or spit-out worthy.

Well, evidently the judges agreed with Lilah, because Mildred won third. First time she'd ever placed at the pie contest. She beamed as she went up to the front. Lilah was glad for her.

Then, inexplicably, considering Callie's taste, Betty's butterscotch came in second. Lilah was happy for her, too.

And shocked. Second was usually Doreen's place. That was what kept giving her hope she could beat Lilah. Hmm. Her new heavenly recipe must've been a big mistake. Or her choice of crust had made them mark her down.

Oh, dear goodness, this would make everything a thousand times worse. Not placing at all would make Doreen into a bear-cat.

Get ready.

Only in the last split second did it occur to her that

perhaps Doreen wasn't second because she'd won first. But, being ridiculous to the point of insanity, Lilah shooed away the thought.

Except . . . the butterscotch *had* placed second.

But then Gladys announced Lilah's Texas summer peach pie as number one and Doreen let out a cackling laugh that sounded like a witch.

Before Shorty could pull her chair out and Lilah could get up and get to the front of the room, Doreen was on her feet.

"I'd like to lodge an official complaint," she said. "And ask for a review of the rules. It was my understanding that each pie that is entered has to be entirely the work of the person entering it."

She turned to look for Elbert, using her flirty, flirty smile—like she had since she was six years old.

"Judge Carson, am I not right about that?"

He stared at her, his fleshy face solemn as the judge he was. "Yes, ma'am, you are correct."

"Then there's been a mistake in the decision for first place. Lilah Briscoe has a crushed wrist and even though it is no longer in a cast, it *is* in a sling, so there is no way she *possibly* could've made that pie all by herself."

Lilah walked faster as she reached the podium, her head held high. She hoped she looked important.

She turned and faced her tormentor.

"My official response to that official complaint is to say that *you*, Doreen Semples, couldn't make my Texas summer peach pie if you used both hands and a hired helper. *I* was raised to be a *Texan*. I'm a direct descendant of three heroes of the Alamo. One broken wrist won't stop me. I have no quit in me."

Applause.

Doreen's face was getting redder by the minute.

"I appeal for justice," she said to Elbert. "That is no answer at all. Lilah should swear on the Bible that she, alone, made that pie. If she can't do it, the blue ribbon should go to Betty Ward."

She turned to look for Betty. "Isn't that right, Betty Lou?"

Betty Lou frowned and shook her head. "Well, now," she drawled, "you know, to tell the truth, I'm just right happy with the red ribbon. I never have even placed in the contest since we went from fifteen places to three and I'm thrilled, just downright *thrilled*, to tell you the truth."

"To tell the truth is what we're asking of Lilah," Doreen said, going from flirty to righteous in a flash, as only a two-faced person could do. She glared at Lilah, then swept a demanding look over her audience. "So? Does anybody here have a Bible with you?"

Well. This was turning into a fine kettle of fish.

Think of something, Lilah. You can come up with a way to turn this . . .

She was too tired to think. She was down to rock-bottom primal level. The only thing that came to her as a possible distraction from swearing on the Bible was to jump Doreen and start a screaming, hair-pulling fight. Her aching wrist would put her at a real disadvantage, though.

And then was the matter of her reputation . . .

"I'm the only witness."

Lilah's head snapped up. Meri's voice was so calm and authoritative it instantly took control of the room. Everything else hushed.

"I came in from making the restaurant deliveries today," she said in a tone that promised an interesting story, "and there was Lilah, making her pie. I was surprised because, like you, Doreen, I didn't think she'd be able to enter the contest this year. But one step inside and I was sliding across the floor . . ."

Lilah's cheeks flamed. Lord have mercy! It was bad enough to have seen her kitchen floor in that condition herself, without having the whole county know about it.

Would you rather see somebody here come up with a Bible? You know there's a New Testament in Sally Blocker's purse. She always carries it.

Meri stood there behind her chair looking like a black-headed angel in that flowery dress she'd bought from Doreen, all relaxed and sure of herself, holding every scrap of attention in the room by confiding that Lilah had used her broken-wrist hand to hold the edge of the dough while the other held the rolling pin in the middle, then all the details about pieces of piecrust and spilled sugar and flour all over the floor, syrup dripping down the front of the stove . . .

Lilah held her breath, but thank goodness Meri remembered not to mention the rhubarb and she didn't give away that it was a mix of strawberries and raspberries, either. Other than that, she poured it all out . . . the whole nine yards.

Without making a big deal of it, she even mentioned crusts already in pie pans that weren't quite perfect enough. Then she wrapped it up.

"I am so inspired by my grandmother's determination and her Texas grit, that I honestly believe I will think about walking into that room every time that I want to give up or quit something. For the rest of my life."

The room erupted in applause that rocked the rafters. Durwood Easton hollered out, "That's our Miss Lilah," and Shuggie Landry called, while wiping tears, "Bless you, Lilah dear. God bless you."

In Lilah's opinion, who God needed to bless was her smart, beautiful, fast-on-her-feet granddaughter.

Doreen had the good sense to sit down then.

The applause went on and on while Gladys presented Lilah with the blue ribbon and the little ceramic rooster that meant she had something to crow about. She already had a whole flock of them at home, of course, but she was so happy to get this one that her hand shook a little when she took it.

Maybe this was a sign Doreen wouldn't get any closer to owning Honey Grove than she ever did to winning the pie contest.

Twenty-four

Lilah shifted the pie basket from her lap to the seat of the truck.

"Well," she said, "here we are."

She and Meri looked at each other and burst out laughing. Meri raised her hand for a high five.

"I thought we never would get rid of Shorty and Caleb," Lilah said. "They're the nosiest two I've seen in a long time."

It was the perfect opening, but Meri didn't say a word about what she and Caleb had talked about.

Still chuckling, she started the motor.

Lilah laid a hand on Meri's wrist as she took hold of the shift lever.

Meri looked at her. "What?"

"Meredith, you were wonderful. Fantastic. Not only did you save my bacon in there, but you made me proud. You knew *exactly* how to take control of the situation and you did it perfectly."

Such a look came into Meri's eyes that Lilah couldn't name all its facets, only the surprise and gratitude and joy.

The whole thing hit Lilah like a lightning bolt. Had nobody ever praised this child before?

Probably not very often. Definitely not the self-centered Edie Jo.

Oh, Lord. Forgive me again for neglecting her.

But joy was joy and to be savored when it came. No clouds from the past allowed.

Lilah leaned forward before she thought and gave Meri a one-armed hug. Meri actually hugged her back. With real sincerity.

Then she let go and shifted into reverse to back out. "I loved it," she said. "The whole evening. That was the most fun I've had since . . . well, since . . ."

"Since the snake in the tomato patch?"

Meri threw her a grin. "Somehow that didn't pop into my mind."

She glanced down at the little trophy, with his slight smile on his chicken beak, sitting amidst the syrupy crumbs in the pie plate between them. "Well? Was he worth it?"

"The sight of Doreen's face when you started talking was worth every inch of piecrust I rolled out with one hand."

They headed out of the big gravel parking lot.

"You and Doreen have always been rivals?"

"Yes. I reckon we've always been what the girls nowadays call 'frenemies.' She's always had a jealous bone when it came to me. Everything from Ed's first-grader's kiss on the playground to his marrying me to my having a daughter—and now a granddaughter—and her being childless. It never ends."

"But why does she want Honey Grove? She has her own business and that big house and a rich husband."

Lilah shrugged with both shoulders and it didn't hurt. Her wrist did, though. Her whole body ached to get out of the sling.

"Because I have it. Really, Doreen's to be pitied, in a way. Life has given her everything except what she wanted most—Ed for a husband and a houseful of children."

"Too bad she couldn't learn to want what she did have. It's sad."

"Exactly. Lawrence is nice as well as rich and he loves her. They have more money than they'll ever live long enough to spend, and she's built that dress shop into a moneymaking machine all by herself."

"What saved us," Meri said, "was that everybody knows she's jealous of you, so they didn't take her accusations seriously. I was holding my breath that nobody else would ask me directly whether I helped you."

"Well, basically all you *did* do on that pie was hold things for me to work with."

"And I protected you from Henry when he came sneaking back down the hall for another run at the syrup pan."

Lilah sighed. "Oh, Lord, every time I think about the mess he made, I don't even want to go home."

"I seem to remember that when I arrived, Henry was locked in the mudroom, yet the kitchen was already wrecked," Meri said dryly.

"Some gremlins had been there."

"Yeah, sure. That's what all the kitchen-wreckers say."

Lilah grabbed that moment and held it in her heart. It wasn't every day that she and Meri could tease and joke. But it wasn't just that. She'd never before heard real affection like this in her granddaughter's voice.

"Don't worry about the mess. I'm cleaning up," Meri said. "You're going straight to bed."

"No, I . . ."

"You *are*. I love to clean, it helps me sort things out and relaxes me, you know that. And I need a chance to think some things through and wind down or I won't be able to sleep at all."

"Caleb got you all wound up?"

Meri shot her a fast glance and even in the dim light of the dashboard, Lilah could see the fast blush on her face.

"Caleb and I are colleagues, working on a business plan. Nothing more."

All prim and proper. But not at all convincing.

Lilah had a sudden surge of hope. If any man could win Meri's trust it was Caleb. He was one of the rare men who liked women so much he took the trouble to try to understand them.

"What kind of a plan?'

"I'm really not free to say at this time," Meri said, still prim. "We'll both tell you about it soon."

Lilah turned to face her granddaughter fully. "I meant what I said about not taking money from you young people. Y'all quit worrying about me and get on with your lives."

Meri said, "Shhh. Not another word. He'd kill me if he knew I'd said this much to you. We want to get some details ironed out first."

Lilah stared at her but Meri wouldn't turn. She drove a little faster, staring out through the windshield at the dark road.

Meri changed the subject. "This town just blows my mind. When I was delivering the produce to Suzy's Cafe, Doreen came out of her shop to try and find out what kind of pie you were making. She'd already heard from the woman at the lunch counter in the Grab It 'n' Go that I'd confirmed you were going to enter, which happened about ten minutes before I got to the square."

"Of course. Charlene Polston. She's on the phone so much I can't believe Terry doesn't fire her."

"Right, Charlene. I don't know why I never can remember her name."

They fell into cozy conversation, a postmortem of the whole day, since Lilah hadn't yet heard how the deliveries and new orders went, and soon they were home, driving down the familiar driveway at Honey Grove. Lilah sat slumped in her seat, realizing at last how beyond tired to the bone she really was, yet still excited by her victory.

"I owe you, Meri. You did a masterful job. Perfect."

"Glad to be of service," Meri said as she drove the truck into its usual spot.

"I couldn't think of a single thing to do and you saved me."

You should quit bossing her so much and trust her judgment more.

It was true. Meri had proved she knew a thing or two about people. She was learning a lot about the farm, too—of course, Lilah would have to keep an eye on *those* decisions—but she needed to back off and let Meri see what she could do. Let her find her own strength. She was going to need it even more when she started building her new life.

She was a grown woman, smart and hardworking, and quick on her feet. She could, and should, make some of the daily decisions.

Lilah could stand aside and let her do that. No problem. No problem at all.

Twenty-five

As it turned out, "no problem" lasted for twenty-four hours. Well, to be absolutely accurate and picky about it, *almost* twenty-four hours.

Which was sad, because she'd done so well, right at first. Last night Lilah'd had no trouble giving Meri free rein to clean up the kitchen and put things where she wanted them.

This morning, she'd stayed out of it when Meri completely rearranged the order of the deliveries. And again when they checked the orchard and Lilah pronounced the Firegolds (her most profitable variety of peaches and, she had to admit, the main reason her peach pies were so good) to be a bumper crop needing to come off in the next couple of days. She had not said one word when Meri called Jimmy, right then and there, and sent him for more peck and half-peck baskets.

And she'd rearranged Lilah's riding lessons schedule to meet with Meri and Caleb so they could tell Lilah all about this new plan of theirs that would not only save Honey Grove but would help it become a thriving business on its own. She'd tried to tell them they were too young to know how fast a bubble of plans could be punctured by reality.

But now, in the late afternoon, when Meri stepped out the door onto the back porch all damp-haired and shower-scrubbed yet dressed in fresh work clothes, Lilah started bossing her to a fare-thee-well, even though she did it in a sweet tone. She wanted some more moments like those last night when they'd felt close to one another.

"Now, Meri, honey. We can haul those baskets up to the orchard in the morning. Don't get all hot and sweaty after you've had your shower."

She scooted over in the swing. "Come over here and sit awhile. You not only cleaned the kitchen 'til after midnight, you've run your legs off all day."

Lilah felt lonely, as if her victory last night was a hollow one because she was in the process of losing the biggest battle of her life. A bit of unhurried companionship would be so nice.

But Meri wasn't interested. "It's okay, Lilah. I'm not tired."

"Those baskets need to be in the barn. If a storm does come tonight, like they're predicting, a high wind'd blow them straight to kingdom come."

"I already tied them down on the trailer. I'll back it under the shed up there."

"Hmph."

She's a step ahead of you. Stick to your vow and let her do things her way.

Meri let the screen swing shut and crossed the porch to the top of the steps.

"If there's unsalvageable produce after the storm, could Caleb and I take it?"

Lilah whipped around to look at her.

"Well," she huffed, "there's nothing like assuming the worst will happen."

Meri looked back with a slow, little grin. "If the baskets blow away, the fruit will be damaged, too, right?"

Lilah sighed.

"We'll pay you for it, of course."

"You two have no idea what you've gotten into," Lilah said, "and it just makes me crazy to think y'all could lose every cent of the money you have to start out in life, and all because of trying to save Honey Grove."

She turned and looked off into the distance, into the black clouds starting to gather in the southwest sky *and* the ones in her heart.

"I've forced myself to try to imagine it," she said. "I *can* live somewhere else. I won't be happy but I won't let myself die of homesickness. I'll find something else to fill my time. There's lot of people who need my help. I'll keep busy."

Every word out of her mouth made her sicker.

Meri narrowed her eyes. "Are you saying you're giving up? So was all that stuff from the podium last night about being a rough, tough Texan nothing but a brag?"

Lilah felt her cheeks redden.

"I'm not giving up yet, but I'm about at the end of my rope. The most I can get from selling the horses that belong to me and every antique I've inherited and my tractor, too, don't add up to anywhere near seventy-five thousand. I've put out feelers about leasing that strip of land along the highway for commercial development, but it'd be too late by the time we got the zoning change, *if* we could get it."

She bit off the torrent of words and took a deep breath.

"Plus Shorty's right," Meri said. "You can't farm without a tractor."

Lilah nodded sadly. "I just can't raise enough money. I've waited too late in the game, even if there *was* some way I could do it without putting myself out of business."

"With all due respect, that's not true. You could say yes to an investment in me and Caleb. You could help us succeed. It's not just *us* investing in *you*."

"Ha. Whoever heard of an investor being *paid* seventy-five thousand dollars the day the deal was made, instead of putting money in?"

Meri shook her head. "Is that all you've got? We went

over and over this with Caleb today. You'd be putting in the
reputation and the name of Honey Grove. And the produce.
And the priceless connections you have to markets all over
Texas and beyond."

"It'd take tons of produce to make all our investments
equal."

"We're not getting anywhere here," Meri said, moving
on. "You can take a couple of days to make up your mind."

Oh. So now she was making decisions for Lilah as well
as for herself.

"It'd be charity."

Meri waved that away as she ran down the steps, in such
a hurry to get away she couldn't even stand still to talk for
another minute.

She called back over her shoulder, "Don't worry if I'm
gone for a while—I need some time alone to think."

"Well, don't overdo yourself thinking about that business."

Meri stopped in her tracks. She looked up at Lilah from
the ground, and Lilah thought of Edie Jo's painting of her
and the little girl Meri.

"It'll save Honey Grove," Meri said. "Imagine again
where you'll live if you lose it."

That made Lilah's stomach clutch even harder.

She and Cale are only trying to help you, Lilah.

"Just *think* of all the equipment and space and help a
business like that would call for. I can't contribute a penny
to that."

"In this recession, all of those things are cheaper. You
just keep concentrating on growing the best produce in
Texas and keeping your customers happy, and Caleb and
I will do the rest."

Lilah looked at the earnest hope in Meri's eyes.

"Honey, you'll be going away soon. You said it yourself.
You need a big life in a big city, big dollars and big chal-
lenges. And now you won't even have your 401(k) money
anymore and you'll have to hire somebody to take your
place and help Caleb."

She wanted, with everything in her, to save Honey Grove. Of course. It was her home *and* her heart. But if she did so at the expense of Meri's and Caleb's futures, the rest of her life would be a misery.

"This idea fills a definite niche in the world of agriculture," Meri said, "and someday it will be making big money. Don't think too long or we'll have to go with some other farm. Honey Grove Kitchens doesn't *have* to be the company name."

She jogged off, then, headed for the overhang where the ATV was parked. Now that she looked for it, Lilah could see its little trailer, loaded and efficiently tied down.

Meri yelled back over her shoulder, "I'll bet *Doreen*'ll go for the idea if *she* buys Honey Grove."

Impudent little jade. Lilah couldn't restrain a grin, even if the remark *did* go through her like a knife.

Then Meri slowed and turned around, walking backward while she hollered at Lilah again, "You know I'm just kidding, right? Can we have the crop if something happens?"

Lilah made a motion for her to go on, but she smiled, too. Meri was giving every sign that she intended to fight for this idea to her last breath. So that meant it might work. Didn't it? One of the truths Lilah had learned in her life was that *heart* was the determining factor in most struggles.

Meri ran the rest of the way to the ATV, mostly running from the sound of her own voice. How could she have been so cruel, taunting her grandmother about Doreen like that? Lilah's hesitation was all sincere concern for her and Caleb and their financial futures.

But challenge was a good tactic to use on Lilah.

Meri had to admit, though, that it hadn't been a planned tactic, it just happened. *You're losing control of your tongue, Mer, as well as your feelings.*

She sighed as she climbed into the driver's seat, turned the key, stepped on the accelerator and shot forward too fast, the trailer bumping and rattling behind her over the uneven ground.

More careless behavior.

Plus what are you doing begging to start a business here? That's only going to add dozens more entanglements to hold you here.

But she couldn't seem to make herself slow down. Last night, while she was scrubbing the kitchen floor and reliving the pie-contest victory, the whole truth had opened up in her mind: Honey Grove, Rock Springs, this entire community was pulling her into it, like a spider into that huge web she'd seen between the open barn door and the wall.

She was becoming much too interested in the minutiae of small-town life. She was even having fun with it! Insane. Some part of her had sensed it after the pie contest when she'd felt so relaxed and easy in the VFW Hall surrounded by all the congratulating, laughing, Rock County citizens. They'd teased and talked to her with such easy affection, as if now she was one of them.

She had to be careful. Definitely, she was getting pulled in.

Honestly, the entire evening had felt *normal* to her. That was the scariest fact of all.

She had to be careful. She had a plan for her life and this wasn't it.

But how could she leave right now? She couldn't, not with Lilah about to lose Honey Grove.

And besides that, damn it, Meri *hated* to lose a fight. She hadn't let poverty and despair win when Edie Jo left her. She'd lost only three courtroom battles in her career.

Then Alan had won a political battle that she didn't even know she was fighting and she'd quit that career. So, by damn, she was *not* going to let Buford Quisenberry take Honey Grove and sell it to Doreen.

Foolish vow. Lilah could be an immovable object.

Alan's machinations had made her feel like a failure. But now she knew she could learn enough fast enough to farm Honey Grove and she knew she and Caleb could make her idea work.

The thought stopped her. She could feel her power coming back and that had something to do with Caleb. She didn't want to look at that fact too closely right now, but it was true. They were learning to get along—really, they were beginning to like each other while working together. That experience of dancing with him had given her (in some weird, inexplicable way) the courage to stand up and make that statement in Lilah's defense, which she knew well was the same as jumping into the intricacies of life in Rock Springs with both feet.

Now she knew she could *never* abandon her grandmother while she was in trouble.

The road to the orchard was nothing but a gravel trail running between two pastures and leading up a long, sloping hill. It was rough but she didn't slow the ATV. The baskets wouldn't fall off, they were tied down.

Being in the orchard would calm her. She loved it up there.

And she loved knowing that orchards needed to be on a high elevation compared to the surrounding area so that during spring frost, the cold air would have easy movement out of the trees. On frosty mornings, Lilah had taught her, temperatures might fluctuate as much as ten degrees from hilltop to the low areas. Too many hours in frosty air killed many crops every year.

Meri felt like an insider, knowing facts like that. She felt like a real farmer. She could be good at this.

The evening was cooler than usual with a breeze from the southwest that grew stronger as she climbed the hill. That was another thing—she'd learned to orient herself to the four directions so she could watch the sky for weather changes. Weather was a huge factor in farming. Most of the storms and rains came from the southwest.

At the top of the hill, she slowed to drive carefully down the aisles between the straight rows of trees, their limbs hanging heavy with gorgeous, red-blushed yellow peaches. Lilah didn't believe in mechanical pickers, so her trees were only seven or eight feet tall. The reason being that, from that height the weight of the fruit could bend the highest branches down to have their peaches picked by hand.

Meri felt her tension slipping away. This was her very favorite place on the entire farm.

The peach trees' narrow leaves were so waxy they caught the light here and there along their dark-green lengths. In some places, they shut out the sun and in others they let it in to glow on the yellow globes of the peaches. Those were a patchwork of the same colors as the quilt on her bed. The first Meredith Kathleen had made it by hand and somehow, when Meri pulled it over her at night, it felt like a hug from her great-grandmother.

Meri sat in the middle of the orchard and turned off the ATV so she could listen to the leaves rustling in the rising wind. Peace in the trees. Mystery on the wind.

You're not just tangled in the community. You're beginning to be tied to this land, too, Meredith Kathleen. Don't. If Lilah doesn't agree, you'll lose it. And you will leave here anyway. You have a plan.

She pushed her thoughts away. She, who was always thinking, always moving, always in a hurry, must've sat there for five minutes just looking and listening and feeling the breeze on her skin. She picked a peach and took a bite of it, groaning with pleasure at the impossibly wonderful taste *and* the fact that juice immediately started running down her chin. She had no tissues, so she wiped at it with her hand, then tried to clean the stickiness off it on her clean overalls.

Deep down, though, strangely enough, she didn't even care. Overhead, a cloud drifted past and blotted out the sun entirely. The gloom was nice, too.

"Hello the orchard! Meri, are you there?"

Her fingers froze on the peach. Caleb. *Darn*. She hadn't even *started* thinking about the business yet. What was he doing here, anyway?

But her heart betrayed her mind with a little thump of excitement.

Oh no, he'll see me with juice all over my face.

He appeared at the end of the row in a faded blue tee shirt and a pale straw hat that shone bright in the dusky orchard.

Then the cloud moved away and the sunlight caught one side of his face as he walked through the line of trees.

She couldn't take her eyes away. Honestly, he was far more handsome than any man had a right to be.

"Had a right to be" was one of Shorty's expressions. Now she was thinking in Tex-speak, no less. Even the language was entangling her.

"Sorry to disturb you," he called, coming closer.

Reading her mind again.

He flashed his mischievous grin. "Not really. You look great with your hair all messed up in the wind."

She didn't like the way he caused her pulse to race, so she used sarcasm for defense. "Thanks so much."

Then he was right there, close enough to touch, complete with his teasing smile.

"But then," he drawled, "you always look good in your farmer's overalls and sneakers. Come to think of it, you remind me of my grandpa. Except he always wore Red Wings."

She glared. "And thank you so much for *that* flattering comparison."

Then, she couldn't resist his smile. "On second thought, maybe it *is* flattering," she heard herself say. "If he had red wings, he must've been an angel."

"Red Wings are *boots*, city girl."

He threw one long leg into the ATV and helped himself to the passenger's seat. "But it's a compliment, all right. Ol' Gramps was no slouch."

He turned to her, pushed his hat back on his head, settled in and leaned closer to confide, "He was skinny, too. But you're a whole lot prettier in the face."

Meri rolled her eyes. "Now I know why you're still single."

Delighted with that reaction, he grinned.

"How about a bite of your peach?"

He didn't wait for permission. He clasped his hand over hers and took a big bite. His lips, soft and warm, touched her fingers and sent a rippling thrill into her blood.

"Ummm, *ummm!*" He straightened up and twinkled at her as he chewed. "State fair, blue ribbon, here we come."

He'd be cute if he weren't so dangerous.

Meri said, "They *have* to start coming off tomorrow. I only hope all our pickers show up."

"Think positive," he said. "Did you know you've got peach juice all over your chin?"

He arched in the seat, causing his shoulder to brush hers with a quick, hot shock, and stuck two fingers into the back pocket of his tight jeans to pull out a bandanna.

"Here, Mer, let me."

Before she could move, he was dabbing at her face with the soft, worn cloth.

Too close. He was way too close. His mouth was way too close.

She pulled back.

He did, too, his eyes sparking into hers for an instant before they flicked to the wheel. The smile teased the corners of his mouth, too. His full, luscious, hot mouth.

And he hadn't made her feel like an idiot for jerking away from him like that. She felt so off balance she couldn't even think.

"Want me to drive?" he said.

She couldn't look away. She couldn't keep from smiling back. It must be true, all that gossip about how irresistible he was to women.

Thank goodness, in Meri's case, that irresistibility went only as far as the smile.

"Why do you ask? I can drive. I drove up here."

He shrugged. "I dunno. It just feels natural to me that the man oughtta be in the driver's seat."

Her jaw dropped. "Give me a break! Even you cannot be that much of a Neanderthal!"

He laughed. "You scared I might grab you by the hair and drag you into my cave?"

Damn. There was just enough of the blue color left in his shirt to make his eyes brighter.

"Which, come to think of it," he drawled, "might not be such a bad idea."

Meri had forgotten what they were talking about.

His fingertips feathered across her cheek as he brushed back a strand of her hair. His eyes, so impossibly blue, wouldn't let hers look away.

Why had she never learned to flirt? Why couldn't she breathe? This was insane. She felt like a high-school girl. No, more like middle school. A high-school girl would know what to do.

What to do? Stay away from him, of course. Any female of any age can see that he is trouble.

But Tim had never elicited a reaction like this from her body, no matter what he'd done. This was a revelation to her.

She drew in a deep, ragged breath. "I . . . uh . . ." She had to work to find some words, then to make her voice keep functioning. It didn't.

He took pity on her.

"Eat your peach," he said, reaching up to pick another one from the tree. "We have to be thorough about quality assurance if we're gonna peddle these big beauties."

So they sat there and companionably ate peaches while she tried to slow her heartbeat. The delicious fragrance and wonderful taste of the big Firegold was the only thing really penetrating the fog in her brain. Juice dripped into her hand and stuck to her lips but she didn't even care. She hardly noticed.

Caleb sat beside her, quietly filling up the ATV, just *being* there with her in her favorite place. No rush, no hurry, no problem.

But the tension between them wasn't gone. She could feel it.

Caleb took a big bite, juice ran down his chin, and he wiped it on the shoulder of his shirt. "Forget the hanky, this is how you do it," he said. "Watermelon, too. Never eat either one in your good clothes, and watch out 'cause the flies and the yellow jackets might get after you."

He looked so much like an earnest, unapologetic little boy offering advice that she had to laugh.

"And don't worry if you hurt your lips on those overall straps. I'll kiss the hurt away."

Her heart gave a hard beat.

He held her gaze with his. She felt color rising in her cheeks and his eyes said he saw it.

Meri, you have to get some control here.

She took another bite of peach, trying frantically to think of a reply that wouldn't encourage him yet wouldn't make her sound like a complete dork. Nothing came to her and finally the silence had gone on too long.

Now she *did* look like a dork. How could she be twenty-seven years old and so inept? She just wasn't used to men flirting with her. At least not men who were attractive to her.

He finished his half of the peach, spit the stone into his bandanna and offered it for hers. She did the same, then she put both sticky hands on the wheel.

"Miss Lilah thought you might want me to back the trailer into the shed for you," he said, in a tone so low and intimate it could've been something like, "you might want me to take you to bed."

His eyes said exactly that. Or was she imagining things? Hard for her to judge. Something about her manner usually prevented men from coming on to her.

She was losing her mind.

Caleb went on in that same persuasive tone. "No offense, Mer, but that shed's not very deep and it'd be easy to ram the trailer right through the sheet metal on the back of it. If you weren't used to judging the depth, that is."

Meri had no idea what he'd just said. She was exploring his face with her eyes. A slant of sunlight highlighted every rugged inch of it.

He lifted his hands, palms up. "Now, don't blame me for being all politically incorrect or something. It was all Miss Lilah's idea."

She didn't know why, but a shard of disappointment stabbed her. "Oh. So she sent you to find me."

Finally, she managed to draw in a deep breath. It smelled like Caleb's sweat and peaches.

"After I asked where you were. What's the matter, Mer? You think I can't figure out on my own that we need to be together?"

Where had she read that a woman, from primeval times, chooses a man based on the smell of his sweat?

Again, a breath caught deep in her chest and couldn't get out.

"Of course we do," she said, frantically wracking her brain for something that made sense. "Did the extension office have those numbers on the unharvested produce?"

His eyes were suddenly serious. She couldn't break the look between them. She couldn't even try very hard.

He shook his head gently. "I'm not talkin' bidness," he said, in his best drawl. "And I'm thinkin' you know that, Meri."

Oh. What had she gotten into, going into "bidness" with him?

Meredith Briscoe! Where is your famous determination?

She turned the key and the motor fired. She tore her gaze from his and fixed it straight ahead as she stabbed her foot down on the accelerator. They roared off so fast, the speed slammed them back in their seats.

"Hey," he yelled over the sound of the motor, "that's clear proof I'm the one oughtta drive."

A clap of thunder sounded, sudden and infinitely more powerful than the noises on the ground.

"No way," she yelled back. "Just hang on to the grab bar. And you're not gonna park it, either."

He flashed her a glance so full of exasperation that she laughed.

"I walked all the way up here to help you out," he shouted, pretending hurt feelings.

"Lilah had no right to send you. I told her I needed time to myself."

"Don't blame her. I jumped at the chance."

She looked around, eyebrows raised. "You're changing your story? Now?"

"No. Her idea about parking the trailer. Me happy to oblige. Both of us hoping to prevent property damage."

She stared through the windshield again, ignoring him, but she could feel his gaze steady on the side of her face.

She rolled her eyes. But she could see why so many women fell for his apparent sincerity.

Meri held her gaze forward and whipped the vehicle around a tree. Too fast for the trailer. It whipped back and forth and Caleb yelled. She lifted her foot from the accelerator.

Meredith! Get control!

"I didn't want you to come up here."

"Oh, yes you did," he said easily. "Don't start lyin' to me now," he drawled. "Really, Meri, I can't go into business with a partner who'll do that."

She could also understand how a woman could be driven to shoot him.

She roared up to the three-sided shed at the end of the orchard, pulled around in a half circle to back the trailer into it and slammed the ATV in reverse.

But she *did* do it slowly. She *was* in control now.

"Take it slow," Caleb said, as if she hadn't even thought of that.

He leaned close to her on the pretext of watching the trailer's path backward. "Easy now," he murmured in her ear, "take it easy. Slow, *slow*. Hold 'er straight now . . ."

"Shut *up*! I can *do* this."

The end of the trailer hit the metal wall with a clash and a clatter. Meri braked, hard.

"Whoa," he said. "That's good, you got it."

"'I already stopped!"

He made a big drama out of jumping out and inspecting the damage.

"Far as I can see, you didn't break the sheet metal. Just bent it some."

Meri made a growling retort, incoherent even to her.

Thunder began again and wouldn't stop. Far, far in the distance, it spoke in a low, slow grumble that went on and on until it rolled off into infinity.

"All *ri-ight*," he said, "we got those baskets under cover just in time."

"We?"

He ignored that, came around and pulled her out of her seat.

"C'mon, gotta go," he said. "Lilah always says that kind of thunder means an overflow. Let's head for the house."

He was a force of nature. Before she could extricate herself on her own, he had her hand folded into his big one and was pulling her through the orchard at a jog. They headed downhill on the little gravel trail.

His hand was huge. Rough. Warm. Callused.

And, to be utterly honest, entirely impersonal. Disappointingly so.

Note to self: Do not get romantically involved with this man. No matter the smell of his sweat. The entanglements with Lilah and the community that you've been worrying about pale in comparison to the pull he could have on you.

Remember, Meredith Kathleen, you have a plan.

But, still, she needed to hear the sound of his voice.

"What does that mean, 'overflow'?"

"Just what it says. Enough rain to make the creeks and rivers overflow."

"We don't have time to deal with a flood. We *have* to start picking those peaches in the morning."

"Don't fret. That thunder is miles and miles away from here."

Huge drops of rain pelted them then, so quick and cold hitting their hot skins that it made them gasp. Meri squealed like a little girl, Caleb ripped off his hat and slapped it onto her head, and they ran, laughing, toward the house, the slick soles of his boots slipping on the wet gravel. His limp slowed them a little, too, or she'd never have been able to keep up with him.

At the bottom of the orchard trail, they paused for

breath, but only for a moment because the big drops were changing into small ones falling in sheets that soaked them through in a heartbeat. Meri would never have thought she could run that far, but they didn't stop again until they dashed up the steps onto the back porch.

Shelter. At last. They stopped instantly in this new world where the rain drummed down on the metal roof instead of on them, grinning at each other as if they'd won a marathon. Caleb let go of her hand.

Their breathing slowed and the grins faded but the look in his eyes held her motionless. She shivered in the cool breeze and couldn't stop.

"Come here," he said.

Meri stepped forward into his arms as if she had no choice and he held her as if there were no consequences.

They stood silent in the rattle of the storm, her cheek against his wet chest. When his hat slipped off her hair he caught it, put it on his own head and his arm around her again, all in one fluid motion.

She didn't even try to think. His heart sounded strong and sure deep inside his body. Every beat it made drove more of the shivering out of her bones. Never, in her entire life, had she felt so warmed. She wanted . . .

Meri, get a grip.

She pulled back, but her arms wouldn't let go of him. His eyes dared her to stay where she was. Her gaze went to his mouth.

He tipped her chin up with one hand, then higher, and bent to take her mouth with his hot one, tilting his head so the hat brim wouldn't get in the way.

She was gone.

Out of herself. Out of the world she'd always known. Out of time.

She opened her lips to him and tasted peach on his tongue, the sweet shock of it destroying her fears. A new shiver ran through her and she twined her tongue with his.

His lips melted all the strength from her body.

He was drawing the very life out of her and pouring it

back again. His arms around her never moved. That steadiness felt precious to her.

She kissed him back. Caleb's scent, mixed now with rain and wet dirt, was more seductive than the sweet peaches. It permeated her entire body on one quick, desperate intake of breath.

Caleb.

His mouth was a warm heaven. She couldn't leave it. At her core, she was coming apart and coming together at the same time, melting into a new woman who wasn't afraid.

But you have to take care. You can't let your guard down like this. You'll want more and more. You'll want him.

Too late. I already do.

But he has dozens of women.

That thought brought the old, iron fears surging back. Everybody always left her, starting with her unknown father and going all the way to Tim.

But she defied the terrors and let her hot, hungry self stay with Caleb one more moment, pressing against his hard body, holding on with her arms wrapped around his hardmuscled back as if he were a rock to cling to in a storm.

Get control, Meri. You can't depend on anyone but yourself.

Even though she was scared by the basic truth she lived by, it took all the strength she could summon to tear her mouth from his. Her lips felt bruised and raw and wonderfully kissed.

Caleb pulled back and looked at her.

He didn't try to kiss her again.

He let her go when she moved to step back.

The new, visceral Meri dropped into an abyss of disappointment. She could hardly talk. She couldn't move any farther away from him.

"Oh," she said. "Oh, Caleb, I . . ."

She could hardly breathe, either.

He waited, looking into her eyes, just the trace of a smile on his lips.

"I just . . . don't think we should do this again."

Sensual Meri screamed in protest. She wanted to feel his arms around her. She *needed* that.

"You didn't like it?"

She wanted another kiss so much her very bones ached.

"No. *Yes*. And that's why I'm saying it's never a good idea to mix business and personal lives. Everybody knows that."

He twinkled, damn it. "They do?"

He smiled and she melted again. That was the reason she had to stand firm.

"I just think . . . it's always a mistake to mix personal lives with business. Let's remember that."

Caleb cocked his head. "Okay by me," he said cheerfully. "Long as we don't let it influence us too much."

Damn. His devil grin was playing at the corners of his mouth and his eyes were shining their brightest blue.

"We have to let it *rule*," she said. "Everything depends on our succeeding with the Kitchens."

Meri ripped her gaze free. She looked back across the yard at the orchard path.

Her brain was nowhere. He didn't answer and she had to change the subject. She said something totally inane.

"Look. It's still raining like crazy but the sun's shining."

"Means it'll rain again this time tomorrow."

She turned to look at him again.

He gave her a straight—and solemn—look. Then the smile again. Oh, yes. His favorite weapon.

But he didn't fight.

"See ya then, pard. We'll have plenty to salvage if the storm predictions hold up."

He picked up his hat, slapped it on his head and clattered down the steps, dashing through the rain for his truck with that hint of a cowboy swagger that was a natural element of the way he moved, despite his limp. Did he always get everything he wanted?

Well, this time he wouldn't. If he wanted to add her to the notches already on his belt. Or whatever that expression was.

She staggered to the swing and dropped into it.

She was glad he was going. She'd needed him to go.

But she couldn't stop watching as he ran to his big pickup and got in. It rumbled to life. He turned it around in the driveway but before he headed out, he rolled the window down and lifted one hand to her in farewell, that laconic gesture Texas drivers used when they met each other on the road.

Nothing personal about it.

Which was what she wanted. What she'd told him.

Yet he'd said that they should ignore the rule.

Which did he intend to do?

She felt shaky all over again, but not only from the breeze on her wet clothes. She was so hot and it was so humid now she wouldn't be surprised if steam came off her body yet she was shivering.

Which did *she* intend to do?

Twenty-six

Lilah drifted toward consciousness to the sound of hail, but in her dream—she and Ed were on their first real date, feeling free and young, driving way too fast down River Road—the noise was gravel, slamming his beat-up old truck half to pieces. Then she woke completely and the truth stabbed her like an ice pick to the heart.

Dear God in heaven, that was *hail*.

And the Firegolds ripe and ready to harvest!

Same for a good stand of okra and the patch of crookneck squash, but they were nothing compared to her big cash crop.

She sat up with a jerk, her heart racing from fear now instead of the fast ride with the handsome boy she loved.

Oh, Ed. If only you were here to help me now.

It was too much. A heartsick feeling washed through her and sucked every scrap of strength right out of her body.

A sinking feeling of being pulled into that Honey Grove Kitchens business before she'd even had a chance to think it all through.

Hailstones peppered the window.

"Lilah! Lilah, wake up, it's hailing outside!"

Meri's bare feet pounded to Lilah's door. She knocked, then opened it before Lilah could respond.

"We can have the salvage, right?" she said, making it the barest of a question at the end as she stepped into the room with her phone in her hand. "Lilah, this may not be such a disaster after all!"

She was half-turned to go but she waited for an answer.

How could Lilah tell her no? She was so excited and ready to prove her idea was good. She was so invested in that idea that her future was riding on it.

But . . . it'd be a worse gamble if she spent seventy-five thousand dollars to save Lilah's skin.

"We'll pay you for it," Meri said, speaking rapidly, itching to be on her way. "You're not committing to a partnership or anything like that. Let's just think about one day at a time."

Lilah nodded. "All right. Just this once. To let y'all test your plans."

"Thanks!" Meri ran.

By the time Lilah got to the kitchen, her granddaughter was outside, holding on to a post of the porch railing as the hail hit and bounced in the yard.

Lord have mercy, the child *still* was wearing nothing but that little black scrap of silk and lace that she called a nightie! In spite of all her worries, Lilah had to smile. Meri's fancy lingerie was such a perfect contrast to her daytime uniform that Doreen ordered for her from somewhere, stylishly cut Meri-the-New-Farmer overalls.

God help the child, she was falling in love with the farming life.

One look at her out there on the porch, with the wind whipping her hair around her worried face, proved that. Though she still occasionally mentioned her plans to move to a city and build the lawyer career she'd always wanted, it didn't seem that Meri was pursuing that idea too actively.

That was another reason Lilah thought her starting that business was a huge mistake. But there wasn't one thing she could about it. She couldn't even take care of her *own* business.

Lightning flashed far away in a dark cloud behind the persimmon tree, bending over now in a swaying arc. Meri gave no sign she noticed.

Watching her granddaughter through the screen, Lilah had a flash of that beautiful face in ruins the night Meri came back from New York. If Meri sank that far into despair again, it'd be Lilah's doing.

Oh, Lord. Why did I let her stay here and fall in love with this place? She's had enough loss in her life.

No matter how heartsick and scared Lilah felt, what she had to do now was buck up and show Meri what this family's women were made of. Show her some courage.

Hope was all anybody ever had that really counted.

Lilah said a quick prayer, reached for her strong voice and pushed open the screen. The wind slapped her gown-tail around her legs so hard it nearly tripped her. The sun broke out of the clouds, but the hail kept on clattering on the roof.

"Meredith Kathleen, you get in here this minute. You'll catch your death out there in nothing but your birthday suit."

Meri startled and whirled around, blinking as if coming back to consciousness. "I'm going up there."

She headed for the door and Lilah stepped out to hold it open. "Right now, let's get dressed," she said in a soothing tone while her stomach tied itself into an even tighter knot at the image of the orchard full of hail-pocked peaches. "The hail never lasts long."

"Do you think it's hailing on the orchard, too?"

"Hard to say. Lots of times hail is really spotty."

Meri rushed into the house as if the wind blew her, went straight to the mudroom and grabbed her bright-flowered plastic boots off the rack as Lilah followed her in. She'd better stop using that credit card for overalls and pretty boots if she was serious about starting that business.

"Oh, honey. Not yet. Please don't go out yet. Didn't you see that lightning?"

"But, Lilah, you said it won't last long and the sun's come out already."

She started hopping on one foot, trying to get the other into the boot. "I'll call you from the orchard," she said. "I'm so torn. I hate for those beautiful peaches to be damaged but it'd be great to have our first project and see how we do. Our help's all temporary, of course, and I've got my fingers crossed they're not working somewhere else today."

Meri rattled on without taking a breath until she had to concentrate on getting her bare foot into the boot.

"Damaged produce has to be processed within six to eight hours," she said, still struggling.

"Meri, calm down. If you'd stop rushing around like your hair was on fire and go find some socks, that boot'd go on a lot easier."

"Six to eight hours isn't very long. Figuratively, Lilah, my hair *is* on fire."

As soon as Meri had both boots on, she snatched an old yellow slicker off the wall hook.

"You'll burn smooth up in that thing," Lilah said. "Slow down. What damage there is is done. And the temperature'll rise faster than steam off the hail. Go put some clothes on."

"I'll call you from the orchard. If there *is* damage, I'll try to estimate how many pickers. I'm so glad I thought of renting Raul's kitchen."

"You did *what*?"

"He's renovating the dining area. And closed on Tuesdays. When he opens again, we can use it only after closing time. We'll get something permanent soon and in the meantime, this is on a needs-only basis, so it's not a constant expense."

Lilah's stomach turned over. That whole business thing had gone too far for her to stop it now. And here she was getting pulled in.

Meri rushed into the kitchen, as fast as anyone could rush in the clompy boots and a flapping slicker, to grab her cell phone. With the other hand, she dumped the apples and bananas out onto the table and slipped her arm through the basket's handle.

"I'll bring back samples," she said and was out the door before Lilah could blink.

She watched her take-charge granddaughter slipping on hailstones and kicking them out of the way, doing that thing called texting—*of course*—with the phone in her hand, while she ran toward the orchard trail. Too bad she'd left the ATV up there last night.

The churning in Lilah's stomach got worse. She tried to calm it with a long, weary sigh as she headed to her room to get dressed. She had to stop this madness, and a nightgown was no kind of armor against a runaway freight train wearing a silk teddy.

The whole time she was throwing on whatever clothes she could manage without hurting her aching, nearly healed wrist, her brain was going ninety miles an hour. In circles.

Only the Good Lord knew what she could do to replace the lost income from this crop. Those kids couldn't pay her even half that for the damaged fruit. Just think of all the containers and hired help they'd have to pay for to save it.

By the time Lilah got back to the kitchen, Dallas and Denton were there making coffee, ready to work, chattering and carrying on so much that she could hardly think at all, much less make a plan. Then, before she could get the cinnamon toast (made from frozen slices of her homemade honey-wheat bread) out of the oven, Meri was clomping up the steps and Caleb was right behind her, with his white one-ton dually waiting at the end of the walk.

Ready to haul produce, evidently. Lilah's heart sank further. Just *think* of all the sweat and money and worry and thought that he and Meri would have to put in. And it was Lilah's poor management of Honey Grove that had even made them think of such an idea.

Pretty soon, the kitchen was filled with cinnamon smells and chatter and the smell of battered peaches. Meri brought the little basket back full of samples to the table and nearly every peach was pocked and torn.

"Oh, is that what you've got in that basket?" Caleb said.

She threw her hair back and squinted at him, a sharp look that mixed irritation and surprise.

"What did you think it was? You saw me crossing the driveway."

"Yeah, but your slicker was blowing open, so I didn't see the basket."

That delighted the Fremont kids and made Meri turn red.

The girl was pouring sweat, constantly pulling the slicker away from her skin to give it some air. But did she go shower and put on some clothes?

No, she did not. She grinned at her tormentors and stayed right there, sweating and suffering, talking to Caleb—who kept sneaking more glances at the scrap of black lace that showed in the low, open neck of the slicker (just one more danger for them both that Lilah felt responsible for)—about plans, and telling Dallas and Denton what to do when they got to Raul's kitchen, for so long that Lilah almost couldn't stand it.

But it was too late now. And if she hadn't let them have her damaged fruit, they'd have bought some from some other farm.

Meri was making lists on Lilah's grocery notepad as fast as she could write, still fanning herself with the slicker, and, when Caleb wasn't watching her, he was punching all the buttons on his fancy phone so fast his fingers blurred. Both of them were talking at the same time, happy and excited as kids on Christmas morning.

Caleb sent the kids to the orchard and took Meri out onto the porch to talk some more. Before they went, Meri asked Lilah to write out her peach preserves recipe with detailed directions. She said she wanted Lilah to oversee the process as the kitchen crew carried it out.

They were into it now. All of them. Here was another business to try to keep afloat, as if the farm wasn't enough.

And there wasn't a blessed thing she could do about it.

Lilah sank into the chair beside her and propped her arms on the table so she wouldn't collapse.

Twenty-seven

"It's temporary," Lilah said to Dulcie, "a one-time deal. I'm just humoring Cale and Meri because it breaks my heart to waste the best Firegolds I've ever had."

Dulcie threw her a wry glance and drove a little faster down the highway.

"You know what your problem is, Lilah? One of them, I mean?"

The tone of the question was light, so Lilah let out a little sigh of relief. She was so tired of Dulcie's gentle pushing her toward partnering with Caleb and Meri that she could scream.

"No, but I'm sure I can depend on you to tell me."

"You've never learned how to be gracious about accepting help from other people. You knock yourself out to *give* help but you've lived all these many years without learning how to accept it."

Well. Forget the relief. This was just another verse to the same old song. Lilah gave her old friend a hard stare.

It didn't faze Dulcie in the least. She just went back to

looking at the road. "All of us human beings need help now and then. It's your turn, Lilah."

"I may need help but I don't need charity."

"You need an injection of common sense. With or without you, Caleb and Meri are in business now. Period. Nothing you can do about that."

Lilah's guilt pricked her again. "I know. And they never would've risked all their money if it hadn't been for me and that infernal loan from Buford. It's all my fault."

"Their decision. You can't control one other person, much less two."

"I *know* that. I learned it with Edie Jo. But now . . ."

"But now you're desperate and your need for control is through the roof."

Lilah crossed her arms and glared out through the windshield at the rapidly passing scenery. "I don't . . ." She bit her tongue. "All right, maybe I am turned that way, but I have to be the boss of my own business . . ."

Again, there was that sideways glance from Dulcie.

"All right. *All right*. What is this? Are you on some kind of a tear to rip open the truth everywhere? I may not have done such a bang-up job with my financial management lately, but I can't just . . ."

"Let go. Those are the words you're searching for. You can't let go and partner on your farm. But you *can*, Lilah. Don't lose your beautiful, precious place—where you need to live until you die—because of your pride."

Lilah snorted. "Ha! My *pride*?"

"Yes, and it'll be all you'll have left if you aren't careful."

Lilah winced.

"I'm sorry, honey," Dulcie said. "I don't mean to sound harsh. But you always want the cold, hard truth straight up. That's what this is. Face it, my dear, old friend."

Lilah slumped in her seat. Her sling knocked the shopping list from her lap to the floor.

"It makes me so sad," she said, "to have come to this. Ed would be so ashamed of me . . ."

"Fiddle-faddle! Ed was a farmer. He'd understand why

you had to get that loan. He struggled through many a drought and many a hailstorm."

"And never lost the place. Or even came close."

Dulcie nodded and swerved around a guy on a tractor creeping along the highway.

"These are different times, Lilah. Way different. None of us knows what'll happen."

"My point exactly, with these kids risking their futures."

"*Theirs*. Not your job."

Lilah shook her head. "And *this* is *yours*? Telling me what to do?"

Dulcie grinned. "Damn straight," she said. "You should've taken the loan I offered. Now you'll have to deal with my renegade son. I just hope you don't have to shoot him."

They laughed but Lilah's heart wasn't in it. Her insides were tied in knots. "If you'll notice, I haven't agreed to that yet."

Lilah took a deep breath. Then another. She forced herself to really see the green fields passing by and the blue sky.

"One thing at a time," Dulcie said. "Meri's given us two hours to get all these supplies and get back to Raul's, so we better have that list made when we get to Sam's Club. You put down sugar and jars and lids and rubber rings and lemons, but do you have gelatin on the list?"

Lilah growled. "You know I don't use it."

"But for such large batches of preserves . . ."

"I brought my wooden spoon. I'll judge when they're ready to pour up. Face it, Dulcie: not your job."

They laughed again, and somehow Lilah felt better.

"Thanks, Dulcie. I just have to think about it some more. I'm not promising you anything."

"While you think, be grateful for the help the Good Lord has sent you."

Lilah turned to her.

"Think about it," Dulcie said, with her green-eyed gimlet look.

Then she looked at the road again, pulled out and passed a dump truck at about ninety miles per hour.

"If I live."

Dulcie raised her eyebrows. "I've never had a wreck."

Lilah decided not to get into that old argument.

"They don't know it, and you don't know it, but Meri and Caleb need this little business as much as you do."

"Dulcie, sometimes I think you aren't aging at all and then you come up with something like that."

"Listen. They each need a risk and a challenge and a companion and something new to do. And . . . do you reckon? Maybe a little romance, too. They're at a cross-roads age and a time in their lives when they both have some things to forget and some to overcome."

Lilah stared at her.

Dulcie stared back. "What? You're too selfish to give them that?"

"Oh no. Why not just turn over my farm and my liveli-hood and my *debts* to entertain the children?"

"You know they could save Honey Grove for you."

They glared at each other, then laughed.

"I have to admit, here lately I haven't been making much of a go of it myself," Lilah said.

"Everything's changing, Lilah. In a big way. We've all got to adapt if we want to stay on the land. Even Jasper's trying to learn how to use the Internet. Caleb and Meri want to bring Honey Grove into the modern world. Listen to them. Give it up. I'm telling you, God has sent them to help you, you old fossil."

Lilah almost admitted defeat but she backed out at the last minute. Her heart didn't know that yet. Maybe, just maybe, throwing in with those crazy kids was the right thing to do.

And then again, maybe it wasn't.

Twenty-eight

Huge mistake.

You're going to lose the little money you had.

You've rushed into this.

You don't have a clue what you're doing.

Caleb's too much for you to control. You don't even know him.

You're giving Lilah a thread of hope that may break any minute.

And yourself. This'll be another failure, not your redemption.

The relentless nagging of her inner critic was making Meri so tense she could hardly drive as she wheeled Lilah's truck into the parking lot behind Raul's. She breathed deep to try to slow her way-too-fast-beating heart. Out at Honey Grove, she'd felt such confidence—actually, she'd felt it since the very moment she and Caleb started working on making Honey Grove Kitchens a reality—but on the drive into town her natural wariness reared its ugly head.

She pushed it to the back of her mind to concentrate on the three-point turn necessary to back up to the door with the load of peaches. Two battered vehicles were already there. Raul had said some guys would be there using the wood-fired, outdoor smoker.

And there it was, attached to the rambling deck/porch of one of Rock Springs's oldest buildings. Lilah said Raul had bought it from a family who'd made famous barbeque there for three generations.

When she opened the truck door, the two men looked up from their work and greeted her with a smile and a wave.

"Hey, how's it goin'?" she said, trying to sound like a veteran Texan.

Smiling made her feel better for a split second, but her stomach knotted tighter as she climbed out of the truck. She wasn't *really* scared, though. Part fear, part excitement, this was the same feeling she always had right before going into court and she was always fine once everything began.

Except you're out of your element now. You've jumped off a cliff this time.

Shut up. I can do this. I can. I have to do something big and do it right.

She focused harder on staying in the moment as she began unloading. Dallas, Denton and friends would be here soon to do most of it, but she might as well take something in as she went.

At the back of the truck she pulled down the tailgate, grabbed a bushel of peaches and started for the door Raul had left unlocked. She smiled because it didn't even cause her to breathe heavily. Working on the farm was making her stronger, faster than any gym time she'd ever spent.

Which, ironically, made a lot of sense. It was all day every day versus a few hours each week.

One of the smoker guys yelled, "Ma'am! Need some help?"

"It's on the way," she yelled back. "Thanks anyhow."

She turned sideways to push the door open with her hip, then looked back when she heard the sound of a big motor and tires on gravel. Darn! Not her helpers.

Instead, it was a big white vehicle like . . . Doreen's.

Surely not. She had to know Raul was closed on Tuesdays. So why was she here?

To poke her nose in, as Lilah would say. And Lilah would be right.

When the door opened, diminutive Doreen climbed down from the huge Hummer with its custom-scripted DOREEN'S DRESS SHOP, ROCK SPRINGS, TEXAS, on the front doors, and hurried around the front of it.

"I was just passing by," she said. "Meri, honey, what are you *doing* here?"

Meri raised her brows, stopped and lifted one knee to help support the basket she held.

"Doreen, your network has failed you," Meri said, trying to keep her tone light instead of irritated. "Everybody knows we're using this kitchen to salvage our hail-damaged peaches."

Doreen, offended, set her fists on her hips.

"Of course I know that. Am I not always the first to know what's going on in this town? I *meant* what are you doing here, putting your grandmother through all this work for nothing? You'll have to place your price point too high to sell more than a couple of dozen jars of those preserves."

Meri's whole body tensed. She didn't need this right now. She didn't have *time* for this. Six to eight hours was flying.

"Thanks for stopping by," she said, turned her back and went on into the kitchen. Lilah was also right when she said Doreen's main talent was to get on a person's last nerve, and do it in a red-hot hurry.

Meri could hear her through the open door calling to the men at the smoker. "Hey, Trace. I'll be right back. We need to talk about Grandma's yard."

Then the screen door creaked and Doreen followed Meri in, saying, "You'll ruin your insides carrying a whole bushel by yourself, Meri, honey. Here, let me help you."

"You want to help peel peaches and slice them?"

"Oh, honey, I wish I could, but I have to go talk to my cousin about mowing his grandma's yard and then I *must* get back to my shop. I hired Kylie Raines for the summer but she's gone to Austin to enroll at UT for this fall."

Meri tried to ignore Doreen so she could look around the kitchen with a different eye than when she'd been in it to make deliveries. It was smaller than she'd realized, filled with well-used and battered stainless-steel tables, hanging pots and pans, built-in ovens, a long grill and a six-burner stove. Three sinks and two big refrigerators.

One freezer that Raul said was full and one that was half-empty. They might need that space to freeze peach slices if they couldn't get them all preserved in time.

Doreen sighed. "Well, I guess I should be going."

"Thanks for dropping by," Meri said again, heading for the pot racks to see how many stockpots and Dutch ovens were available for cooking peaches.

The Fremont kids burst in through the door, each carrying as big a load as possible, Dallas calling, "Meri, where do you want us to put these?"

"A couple of baskets at each of the sinks and the rest over there by the wall. Once you've unloaded, let's start washing and peeling."

There was no time to think or make lists. She'd have to do this on the fly.

"Well, I'll go now but I wish you luck," Doreen said, coming around the table to give Meri a little hug. "I hope I didn't bother you, sugar, but I'm just trying to help."

Thank goodness, she began moving toward the door as she talked.

"I know Lilah can't afford to waste a penny right now and you've never breathed a word about any food packaging experience in your background, so I just wanted you to know that I can make some pretty mean peach preserves. You call me if you need more help."

Doreen's tone was so . . . wistful, maybe. Not quite reproachful, but almost. As if she'd been left out of something and was forgiving Meri for it. Did she think she should've been personally informed of the plans at Honey Grove?

Just the thought irritated Meri. She had enough to think about already.

But she also felt as if she still owed Doreen. It was like a little guilt burden that she felt every time she saw the woman.

"Doreen, please don't worry about us. We'll be fine."

She tried to breathe deep as she started walking Doreen to the door.

But Meri'd sounded more abrupt than she'd intended and Doreen looked hurt as Meri opened the screen for her. She went out but then she stopped.

Softly, she said, "Meri, I loved your mama to pieces and Lilah's been my friend since kindergarten. We aggravated each other, even then, but I'd do anything I possibly could for her. And for you."

Meri's shoulders sagged. Doreen, too, thought Meri owed her. But *what*?

These small-town people were so weird and so touchy and Meri still didn't know the culture well enough to know all the rules of behavior. Doreen had refused money that day, so Meri had sent her flowers as she was rushing to the airport. What else should she have done?

Right now, she'd have to take time for an apology. "Doreen, I'm sorry if I was too abrupt just now. I do appreciate your dropping by and your offers of help and I still remember how great you were to volunteer to stay with Henry when he was hurt. I owe you for that."

She gave Doreen a big smile. "Really. Monitoring a cat's urine *can't* be a very pleasant job."

They chuckled at that and Doreen patted her arm as they stepped out of the way of the competing Fremonts who came charging back out the door, headed out for another load of peaches. A car and a truck carrying the rest of the Honey Grove Kitchens crew came roaring into the parking lot.

Meri said, "See you later, Doreen," and went out to help them unload. The faster that was done, the faster the truck could go back for more peaches.

But Doreen came, too. "No worries, honey," she said. "You and I, we're good. Oh, and nobody's going to blame you for *this* fiasco. Everybody will give you credit for trying to help your grandma."

Meri's eyes flew wide. "It won't be a fiasco," she said in a tone so firm she hardly recognized it. "I know what I'm doing, Doreen."

Doreen sniffed. "Well. At least you're confident, Meri. That's half the battle." She gave her another pat and headed for Cousin Trace at the smoker.

Meri watched her go, suddenly feeling stronger. Much stronger. A good challenge never failed to inspire her.

Doreen glanced back, trilling over her shoulder at Meri, "I'll come back by when I close the shop this afternoon and see how it's goin'. I can stay and help then if you need me."

She meant that. She *would* help.

Meri sighed. Small-town relationships had their good points.

And their bad.

Two hours later, Meri was happy. Things were going so well—and that was because she *did* have the organizational skills to run a business, she'd decided. So did Caleb. He was supervising the picking and hauling of the fruit and reporting to Meri when each load left Honey Grove headed for the processing kitchen.

The Fremont kids were peeling and slicing. Their two best friends, both boys, were washing peaches, and Lilah and Dulcie stood at the six-burner stove, each with three pots of sugar and peaches cooking. They watched their mixtures constantly, stirring and testing until Lilah said that the syrup dripped from the wooden spoons just right. The entire restaurant smelled delicious.

Meri and the teenagers Dallas and Denton had recruited were boiling jars and lids on the smaller stovetop, drying and setting them out to be filled. Four dozen short, fat jars stood in a golden row, full and capped. The whole process was moving amazingly well, and Meri had made it up as she went!

Her most brilliant piece of management may have been the one to keep all her employees happy: the rule that the music playing must alternate between a teenager's choice on Dallas's iPod and a choice by either Lilah or Dulcie on Dulcie's iPod.

That great stroke of genius had created a real camaraderie among them all as well as a lively discussion of outlaw country versus something called Red Dirt music. Now they were arguing about whether that began in Texas or Oklahoma.

Meri smiled to herself. She hoped Doreen *did* come back by later, just so she could see that there was no "fiasco" here. Quite the contrary. It was all peach preserve production and music education.

She was glancing at her phone to see what time it was, since Caleb had called twenty minutes earlier to say the next load of peaches had just left Honey Grove, when she realized something was going on outside. Trace and Lonnie (they'd been in and out several times to visit and eat peaches since Lilah arrived) were yelling now and there was a growing crackling noise.

Then Trace jerked open the back door and yelled into the kitchen.

"Miss Lilah, y'all better git out. We just called 911 for this fire out here. Go through the front, don't come this way."

He took off at a run. Meri froze with the phone in her hand.

How could this be? And just when she had everything under control!

Pandemonium erupted as the chattering kids ran to the windows to see the fire. Oh! She was responsible for these teenagers . . .

The thought almost panicked her. She didn't like being responsible for anyone but herself. Probably, Tim had been right when he said she didn't need children.

"You heard Trace," she shouted over the din. "We need to get out now."

Nobody so much as turned to look at her. They certainly weren't going to do as she said.

Denton yelled, "Come on, guys, let's go help Trace and Lon fight fire!"

"Yeah! Good idea . . ."

The excited boys headed for the door.

Lilah stepped in front of them, yelling over their noise, "You'll do no such thing. We're going out the front . . ."

Dallas turned away from the window, stopped the music and whistled through her fingers with such a piercing shriek that complete silence fell. Meri stared. She and Lilah were hopeless, but Dallas Fremont had no problem taking control.

"Let's move our stuff, guys! The fire's not even on this side of the patio yet and the firemen are coming. Come on, hurry! We *can't* waste all our hard work."

"No!" Lilah cried. "Your lives are more important than these peaches . . ."

But Dallas ran to the stainless-steel work table holding the finished jars of preserves, pushed it to the counter and began adding baskets of unpeeled peaches to its second shelf.

"Leave the peeled ones," she called to her minions. "They'll be all brown by the time we get to another kitchen. But load up everything else. We'll bring Raul's stuff back later."

Meri, the brilliant organizer/manager/leader in control of this operation, noticed for the first time that the stainless-steel work tables were all on rollers. She ran to the window to see the fire for herself. Dallas was right, so far, but the wind could change in an instant.

Lilah was flapping her arms, yelling, "Listen to me. You all go out through the front door and do it *now*!"

But the six teenagers, including the shy girl who didn't speak, even when Dallas had introduced her at Honey Grove, were moving like a whirlwind with a purpose, grabbing baskets and peaches and equipment to pile on the tables. Lilah kept trying to herd them toward the door but they were oblivious, as if they'd been trained for this exact task.

Meri had never felt so *not*-in-charge since the huge show-down with Alan over her job assignment. Even then, she'd reasserted control, even though she'd had to quit to do it.

She couldn't quit now.

"If we help them, it'll get them out faster," she called to Lilah as she headed for the boxes of empty jars.

She hated to give in, but she had to get them out of danger before she had a nervous breakdown.

Dulcie had come to the same decision. She was throwing kitchen towels and tablecloths into empty baskets to make nests for the pots she'd just taken from the stovetop. Lilah began gathering the paring knives, wooden spoons and utensils, about all she could do with only one hand.

Meri's phone showed that only five minutes had elapsed when the efficient, stubborn kids began pushing the loaded tables through the swinging doors that separated the kitchen from the restaurant's dining room. After checking to make sure the gas was turned off on the stove, the three women followed, Meri carrying a last half-bushel of peaches that didn't fit on the burdened tables.

Yelling and talking, the kids pushed the tables down the sidewalk to the corner and around the side of the building, heading for the parking lot, running when they passed the fiery patio. The siren at the fire station was wailing on and on to call in the volunteer firemen, and the first—maybe the only?—fire truck was screeching toward them from the opposite side of the square.

Trace and Lon had a hose turned on the flames but that small amount of water couldn't dent them. They were already spreading over the open "roof" framework of the patio and licking at the brick wall of the restaurant itself, near the old wooden frame of a window.

The heat was so intense everyone moved a lot faster, despite being out of breath from carrying baskets and pushing the tables.

"Git y'all's trucks outta the way of the fire engines," Lon

yelled at them as the first one came screaming around the corner. "This is gonna get worse."

"Raul's gonna kill us dead," Trace yelled.

Meri looked at him, then did a double take as she glimpsed someone behind him. Doreen—yes, it *was* Doreen, in a bright yellow pencil-skirt dress, which she had not been wearing earlier—taking tiny steps as she dragged another water hose wound on its plastic holder across the gravels.

In front of Meri, Lilah and Dulcie stopped in their tracks, Lilah waving her favorite, wooden, jelly-making spoon in the air.

She screamed, "*Doreen?* Merciful heavens! What are *you* doing here?"

There was so much noise from the fire, the sirens coming nearer, and all the voices that Meri, right beside her, could barely hear her. Doreen hadn't even *seen* her.

Meri shifted the basket she was carrying to her other hip and they all rushed faster to move their cars. Sure enough, there was Doreen's Hummer, parked in the shade at the back of the lot near the alley.

The heat was already so intense the vehicles felt hot to the touch.

Denton jerked his truck door open, then stopped with one foot on the running board and yelled, "Where to, Miss Lilah? Where's another kitchen we can use?"

Lilah whirled and stared at him, taking a deep breath, clearly trying to think where to go while Dallas and the others were unloading the tables into Denton's truck. Dulcie hurried to her Escalade and opened the hatchback, then went to help Dallas sort things out.

Meri realized her heart was beating faster and she was holding her breath.

Could they really pull this project—literally—out of the fire?

"First Baptist Church," Lilah yelled back over the roar of the fire. "Everybody meet up there."

Meri's surge of relief turned to worry.

That was a public kitchen, yes. Sort of. But would it be legal to sell what they made there?

Could they reenergize and organize like they did before? Get their rhythm back?

Twenty-nine

Lilah and Dulcie brought up the rear of their ragged caravan headed for the church, dodging and weaving around the square through the mess of vehicles already rushing to either watch the fire burn or help fight it. *Then*, on top of trying not to wreck, after surviving hailstorms and fire and sticky pots of half-cooked peach preserves, they had to contend with old Hub Morrison wobbling around in the middle of Lamar Street, taking it upon himself to direct traffic.

He let Meri and the kids go on but he held up his hand to stop Lilah and Dulcie. Once they halted, he turned his back on them and started the cross-traffic moving. There was a long line of it.

Lilah wanted to scream. All this on top of worrying about Caleb and Meri and whether to throw in with them or not! There was so much going in her head underneath all these emotions that she couldn't get a handle on anything.

"I know Johnny Martin's busy right now," she said, through gritted teeth, "but the very least he could do is to keep Hub out of the road."

"Johnny was elected sheriff to keep the peace, Lilah, not to babysit the old folks."

"Well, if he's gonna let him hang around his office all the time, then he's responsible for stopping him when Hub tries to go into law enforcement."

Lilah twisted around in her seat. "Let's go around. That's Jenny Sevier behind us, so motion to her we want to back up. I'm *not* going to let Doreen stop us now."

Dulcie turned to her with that calm, green-eyed look that could be beyond irritating when used at the wrong time. Like right now. She was shaking her head no.

"She's always had a mean bone," Lilah argued, "so why am I surprised she'd try to burn us out in our hour of need?"

Dulcie sighed. "Lilah, darlin', Doreen couldn't have started that fire. She wouldn't have gone *that* far. You're sounding a little bit paranoid here."

"Then what was she doing there, dragging that hose around? She was there earlier, too. So why, if not to make the smoker's fire flare up high enough to catch the patio?"

Dulcie shook her head. "Too far-fetched, too *evil*. Doreen is mean sometimes, I'll grant you that, but not to the point of arson."

"A woman who'll steal another woman's daughter will steal her farm, too, even if she has to criminalize herself to get it done."

Dulcie sighed. "Listen to me, Lilah. That fire put Trace in danger and she loves him. And she wouldn't put all of us in danger, either. Don't you dare breathe a word of this suspicion to anybody but me. They'll start saying you're losing your mind."

"Well, I have every right to do just that." Lilah rolled her window down. "Get out of the way, Hub, you old coot," she hollered, over the noise of more oncoming sirens. "I swear to my time, you're gonna get yourself run over. Get out of the road!"

"So says the nosy old hen," he yelled back. "What's yore hurry?"

"You're letting out all the air-conditioning, Lilah," Dulcie said, fanning her face with her hand, "and I think I'm having a hot flash."

Sirens and that awful bleating noise that they installed on all the new emergency vehicles nowadays nearly deafened them. Lilah sat drumming her fingers on the door handle while Rock Springs's new fire truck, the old water truck and two ambulances came blasting through the intersection, all of the drivers determined not to miss this chance of being seen being useful.

At long last, Hub waved them on. Dulcie turned and drove up Lamar, still at a snail's pace because of the traffic. Lilah rolled her window up.

Dulcie shot her a sideways glance. "Feel better now? After taking out your frustrations on a helpless old man?"

Lilah snorted. A big red dually pickup with a winch on the front was coming into town way too fast, lit up all over like Christmas and blasting its horn.

"Those volunteer firemen just live for a good emergency," she said. "Only thing better than a fire on the square would be an ice storm where they could use their winches to pull people out of ditches."

"Don't try to change the subject. You still haven't promised not to accuse Doreen."

Lilah gave her her killer look.

Dulcie looked back with an eyebrow raised and a threat in her eyes.

Then she smiled. "If you jump Doreen, you'll be pulling me and B. J. and Parmalee into the fight, too—your whole *prayer* group. Is there something about that sentence that doesn't quite compute?"

It *was* funny, but Lilah refused to smile back. Dulcie wouldn't let her break the look.

"Watch the road," Lilah said.

Dulcie dodged a flatbed with a feeder on the back, its cab jammed with more young men hoping to get to the fire before it was too late.

"We haven't had this much excitement in Rock Springs

since that escaped convict got off the Greyhound and tried
to rob the Grab It 'n' Go with a pencil under his gimme cap."

"Right. And I've enjoyed almost more of it than I can
stand," Lilah said. "Starting with that infernal hailstorm
that dragged me into Meri and Caleb's wild-eyed scheme.
Now it's wearing my nerves to shreds trying to save those
peaches and make a dollar or two, which would be a drop
in the ocean of what I need."

"Take a breath. Then take one step at a time," Dulcie
said. "One day at a time. That's all we can do."

"Just pray we can make these preserves as good as they
usually are. We don't want to ruin the Honey Grove brand
at this late date."

Dulcie glanced at her, grinning a little.

"It's *temporary*," Lilah hastened to add. "I haven't
signed anything or agreed to anything. This is a one-time
deal I'm doing for Honey Grove Kitchens."

"But that *is* the name?"

"It's temporary," Lilah said, trying for a tone firm
enough to close down the discussion.

Dulcie swerved to miss a car marked DEPUTY SHERIFF,
whipping out of the alley on the wrong side of the street.

At the top of the hill, they turned off on Lamar and into
the drive at First Baptist.

"Turn here and go behind the main building, Dulcie.
That'll put us right by the door to the fellowship hall."

Dulcie shook her head. "You Baptists," she teased,
"all y'all do is eat. Fellowship dinners, prayer breakfasts,
ladies' luncheons."

"Well, if the Presbyterians would loosen up and break
bread together once in a while, y'all'd feel a lot closer to
God."

Lilah actually smiled in spite of herself as she showed
Dulcie where to park. They'd exchanged those taunts too
many times to count. Nothing like an old friend. Even if
she *was* too calm to be any fun sometimes.

"Several cars here," Lilah said. "Maybe there's a dea-
cons' meeting."

Meri and the Fremonts and the rest of the crew were already unloading peaches.

"This door," Lilah called. "The kitchen's right in there through the dining room. We'll have two cooktops but they're not as big as Raul's."

As Dulcie opened the back door of her SUV, Meri came over to Lilah.

"Once we got away from the fire, I realized there's a problem," she said quietly. "If this isn't a licensed commercial kitchen, it won't be legal to sell what we make here. Do you still want to go ahead?"

That rocked Lilah back on her heels. But only for a moment.

"We'll give it away if we have to."

If for no other reason but to spite Doreen, I'll finish this job if it harelips the governor.

"Really, Meri," she said. "Even at best, we can't sell these preserves for enough to pay Buford's note."

Meri went back to help the kids; Lilah picked up as much as she could carry one-handed.

She led the way into the fellowship hall through the double doors and along the wide windowed hallway that curved into the dining room. They could set up the peeling and slicing in there. They would have to. This kitchen was much smaller than Raul's. She walked faster.

". . . and, Father, please teach us to *listen* when we pray instead of doing all the talking. A—"

Lilah stopped so fast she nearly lost her balance, which was a little off, anyway, since her arm was in the sling.

"Merciful heavens," she blurted, "Help us all. I completely forgot about Tuesday Bible Study."

"—men." Modean Blocker, standing at the teacher's podium, lifted her head and stared at Lilah, blinking as if she couldn't believe her eyes.

A couple dozen more women sat with their Bibles and notebooks on the tables in front of them. They looked astonished, too.

"I'm *so* sorry, y'all. Everything's just so hectic I don't even know what day it is."

"Now don't you worry about that for a minute, Lilah. That was our closing prayer," Modean said in her sweet way. "We're done."

"I should've been thinking what I was doing," Lilah said. "We just came in to use the kitchen because the one at Raul's caught on fire, and . . ."

Everybody started talking at once as Lilah's crew came pouring in behind her with loads of produce and supplies. The wonderful smell of sun-ripened peaches warmed the room, which, thankfully, was much cooler than Raul's, at least until the cooking began.

"Is that what the sirens . . ."

"*Fire?* Raul's?"

"What happened?"

"Is it bad? Anybody hurt?"

"Not when we left there, but the patio was blazing and the building itself was about to catch."

The excited women began gathering around Lilah, wanting to know what she had been doing at Raul's in the first place, talking about old buildings and town history and the dry weather and the wind and the possibility of a conflagration sweeping through all of the old downtown. It had happened to other towns.

"Trace and Lonnie were fine when we left," she said, "doing the best they could 'til the firemen came . . ."

The sound of Trace's voice yelling that warning echoed in her head and the sight of the flames trying to eat up the old building that had been standing as long as Lilah could remember came back to overwhelm her for a minute. The whole town *could* burn.

The whole world was changing too much, too fast. Soon she might even lose Honey Grove.

She let her sack of jar lids drop onto the nearest table and sank into a chair.

"Lilah! What were y'all doing using Raul's kitchen, anyway?"

She did not have time for this. She needed to sit, though. She would, but just for a second.

To keep from thinking about her situation, she started telling the whole story. A minute or two into it, somebody leaned over her shoulder to put a cold bottle of Coke into her good hand.

She looked up into her granddaughter's worried eyes. "You okay, Lilah?"

Meri's concern sent a sudden knot into Lilah's throat. Honestly, she was an emotional wreck. She had to get ahold of herself.

At first she could only nod; she took a drink of the sharp, fizzing soda so she could say, "Go ahead and get started, Meri. I'll be there in just a minute."

"So what made the flames flare up in the smoker?" Naturally, that was Pansy Carter. She always questioned everything that happened like she was some kind of scientist, when really she was just lonely and wanting for conversation.

But the question stirred Lilah's simmering suspicions of Doreen.

"Fat dripping into the fire, I guess. You'd have to ask Trace or Lonnie."

She couldn't keep herself from adding, "Or ask Doreen. She was out there with them."

Her hands were shaking. This was ridiculous.

She pushed her chair back and stood up. "Girls, I've got to get busy—there'll be at least two more loads of peaches coming in and they have to be processed within a few hours."

Plus, she needed to call the church office and let somebody know she wanted to use the kitchen, although she was sure it wouldn't be a problem.

"I've got to get these kids organized. Y'all stay away from the square if you want to get home before dark. It's a mess of traffic."

They were all gathered around her, hugging good-bye, some asking her to put some preserves back for them—as if there'd be a run on the batch when it was all done—some offering to stay and help with the process. Lilah turned to wave when Ruby Baxter called good-bye to her and there, coming into the room, was Doreen, still in her little, tight yellow dress. She was with a short, middle-aged man who was a stranger to Lilah. She couldn't care less who he was. All she could think about, all she could really *see*, was Doreen.

Lilah's whole body stiffened. Her heart was racing like crazy and she didn't care about that, either. If she was only going to live one more minute she'd spend it telling the truth.

"You have more *purely unmitigated gall* than anybody I've ever seen, Doreen Semples. You want to burn us out here, too? I'd think setting fire to your own church would be one step over the line, even for you."

Doreen stopped in her tracks. Her head rocked back and her jaw dropped. Eyes wide, she stared at Lilah.

"You were the worst actor in the junior class play," Lilah said. "Don't even *try* that innocent look on me when you oughtta be hangin' your head like a sheep-killing dog."

Doreen didn't need much time to recover. She never did.

She used her most incredulous tone. "Are you implying that I'm an *arsonist*? Where did *that* come from? My goodness gracious! Lilah, what are you talking about?"

She opened her arms in a helpless gesture and glanced around at their audience, all frozen in place, staring at the show with bated breath. Lilah didn't care about that, either.

"Honey, are you still on some kind of medication from when you took that hard fall out of the tree and crushed your wrist?"

Doreen's bright eyes found Dulcie in the crowd. "Dulcie? Do you know? Something's affecting Lilah's mind. Is she taking too many pills or is she in so much pain she needs some?"

Lilah snapped back, "Don't try that old dodge. Why else would you be hanging around that smoker when Dulcie and I got there and then again a couple of hours later when you've got a business to run? What'd you do, throw too much wood on the fire when Trace and Lonnie were inside talking to us?"

Doreen truly did look astounded.

"Or maybe add a little dash of lighter fluid?"

Doreen blinked. Her mouth opened but she didn't say a word.

Lilah felt a little twinge of doubt.

But surely she wasn't in the wrong here. No. That couldn't be.

"Paranoia," Doreen said. "That's what this is. Lilah, you need to get down to that new mental health place they've put in there by the post office."

Even more heat rushed into Lilah's face. She felt like she might explode, she was so wound up inside. She clenched her teeth.

"Answer the question, Doreen. What were you doing in the parking lot at Raul's this morning?"

Doreen rolled her eyes and glanced around as if to say, *I'll have to humor her.*

"The first time, I was talking to my cousin Trace. About when he would either mow his grandma's yard or hire somebody to do it."

Then she added—as if Lilah had not only lost her mind, but her memory, too—"She's my aunt Flossie and she's in rehab in San Antonio from a broken hip."

Little Miss Innocent.

"And the second time? Why'd you come back during business hours for your shop when you don't have any employees?"

Doreen smiled her sweetest smile and used her most reasonable voice. It even held a little sympathy in it for Crazy Lilah.

"To bring Trace the key to aunt Flossie's shed, where she keeps the lawn mower."

Then she shrugged, eyebrows lifted, looking around again with her hands open in helplessness.

Pansy Carter was nodding in response to show she accepted Doreen's excuse, hook, line and sinker. Pansy should've gone on home when the Bible study broke up.

But no. She'd had to hang around and poke her nose into Lilah's business.

Actually, several people looked at Doreen as if they believed her. Then they looked at Lilah as if they really *were* questioning her sanity.

This was nuts. They ought to know better than to believe a word out of Doreen's mouth. She'd lived here all her life. Hadn't they been paying attention?

But, much as she hated to be wrong, Lilah, too, had to admit that those excuses made sense. Even worse, they sounded sincere.

She swallowed hard. "And just exactly why have you followed us up here to the church kitchen?"

Doreen's smile widened and she turned to the man beside her.

With a graceful gesture, she said, "Y'all, this is Fred Edson out of Brenham. He's the restaurant inspector for the county. I brought him up here to see if he can give our church a commercial kitchen ranking or at least start that process so it'll be legal for Lilah to sell these preserves and jams that she's making today."

This time it was Lilah's jaw that dropped. She couldn't pick it up.

Even if she could, she couldn't find her voice or her heart, which had just gone through the floor. And through the ground. All the way to China.

Lord help her, she was wrong. Ooooh! She *hated* to be wrong.

Especially in front of the entire town. People'd be retelling this for months. All the way through next winter. They'd be talking about it for *years*.

What a chapter in the saga of Lilah and Doreen!

Lord, please help me now.

The *only* light she could see was the fact that she hadn't had time to move on the next thing she would've naturally said, which was to point out that Doreen wanted Lilah to fail so she could get her hands on Honey Grove.

That would've painted Lilah as paranoid, for sure.

But really, who could blame her? Who, in this town, knowing Doreen and the history between them, would ever have believed Doreen would do something nice for Lilah? Something that would actually *help* her?

She came out of herself enough to really look at Doreen. Her eyes were bright. But it was more than triumph this time. Could those possibly be *tears*?

Doreen broke the look with Lilah to look at the restaurant inspector.

"Fred is another one of my cousins," Doreen said, "and he was doing his inspection of Suzy's Cafe today, so it's just a godsend that he was here when Lilah needed him."

She introduced Lilah individually and Fred nodded. Clearly he was a shy man.

"Nice to meet you, ma'am. Glad I could help. Well, let me look at this kitchen before ya'll get going here."

He fled to the kitchen but no one else moved. Lilah could feel all eyes on her and Doreen was looking at her again.

Gotta do it, Lilah. Be fair. Face up to your mistakes.

Lilah had to swallow twice and scrape her throat to clear it, but finally she said, "I apologize, Doreen. I am sincerely sorry that I accused you. I was totally wrong and I hate that *so* bad. I can't tell you how much."

Doreen didn't say a word. But, incredibly, those *were* tears in her big brown eyes. She waited.

Lilah cleared her throat again. "Will you please forgive me?"

Doreen kept staring at her.

At last, she nodded. Thoughtfully.

"Yes, I forgive you, Lilah. And I hope you can forgive me for any wrongs I may have done you over the years."

Oh, yeah. *Any* wrongs I *may* have done. Typical.

"I want us to be better friends," Doreen said. "I've wanted that for a long time. Can you learn to trust me, Lilah? Can we be real friends instead of frenemies from now on?"

Hmpf. Nothing like holding a "friend" hostage in a

public forum, when this whole thing should be entirely between the two of them!

If that wasn't tacky, Lilah didn't know what was.

But. Doreen's behavior (when other people were around) hardly *ever* crossed the line from tasteless into tacky. So this might be sincere.

The hope in her voice certainly was and so was the soft look in her eyes. They were extremely rare. After all, she'd known Doreen since the first grade.

Lilah was touched.

You've been praying for the heart to forgive Doreen, haven't you? Here it is.

Looking back over the long years, Lilah knew that holding a grudge had damaged her more than it had Doreen.

And you created it, Lilah Briscoe. You chose it. You clung to it. So you wouldn't have to look at the real truth.

That cold fact hit her mind and her heart like somebody had slapped her sideways. It knocked the wind out of her. She needed to push it back into the dark corner where she must've been keeping it all these years until this turmoil swept it out of hiding. She wanted never to look at it again.

But if she didn't do the right thing now she would never have another scrap of respect for herself. She took a deep breath and swallowed hard.

"Doreen, I should never have blamed you for my daughter's troubles and her wild ways. That was her nature and I didn't recognize it until it was too late. I expected her to be like me instead of who she was."

Astounded, Doreen stared at Lilah. Everyone did.

"You didn't hold a gun to Edie Jo's head and run her out of Texas. Nothing you or anybody else did or didn't do could've made any difference in the choices she made. I ought to know, since I raised heaven and earth trying."

Doreen was to be pitied. She'd never had the joy of carrying a baby in her body *or* in her arms. At least Lilah had had those sweet early years with Edie Jo.

And the man Doreen had loved had loved Lilah instead.

"I've done you a great wrong," Lilah said. "I need your forgiveness for much, much more than my mistake today."

"I forgive you, Lilah." And she really did. Lilah could tell by her tone and the look in her eyes.

Lilah waited, since Doreen rarely used such few words, but there weren't any more. Doreen just walked toward her with her arms open wide and they hugged. A long hug.

Lilah felt a great burden lifted.

But as they parted, she wondered. They could be friends, yes, with the big wedge between them gone, but what about the little frictions of day-to-day life? Would they ever really be heart-friends?

Tormenting Lilah had occupied many an hour of Doreen's life.

Time would tell.

Thirty

Three days later, Meri drove off the highway into the winding driveway at Caleb's place, exactly 10.2 miles on the opposite side of Rock Springs from Honey Grove and a hard right turn because of the angle of the hill, just as Caleb had said. She took it too fast and the rear of Lilah's truck fishtailed as it rattled across the cattle guard.

She wanted to get through this first meeting alone since the kiss, confirm that their business relationship was solid and singular and that that would be their agreement going forward and get back to Honey Grove as fast as possible.

She was driving more slowly, though. The narrow, white-gravel road hugged the side of the hill but on her right, pastureland with grazing cattle rolled on and on toward gray granite bluffs. It was seductive. Like its owner.

But she could handle him. She had set the rules and he'd seemed to agree. And she was in full control of herself.

On one level, she still couldn't believe she'd been so impulsive as to ever get into this situation, especially knowing that a few months from now she'd be a long-distance partner. That was one item on the agenda for the day.

The major one, though, was Lilah and her obstinance. If Caleb had known her since he was a little boy, maybe he'd think of a tactic that would work. So far, everything Meri had tried, including challenge, had failed.

She set her jaw. She had risked almost all of her savings to try to save Honey Grove. Yes, this would finally be a profitable company. Yes, she was loving seeing her idea become reality. But, by damn, she had started all this to try and save Honey Grove and she intended to find a way to make Lilah let her do it.

It was a little over a mile from the highway to the house, Caleb had said. But he hadn't said that traveling that distance would make her want to stop and get out of the truck and do nothing but breathe in the air of this place and look in all directions. It was even more beautiful to look in the rear-view mirror. The back side of the hill was more white bluffs trimmed in dark green cedar and other trees she couldn't name. An eagle flew from one of them as she watched.

And when she looked through the windshield again, the road sloped down to a river and the low concrete bridge across the clear water running fast over rocks. She stopped in the middle of the bridge to look at it, then rolled down her windows to listen. She loved that *shush*ing sound, so peaceful and full of motion at the same time.

The air smelled like cedar and fresh water and, faintly, from far off, of grass and cow manure. She didn't even mind that.

Get going. You have a dozen more items on your list for today.

She stepped on the accelerator, drove past a shadowy grove of big old trees that she thought might be a pecan orchard and around the next bend was the house.

Calling it that was an act of charity. She braked.

She'd never been so shocked. Caleb drove a new pickup truck and wore custom-made boots. And *this* was where he lived?

It was a limestone and weathered barn-siding shell of a house nestled in a grove of enormous, ancient live-oak trees with Spanish moss hanging from the branches. The rambling structure looked to be about the same age as the trees.

The low, stone wall around its dusty yard lay in pieces.

There were sawhorses set up near the porch with planks across them and some kind of a saw on its own little table plugged into the house with a long cord. This place was wired for electricity?

One end of the porch roof sagged on its post but the walls of the house itself looked basically solid. It rambled on and on, long and lean, a mix of rough, limestone-block walls and wooden siding as silvery gray as any she'd seen on barns so old that they were falling down. The porch ran the entire length. Lots of windows—some cracked. Weathered wooden shingles, some missing.

Meri slid her bag onto her shoulder, picked up her agenda, her notes, her laptop and her phone, got out and started up the newly laid flagstone walk.

The screen on the front door banged open and Caleb came out to meet her with that purposeful, fast stride that he always used in spite of the limp.

"Mi casa es su casa," he said, as he crossed the porch. "Welcome to Indian River."

"That's the name of your ranch?"

He shrugged, his boot heels pounding down the raw, new steps. "It had the name long before I got here. Legend is, the Comanche used to follow this river to and from their raids down into Mexico."

He met her halfway up the walk and took some of the load out of her arms. He smelled like . . . sunshine. And Caleb.

"Looks like you're movin' in," he said in that low, slow teasing tone that was like a hand stroking her skin.

It got her every time.

She blushed; then, irritated with herself, she straightened up and shook her head.

"The website's up and I want you to see it on a bigger screen than my phone's. It's gorgeous and the designer's giving us a discount because his grandmother knows Lilah."

She stopped in her tracks. "Oh! But I don't know if my aircard will work way out here. Where's the nearest tower?"

He got them moving again. "No problem if it won't. I don't care. That website stuff's all yours."

"But I want you to see how great it is. If you can't see it today, I'll show it to you tomorrow when you bring the preserves in to the farmers market. Oh, and I've decided we should go ahead and get a Facebook page, too."

They climbed the wide steps side by side. Somehow, there was an easiness between them she hadn't expected after the way they'd parted.

"Whatever you want," he said. "Just don't put my phone number on there. Watch your step, now. Stay on the new part of the porch."

"Why not?" she teased. "Scared all your old girlfriends will be calling?"

He grinned. "Hey. You sayin' I don't have any *new* girl-friends?"

Her lips parted but his eyes were looking deep into hers. A significant look. It held her silent for a long, slow beat of her heart.

"I didn't mean that."

He raised his eyebrows. "Oh?"

"I'm sure you have several, judging by what I've heard about your past."

She sounded too prim to live. She hated that.

"No," he said, still watching her closely with that care-less grin lurking at the corners of his lips, "you were right the first time, Mer. I *don't* have any new girlfriends."

"Don't try that pretend-pitiful tone with me," she said, trying to sound brisk like Lilah. "You could have a dozen new girlfriends if you wanted."

Ooops.

Now the grin became full-sized. "But, Mer," he teased. "I don't want anybody but you."

She forced herself to meet his gaze. Never mind the grin. His eyes were entirely serious. Her breath caught.

I am in complete control. Of my imagination, my sensual self and my emotions.

"Do you have any coffee?"

He made a regretful noise and reached around her to open the door. Again, his scent tugged at her, *deep* inside her. She resisted turning toward him.

If he so much as touched her now . . .

But he didn't.

"Coffee? Dang it. I knew I was forgettin' somethin'."

She stepped into the wreck of a house and took a deep breath of the delicious smell of really fine coffee.

"Good try," she said dryly.

"This way," he said as he ushered her across a large, high-ceilinged room with power tools, pieces of wood and cans of paint scattered everywhere. Sacks of plaster or concrete or something like that were stacked against one battered wall.

"So," she said, and her voice came out normal. Almost. "Are you doing the renovations yourself?"

"Yep," he said, and his voice came out without the teasing tone. "It's slow but once we get the business really rolling, maybe I'll have more time for it. Thanks for comin' out. It saved me the drivin' time. I need to finish the porch floor today."

Her heart dropped, entirely without her permission.

So. He wasn't trying to get you alone for a rendezvous, Miss Let's-Keep-It-All-Business. He meant nothing by that teasing. He has no problem accepting your rules. Which is good. Exactly what you want.

Then he touched her on the small of her back and the heat of his hand through her thin tee fired her blood like a torch held to paper.

Get control. Get. Over. It.

"Umm, so, uh, how long have you been working on the house?"

"I bought the place six months ago when I came back from Montana and started on it right away." That low velvet voice again. But impersonal.

But his fingertips were still there, on her spine, guiding her in the direction he wanted her to go.

Meri nodded thoughtfully, although she could hardly move her neck without letting it turn her head toward him. Right now, she did not want to see his chiseled, compelling face. She wouldn't be able to look away.

"Um, Lilah told me you're in and out of Texas. She says you're the restless kind."

She bit her lip. Darn! Now she'd told him that she'd been asking about him.

"There's that," he said, still careless. "And also the fact that sometimes even Texas ain't quite big enough for me and Jake both."

Her brows went up. "Jake? Jasper? Your dad?"

He nodded.

She let herself glance at him. "I called my mom Edie Jo."

He met her eye, entirely serious now. "I know. So I'm thinkin' you probably have a clue what I'm talking about."

"Except our problem was I *wanted* to be with her."

Shut up.

She tensed and turned away, hoping he wouldn't say any more about that.

He didn't.

She was the one who wanted to ask questions. Why did he feel that way? Jake Burkett had never abandoned his family, as far as she knew. And Dulcie most definitely seemed to dote on Caleb.

No. You're the one who wants this to be all business. Jake isn't in it. Neither is Edie Jo.

His touch took her toward the door to the kitchen instead of the one to the hallway. On the other side of it, she glimpsed a rumpled sleeping bag and super-starched shirts and jeans hanging on the door, still wrapped in dry-cleaning plastic.

"What were you doing in Montana?"

"Outfitting in the Bob Marshall Wilderness."

Before she could ask what that meant, exactly, he said, "Before that, I was roughnecking in Wyoming."

"But you're a veterinarian. Right? Or do you only play

one on TV? Did I take poor, crushed Henry to a veterinary impersonator?"

"I got the credentials," he said. "But then I realized Jake wanted them a whole lot more than I did."

"So you won't use them? Good grief, Caleb. I never had even *one* parent who wanted *anything* good for me."

She clamped her lips closed.

What is it about him that makes me say things like that? I have to know so I can stop this from happening.

But he threw her such an empathetic look that tears sprang to her eyes.

She looked away, set her jaw and swallowed hard as she walked through the door into the kitchen. He followed without saying a word.

Get off yourself. Make it all about him.

"You seem so . . . I don't know," she said. "Settled, or something. I was surprised when Lilah mentioned your wandering. If I didn't know, I'd have guessed you never left Texas."

She chanced another glance at him.

He grinned and drawled, "What? I don't seem like a world traveler to you? You think I'm an unsophisticated redneck?"

Good. Let's lighten up.

She grinned back. "No, and there you go again with that fake-hurt tone. You care less what people think of you than anyone I've ever known."

Mistake. More proof you've been thinking about him.

But he didn't care. He threw her a smile and headed for the 1940s stove, where there was a covered skillet waiting. "I care what *you* think, though," he said sweetly, as he tucked her laptop under his arm and lifted the lid.

After a beat, he added, "Come here and tell me what you think about my cooking. Isn't this the prettiest breakfast you ever saw?"

Comfortable. Caleb Burkett's comfortable in his own skin. That's another way we're total opposites.

She went to look at his masterpiece. It smelled so good it made her mouth water. Scrambled eggs with red and green peppers, bacon bits and cheese.

"It's gorgeous," she teased, "but maybe I think that because I'm starving."

"You're about to make me cry, heapin' on the praise like that," he said. Then he turned brisk. "Let's get this stuff out to the patio and you set us up for a power breakfast while I bring out the food."

On the way through the long room to the back door, Meri tried to see everything in the kitchen. Gold-colored refrigerator from the seventies, rickety old cupboard like the ones Lilah called a "pie safe," big old deep sink with one narrow, built-in cabinet that had a battered wood top.

But so what? The whole room smelled like coffee and bacon and was full of sun from a whole wall of big windows standing open to the breeze. The opposite end of it held boxes and boxes of jars of Honey Grove Kitchens' first product: the precious, hard-won peach preserves stacked on tables he'd made from battered doors and sawhorses.

There was another beat-up work table with a worn chair. Nothing else.

He took her outside onto a patio made of more newly laid flagstones like the ones in the front walk, put her laptop and agenda on the big, wrought-iron table in the shade of yet another live-oak tree and turned to her.

"Coffee. Black, right?"

She nodded, her traitorous heart lifting a little with pleasure that he'd remembered.

"Only way to drink it," he said, and went back in.

He remembered that because he drinks it that way, too, you ninny.

She made herself quit thinking and work quickly, laying out her lists, her other written notes and opening up the laptop. Caleb came back with heavy paper plates of breakfast burritos with salsa on the side and napkins, then went back in for the thick mugs of coffee.

Meri held hers in both hands and sipped carefully. Then they ate hungrily.

"You're a good cook," she said. "Are these Brandywine tomatoes in the salsa?"

"Yep. You're a tomato farmer, for sure. My mom made the salsa."

She said, "Great! I'll ask her for that recipe for the next time there's a surplus of tomatoes. Especially the Brandywines."

Caleb's eyes brightened. "Oh, yeah, I closed the deal for the kitchen. Or I should say *kitchens*."

She froze with the burrito at her lips and stared at him.

"What? You're talking about building more than one? You already made the deal?"

He took a big bite while he nodded yes, waggling a forefinger to say "wait a minute."

When he swallowed, he said, "J. B. and I were just sittin' around shooting the bull after I'd hammered him down to a price we can live with, and I got the idea of doing baked goods to cope with the winter produce lull and use a lot of the surplus we freeze. You know, strawberry cupcakes, zucchini bread—my mom even makes zucchini chocolate cake. Don't you love it?"

He beamed at her while he ate more of the burrito.

Meri tried to cope with the sudden anger assaulting her. It was fear, too.

"You contracted for *two* kitchens without consulting me? What will you do when I'm in New York or Chicago trying to hold up my end of this business long-distance?"

He nodded calmly as he finished the burrito in one huge bite.

That done, he sipped coffee and said. "You've got the virtual stuff covered. I'm your real-life man."

He held her gaze with his long, steady, warm, blue one.

He set his cup away and reached halfway across the table to lay his big hand down, palm up and open.

Such a wave of longing and desire flooded through her that it almost washed away the anger and the fear.

But not quite. This was danger like she'd never known.

"Caleb. You need to know that if we can't talk Lilah into letting us save Honey Grove, I want out of this business."

His eyes warmed even more.

"Meri. I could write you a check for your half right now and you wouldn't take it."

"Because I haven't given up on Lilah yet . . ."

He shook his head, still looking deep into her . . . *self*. Her real self. There was no place to hide.

"Here's what you need to know most of all," he said. "I have no intention whatsoever of keeping this relationship with you all business. None. We will make a hell of a pair and that's not me talking. It's meant to be."

Shocked, she couldn't move. Her hand ached to move closer to his, to touch it. She couldn't breathe.

The leaves overhead rustled in the breeze.

"If you can't live with that, get up and walk away. I won't promise that'd stop me from coming to New York or Chicago or London or wherever, but I will write you that check right now."

She tried, oh, she tried to be strong. She even called on her hurt feelings and managed to speak.

"How can I trust you? You told J. B. you wanted two kitchens before you even told me."

"Well, hell, J. B. was sittin' right there. I don't know where you were."

He grinned, then, that devil grin and she found out she was way more susceptible to him than she would ever have believed.

She laughed. They both laughed more than the joke deserved and somehow, during all the laughter, she laid her hand in his.

It cradled hers, easy and warm, his calluses comfortably rough against her skin. The feeling she'd had when he held her in his arms bloomed full in her blood again. Safety. Here was safety.

Their fingers twined. He squeezed her hand and before she could think, she squeezed back.

Thirty-one

Those two were thick as thieves this morning. Ever since Caleb had arrived at Honey Grove at sunup to help Jimmy load the produce for the farmers market (first time Cale had done *that*), he and Meri had been different with each other.

Caleb said he'd come out to help so Lilah wouldn't do too much and lift more than five pounds now that Doc had taken off her sling. And that might be right, because he loved Lilah a lot. But that wouldn't account for the change in the way Meri looked at him or for the more relaxed way she behaved. Would it?

No, it would not. She'd known they were falling for each other when Meri was in her teddy/slicker outfit. So, likely they were planning to double-team her today about throwing in with them as partner. But, Lordy! They said they were going to build *two* kitchens, and that meant they'd need that seventy-five thousand dollars more than ever.

Last night, Lilah went to bed still exhausted from all the work and excitement of the peach preserving and the fire and all the work and worry she'd had since, but she hardly

slept a wink for trying to imagine what life would be like if
she lost Honey Grove. *When*, to tell the truth. Not *if*.

Because she'd done everything she knew to do to try
to save it. Right now, she felt like the heartbreak would
kill her.

It'd be even worse, though, if Honey Grove Kitchens
failed. The guilt would eat her alive.

Yet she was so selfish, she was sorely tempted to tell
them she'd take their offer and then work like crazy to help
them succeed.

She was so beyond sick of all this indecision that she
was probably imagining there was something different
about the kids just so she could have something new to
take her mind off the money problems.

Now that they were in town and setting up the booth,
they kept trying to make her sit in the truck until they got
the booth set up. She had humored that notion for ten minutes now and that was enough. There were things she could
be doing to help.

Also, from here she couldn't hear a word they were saying.

She opened the door and got out. Farmers market booths
formed a line down the middle of the square and the traffic went around on the days it was open, creating sort of a
mildly carnival atmosphere. Lilah would try to enjoy that
today and live every moment that she was still a farmer.

Lots of sellers were here today and tents were popping
up fast. Now, if the customers would just come, they'd have
a good day. The weather was beautiful, a little bit cooler, so
maybe some of the organic, fresh, eat-local foodies would
take a drive today and come out from San Antonio and
Austin.

Lilah opened the back door of the truck, took out the tall
folding stool and the cash box and carried them across the
square to the spot Meri and Caleb had chosen for their tent.
They had it up and almost all tied down already. Neither one
of them was the kind to let any grass grow under their feet.

They scolded Lilah a little for carrying the stool but

she'd done that with her stronger arm and tucked the cash box under the other, so she was good. She set up behind the front counter while they began bringing boxes of produce and preserves on the rolling dolly they'd hauled in the bed of the truck.

Lilah kept one observing eye on them while she arranged the jars of preserves and divided the okra and the last of the Big Boy tomatoes into peck baskets. It was such a pleasure to have both arms free now, but her left wrist was still weak enough that she used it in a gingerly way instead of trying to push it back to normal immediately. Doc would be shocked to see that but she'd learned a lesson when it took so long to heal.

She must be getting old. Probably, she wouldn't ever climb another tree.

She'd noticed that Shorty had quit starting his colts himself. And Dulcie used one of the Burkett Ranch pick-ups now to haul her art equipment down to the river for landscape painting instead of crossing the pastures on horseback like she always used to do.

Lilah smiled to herself. Ironically, getting old seemed to make people less reckless with their bodies and more reckless with their words and attitudes, because they cared less and less what other people might think. She loved that about her age right now. It was downright amazing what wasn't the least bit important to her anymore.

It was also amazing to realize that she could do any-thing she had to do. If she decided to let Honey Grove go for Meri's and Caleb's sake, she could do it.

Meri and Caleb were still all wrapped up in their busi-ness talk—nodding one minute in agreement and having a hard-gesturing argument the next. They were fun to watch, taking a minute to sit on the opened tailgate of Caleb's pickup and look at some papers Meri had brought in her big bag.

Lilah grinned, remembering her first sight of Meri as an adult. In that moment, she would never have visualized the citified Meri sitting on the tailgate of a pickup parked on the square. Her granddaughter had changed a great deal in a short time.

More customers for the farmers market began to drift in and park along the square. Lilah checked her watch. Nine o'clock. It was about time things picked up.

Shorty walked past on the sidewalk on the north side of the square and waved at her, motioning that he'd go on down to the coffee shop for a while. He'd keep watch out the window, she knew, and come to help at the booth if they were really busy.

If not, he'd end up standing under the big pecan tree in front of the saddle shop, arguing the Bible with old man Mitt Burlingame the way they always did. She shook her head in wonder. Neither one of them knew enough Scripture to wad a thimble.

Lilah wished he'd come over here right now and listen to her worry over what to do about this mess she was in. But Shorty was sick of hearing it and already to the point where men go so quickly. Make up your mind. *Do* something so you'll quit talking about it.

Lord knew she would if she could. But she still didn't know what was right. She was worn smooth out with thinking about it.

Never make a decision when you're tired.

She could hear those wise words in her mother's voice as surely as if she were with her right now in the flesh as well as in spirit.

Her mother and grandmother both had seemed very close lately. No matter how old a person got, when she found herself in deep trouble she still wanted her mother.

Precious little Meri had never had that comfort.

Instead, she'd had a mother she couldn't bear to think about. And her only grandmother hadn't tried hard enough to find her.

It'd be morally reprehensible for that grandmother to come into her life twenty years late and become a burden to her.

Meri and Caleb needed her decision within the week so

they could get the money together to pay Buford. Lilah's hands shook a little.

But she still had a couple of days to feel a leaning toward which way she should go. The answer would come when she least expected it.

She sneaked another glance at her granddaughter and Caleb.

If Lilah did go in with them, then they'd feel trapped in the business forever. Even if things went sour between them and they ended up hating each other, they'd keep hanging on for her sake. Without Lilah, they'd be free to split up and go their separate ways if it all went south.

Really, she *did* need to know what was going on between them. If only Meri would open up to her! Confidences over cocoa and cookies while curled up on the sofa was supposed to be a perk of grandmotherhood, wasn't it?

Caleb and Meri finished unloading all the produce, and the three of them arranged it on the table and around it on the ground. Then the two young people left to visit the other booths, handing out brochures about Honey Grove Kitchens, spreading the word. Their excitement was contagious.

Verna Carl Brassfield stopped at the booth, chattering away about how she really believed that coolness in the air early this morning was a sign of an early fall and how pitifully weird the square looked with Raul's all burned down. Not to mention the smell of smoke that still hung in the air. But mostly she went on and on about how sorry she was that she'd missed all the excitement the day of the fire, including the work at the church.

She tried to make up for not helping by buying six jars of the peach preserves to use for gifts. Lilah wrapped them in newspapers so they wouldn't break and packed them in the bottom of a big bag. As she handed it to Verna Carl, she saw Doreen on the sidewalk in front of Suzy's.

"Who's that Doreen's talking to? I don't know that girl."

Verna Carl turned to look. "Oh. She's the mysterious young woman who came into town on the bus."

"What! I haven't heard about that. When?"

"The day after the fire, I think it was. Nobody knows who her people are or where she's from, not anything about her, really, but Doreen latched on to her."

Lilah sighed. "Of course she did. You mean that girl just picked Rock Springs at random? Why in the world?"

Verna Carl shrugged and glanced at her watch. "Doreen has taken up with her in a big way, so maybe we'll find out why one of these days."

Then she rushed off to pick up her granddaughter from cheerleading lessons, and that pushed Doreen and her latest protégé to the back of Lilah's mind. Carly was only thirteen years old, so she probably *did* share confidences with her grandmother. Would she still do that when she was twenty-seven?

After that, Lilah sold two pecks of tomatoes and one of okra to a family who'd driven out from Brenham because of the "new" idea that it was better for people to eat locally grown foods than to pay extra to have them hauled in from the ends of the earth. Good. Maybe the concept would turn out to be more than a passing fad.

Lilah looked to see what Meri and Caleb were doing. They were in front of Aunt Annie's Handmade Soaps. Derek Hornbuckle had walked up to talk to Caleb. Meri was gazing off across the square with the strangest expression on her face.

Lilah turned to follow her gaze. A young man stepping off the curb had his eye on the Honey Grove sign and was headed straight for Lilah. He didn't look familiar and he was dressed all wrong, even if he *was* wearing jeans.

He had on high-topped hiking shoes and a plaid . . . was that a *flannel* shirt with the sleeves rolled up? Surely not. But it was. At least, it was thin flannel. He must be from up north and cold-natured, to boot.

Lilah double-checked. Yes, he was what held Meri's attention. She'd gone paler than ever before but her cheeks were slashed with red. She was furious. And surprised to the point of shock.

All at once, Lilah knew. Could this possibly be the boy-friend from New York?

From the corner of her eye, she saw Meri start in her direction.

They arrived at the Honey Grove booth at almost the same moment.

Lilah was right. Of course. That feeling never failed her. If only it'd come to her about the farm.

"Tim," Meri said, in a new, hard voice. "Why are you here?" Fierce Meri.

The tentative smile vanished from Tim's face. He jerked back, mute and miserable, and looked at Meri. But he didn't turn tail.

"Meri." His eyes were red-rimmed and tired. This young man was exhausted. "I need to talk to you."

"I said all I'll ever have to say to you the day I left New York. Go away."

"I'll talk. I want you to listen." His voice was stronger now. "There's a lot you don't know."

Oh no! Her curiosity might pull her in.

And no good could come of this. Lilah remembered what Meri looked like when she'd come back from that day in New York.

Meri was still looking at him, blank-faced. "Go."

He blurted, "I can't think about anything but you."

Oh no! That really did sound like he meant it. And that he'd suffered over it. But how could he really care for her if he hadn't stuck up for her at the law firm?

Meri gave no sign but Lilah could feel her soften, just a hair. Her glare moved from his face to his shirt.

"I know all of flyover country's the same to you, Tim," she said, in her most sarcastic tone, "but your plane has landed in Texas. In the summer. Hard to confuse with Colorado."

Tim swallowed hard. But he took hope, of course. Because she'd said any words at all that weren't ordering him to leave.

He tried a small smile. "Don't be sarcastic. That hiking trip was our best time together, Meri. Don't you remember?"

"Oh, yeah. And I also remember how you threw me under the bus the first time office politics threatened your career. For some reason, I remember more about *that* than the Rockies trip."

"I must talk to you."

"You're a couple of months too late on that."

"You wouldn't listen before."

Meri set her fists on her hips. "And I won't now. Get out of here, Tim. Get out of Texas. I never want to see you again."

Caleb walked up behind Meri but she was unaware.

Tim saw him, but he didn't flinch. Maybe he was tougher than he looked. He straightened, stood taller and squared his shoulders.

Still, he couldn't compare with Caleb. Lilah looked from one of them to the other. There was no comparison at all, apples and oranges. Tim could never hope to win if Lilah was right about the hints of a budding romance between Meri and Caleb.

"Give me a time and a place and I'll meet you there. I'm not leaving this town, much less the state, until you hear me out. Which, I promise, you'll be glad you did. Even if you never see me again after that."

His face changed. His voice, too. "I miss you too much, Meredith."

Meri didn't say a word.

Lilah's breath caught. She remembered, too, how the heartbroken Meri had said Tim was her only long-term relationship because they were perfectly matched. She'd said it more than once.

The feeling that no good could come of this grew to the size of a bowling ball in Lilah's gut. Her intuition never failed her. The wind shifted and brought the stink of smoke, like a bad omen, from the burned hulk of rubble that used to be Raul's.

Stick to your guns, Meri. Make him leave.

"I can explain everything," he said. "Please, Meri. I love

you. I'll never love anybody else. You owe me a chance to set the record straight."

Lilah's heart sank into a growing, sickening feeling while Meri just stood there, looking at him.

This was a child who'd been abandoned too many times. Here was somebody she'd loved coming back to claim her.

Plus, what woman could resist at least hearing some more of that kind of talk?

At last, Caleb said, "You want me to run him off, Mer?"

Tim startled and looked at him but didn't back down.

Meri shook her head without turning around.

And, sure enough, her look wasn't as hard as she stared at him.

"Thirty minutes of your day," he said. "That's all. Nothing was like you thought it was at the office, Meredith, and I have proof over there in my rental car. I did not betray you. I didn't know Alan would *fire* you. All he said to me when he took you off the team was that you were too much into details, and that was slowing us down."

"And . ."

"That you're too controlling, too much of a crusader, too argumentative and too sure you know what's best."

"And you didn't bother to pass that on to me?"

"All that was after he'd let you go. Not before. I have proof," he said. "Right over there in my car."

Lilah clicked her tongue in dismay. Meri was an attorney. She was a doubter, and for good reason. She would not be able to resist seeing the evidence.

Meri said, "You destroyed my life, Tim Montgomery. While I was planning for you to share it."

"I'm *not* complicit. Alan fired me, too. I'll tell you all about it. And if you want to stay here, I'm going to look for a new position in Austin. Or Dallas. Texas has more jobs than the rest of the country. I've done the research."

Meri kept her eyes on him. Lilah willed him to go away. She decided he was telling the truth, at least the part about him losing his job.

Sure enough, Meri did what Lilah thought she would.

"All right," she said. "You have thirty minutes." She led the way, headed for Suzy's Cafe.

Caleb watched them go. "He doesn't know her," he said, almost talking to himself.

Startled, Lilah stared at him. "Do *you?*"

He gave her that grin. "I'm learnin'. And I'm bettin' she'll send him on his way."

Lilah's worried heart thrilled at that. There was a weight in Caleb's voice that showed he knew more than he was telling. She would try to feel him out—without prying, of course.

She shook her head. "I don't know, Caleb. If he's got proof that convinces her he had nothing to do with her losing her job, then he'll fit right in with her plan to move back to New York and work on the kitchen from there."

"Forget that," he drawled. "This is where she belongs. The ties are here. She just doesn't know that yet."

Lilah felt a smile take over her face. "Oh, Caleb. I do hope you're right."

He cocked his head and twinkled at her. "Of course I am. When have I ever been wrong? In my whole life?"

They laughed, remembering the tumult of his growing-up years.

Then he touched her hand, just the way he used to do as a kid. "Guaranteed she'll stay," he said. "Put it out of your mind. Now, you got anything you need me to do right now, Miss Lilah?"

"Can't think of anything."

"I'll get back to work. Call if you need help. Lift nothing heavier than five pounds, remember that."

Somebody hollered at him and he was gone, leaving Lilah torn between smiling at the warmth of his warning and gnashing her teeth over Tim's arrival. She'd only *thought* she had troubles before.

If that young man broke Meri's heart again, she'd have to hurt him.

If Caleb didn't beat her to it.

But Lilah would not say a word. Not one. She'd sworn

to let Meri make her own decisions and she'd hold to that, even though it'd be the hardest thing she'd ever done.

Even if her little voice *was* screaming that Meri shouldn't take Tim back. Her only comfort was another truth: Nobody could or should ever try to pick another person's mate for them.

"So," Caleb said, "what happened?"

He glanced both ways, then pulled out onto the highway. He'd waited until they were out of Rock Springs and headed to Honey Grove before he asked the question Meri had been expecting. She'd known it was coming ever since Shorty announced he was taking Lilah to Sonic for a limeade chiller before he brought her home.

Strangely enough, she didn't resent the question. In fact, she welcomed it. Her mind was whirling with all the memories Tim had stirred. Her insides were in turmoil and she had an unfamiliar urge to talk things out.

"He showed me a stack of e-mails he'd printed and supposedly all the memos from Alan and yada, yada, yada, on and on. Supposedly they prove he didn't know that Alan was planning to push me off the CRT team until the minute it happened."

"You believe it?"

She shrugged. "I don't know. It's impossible to prove a negative. I do know he never said a word in my defense, never took one risk that would cause him to follow me out the door. Yet it happened anyway. They're cutting back like crazy."

He gave a judicious nod. "Sounds like you still don't trust him."

She stared out the windshield at the green-and-brown fields stretching away from either side of the narrow asphalt.

"I don't know how I ever trusted him enough to plan a life with him. Why *did* I? *How* did I? I should've known myself better."

"I've been there," he drawled.

She twisted to face him as much as she could inside her seat belt.

"Caleb." For some reason, she had to take a deep breath and make herself go on. "I have huge problems with commitment because . . . of my mother. I shouldn't have committed to Tim, and I don't think I ever can do that again."

He threw her a warm glance and that devilish grin. "Happens I have a history of that kind of difficulty, myself."

She couldn't resist grinning back, which made her feel better than she had done since the moment she saw Tim in the square.

"So I've heard," she said.

The grin widened. "I'm sure you have. I've been the favorite topic of gossip in Rock County all my life."

They held the look.

"Most of what you've heard's probably true, even if maybe exaggerated," he said. "The one story that's not true is that Ronnie Rae was still married when she shot me. Foolin' around with married women has never been my style."

Meri nodded.

"No matter what you hear, remember that."

Suddenly, her good feeling was gone. She believed him implicitly but that only pulled her more strongly to him. She didn't know how to have a lasting relationship with a man. And she knew, like a strike of lightning, that she was falling for Caleb—and that if she let herself fall too far, it would literally kill her if it didn't last.

She said. "And trusting my heart has never been mine. Remember that."

He looked at the road, then back at her. His smile was gentle this time.

He nodded. "Got it."

He looked at the empty road again, then back at her. She was still looking at him, memorizing his rugged jaw and straight nose and perfect profile. She couldn't take her eyes off him.

"I love you, Meredith Kathleen. I've known since I saw you that you're my soul mate."

She stared. "How can that be? We're opposites and we fight and I may go back to New York. I told you that."

"Heard you," he said. "But you might not. And I'm a wanderer, anyhow. Let's just give it a shot. You'll find out that I'm right."

Her idiot heart leapt, thrilled, but she didn't trust it.

"But, Caleb . . ."

He checked the road again and then his eyes were smiling into hers.

"Shhh," he said. "No worries. It'll work out or it won't. We'll just take it one day at a time, how about that? Do we have a deal?"

She was not a strong enough person—there wasn't one in the whole world—to resist that grin. This time it held such sweetness.

He took one hand off the wheel and rested it on the seat between them, palm up and open.

Meri laid her hand in his. It cradled hers, still easy and warm, his good calluses rough in the same places against her skin. The feeling came back, too, surging into her blood. Safety. Here was safety.

When the back screen door slammed, Lilah startled awake in her easy chair so fast she nearly knocked Henry out of her lap. She'd been sleeping through the six o'clock news again. Dang! She was getting to where she couldn't even stay awake to hear about the weather. She'd have to tell Shorty he should've stayed for supper so he could keep her awake.

She got busy stroking Henry's back, nose to tail, trying to soothe him out of his yowling complaints.

"Lilah?"

"In here, Meri. I'm supposed to be watching the news."

Meri came through the doorway with her fast, purposeful

walk, sat down in the other wing chair and arched her perfect brows at Lilah. "*Supposed* to be watching?"

Thank goodness Henry settled down enough they didn't have to yell.

Lilah smiled sheepishly. "Nodded off before I knew what was happening."

"I've got news that'll wake you up."

Oh, Lord. Don't let it be that she's back with Tim already.
"What is it?"

Meri gave her a fleeting smile, then looked at the television screen. "Give me a minute. As soon as I said that, I got shaky."

"Lord have mercy! You can't come in here and do that to me."

"I promise. I *will* go through with it. Just let me sit a minute."

Go through with what? Oh, God forbid "it" should be a wedding!

No, Meri wouldn't do that. Not this soon. Lilah had to get the fog out of her brain so she could think straight.

She fixed her eyes on the screen to keep from staring at Meri. Truly, bless her heart, the child was breathing hard. But she wasn't saying a word.

"I really appreciate that newsgirl right there," Lilah said. "At least she isn't dressed for a cocktail party with her neckline cut so low it shows her whole boobies and half her navel."

With a smile in her voice, Meri said, "You think she's had some good raisin'?"

Well, if Meri was in a teasing mood, whatever she was working up her nerve to say surely wasn't *too* bad.

"I do," Lilah said, "and Southern raisin', at that, although they've trained her to talk like a Yankee up there on the national networks. That right there is a girl who knows you don't wear velvet after February or white shoes before Easter."

"I think you're right."

"But then again," Lilah said, "we don't know if she's ever been tempted to go along with the crowd. Maybe her boss never has asked her if she'd like to wear a slut costume like all the other girls."

They were laughing at that when Meri jumped up again like she'd been sitting on sticker burrs.

"Iwanttolookatmymother'sthings," she said, so fast that it was all one word and it took Lilah a minute to grasp its meaning.

Lilah stood up alongside her granddaughter. "Then let's just do that very thing," she said, and was so proud that her voice came out completely calm.

This just goes to show you never can tell. Keep on keeping your mouth shut, Lilah Briscoe.

She let Meri lead the way back through the kitchen.

But she couldn't keep her tongue from saying, "What brought this on, sugar?"

"I have to do it. I can't go forward in my life, not really, until I find some kind of closure about . . . my mother."

Go forward? You mean, like marrying? But Lilah did not say it.

"Tim was my only long-term relationship and the first time I ever realistically hoped I might have a family of my own. Now I know I'm not ready for that yet."

Lilah got her mind around all that as they went down the back steps, Meri's hand under her elbow as if Lilah were a feeble old thing. But she let it be.

Her heart was beating faster. She sent up a little prayer that she'd have the right words for Meri as they looked at Edie Jo's things. That seeing them and talking about her mother would bring Meri some measure of peace.

And she prayed to be a good actor so Meri wouldn't know that she'd already seen the pieces of Edie Jo's life. If Meri knew Lilah had broken her promise, she'd never trust her again. But she couldn't have not looked at them. She had to be sure there was nothing there that would damage Meri even more.

Not to mention she had to check for insects dangerous to the farm.

Thank the Good Lord Meri finally had come to this decision.

"Even as old as I am, it still shocks me sometimes that life's so full of surprises," she said, as much to herself as to Meri. "Anything can happen."

"That is so true," Meri said wisely. "I could not believe it when I saw Tim coming across the square."

Gold star for Lilah. Not one question passed her lips.

The wind was rising, rustling the persimmon tree against the dusky sky as Meri hurried them across the yard toward the springhouse.

They left the door open to the cooler evening air and Lilah flipped on the light.

Meri stopped still in the middle of the small room and Lilah got scared she was changing her mind. The boxes sat waiting, rewrapped. Their red strings shone in the light against the white walls of the little building.

"Let's get to it," Lilah said briskly. She went to the nearest plank table and slipped the string off the first box she touched. "How about if I just open all four and you start spreading things out on both tables?"

The first one she was opening was the one that'd help Meri the most.

Sure enough, Meri had the same shocked reaction Lilah had felt the first time she opened that box. It held only pieces of tin with bright pictures painted on one side.

"What? Pieces of art? Edie Jo was never interested in art."

Her voice trailed off as she picked up one and then another of the colorful pieces. As she studied them, her eyes widened. Lilah didn't say a word. She turned away to open more boxes, holding her breath to see if Meri saw what she had seen in those paintings.

"Maybe that guy who took her to South America was an artist," Meri said, spreading them out on the table. "Are these those religious paintings?"

"Well," Lilah said, "when I knew her, Edie Jo was never interested in anything spiritual."

Meri said, "All of these look like the work of the same person . . ."

"Umm-hmm." Lilah took out Edie Jo's scrapbook. And then a packet of letters and some old photos of Edie Jo at different ages. Then a small cedar jewelry box with Lilah's mother's garnet ring and a high-school ring that looked to have belonged to one of the many boyfriends, and some diamond earrings Lilah had never seen.

Meri came over to riffle through all of that. Lilah gave her the ring handed down from her namesake great-grandmother and they talked about it. They looked at Edie Jo's publicity photos and her scrapbook of mementos from the few small-time acting and dancing jobs she'd managed to land, then Lilah drifted back to the paintings.

"Your mother wasn't a collector," she said. "Of anything. These really surprise me."

"Me, too," Meri said. "And you're right—we left lots of stuff in every apartment we moved out of. She never kept anything."

Meri kept moving from one painting to the next.

"I love the colors in these," she said. "And the Impressionistic feel. I wonder if that guy who took Mom to South America *was* an artist."

Lilah tried to hold her tongue again, but failed. "They're signed," she said.

It took a long minute before Meri muttered, "E.J.B.? Is that what the initials are?" It took her a minute. "Edie Jo Briscoe? No. It can't be . . ."

She whirled to look at Lilah. "Did you know she could do this? Was she artistic as a child? In high school? I could never even get her to color in a coloring book with me. Crayons used to be my favorite thing."

Lilah could almost hear her heart beating. And Meri's.

The girl was staring at the painting in her hand. It was the most important of the lot.

"But this is Honey Grove," Meri said. "No mistaking the barn and the beehives . . .

"Oh, and it's you, Lilah. The way you're standing . . . and Mom, when she was a little girl . . ."

"Look again."

Meri glanced up, frowning. "Of course it's you."

Lilah held her granddaughter's puzzled gaze. For a long moment. She looked at the painting again as if she'd never studied it before.

"And you."

Meri's eyes flew open even wider and her cheeks reddened underneath the yellow glow of the bare ceiling bulb. "Not likely," she said wryly.

She couldn't keep from looking at it again, though.

"Your mama had red hair from the day she was born," Lilah said. "That little girl's is black."

Meri stared and stared at the little girl in the picture. Finally, without lifting her head, she began to nod agreement.

"She wanted you to be here at Honey Grove with me," Lilah said softly. "Or she wouldn't have painted that. Your mother was sorry she kept us apart and, in her imagination, she tried to change that."

It took a long time but Meri didn't look up.

"Don't you agree with me?"

When Meri lifted her gaze to meet Lilah's, her eyes filled with tears.

"She loved us both, Meri. In her own selfish, twisted way, she really did. Otherwise, we wouldn't have been in her mind. In her heart."

Meri sank down on the bench attached to the table. "I guess she did, in her own selfish, twisted way. She told me all kinds of bad things about you," she said, lifting her eyes to Lilah's as she confided that. "Until I finally quit asking."

"And then you forgot me."

Lilah went to sit across the table and leaned toward Meri. She told her everything then. Edie Jo's vindictive fury when Lilah wouldn't lend her any more money, and how she tried to get Edie Jo declared an unfit mother so she could keep Meri at Honey Grove. The three expensive but unsuccessful detectives she'd hired to find the two of them when they left town. The years and years of tears and prayer.

"We moved all the time," Meri said. "One year I went to school in five different cities. I was always the new girl, the outsider and shy as could be, so I finally quit trying to have friends."

"I'll never forgive myself for quitting the search," Lilah said with a hitch in her voice. "Oh, Meri."

She dragged in a deep, ragged breath. "You needed me to tell you I loved you and I needed you to tell me the same. Your mama never would."

Meri shrugged. "Me neither. But she did hold me and stroke my hair sometimes. And she didn't give me away."

She kept looking at the painting. "Until I was fourteen. And at least that gave me all of high school in the same place. Even if I didn't really belong to the family I was with."

Lilah reached across and took her granddaughter's hand. Meri didn't pull it away.

Thirty-two

The next morning, Meri sat on the back porch still swinging gently long after first light had come and gone, the first Meredith Kathleen's scrapbook forgotten in her lap. She kept having flashes of Edie Jo's paintings and thinking of the fact that her mother had had a wonderful talent Meri never suspected. But it was the painting of Lilah and Meri together at Honey Grove that she could see in every detail when she closed her eyes.

It must be the source of the gut-level decision that her mind had presented to her as a done deal in the middle of the night: She would stay in Texas. This was without precedent for her. Always, all her life, her method was to think through every detail and every pro and con before she reached any important decision. This one was forgone. She'd spent hours now, looking at it from every angle, and it had stayed the same.

She loved every inch of Honey Grove. She cared about Lilah far more than Edie Jo had ever cared about Meri. And she knew in her heart Lilah cared deeply about her, or she would not have put concern for her and Caleb ahead of saving Honey Grove. She loved this farming life, which offered a new challenge and new hard work every day, yet the rewards at its bedrock core never changed. She'd never felt so alive in all of her senses.

She wanted to be here all the time for Honey Grove Kitchens, too. Doing only the online work and living in New York would cause her to miss all the on-the-ground excitement.

And she would admit, to herself only, that Caleb was a big part of her wanting to stay. She *needed* that feeling of security that she'd never had before. And romance. She wanted a real, honest to goodness chance at romance.

But she'd told him the truth. She didn't know if she'd be able to do it. She was willing to give it a shot though. No fear. And sexy Caleb there to help her. She smiled.

The screen squeaked and Lilah stepped out the back door holding her first mug of coffee in one hand and a large brown paper bag in the other. Meri jumped up to help her.

"Stay there," Lilah said. "I need to use my wrist to strengthen it. Sit back down."

But Meri couldn't. "That bag looks heavy. Are you sure . . ."

"It's *not* five pounds. And you need to rest, not to wait on me hand and foot. I heard you get up before the crack of dawn, tired as you must be from all the work and the emotional strain from that *Tim*."

The disgust in her voice made Meri smile. Lilah was loyal to *her.* Lilah cared about her. Meri knew that now, all the way to her bones. She loved knowing that.

Lilah held the door open with her back against it until she got everything through, using her foot to keep Henry—who sat down and glared at her—inside as the screen door closed. She came to sit down beside Meri.

Take it easy, Mer. Don't rush into it. You know a little bit about how to deal with her now. Pretend you're in court and persuade her.

Once she was settled, Meri said, "All right, Lilah. I want to ask you about this recipe for Christmas cake. Is this the one you were saying my mom always liked so much?"

"That's it and that's the first time it ever got written down," Lilah said. "Before that, it was just passed on by word of mouth from one generation to the next, since way back before our people came from Tennessee to Texas with Sam Houston."

She leaned back, took the colander full of fresh green beans out of the bag and shook it open at her feet to catch the ends of the beans when she snapped them. "It's so nice to have both hands to use," she said. "This is my favorite place to sit and snap beans."

Her voice broke on the last word. Meri saw tears in her eyes as she sipped her coffee. She must be thinking that this might be the last time she did that at Honey Grove.

"No hurry today," Lilah said, her voice a little stronger. "Sunday got here just in time. We both need a little letup on the working and rushing around."

"Are you going to church?"

"Yeah, but there's plenty of time to get dressed. I'll help you at the barn first."

"I'm going to learn to make this cake," Meri vowed. "It looks complicated but it sounds delicious."

"It is, and it is. I'll teach you how."

She took another sip of coffee. "Not to get all sloppy sentimental," she said, "but I want you to know it makes me so happy that you've fallen in love with this scrapbook and will treasure it when I'm gone."

"I *will* treasure it," Meri said. "I want Honey Grove, too."

Lilah caught a breath. She threw Meri a sharp look.

"That thrills me to hear," she said, keeping her tone very even. "But, honey, that seventy-five thousand might pull y'all under. You don't want a bankruptcy on your record."

Meri held her gaze, trying to keep her impatience out of her eyes.

"And you never can tell what's going to happen," Lilah went on. "If Tim's going to hang around here and hunt for a job in Texas . . ."

"That's not relevant. We might be friends. Or not. But definitely nothing more."

"And who knows how you and Caleb will get along over time, since you both need to be the boss . . ."

They turned toward the sound of tires crunching on gravel. A big maroon car crept down the driveway.

"Who in the world," Lilah said, "at this time on a Sunday morning?"

At the end of the walk, the car drove right on up into the yard with no regard whatsoever for the grass.

Lilah and Meri both stared at it.

Buford Quisenberry rolled his windows down and sat there, looking the horse pasture over. And then the truck patch. And the beehives full of honey in the sweetgum grove.

"Is that who I think it is?" Meri asked.

"It is. Acting like he owns the place already. Surely he wouldn't drive out here and do business on a *Sunday* to call the note."

"It isn't due for another week, so, legally, he can't."

Lilah picked up a crisp green bean and snapped it.

"Buford," she called, "what can I do for you?"

He opened the door, got out, and walked around the front of the car, coming toward them.

"Just checking," he said. "From the looks of things, I'd say in the right hands, this place could service its own debt."

"Sorry sumbitch," Lilah muttered.

Startled, Meri looked at her.

"Is that why you drove all the way out here? To insult me?"

His face reddened as he walked closer to the porch. Meri noticed that Lilah didn't invite him onto it to sit down.

"Meri, this is Buford Quisenberry," she said. "Buford, my granddaughter, Meredith, the attorney."

He nodded at Meri and gave her a wide smile. "Nice to meet you, Miss Meri. I heard all about your speech at the pie contest. You're quite the celebrity in Rock Springs."

"Thank you," Meri said.

She would let Lilah handle this. For now. It was Lilah's business.

Buford turned to look at Lilah again. "To answer your

question, Miss Lilah, no. I came out this morning to remind you of the due date on your note. That's all. I hadn't heard from you and I thought it might've slipped your mind."

"That's not likely," Lilah snapped.

"We're fully aware of the deadline," Meri said. Her tone dismissed him.

Inside the house, Lilah's phone rang. She ignored it.

"Do you often do business on a Sunday, Buford? Did you think I'd already be gone and you could snoop around all you want? Do you even know what time Sunday School begins, Bufe? I haven't seen you there in a long, *long* time."

He glared at her. Then, brusquely, he nodded. "Ladies, have a good day."

Without a word, Lilah and Meri watched him until he was in the car, turned around and gone.

"Buford's like Doreen," Lilah said, "in that they've both wanted this place for a long time. And, if the truth were told, either one of them probably *could* make a profit here."

She went back to snapping the beans.

"Because either one of them has the capital to do that," Meri said, trying to keep both the urgency and the pleading out of her tone. "So can you if you'll accept it. You should learn to accept help, Lilah, instead of always being the giver."

"You sound just like Dulcie. Have you been talking to her?"

"No. I've talked to no one but Caleb about your business. We agree that your participation would increase our chances of success, not hinder them. In fact, we're realizing you're *vital*. You'd be *key*."

Lilah looked up to give her a quizzical, skeptical stare.

The phone in the kitchen rang again, longer this time. Henry matched it, yowl for ring.

"Want me to get that?"

"Let it go," Lilah said. "I can't deal with anything else right now. Listen to me, Meri. I love you and Caleb more than words can tell, so I can't chance it, sugar."

The phone quit and, mercifully, so did Henry.

"You'll be gone and . . ."

"No, Lilah. I'm staying in Texas. I've decided not to go back to New York."

Lilah's mouth fell open in surprise and Meri felt her deep stare as she searched her face. Meri could practically see the wheels turning in Lilah's mind, no doubt looking for a clue as to why she hadn't already guessed this.

Meri laughed. "I know you don't understand why you didn't know that I'd stay before I did. Don't worry, Lilah, you don't have a bug on your grapevine. I didn't know it myself until the middle of last night."

She loved the way Lilah's eyes lit up. She was *happy* for Meri to stay.

"You're sure?"

Meri nodded. "More sure than I've ever been about anything."

Lilah squinted. "It's not because that *Tim* said he's staying in Texas?"

Meri laughed again. "*Tim* is not a blip on my radar screen."

"Caleb?"

Heat rose in Meri's cheeks. "Not because of any man."

"Oh no. You're not staying to take care of *me*? Because if that's it, then I won't have it. No! You have a life to live . . ."

"Whoa," Meri said, like the Texan she was, "I want to live it *here*. I want to be with you, not take care of you. I want this business and Caleb's friendship and I want first light under these trees, looking over these fields to that white bluff. And I want that every morning."

Silence fell and their eyes locked. They looked deep into each other's hearts.

Finally, Lilah heaved a huge sigh. "Well, then," she said, "give your old grandma a hug."

Meri reached across the scrapbook and Lilah across the colander of beans. They hugged for a long moment, cheeks pressed together.

When they parted, Lilah looked at her straight and spoke in her tart tone. "But I'm still not coming in on that

Kitchens business, Meredith Kathleen. Don't think that. You can lose your money from here just as fast as you can long-distance."

Lilah snapped beans again to have something to do with her shaky hands, her mind running a million miles a minute. *What* a kettle of fish this was turning out to be!

Now it'd be even harder on Meri if Lilah let the bank take Honey Grove. The girl loved this place in a bone-deep primal way, the same way Lilah loved it.

Oh! What should she do?

She felt empty and hollow, yet full to the top with feelings she couldn't even name. The only other time she'd *ever* felt this vulnerable was when Ed died. It was awful.

Better get yourself together, girl.

But for once in her life, she didn't even know how to start.

Meri said, "Lilah, try to hear me. Try to listen with an open mind, *please*."

That remark just chapped Lilah's hide. "I *always* have an open mind."

"Sorry," Meri said, "but there's no time to debate that now."

And she had the nerve to give Lilah an impudent little smile.

Lilah refused to smile back at her, although maybe she *did* have a point there.

"Caleb and I need you more than we even realized before," Meri said, trying to keep her tone casual but not succeeding too well. "If you want us to succeed—and I know that you do because you love us both and you're so worried that we might fail—then you have to help us. This far in, we're beginning to see that in order to really go big the way we need to do, we'll have to have you . . ."

Lilah snorted and stopped working. She glared at Meri. "Don't patronize me. I'm in no mood for charity right now."

"Don't underestimate us," Meri shot back. "We're not stupid. We aim to run a successful business and neither one of us can afford to lose our investment. We've done our due diligence. We need you."

"Oh?" Lilah said, wanting more than anything to break down and cry. "And what story have y'all concocted for the poor old grandma who can't pay her own debts?"

She scooped up another handful of beans and snapped one. She couldn't look at Meri. If she did, she'd burst into tears.

In the calmest voice in the world, Meri said, "The name Honey Grove . . ."

"Don't *even* try to tell me that."

"Hear me out."

It was a *command*. Lilah looked down at her beans and shook her head proudly. She could just see this girl in a courtroom.

Meri started up again. "The name and the reputation of Honey Grove, both for the produce and the honey, is golden. So are your contacts in agriculture, your connections in Texas that go back for decades *and* your Firegolds, which nobody else has."

Lilah looked up to meet her granddaughter's eyes. She could begin to see what she was talking about.

"We foresee canning, preserving and freezing to start, as soon as we get our kitchens built. That's summer. To keep the kitchens working during the winter, we'll expand into baked goods, casseroles and soups. I'm thinking eventually maybe catering, too."

Lilah couldn't look away from the light in Meri's eyes. The girl was in love with this business as well as the land.

"So you see? We'll need your recipes and your supervision of the preparation process. Your reputation as a cook guarantees automatic sales. The more people I talk to, I'm learning that you're famous for your food all over this part of Texas. I put the Firegold preserves on the website three days ago and we're already filling orders."

It made no more sense than a donkey reading a book, but Lilah felt a sharp surge of hope. It started her resolve crumbling.

"I would have to oversee the use of my recipes."

"You will have to be the backbone of the entire operation.

Total control in quality assurance. Input into packaging, marketing, shipping, you name it. For our home products, both the baking and catering would be marketed under the Honey Grove Kitchens brand. So would your jams, jellies and honey—we might want to put the beekeeper on contract with us. Then, other farms' produce will be under the Taste This Texas banner."

"I'd still have to oversee the growing, too."

"Of course. You just wouldn't have time for as much hands-on in the fields. And that might not be such a downside."

"Not at all."

Not at my age.

But, of course, she didn't say that.

"You really think this will work? That it'll save Honey Grove?"

Solemnly, Meri nodded. "And maybe several other family farms, too, eventually, since they won't have all that loss through waste. Salvage of unsold produce is a niche, Lilah. Nobody else is in it."

"Well, then. If I can be a help to y'all instead of a hindrance . . ."

Meri looked at Lilah and nodded. "Just *think* of all the experience you'll bring . . ."

". . . and if you all will listen to what I tell you . . ."

Her words trailed off. Already, in her head, Lilah was into it, her imagination racing into the future.

I'll take the reins of this operation and get it lined out just right. Oh! And I can do so much more, once we get everything rolling and people hired to do the paperwork and the deliveries and all that grunt work I don't like. Education! How exciting! I can incorporate eating local into my Texas history talks and vice versa! That'll help with the marketing, too, and . . .

Really. These kids have been right all along. I truly can be a huge help to them. They probably can't do it without me, just as they've been trying to tell me.

Meri's voice reached her faintly.

"So you're in? I can call Caleb and we'll get the money together to pay Buford?"

Lilah took a deep breath. "I'm in."

She held out her open hand. Meri, with a smile as wide as the Texas sky, laid hers in it. They twined fingers and squeezed at the same time.

Meri was beaming. "Do not worry. We can do this."

"I know we can," Lilah said, and all her strength came pouring into her backbone. She should've given in to do this a long time ago and saved them all so much agony.

It wouldn't do to tell Meri and Caleb that, though. They'd value her much more for having had to work so long to get her.

"Remember this, Lilah. Honey Grove Kitchens will revolve around you."

I'll be a truly fair CEO and good to everyone. I'll handle every problem with kindness and grace. People will say that I'm lovely to work for and the staff that follows me around to my talks and my meetings and my trips to buy other people's produce will all adore me. We'll have a lot of fun together.

Meri's cell phone played the song that was her new ringtone. It made Lilah smile: Bob Wills's "Roly Poly."

"You really are a Texan now," she teased as Meri started digging in her pocket to find the phone.

Her whole heart lifted. The decision was made and it was going to turn out wonderfully well.

Maybe, in her gut, she felt better than she had a right to, considering the fact that she'd just agreed to join these two kids who were flying into the face of all reason, but if they ran into trouble, she'd be there to save them.

She felt more hope and happiness than she had in months. Or maybe it was just the absence of loneliness. *We can do this.* They were in it now, all three of them. And Honey Grove was saved.

Meri looked at her phone. "It's B. J."

She answered, then held the phone out to Lilah. "It's for you."

"Lilah! Why won't you answer your phone?" B. J. was breathless.

Lilah's heart constricted. "What's wrong?"

"Doreen's been in a terrible wreck."

"Oh no! What happened? Where? I thought she was gone to market in Dallas."

Lilah held the phone so Meri could hear, too, which was no problem, since B. J. was so worked up she was practically yelling.

"Lawrence went with her and they took the back roads. Just outside Pilot Point, they were stopped to make a left turn to go see Lawrence's nephew at his ranch there, you know? Somebody who was half-flying up behind them tried to pass on the right and sideswiped them with a six-horse trailer."

"Oh! Dear Lord!"

"They were in Lawrence's new pickup. Probably would've been better if they'd been in the Hummer . . ."

"B. J. Who's hurt and how bad? Was anybody else with them? Oh! What about that young woman who's new in town that took up with Doreen? Dulcie told me on the phone last night that she heard that Doreen has hired her to work in the dress shop."

Lilah stopped herself. "But no. Doreen would've left her to keep the place open while she's gone."

"Lawrence got a hard lick to the head but he'll be okay. He's still addled. But Doreen's arm's broken and her right leg was smashed to pieces. Lilah, they think she might lose it."

Lilah went sick to her stomach. "No! No! Oh, I am so *sorry*! I just can't believe it. Bless her . . ."

"Lilah, she's asking for you. She's in the hospital in Plano and she wants you to come."

"Me?"

"Yes, you. You're gonna have to go up there."

"Merciful heavens! On top of everything else . . ."

"Lilah."

"I know. I know."

"She'll have to have a bunch of surgeries and she's

lost so much blood they thought she was gone. Twice, she nearly died."

"I'm going. Just give me a minute to get my mind around it. I was supposed to teach the first-grade Sunday School today. You'll have to take my place."

"I will. Now go get ready but don't go by yourself. The MRI on my back's set for tomorrow and I can't wait for another appointment. I've *got* to get something done about this pain or I'd go with you."

"Don't worry about it. Maybe Dulcie can go."

As soon as Lilah said good-bye and started looking for a way to hang up the phone, Meri reached to take it from her.

"*I'm* going," Meri said. "Your wrist is still too weak for you to drive long distances."

Warmth sprang up and ran in Lilah's blood. Spoken like family.

"Well, all right," she said, and her voice trembled a little bit with unshed tears, "I'd love to have you come. But remember, you may have to put up with a bit of my driving advice from time to time."

Meri looked into her eyes, smiled and shook her head.

"Don't you think I already know that? *Really*, Gran!"

October 1, 1940

This scrapbook belongs to

Meredith Kathleen Rawlins

For my children and to be handed on down

> *Blessed of the Lord be this land,*
> *for the precious things of heaven,*
> *for the dew and for the deep that coucheth*
> *   underneath*
> *And for the precious fruits brought forth by*
> *   the sun*
> *And for the precious things put forth by the moon.*
>
> —Deut. 33:13–14

How to Sweeten Persimmons

BEFORE FIRST FROST

Wrap individually in cheesecloth. Put in icebox near enough ice block to freeze. Leave overnight. Take out in morning and thaw. Rewrap and refreeze. Do this several times. They will be good and sweet for fresh eating or baking, either one.

BISCUITS

Oven at 450, heat two pie plates thinly covered with oil.

Sift 2 cups flour with 4 teaspoons baking powder, 1 teaspoon salt, 1 teaspoon baking soda. Make well in center. Add 8 tablespoons oil and buttermilk. Maybe ¾ cup, don't get too wet. Mix only until batter cleans inside of bowl. Turn out on floured board and work gently. Take pans from oven, cut out biscuits, turn once in the hot oil and bake.

Sausage Gravy

Slice a roll of good country sausage. Hot is best but use mild if you must. Fry in iron skillet until well done and slightly crusty. Remove to platter, leaving crumbles and not too much grease. Maybe 2–3 tablespoons. Sprinkle evenly with a thin layer of flour, salt and pepper and cook until browned. Add milk gradually, stirring constantly. Let the milk cook a little, until bubbly and pour up. If you leave it on the fire, the gravy will shrink. Use milk that hasn't been skimmed too close. Use thin milk and you might just as well not make gravy at all.

*The best way out of a difficulty
is
through it.*

Lemon Chess Pie

Cream ⅓ cup butter (room temp) with 1¼ cups sugar. Add 3 eggs (room temp) and beat well. Mix in juice of 2 lemons (maybe about ⅓ cup) and 2 small pinches of salt until smooth. Pour into unbaked crust, put in preheated 425 oven about 13 minutes until filling starts to brown. Lower the temp to 300 and cook about 20 minutes until pie is set. Let it cool. Very tasty for so little effort.

Fear is a lonely thing.

Even those who love us best cannot get close to us when we are afraid.

For God hath not given us the spirit of fear but of power, and of love, and of a sound mind.

—II Timothy 1:7

Children, this is true. Don't let your fears rule you. Fear is the most destructive force there is because it stops you before you even try. Hot corn bread with butter is always a strengthening thing.

Grandma Talitha's Corn Bread

Oven at 450, grease heating in small iron skillet

    1 generous cup cornmeal
    2 teaspoons baking powder
    Pinch (not quite a ½ teaspoon) baking soda
    1 scant teaspoon salt

Mix, make a well, add an egg and buttermilk enough for cakelike batter. Pour into hot grease in skillet and bake until you smell it baking, about 20 minutes (test with a toothpick). A little more if you like thicker crust.

If we would read the secret history of our enemies, we would find in each man's life a sorrow and suffering enough to disarm all hostility.

—LONGFELLOW

A friend loveth at all times.

—PROVERBS 17:17

Cowboy Cookies

Preheat to 350

Cream 1 cup butter, 1 cup white sugar, 1 cup brown sugar. Beat in 2 eggs. Mix 2 cups flour with 1 teaspooon baking powder, 1 teaspoon baking soda, 1 teaspoon salt. Add gradually to creamed mixture. Add 2 cups oats. Drop by teaspoonful on lightly greased cookie sheets. Bake approximately 9 minutes or until lightly browned.

Make a double batch . . . and take some to a neighbor.

Pray as if no work could help
And work as though no prayer could help.

—GERMAN PROVERB

A proverb is a short sentence based on long experience.

—CERVANTES

Overheard: "If only I could get away from men for a while, I would let my eyebrows grow out."

—"ASK ANY WOMAN," *LADIES' HOME JOURNAL*

Why is it that everybody loses gloves but no one ever finds any?

A woman whose marriage failed says that if she were a bride again, she would continue to plan how much housework could be done in a day but then she'd do only three-quarters of that amount. That would assure enough time left over for companionship with her husband.

Sweet Tea

While loose tea leaves in water come to a boil in a small saucepan on the stove, put a cup of sugar in a large ceramic bowl. Pour boiling tea water through a strainer into the bowl. Let it melt the sugar, stir and leave syrup to sit until cool. Then add cool water and pour into pitcher.

> *I will lift up mine eyes unto the hills, from whence cometh my help.*
>
> —PSALM 121:1
>
> *A man may go by signs*
> *And things that were;*
> *A woman knows, for earth*
> *Is kin to her.*
>
> —FROM "FARM WOMAN," ALMA ROBISON HIGBEE

About the Author

Genell Dellin grew up in a household of seven, including Grandpa Grady, who raised vegetables in a big truck patch and hauled fruit from the Rio Grande Valley to sell door-to-door, and Gram (Ara), well known for her down-home Southern cooking. Several of her recipes now are Lilah's. Genell has written both historical and contemporary romance, and she loves to hear from her readers. Please visit her website at www.GenellDellin.com.

Now Available

from *New York Times* Bestselling Author

JODI THOMAS

Rewriting Monday

With her career as a big-city reporter over, Pepper Malone has escaped to Bailee, Texas, to pull herself together before moving on. But when she bursts into the office of Mike McCulloch, editor of the *Bailee Bugle*, demanding a job, neither of them is prepared for the madman targeting this sleepy little town's newspaper staff—or for the feelings growing between them.

Jodi Thomas is...

"A masterful storyteller."
—Catherine Anderson, *New York Times* bestselling author

*Enter the rich world of
historical romance
with Berkley Books . . .*

Madeline Hunter

Jennifer Ashley

Joanna Bourne

Lynn Kurland

Jodi Thomas

Anne Gracie

Love is timeless.

berkleyjoveauthors.com

Penguin Group (USA) Online

What will you be reading tomorrow?

Patricia Cornwell, Nora Roberts, Catherine Coulter,
Ken Follett, John Sandford, Clive Cussler,
Tom Clancy, Laurell K. Hamilton, Charlaine Harris,
J. R. Ward, W.E.B. Griffin, William Gibson,
Robin Cook, Brian Jacques, Stephen King,
Dean Koontz, Eric Jerome Dickey, Terry McMillan,
Sue Monk Kidd, Amy Tan, Jayne Ann Krentz,
Daniel Silva, Kate Jacobs...

You'll find them all at
penguin.com

Read excerpts and newsletters,
find tour schedules and reading group guides,
and enter contests.

Subscribe to Penguin Group (USA) newsletters
and get an exclusive inside look
at exciting new titles and the authors you love
long before everyone else does.

PENGUIN GROUP (USA)
penguin.com